Nobody Believes Me

Molly Katz is a former stand-up comedian and the author of *Jewish as a Second Language*, a humorous guide to intermarriage. Her stories and articles have appeared in *Cosmopolitan*, *The New York Times* and *Psychology Today*. She lives near New York City.

80p

MOLLY KATZ

NOBODY
BELIEVES ME

HarperCollins*Publishers*

HarperCollins*Publishers*
77–85 Fulham Palace Road,
Hammersmith, London W6 8JB

A Paperback Original 1995
1 3 5 7 9 8 6 4 2

A catalogue record for this book
is available from the British Library

ISBN 0 00 647602 3

Set in Sabon

Printed in Great Britain by
HarperCollinsManufacturing Glasgow

ACKNOWLEDGMENTS

My thanks for their help, alphabetically, to:

Paul Black, Eagle Investigations, Inc.; Candace Coakley; Dr Ellen Gendler; Joan Gurgold; Leslie Holland; Joann Kunda, Rebus International Investigations, Inc.; Dr Ann McMahon; Julie Morrison; Toba Olson; Dave Peretz; Dolores Walsh.

I am especially grateful to these special people:

Elegant, extraordinary Linda Grey;

Danny Baror – fearless, brilliant, and full of surprises;

Joe Blades, who edits beautifully from the inside;

Detective Mike Marculescu – thank you for being so patient, and so generous with your time and effort.

CHAPTER ONE

With delicate pink-nailed fingers the woman pulled her left sleeve up. Camera 1 moved in for a tight shot of the bluish area on her shoulder. It was incongruous, a multicolored blight on clear, gleaming skin.

'This is permanent,' the woman said in her soft voice.

Lynn Marchette, standing in the center aisle with her back to the audience, peered at the nearest monitor.

'Permanent?' Lynn asked into her hand mike. 'Is it a tattoo?'

'No. It's a bruise.'

'Bruises aren't permanent. But you're saying this one is?'

The woman nodded. 'If we were driving somewhere and got lost, my husband would punch me here. He did it so much, finally the bruise stopped going away.'

The other guests on the set, all women, gazed at her in sad understanding. Lynn asked, 'Why did he need you to direct him?'

'I didn't direct him.'

'He just punched you anyway.'

'Yes.'

None of the other guests looked the least bit surprised. Veterans of abusive marriages themselves, they were accustomed to routinely insane behavior.

'You never said or did anything, but your husband would punch you if he lost his way on the road.'

'Yes,' the woman said.

'Taking out his frustration. Using you as a punching bag, literally.'

9

'Right.'

Shaking her head, Lynn turned to take audience questions. She held the mike out to a thirtyish black woman.

'I'd like to ask all the ladies what finally made them go for help.'

While she moderated the responses, Lynn scanned the audience for other questioners. The preshow hour she spent getting acquainted with everyone gave her some idea who would ask what. This ability to sift likelihoods, while assigning a variety of other tasks to each eye and ear, was a precious talent. Oprah and Phil and Sally Jessy had it. She only hoped she had the rest of what they had. The Channel 3 management seemed to think so.

Once in a while even Lynn thought so.

A muscular young blond man asked if some of the women might not be overreacting. As boos rose from the audience, Lynn gently silenced the guests vying to be heard. She addressed the only silent panelist, a gray grandma with haunted eyes, who was pulling her hair back from her face.

'What are you showing us, Vera? Can we get a shot of Vera, please?'

In a second all the monitors showed a wandering inch-wide scar from Vera's ear to above her eyebrow.

'How did that happen?' Lynn demanded.

'He came at me with a chisel. Scraped it right down my face.'

Taking a signal from the floor director, Lynn turned to the camera. 'We'll be back in a minute with more from these courageous ladies.'

As the guests filed out of the Green Room, Lynn shook their hands and wished them well. A few hugged her.

Her feelings about her guests tended to jump between extremes. She loved to confront slimebags like criminally

10

negligent landlords on the air, but loathed being near them afterward. The troubled victims, she wanted to take home and make pea soup for.

Kara Millet, her producer, patted her shoulder as she was saying goodbye to the last battered wife. Kara was plumpish and copper-haired, and wore long Gypsylike skirts.

'Great show.'

Lynn turned. 'Thanks.'

'Aren't you going to remind me I didn't want to book yet another one of these?'

Lynn smiled, shook her dark curls. 'I knew I was right. There's no such thing as too many programs on family violence. People snarf it down and howl for more.'

'It's the way you handle the topic. You don't hide what you think. You've got the viewers in your pocket because they don't have the uncomfortable suspicion that you're exploiting the guests or the subject.'

Lynn plucked a chunk of doughnut from the debris around the coffee machine. 'Everyone on the air is chasing their tails, looking for the new wrinkle. Here's *Geraldo*,' she said, striking a pose, 'with kleptomaniac nuns. Here's *Sally* … with schizophrenic mother superiors. The real problems, because they seem mundane, get buried under the entertainment factor. "What, another battered wife? Yawn, burp. Is there a game on?"'

'Don't eat that.' Kara took the doughnut fragment. 'I'll get you a fresh one.'

Lynn took it back. 'I only want a nibble. I'm going to my brother's for dinner. He gets upset if I don't stuff myself.'

'Oh, your sister-in-law called. She wants to know if you're bringing a date.'

'I already told her I'm not.'

The wall phone rang. Kara punched the lighted button. '*Lynn Marchette Show*. May I help you? … Yes, she's right here.'

11

Kara pressed the phone to her chest and mouthed, 'Orrin.' Lynn grabbed it.

'Dennis?'

'Hi, Lynn. That was a hell of a show.'

'You liked it?'

The general manager chuckled. 'I did, but I wasn't the only one. Five people from QTV watched with me in my office.'

Her heart pounded. 'What did they think?'

'They were impressed. They're talking syndication.'

'They *are*? Oh, my God. Dennis, why didn't you tell me they were going to be here?'

'I wanted them to see you at your natural best. And I hadn't much notice myself. They flew in this morning, and they're already on their way back to LA.'

'But they really liked it?'

'They were mesmerized. When you orchestrated that moment where the woman showed her scar, none of them breathed.'

'I don't orchestrate –'

'I know, I know, but whatever you call it, the communication is what they saw. All the guests, that whole audience – they could be your brothers and sisters.

'These suits have been sampling shows all week around the country. They were glazed when they got here. They barely knew they were in Boston. But you woke them up.'

Lynn clenched her hands. 'What happens now? Will they call me?'

'They want you to come to LA next Wednesday.'

Even the choke of traffic on the Tobin Bridge didn't bother Lynn tonight. She kept the Lexus windows down and let the chill work on her heated face. The radio was on, but she barely heard it, couldn't concentrate ... didn't once do her dial-around for local call-in shows.

She didn't care how the rest of them were doing their

jobs. She was fine without that particular compulsion just now.

Amazing what a call from Hollywood could do.

She couldn't wait to get to Booboo and Angela's and tell them.

Her brother would whoop and stomp and bend his big frame to wrap her in one of his python hugs. Angela would be circumspect, raising questions, trying to calm the two of them down. But still Booboo would savor it all with her, help her believe it wasn't going away.

Good fortune wasn't real until she'd shared it with Booboo.

'Won't you need clothes?' Angela asked, pouring coffee. She sniffed. 'Is this the French roast again? I thought we were going to try the java blend tonight.'

'I just grabbed the nearest bag,' Booboo said. 'We'll have the java for breakfast.'

Lynn sipped. 'This is delicious. A dress, I guess. Or a suit. Or I might not buy anything. I have tons of daytime outfits.'

'But it's *California*,' Angela said. She touched her fashionably wispy black updo.

'But I'm Boston. They know that. They're buying that.' Lynn studied the table absently, mentally thumbing the racks of her apartment closet. But she was still too euphoric, with the attention span of a kitten.

'I think I have everything I need,' she told Angela.

Booboo smiled. 'Except confidence. Too bad there's no Spiegel catalogue to get that from.'

'Just you.'

'Not *just* me. Me plus. *Plus* your boss and your producer. *Plus* all those people who watch you, and the ones who write about you, and now this syndicate.'

Kara gazed at a pair of mannequins in evening dresses.

13

Lithe womanoids with impossible hipbones; who the hell's pelvis ever stuck out of her clothes? But one of the dresses was wonderful, just right for Lynn.

She found a pay phone.

'I promised myself I'd stay in today and get ahead,' Lynn said. 'I'm going through mail. There are a few good show ideas –'

'I'm fifty feet away from the most gorgeous dress I've ever seen. You have to come and look. Don't use your Saturday for the mail.'

'But I'll be away three days next week.'

'We'll *handle* that. Please check out this dress.'

'Are you in one of those places where they bring clothes out to you? You can't see the racks?'

'No. I'm at Lord & Taylor's. Second floor. I'll meet you by the escalator.'

She was there in twenty minutes (very Lynn), wearing leggings and sneakers and slouch socks beneath a long, oversized sweater (very un-Lynn). So much of their time together was spent in a work-related context that Kara always forgot Lynn could look like this – eighteen rather than thirty-eight, dorm president instead of TV pro.

'I don't know why I'm here,' Lynn grumbled before the escalator was all the way up. 'I don't need anything.'

'A friendly hello to you too.'

'Ugh. Sorry.' She squeezed Kara's generous shoulders in a hug. 'I'm not myself.'

'You are yourself. Obsessing about your trip. Maybe this will take your mind off. Over here.'

'Oh, my God.' Lynn moved closer, looking from the wide sweetheart neckline to the shoulder-baring drop sleeves ... to the all-over cascade of huge sequins. Reflecting the light in pastel glimmers, the mother-of-pearl disks were the size of half dollars. They covered the fabric and dangled at the short hem.

'Try it on,' Kara said.

14

'I don't dare. I might love it. But I have no use for it.' She checked the tag. 'Four hundred and ninety dollars? Not a chance.' But she didn't move to leave.

Kara touched a sequin. 'You're flying to the West Coast. You're about to be syndicated. There will be parties.'

'If there are any, I can buy something then.'

'No one ever finds a dress under pressure. It's a law of nature.' She pushed Lynn closer to the mannequin. 'This shiny stuff will be great on you.'

A sales clerk who looked like Cher's grandmother led them to a dressing room. She eyed Lynn's sneakers, went out, and reappeared with well-worn spike-heeled pink pumps.

'I was right,' Kara said when Lynn had everything on. 'Do you like it?'

'Yes.' Lynn reached to adjust a sleeve. She made a face. 'Too much flab here,' she said, moving her upper arms so the flesh jiggled. 'I'll have to tighten it up.'

'Or get a tan. You're allowed to have a lot more skin when it's tanned skin. So you'll take the dress?'

Lynn looked resignedly at Kara in the mirror. 'Yes.' She turned to get a side view, snagged a needle heel in the carpet and stumbled.

Kara caught her. 'Remember that move,' she said, laughing. 'Never know who'll be there to rescue you.'

'How desperate do you think I am?'

'Moderately to very.'

Lynn watched her own ironic smile form.

'I shouldn't spend the money,' she said. 'You only put on a dress like this for someone special who's nuts about you. And if there are any of those around, they're keeping themselves well-hidden.'

'Stop that. Take the dress. All you have to do is put it on to bring the men running. But just in case,' Kara said, unzipping it, 'let's see how much they want for these shoes.'

* * *

15

Lynn couldn't stop looking out the plane window. She didn't care if people thought she was provincial.

Didn't care enough not to look, anyway.

She'd flown so little in her life. Her success so far was local. Now maybe that would change.

But she couldn't count on it. These syndication possibilities could go either way. She'd been around TV long enough to know that, had seen enough Boston hotshots get all lipsticked and powdered and wined and dined – and dumped.

Nothing person. She truly understood. To go nation-wide, you positively had to be the best. If you turned out *not* to be – well, you didn't open a vein, but you didn't become a national personality either.

Now it was her turn to find out.

They were flying over Iowa. Below the puffs of cloud, the terrain was scored by farms, squares of green and brown, the gray glaze of ponds, huddles of buildings. She was up too high to see animals, but Lynn knew they were there. She knew a lot more than that.

As a little girl, she'd cared for the chickens and hogs on her parents' farm in East Tennessee. It was only one of many duties, but it was her favorite, because when she was done each day, the animals became her audience. She would read them her school essays and the poems she wrote. They were the only ones who had time to listen.

So really, she *was* provincial.

She turned from the window and picked up the magazine she'd been not reading.

Back then she'd looked the part, with her skinny hips and wildly rippling dark hair that flew all over. At least now those traits were in fashion. She'd had to change her way of speaking – not just her accent, but the over-the-pasture expressions that made farm kids sound like septuagenarians. Her brother's speech patterns still betrayed his roots. His friends and banking associates teased him all the time.

But a lot of media stars were provincial to start with. Everything she knew professionally, she'd learned from Phil Donahue – enough of a provincial himself to have begun his own magic in Dayton, Ohio.

Lynn had watched his process her first year in college, as Phil worked the audience of his Dayton show.

'I need your help,' Phil told the audience. 'The show is you. I need you to ask good questions, so I won't look stupid.' He learned their names. Talked to them during commercial breaks: 'How you doin', Betsy? Think of a good question for the senator here, Joe.'

Of course, they were thrilled to help, couldn't wait to do what Phil needed. And because they did, all the home viewers felt like *they* were standing up and asking the senator questions.

'You live and die by your audience,' Phil had been quoted as saying. And Lynn had taken that admonition as seriously as any classroom lesson.

If she began as provincial as Phil had been, she only hoped she now exhibited half his skill.

So to be honest, wasn't provincialism a red herring? What she was really worried about was that she wouldn't get the syndication.

Wasn't good enough.

Or much more likely, *was* good enough, and would get it. And would sabotage it. Return to some of her old destructive habits. Screw it up for herself because she didn't deserve it.

She put down the magazine and hunched over again to look out the window.

After the meetings, they took her to a beautiful restaurant in Malibu called Geoffrey's – one of *the* Hollywood hangouts, they said. It was right on the Pacific. They sat outside at a table for six, amid urns of intoxicating blooms. Heaters mounted on posts warmed the salt breeze.

Lynn sat between Vicky Belinski, QTV's national syndication vice-president, and Len Holmes, the programming VP. The afternoon had consisted of three hours of deceptively laid-back chitchat in quiet mauve offices, conversation that had revealed every fragment of a thought Lynn had ever formulated about TV, every breath of a plan. Her background. Who-do-you-know. Direct questions, sideways questions, nonquestions. Vicky had a ready, boisterous laugh; Len was more conservative.

She hadn't prepared, other than to have Kara toss her a few practice balls. To overrehearse would have been a mistake. Her spontaneity was what they were looking to purchase, and there was only one way to give them that.

But she was exhausted. Even this friendly dinner was tiring. The title bout was done, but she was still being weighed by five people who were considering investing a fortune in her personality ... not quite the casual get-together.

Vicky passed her a basket of bread. The basket was lacquered pink and silver, the slices within its warm napkin crusty-soft and oatmealy. The aroma brought her suddenly from indifferent to starving. She took a big piece and buttered it.

The surf whooshed below; mist eddied around the heaters. The nourishment relaxed her a bit. And as she relaxed, she began to feel better, to welcome the euphoria of what was happening.

Because it was. She knew she'd passed whatever the tests were, was continuing to pass them as she sat there. QTV, one of the heavyweight syndicators, was most deeply interested in acquiring her show. In making her an Oprah, a Sally Jessy.

A Lynn Marchette.

With that thought she gobbled the rest of her bread and took another slice.

* * *

Nine years ago, on a night as frozen as this one was balmy, she'd held bread in her hand. But it wasn't warm and grainy. It was white, and sodden with mayonnaise and tuna juice.

Her apartment then consisted of two tiny rooms over a pizzeria on Huntington Avenue. It cost $280 a month, barely affordable on her salary as a screener for the Carl Cusack show on WBHJ radio – a job she'd eagerly taken, despite the feudal pay, because Carl was known to put assistants on the air. For a would-be talker who was brand-new to Boston, whose radio jobs to date had never offered such a chance, it was a dream find.

What wasn't as well-known was the fact that Carl exacted a price for the exposure. Nothing flat-out dirty – that didn't happen to be how the man took his pleasure. Rather, Carl Cusack liked to rage and storm and humiliate people. He baited them and set traps.

So far, Lynn had managed to step around him, responding to his jibes with silence or calm, logical answers. She hadn't yet been Victim of the Day – and she hadn't gotten on the air either. Because she hadn't yet figured out that you had to react – to cry and shake and shrink from the dragon – to earn your reward.

On this January night, she arrived for work with her cheek swollen from gum surgery. The dentist had insisted she go home and lie down with an ice pack, but she couldn't; the payments on the long-delayed treatment had used up everything, including most of the current month's rent. Carl didn't pay you if you weren't there.

'What did you do, eat half a chipmunk?' Carl greeted her. His swift, dry wit was one reason he was popular with columnists as well as listeners.

'Dental work,' Lynn said, speaking as clearly as she could around a tongue that felt as if someone had stuffed a whole egg in her mouth.

Carl raised his eyebrows.

19

'I'm all right,' Lynn said before he could question whether she should be there.

Error. 'I don't recall inquiring into your welfare.'

Lynn nodded, eyes down as she sifted through commercial tags on the desk the assistants shared.

'Yes?' Carl bellowed. 'Was that a *yes* you gave me? To what question, might I ask?'

Lynn looked up. His eyes, permanently reddened around the gray irises, as if he'd always just gotten shampoo in them, were wide and fixed on her.

'I was just acknowledging what you said.'

She wasn't speaking very well; the long word had come out missing a syllable. And the novocaine was going, leaving a burning-sore crater behind her right upper molars.

'Recite the Preamble to the Constitution,' Carl said.

Lynn frowned. 'Pardon?'

Carl bent so his face was level with hers. '"We ... the ... people,"' he drawled. 'Go on. "We ... the ... people ..."'

'I'd rather not.'

'Don't know it? Here's an easier one – the Gettysburg Address. "Fourscore and seven years ago" Finish that, please.'

'You want me to say the Gettysburg Address?'

'Thaaat's right,' Carl said with burlesqued patience.

Lynn bumped the crater with her tongue and winced. An ache was spreading over the right side of her head. She knew these headaches much too well, knew dental pain exacerbated them.

She looked hard at Carl and decided the best way out was through.

'"Fourscore and seven years ago ... our fathers brought forth upon this con ... con ..."'

'*Con-tin-ent.*'

Lynn leaned away from his glare and his breath. '... a new nation, conceived in liberty and ..."'

She had to stop and rest a second. Her cheek was

grazing the crater on certain sounds, and every touch shrieked pain.

'"... dedi ... dedicated to the ..."'

Carl thumped the desk. 'Get out.'

'What? No, please ...'

'How dare you inflict yourself on my program when you're worse than useless? I need effective screeners on my phones, not a lisping, mumbling idiot. This is unconscionable. You've left me short-staffed at the last minute.'

'I can work. I –'

'Get *out*, I told you. And take your belongings. You don't work for me any longer.' He turned and strode away.

Lynn's gasp was nearly a sob. She ran after Carl, caught his wool jacket. '*Please*. I need this job. Just let me take some more Excedrin. I'll be –'

'How *dare* you!' His breath blasted her. '*You* need the job? Therefore, I should permit substandard performance in a pivotal role on a top-rated program?' He raised his arm as if to hit her, but only banged the wall. 'What you *need* is a lesson in judgment, but I haven't time to provide it – I have to find another screener so I can go on the air.' He hit the wall again. 'Don't bother slamming the door on your way out. You'll never make as much noise as I can.'

Mel Medoff, the program director, was still in his office. He listened to the barest start of Lynn's story, rolled his seen-it-all dark eyes, and hustled her down to the coffee shop across from the station.

Some survival instinct took hold, and despite the palpitating hole in her mouth, Lynn was hungry. She crammed down chowder and most of a tuna sandwich while Mel laid out the facts of life for her.

'The station doesn't hire, fire, or pay Carl's people. As you know. You're right – he's a prick. But I can't intercede.'

'Are there other jobs open at the station?'

Mel was shaking his head before the sentence was

finished. 'Carl would shit a brick if we hired you.' He spread his hands. 'What can I say? You got screwed. It's not fair. But he has the numbers ...'

She walked home carrying a slice of bread in a napkin, all that was left from her meal; she wouldn't even be able to look for another job until she was healed enough to speak, and her kitchenette was as bare as her wallet.

There was no one to borrow from. The pizza guys found her a lot less cute when she owed rent, and Booboo, his banking days still way ahead, was barely surviving back in Tennessee, trying to hold on to what remained of the farm.

As she dropped into sleep after icing her forehead and swallowing four Excedrin, her last thought was of the irony.

Already she was hungry for the wet bread slice that, like Jack's beans, would have to be apportioned as the next day's sole nourishment.

Boston was supposed to have been her breakthrough: the Cusack show and then another and another, and they'd be wining and dining the new star ...

By the time coffee came, it was dark. The outdoor lights, the flowers, the warm gusts from the heaters wove a tropical net that had settled over Lynn. After several glasses of wine and exquisite California food, she couldn't seem to stop smiling.

Her table had fallen into conversation with the next one, a group from a Los Angeles advertising agency. A couple of the agency people knew one of the QTV men. Lynn drifted away from the talk to gaze at the ocean for a while, tasting the heady possibility that settings like this would be common for her soon. When she tuned back in, Len Holmes was passing her chocolate torte to the other table.

'You don't mind, I hope?' Len said. 'We get to taste their plum mousse.'

Lynn laughed and took the plate being handed over. She tried some of the purple fluff. It was fabulous. Everything was fabulous.

'Great, huh?' a petite feline-looking woman at the next table asked her. 'Please, take more. The less there is when it comes back to me, the less I'll eat. By the way, I'm Joanne.'

'Lynn. And what you're doing is self-flagellating food mechanism eighty-two B. I know it well.'

'A sister!'

'You too?' Vicky said.

Lynn passed her the mousse. 'See what we're doing? We're all thin, more or less, and attractive and successful. And there's some creature in us that won't relax with that. We keep pistol-whipping ourselves.'

'Have you done a show on that?' one of the QTV people asked.

'Several. The syndrome takes many forms. I could do a hundred shows on it.'

'Because it's out there,' Vicky said.

Lynn nodded. 'It's an epidemic.'

Len leaned toward her. 'This is what stands out about you, what drew us. You're more, shall we say ...'

'Marginal,' Vicky said. 'And you give a shit.'

For a crazy moment Lynn imagined a billboard for her new national program: THE LYNN MARCHETTE SHOW. SHE GIVES A SHIT. To keep from giggling, she drank some coffee.

'Your rapport with an audience ...' Vicky shook her head. 'Amazing.'

More coffee was ordered; a couple of the QTV people went home. There were goodbye hugs between people at the other table before some of them left; then Joanne and two men moved over to Lynn's.

She should have been jet-lagged, but she was too excited. She felt more awake every minute. This was a dream place in a dream situation, where people laughed and embraced and had a great time. She wanted it never to stop.

'What did I hear about a show?' Joanne asked.

'Lynn hosts a TV talk show in Boston,' Len told her. 'We're preparing to syndicate it.'

Preparing. Lynn's heart jumped.

'So you're from Boston?' one of the advertising men asked. He was tanned and solid-looking, with an uninhibited smile. 'How do you like la-la land?'

'I think I like it a lot. I haven't seen much.'

'Well.' Vicky slapped the table. 'How rude can we be? Here a whole day and you haven't had a tour.'

'No tour?' Joanne asked. 'That's no way to treat a stranger. Let's do it now.'

'Why not?' Len said. 'Lynn? Are you up to it?'

'Absolutely.'

The checks were paid, and they got into Vicky's car, a big Mercedes. Lynn sat up front between Vicky and Len. Joanne rode in back with Greg, the nice-smile man.

They drive through Bel Air, saw Melrose, and the stores on Rodeo Drive.

'Mann's Chinese Theater,' Vicky said. 'We have to.'

Lynn gaped at the handprints and footprints, the names written in cement. She bought a Lassie butter dish for Kara. Everything she did seemed unreal and yet acutely genuine, like action viewed through fine binoculars.

It was after eleven by the time Vicky drove back into the restaurant lot in Malibu.

'I'll take Lynn to her hotel,' Len said. 'Vicky lives right near here,' he told Lynn.

'You're staying in town?' Greg asked.

'Yes. The Hyatt Tower.'

'Why don't I take you? It's on my way home.'

The Hyatt doorman, a crew-cut teenager, extended his hand to help Lynn out of Greg's BMW.

'Thanks,' she told Greg. 'For the tour and the ride.'

He gave his wide smile. 'The tour wasn't the mega version. But I hope you liked it.'

'I loved it.' She shifted to get out.

'Home to Boston tomorrow?'

'Yes. I hope I get back here soon. I didn't see nearly enough.'

He bent closer to her. 'You don't look tired. This is awfully late, Boston time, but am I right? You're the kid who can't stand to leave the birthday party while there's ice cream and cake left.'

Lynn laughed. The image made her think of the white sequin dress in her room upstairs. Painstakingly carried all this way in tissue, it hung in the Hyatt closet that was as big as her first Boston apartment – waiting for ice cream and cake.

She hadn't needed it. But it seemed to have done what it was supposed to do anyway.

She glanced at the doorman, who appeared unaccustomed to having any Hyatt Tower guest vacillate before taking his hand. He held it dangling in abeyance.

Greg snapped his fingers. 'Farmers Market.'

'I've heard of it. What is it?'

'An LA phenomenon. Not to be missed, especially at night. It's an outdoor maze of stalls that sell everything; food, produce, souvenirs.' He tapped her hand with his finger. 'I saw that butter dish.'

'It's for my producer. We have a tradition of bringing each other horrendous mementos. When you get one, you have to use it for company, with no explanations.'

'We can do a lot worse than the butter dish at the Market.'

Lynn clapped her hands. 'Let's go.'

The doorman still dangled. Greg leaned across Lynn and grabbed the door handle. 'Thanks, but we're leaving.'

The boy scratched his meager fringe as they drove off.

* * *

'But I already had dessert,' Lynn said. 'A few, I think.'

'Just bites. There was so much sharing, you couldn't have absorbed much. But wait. I have the answer.'

He took her hand and led her around a series of fruit stands. 'Look.'

She wasn't sure what she was supposed to see.

'There,' he said.

He held her head and gently positioned it so she was looking at a frozen yogurt counter with rows of fresh fruit sauces. The scent she'd caught when he leaned over her in the car filled her nose again, a spicy, sexy, incenselike cologne.

'Guilt-free sundaes. Where else but in California?' he said. 'I'll get one for myself, and you can taste before you decide.'

While the sundae was being made, Greg took her hand again and brought her to a wall of souvenirs. He was right; they made the butter dish look almost refined.

Lynn picked up a set of napkin rings. Each showed Elizabeth Taylor with a different husband.

'What did I tell you? No, let me,' Greg said as she opened her purse. 'I'm buying some other stuff anyway.' He opened his hand to show her a three-pack of Tums and a book of stamps.

She started to protest, but gave up. It didn't matter, really. A sweet gesture; she needn't turn it into a courtesy contest.

Everything was so easy when you were on top of the world.

'Try this.' He gave her the sundae. Before he was back with the purchase, she'd nearly finished the fruity concoction. Another thing she'd never have done on an ordinary night.

They walked the aisles and alleys. The glow of the paper lanterns overhead, the press of festive people, made it seem like a native bazaar.

'Even the fruit is different,' Lynn said. 'We get one or two types of peaches in Boston. Never a selection like this. There must be eight or ten kinds. What are these huge red ones? They look delicious.'

He picked one up.

'No,' she said. 'I'm stuffed, and it's too fragile to travel. Good Lord, the artichokes. They're as big as pumpkins.'

Greg laughed. 'You're not always like this, are you?' he asked, stroking her hair. He fluffed a thick ringlet. 'This is your time, your night. You give off a … sparkle. It's a pleasure to be part of it.'

Suddenly grateful for the understanding, Lynn touched his arm. 'Thank you.'

They stood for a moment in the half light of an orange lantern, looking at each other. She was barely five-four, and he had to dip his head.

'Yogurt,' he said, and thumbed the smudge off her chin. But instead of taking his head away, he lifted her face and kissed her mouth.

His scent enveloped her again, but his whole scent this time, not only the cologne. It was warm and male, and as exquisite as everything tonight.

Slowly he pulled back. A dot of moisture shone on his upper lip. Lynn fought the impulse to rise on tiptoe and lick it off.

'Better take you back,' he said softly, 'before you turn into an artichoke.'

The doorman must have been on a milk break. There was no one bounding out the hotel door to the car. Greg pulled to the curb.

Lynn had wondered if he'd want to come up, and what she'd say if he did. *No*, of course, she couldn't go around sleeping with an associate of her about-to-be syndicate on her audition day, but what gradation of no, what nod to the future?

27

She needn't have been concerned. Like everything else in California, the moment transpired perfectly without her having to do a thing.

'I know this isn't the time … yet,' Greg said. He put two fingers on her lips. 'Not that I'm not tempted to push. I just found you, and now you're leaving.'

Her mouth tingled under the touch.

'But I'm not giving up. Just willing to be patient. A little patient.' He took his hand away, then pulled a pen and pad from a door compartment. He looked up questioningly.

'Three eighteen Harbor Landing, Apartment 3805, Boston 02156.' She recited her home and work phones.

He wrote intently, tore off the page, held it for her to verify. He folded it, put it in his shirt pocket. He looked at Lynn, a heated gaze from cat-gray eyes. It was this that finally got her attention, yanked her from the happy distraction that had been her mood all day and evening.

She knew in that instant that he wanted her, and she wanted him. In a quick whirl of images, she saw those eyes above her as she lay on her back. She saw them reflecting the frenzy of what they were doing together. His shoulders moved with the rhythm of …

Stop.

She moved aside on the car seat.

Too bad there wasn't a yogurt substitute for this.

'I have to go in,' she said.

'I see that.' There was a chuckle in his tone, or was she imagining it?

'Are you laughing at me?' she asked.

'Yes. In the nicest possible way.' He leaned back and stretched, the tanned arms going behind his head. He had long since ditched his suit jacket, and the short shirtsleeves revealed thick muscles, forearms covered with dark hair.

'I see a lady striving to keep her priorities straight. A passionate woman, beautiful inside and out, who knows that for a hundred reasons she has no choice but to get out of this car, go upstairs, take her vitamins, and go to sleep ... but who is very tempted' – he leaned over and kissed her, a quick, sweet touch of his mouth and tongue – 'very tempted to say, the hell with the reasons. I want to be under this guy.'

He looked directly into her eyes with the last words. He was so perfectly right that she couldn't think of a response. But her hand went for the door handle, as if to remind her that just in case other parts might mutiny, this one was staying sensible.

'That's why I was laughing,' he said. 'Because your thoughts were so clear in your face. And I was flattered.'

He got out of the car and came around in time to meet her as she stood.

'I'll say goodbye here,' he said, his arms going around her waist. 'Just remember that one day soon we'll be ending an evening somewhere and the reasons won't be there. At that time it will be my great pleasure to bring your imaginings to life ... Star.'

Both hands pressed her to him. There was no one around, and she was going upstairs, alone, and she was going to be a national television star. And so she returned the kiss eagerly, her hands exploring through his shirt the back she would know much better sometime soon.

CHAPTER TWO

'He sounds wonderful.' Kara hugged her. 'I'm thrilled for you.'

'He's the one responsible for your present.'

'He bought this?' Kara picked up the butter dish.

'No, the napkin rings. He was there when I got the butter dish, and when he mentioned it later, I told him about our tradition. That was when he said I had to go to the Farmers Market. He promised I'd find things there that would make the butter dish look conservative.'

Kara placed the butter dish carefully away from the containers of takeout Mexican food that covered Lynn's glass coffee table. She dipped a pretzel in salsa.

'For God's sake. Take a Dorito.' Lynn pushed the bag toward her. 'We're celebrating.'

'We can celebrate without fat grams.'

'Ugh. *Hot*.' Lynn grabbed for her water glass.

'Did you tell him about this particular tradition? How you always order the hottest salsa, and always complain about it?'

Lynn wiped away a tear. 'No sense loading all my craziness on the man at once.'

'Well, it sounds like everything went great. You met a nice guy, and you aced the meetings.'

'Even I can't believe how I aced them. I wish you could have been there.'

'Do you think ... QTV wouldn't try to assign you some other producer for the syndication, would they?'

Lynn looked up. 'It wouldn't matter if they did.'

'You'd hold out for keeping me?'

'I'd never do the show without you.'

She watched Kara's shoulders drop in relief, and felt lousy. Why hadn't she thought to reassure her sooner? How insensitive and self-absorbed, to forget that she wasn't the only person in television who'd ever had an ambition.

'So,' Kara said, 'how did your new friend handle the fact that you're going to be a national celebrity? No problem?'

'He seemed dazzled.'

'Wow.'

'He's smart, funny, he *listens*. He makes interesting observations. He's romantic.'

'That whole night sounds like a movie. The ocean, the mist, the gorgeous stranger, the sightseeing ...'

'He's the most – well ...' Lynn lowered her voice. 'The way he talked to me ... the sexy things he said ... I mean, Kara, I'd known the man, what, a few hours? And here he was talking about what he wanted to do in bed, guessing my fantasies – and I not only let him, I *enjoyed* it. This is happening so fast.'

Kara squeezed Lynn's arm. 'Congratulate yourself. How many shows have we aired on the trouble people have being intimate? And who is poster girl for the problem?'

'Would you believe I almost slept with him right away that night?'

'You? No.'

Lynn laughed. 'I guess I've discovered something. The only prerequisite to meeting a guy who's good for me was that my dreams had to come true.'

'So that's all you needed. Stardom.' Kara scooped the last drop of salsa from the dish. 'You should write an article. That simple formula will be reassuring to all the *Cosmo* girls.'

* * *

31

Dennis Orrin's office was filled with pictures of past and present local Channel 3 celebrities. When Lynn opened the door, Dennis was rehanging her picture on its own wall, having removed it from the grouping.

'What's this?' she asked. 'Target practice?'

Dennis turned. He grinned, came over and hugged her hard. 'QTV called. They want to make a pilot.'

'*Ha!*' Lynn pounded his back.

'I knew they would. You should have known too.'

'I sort of did. But they took a whole *week*.'

'How many times do I have to tell you? They dork around forever making these decisions.' He swept a hand over what remained of his light hair. 'But you convinced QTV you're a powerhouse. They think you're Barbara Walters.'

'They do?'

'You blew them away. To decide in a week is like overnight.'

Lynn shrugged. 'It was magic. All the talks went well. We all got along. Everything clicked.'

'How soon?' Kara grabbed her notebook. 'Where?'

'A couple of months. Maybe here, but with the set glitzed up; maybe somewhere else, if they want a larger audience.'

'And ... I'm producing?'

'Of course.'

Kara put the notebook down. 'Thank you.'

'Don't thank me. I need you.'

'I'm producing a national pilot. Oh, my God.'

'And it isn't just the pilot that has to be great. QTV wants to start test-marketing, so any show we do from now on could be one they choose for several markets.' Lynn paced her office. Fiery October sun shot in through the triple window, beaming on her. 'I'm so excited. I can't even sit.'

'I've been working on a list of topics. We can use it to brainstorm. Oh! I forgot.' Kara hurried out and came back with an enormous package she could barely carry.

Together they set it on a table. Lynn peered at the label. 'Next-Day-Air. From Los Angeles.'

Kara slit the tape and they opened the box. Inside was a crate of lightweight wood, intricately built so that each square was a protective compartment for a peach.

Beautiful peaches, six varieties.

Lynn opened the card.

In Greg's handwriting it said, *Peaches for a peach. Do you miss LA? I hope so, because I miss you. Love and kisses, Greg.*

Kara caressed a big red fuzzy globe. 'I've never seen anything like these.'

'That's what I said at the Farmers Market. And he sent them. Where do you suppose he ever got that crate? He must have had it made.'

'Whatever he did, it was a lot of trouble. This guy really likes you, Lynn. And *you* were worrying because he hadn't called.'

Lynn blinked. 'I never said that.'

'You think I can't spot the why-doesn't-he-call clenched-teeth look after this many years with you? So. Will you call him?'

'I don't have his number.'

'I'll call QTV.'

'Thanks. Ask for Vicky Belinski. Say you want the name of the ad agency Greg Alter works for. I don't remember it.' She smiled. 'It's amazing I remember what hemisphere I was in that night.'

Kara finished scribbling and went out.

Lynn lifted a peach from its cube. The skin was fuzzy as suede. Its color went from deep red to butter yellow. It was perfectly ripe, just yielding to her thumb.

She fumbled in her desk for something to cut it with and

33

found an old letter opener. She put the peach on a tissue, sliced off a hunk, and bit into it. Juice ran all over. She'd never tasted anything so delicious.

She finished that, cut more and went to the window. Absently chewing, she watched the traffic on Morrissey Boulevard twelve stories below. It was snarled as always in the late afternoon, everyone hurrying to beat everyone else.

She watched a Camaro darting from lane to lane. The driver wasn't finding an opening to pass and wasn't going to, using all his energy zigzagging.

For years Lynn had spent her resources that way – all movement and no direction. Stuck in her work, stuck in her life. Moving from job to job in radio and then in TV production, always hoping to get on the air.

Finally she'd begun to understand that hoping wasn't doing. If she wanted a show, she couldn't slog around waiting for management to anoint her.

So she'd watched and learned and begged and reminded, until finally Dennis Orrin had started using her as a substitute host.

Lynn Marchette. The person in charge of the mike, the audience, the whole *studio*. Not lambs. Not sows. People.

A wonderful achievement for an invisible girl from a family that aspired to blue collar.

But she always had to be on guard when life was going well. Rejection she could take just fine, but success ... whatever demon inside thought she wasn't entitled, tried hard to make sure she couldn't attain it.

When something wonderful happened, like finally getting her chance on the air, then her regular show, right through to the miracles of the QTV deal and meeting Greg, then she could shake for hours or days, until the permission kicked in. Until she accepted that she *did* deserve it, she *would* enjoy it.

Learning to own the good parts ... Of all she'd had to

master to get on the air and stay there, that had been the toughest.

She could trace the influence of pills on her life back to her first days in Boston, when she'd had to self-medicate because she was the only doctor she could afford.

Pain in her teeth was a constant, debilitating force.

Of course there had been no money for dental care when she was growing up. By the time she was eleven, toothaches kept her awake, and for really bad ones, her mother would walk her into the Little Red Hen, Greeneville's only restaurant, on Sunday noons, when Dr Fenton Cabell, Greeneville's only dentist, was having his dinner. Dr Cabell would put down his knife and fork and go into the john and wash, and let his pork loin sit there while he probed Lynn's sore mouth.

He always prescribed something to put on the tooth, and asked Lynn's mother to bring her to the office on Monday, when he'd fix her up and make no demands for prompt payment. But the office visits never took place. When the next acute toothache occurred, the Sunday process would be repeated.

Lynn never actually sat in a dentist's chair until she was in her twenties. By then she needed an enormous amount of work. There was no way to afford it, so she had what little she could pay for: a filling here and there, scraping and cleaning. Gum work when the dentist folded his arms and insisted.

But after the years of neglect, the toothaches persisted, evolving into excruciating headaches. She'd be awake at one or two and have to take so much Excedrin – nothing else cut the pain – that the caffeine in it would prolong her insomnia.

She came to dread the whole routine.

When she began dozing off at work, she grew desperate. She was an assistant producer by then. She couldn't lose her job; the money would increase as she got promoted, she rationalized, and with it she could afford more treatment. But if she kept losing sleep and was fired, her teeth would stay bad and the headaches would never stop.

So she learned to take a Valium with the Excedrin.

But her body needed more of the Excedrin for the pain, and more Excedrin led to more Valium.

She only took it in the night. But the effect lasted longer than she wanted. More pills caused more effect.

At precisely what point her pain-Excedrin-insomnia-Valium syndrome had become a dependence, she didn't know. Lynn only knew that on the day her brother arrived at Logan Airport to do what she had been pushing for since she'd come to Boston – settle here – she had to monitor herself every minute so she didn't act drugged.

He got off the plane hungry, so she took him to a Friendly's. They ordered vanilla shakes – frappes here, iceburgers back home – while they waited for their sandwiches.

'I hope you like your place,' Lynn said for the third time.

'If I can cook on more than one burner and the ceilings are higher than my head, I'll like it,' Booboo said. 'I'm not too picky after the last couple of years. First room I took after home had a hole in the wall a hawk could have fit through.' He grinned. 'Plugged it with my pillow. Then I was set to buy another one, but I got used to doing without. Now they all say it's healthier to sleep without a pillow.'

'Yes,' Lynn said. 'A pediatrician explained that on the show. Start the baby sleeping flat, and avoid back trouble later on.'

Booboo was staring at her, and she was suddenly afraid he could spot something in her eyes. To show how sluggish she wasn't, she grabbed her frappe and drank thirstily.

But it had been brotherly pride, not suspicion, in his gaze. 'I can't wait to be ringside when you do your show.'

'I can't wait for you to be there.'

'My big sister, a television powerhouse. Who would have thought?'

Playfully, Lynn swatted at him with her napkin, but didn't come close. Alarming only to her, of course. He didn't know her aim was off by half a foot.

The apartment she'd found him was in Marblehead. Lynn finished her sandwich and every drop of her shake so the nourishment would equalize the drug and prevent it from interfering with her driving. It worked; she felt fine, drove fine. Booboo was delighted with her choice.

'How far is the water?' he asked, sniffing at the window he'd just opened.

'Two blocks. It was as close as I could get without committing you to a gazillion-dollar lease. Isn't this great?' She raised two more windows, pushed over a cushioned rattan easy chair and set it between them. She sank happily into it. 'Smells like a beach cottage. I was so excited when I saw this. I can't wait till I can afford a place *right* on the water, *right* in the city.'

'And how many minutes is it till then?'

They laughed together, the way they used to when the piglets tickled their hands, lapping up the treats saved from supper.

The memory was strong just then. Sitting back against the fresh-smelling cushions, Lynn could feel the sensation of a soft-whiskered snout in her palm. She laughed again as the damp tongue brushed her wrist.

The smell was mud now instead of sea air. The familiar odor was all around, the earthy tang of the bog beneath the dining room window that never dried up, even in arid summer when the grass went brown.

Lynn heard her mother sorting eggs in the kitchen, the *tink tink* as her old-looking fingers set the big ones in the blue bowl, the small ones in the yellow. Muttering about how many small ones now … smaller hens, smaller eggs, everything was getting smaller, especially the budget for feed, so what could you do?

Suddenly the mud smell and the sounds went away. Lynn was dizzy, terribly dizzy. Dorothy and Toto in the whirlwind. Her stomach was rattling around inside her as she tumbled.

But she'd coated it, hadn't she? Put a coat on it? In it?

Lynn pressed her hands to her belly to lock it back in place.

That stopped the tumbling.

She looked down at her hands, kept looking, looking, as she became reoriented. Saw her watch and gasped without sound.

Eight minutes gone.

'You sure conked there.' Booboo was on the floor examining a phone jack. 'I figured I should let you nap.'

Lynn got up and went into the bathroom.

It hadn't been a nap. She was pretty sure she knew what it was: a blackout. The kind drinkers had.

If she was drugged enough to black out, she had been too drugged to drive.

Yet she had driven a car with her brother in it.

She leaned against the closed bathroom door and quietly sobbed.

She was finally on the air. She finally had her brother here. Despite her good intentions and what she'd wrongly assumed was her good judgment, she'd done something potentially tragic.

It was enough to shock her into throwing out the Valium.

But once she'd learned to endure the anguish of the pain and no sleep and no pills, her unentitled self still found ways to sabotage her. Her taste in men was the subject of endless jokes. Kara said her ideal date had a perpetual scowl and an unemployment check.

Lynn couldn't argue. 'Line up six guys in front of me,' she'd told Mary Eli, Kara's psychiatrist friend, when Mary had appeared on their 'Smart Women, Foolish Choices' show, 'and I'll head straight for the one who'll give me the most trouble.'

Could it be that those days were over now too? Was she done beating herself up?

She was being courted by one of the biggest and most successful television syndicates. A man was missing her, thinking about her, admiring her, sending her exquisite treats – not a punishing misfit, but a smart, effective, beautiful, real person.

Professionally and personally, she'd struck gold.

Smiling, still holding her sticky peach pit, she turned from the window and went to find Kara.

The ice cubes clicked as they settled in the black-glass carafe on Dennis Orrin's desk. The carafe had come with its own tray and two trendy goblets. It was trimmed in brass, and the brass was kept polished, just as the carafe was kept filled with fresh ice, by the maintenance staff.

They performed these tasks faithfully because even they – or, Dennis Orrin sometimes thought in his cynical periods, *especially* they – understood the difference between this carafe and the lower-echelon ones.

He poured water and sipped it while he watched the tape that had just been FedExed from Cleveland.

Not bad. The boy could read, at least. A shocking number couldn't; you watched them mouth words phonetically like one of those nonEnglish-speaking rock groups.

But essentially another newschild trolling for a grown-up anchor spot. And if there was one thing Dennis insisted on in his grown-up spots, it was grown-ups.

Five months left to find one – who could read, could be depended on to show up nightly in televisable condition, and had *it*, the trustable authority that prompted people to turn on Channel 3 right before, after, or during dinner with the same faithful regularity with which they padded down the driveway and picked up their paper each morning.

He rewounded and ejected the tape and put it on the Out table for return. He went to his desk and called Cleveland and ruined the newschild's day.

He stepped into his bathroom and washed up, a silly habit; years ago he'd begun to notice he did it after rejecting people. Then some psychologists on a Marchette show had talked about a bunch of compulsions, including what they called Lady Macbeth handwashing. Dennis had listened carefully to that, sifted what he heard, subtracted a small percentage for the kaleidoscopic TV context, and still been left with relief. Just an odd habit.

Back at his desk, he looked over the rest of his stack of cassettes and decided to wait awhile before viewing the next one. Watching too many at a time fuzzed his judgment.

Hearing that once, Lynn Marchette had chuckled and said, 'Like perfume.'

'Hm?' he asked eloquently.

'They always tell you not to sample more than one perfume. In a store. You lose your nose.'

He looked at Lynn's picture, newly alone on its wall.

A quick sense of humor, even better on camera than off. Truly a grown-up. QTV had made a wise choice.

For a while a few years back he hadn't been so sure Lynn would get to this point. Headaches, insomnia ... He had actually seen her asleep at her desk more than once. She had confided that she was afraid she was getting dependent on tranquilizers, and so had quit them.

She seemed to have all that behind her now – the tranquilizer part, at least.

Not that he was unsympathetic. His pot days were only a little further in the past than Lynn's problem, and she'd halted hers a lot faster. He remembered most acutely the innocent start, then the nightly use, then smoking in the day, the joint like a cigarette with his coffee. Then the joint *instead*.

But he'd had to make a decision, and he'd made it.

This was his strength – what had earned him the carafe. His ability to parse a situation and assign priorities. It was what the magazine pieces about him hooked on to. That he instinctively knew to pick up the phone and call a kid waiting by it in Cleveland, rather than waste time dictating and observing protocol.

That he could elect to be a penniless loser of a creative doper, or a bored but top-shelf major-market honcho with a well-kept family.

He aimed a small smile at the picture of Bern and the girls, poured more ice water, and slipped another cassette into the player.

Lord knew how he got up the three stories, but a resilient chipmunk had become a regular visitor to Lynn's harbor-front terrace, lured first by the seed she put out for the birds. After a year of talking to him through the screen door in a special chirpy tone she and Kara called her chipmunk voice, he had started eating from Lynn's hand.

She felt silly enough today to treat Chip to a bit of peach. He sniffed it, his little tail with its identifying hairless patch quivering, then gobbled it.

'My opinion exactly,' she chirped at him.

The phone rang while she was enjoying her fourth peach of the day. She clicked down the TV volume and ran to answer in the kitchen.

'I hope you're not disappointed,' he said. 'Do they taste as good as they look?'

'Greg!'

41

'How are you, Lynn?'

Her heart was banging away. 'Great. And you?'

'Good too. I can't wait to hear about your syndication deal. Do you have any news yet?'

'Just today. They want me to make a pilot.'

'Fantastic!'

'I was biting my nails, but my boss says this is fast. So your timing was great on the peaches. They were like a congratulations present. They're delicious. I can't stop eating them.'

'That's what I wanted to hear.'

'I would have called you, but I didn't get your home number, and they couldn't locate you at the Bailiss Agency. Anyway, thanks. This is so thoughtful.'

'I wanted you to have a taste of Los Angeles. How did the napkin rings go over?'

'Kara was hysterical. She would have told you herself if she'd reached you this afternoon.' Lynn picked up a pencil. 'Give me your number now while I'm thinking of it.'

'I can do better than that. I'll come up there and hand it to you.'

Lynn dropped the pencil. 'Where – Where are you?'

'About fifteen minutes from your building, if I'm reading the city map right. Is tomorrow better? I could take you and Kara to lunch.'

Lynn smiled and grabbed a napkin to wipe the ubiquitous peach juice from her face. 'Tonight is just fine.'

He brought a red wine that was as lovely and as unfamiliar as the fruit.

'St Leu,' he said when she asked again, as he was pouring the last of it into her best goblets. She watched him in a haze of excitement. He gave off a galvanic sexuality that was irresistible.

'Not that I'm so chauvinistic about California wines,' Greg went on. 'But I wanted to bring you something unique, and I knew you wouldn't have this in the East. It's from a local vintner. Do you like it as much as the peaches?'

'That's ...' She started to giggle. 'All I can think of is apples and oranges.'

He said, 'It's peaches and grapes.'

She fell back on the couch, laughing. Greg had eaten dinner before arriving, and she had been too busy with the peaches. The cheddar and pumpernickel she'd brought out sat nearly untouched on the coffee table.

Except for a hello hug, he hadn't touched her. But her head had just landed on his arm, and now he was lifting her chin to kiss her.

The memory jolted her, the taste of Greg's mouth, sharpened by the wine, the spicy scent. She felt again the heady joy of being in LA on a miraculous adventure. Paired with this delightful man who was a part of that, and more important, willing and eager to share in *her* part. When had she ever picked – no, happened to meet – no, *picked*, it was the principle that Mary Eli, now Lynn's friend too, was always banging her over the head with ... When had she ever picked a man who wasn't threatened or angry or at best indifferent to her success?

Greg pulled her closer and slung a leg over both of hers. She touched the ridge of thigh muscle. Wine-bold, she moved her hand higher, inside the thigh, and felt him jump.

He took the hand in his and lifted it. Still holding it, he said softly, 'I have a hotel room. I'm planning on sleeping there tonight.'

He watched her face.

Her reactions, which were so clear to Kara, were probably no mystery to Greg either. Everyone said her transparency was part of her strength. And if all of Boston could read her feelings when she interviewed a teacher accused of child molesting, or a discriminated-against teenage lesbian, she probably didn't even have to answer him in words.

But she said, 'Please stay here.'

'I don't want you to think I expected to.'

'I don't.'

Still looking into her eyes, he pressed her hand to his erection.

He felt familiar beside her in her bed, as if a place had been reserved for him all this time. Probably she'd dreamed of him here, and hadn't remembered until the sense-recollection prompted her.

He made love to her with an intense concentration, caressing her legs and kissing her knees and ankles. He spent long minutes moving his mouth along her shoulders and the insides of her arms before bending lower. No one had ever loved her so slowly and methodically, so selflessly.

When she finally went to guide him on top of her, he smiled and shook his head. 'I want you to come,' he whispered.

And so she gave in to Greg's probing tongue and covered her mouth to keep from shouting out as he sent her barreling to a neon climax, her feet thrashing the mattress.

Greg woke first; he was leaning on an elbow, looking down at Lynn, when she opened her eyes.

'I don't smile in the morning,' she said huskily, trying to and not succeeding.

He grinned and sat up. 'How about if I make us coffee?'

'That won't do it. Nothing works.'

He laughed. He looked as attractive in the early daylight as he had at night; more so, because the little creases and flaws humanized him.

Lynn knew, because she had to see her own face in the mirror every morning, that it was pale and puffy, with vestiges of mascara under her invisible naked lashes. In one of the many magazines that crossed her desk, Cindy

Crawford claimed that was how she knew she was loved: her husband could look adoringly at her morning face.

Greg must have gone to the same school. He was gazing at Lynn now as if she actually appeared normal.

Self-conscious, she sat up and put on her slippers. 'I'm going to wash,' she said with a last, futile attempt at a smile.

They sat on the tall stools at the breakfast bar off her kitchen. Like so much of the apartment, the area was designed for maximum enjoyment of the view. A window wall framed the harbor; a barge skimmed past, trailed by eager gulls.

Just the scene she'd pictured when she moved in – hopefully, naively, a brochure emotion: a man on the stool beside her, sharing a tender moment before work, as the sun showcased the panorama.

'Can you take today off?' Greg asked.

Lynn shook her head. Her hair was tamed, her face and panty hose on; she was almost ready to leave.

'Half a day, then. Just the morning, plus lunch. Then I'll give you up until evening.'

'I really can't.' She reached into a flowerpot where she kept odds and ends. 'Take a key. Then you can go around and sightsee, and come back here when you've had enough.'

He pocketed it, sipped coffee. 'Let me guess. You don't take a lot of vacation time.'

'But I do. I try to get in four weeks a year, more if I need it. I go away on trips with people, or alone. I just work very hard when I'm here.'

'Okay,' Greg said. He stood, put his hands behind his head and stretched. They were beautiful hands, large and angular, the fingers wide. Looking at them, Lynn remembered sharply their knowing ease on her hips.

She turned away and drained her mug. 'Good coffee. Thank you for making it,' she said.

'It isn't really.'

'No?'

'No. If you were taking that half day off, I'd buy you some. With a nice buttered bran muffin. Raisins in it.'

Lynn got their coats from the closet and opened the front door. The hallway was bright from the skylight, the waterfront smell heavy in the warm air. The corridor window showed the barge in the distance, too far for the gulls to be visible.

Again the memory of that hopeful feeling. She was finally living the picture.

'Oh, hell,' she said.

She showed him the waterfront, all the contemporary buildings like her own, the hotels and restaurants and shops. The breeze chilled, but the sun was intense, and Lynn felt lustily proud of this turf of hers. Greg came from a place of jacaranda and palms; here was the other side, the antipalm, *her* waterside city.

They got coffee in plastic cups and sipped as they walked along, the steam whipping away on the wind. At a souvenir shop Lynn bought Greg a beanpot that had a cod for a lid.

'Does this mean I can be in the game?' he asked.

She nodded. 'You have to put it out for company – preferably with beans in it.'

'And not say it's a joke.'

'You can't say anything.'

Greg laughed delightedly. 'It's so ...'

'Garish. The tackier the better. Once Kara brought me sunglasses from Maine in the shape of two lobster claws, and made me wear them to the beach.'

'Speaking of that ...' Greg finished his coffee and dropped both their cups in a trash bin. He stood facing Lynn and gently took off her sunglasses. 'Better,' he said.

'What was that for?'

'You have great eyes. I love looking into them.'

'You're supposed to wear those so you don't get wrinkles from squinting,' Lynn said, but she put them away.

'There's nothing wrong with wrinkles. We earn them. *Look* at that.'

He'd stopped at a swimwear store and was pointing to a jade-and-black bathing suit in the window. It was a kind of one-piece bikini, the top and bottom attached by a silver circle at the waist in front and back.

'Let's go in,' he said.

Lynn shook her head.

'Oh, come on. Try the suit on. You bought me a gift. I'd like to reciprocate.'

'Are you kidding? It's hard enough trying on bathing suits alone. All that untanned bulgy stuff under fluorescent lights. Forget it.'

He slipped his hands inside her coat, under her sweater at the waist. 'How,' he asked with burlesqued hurt, 'could you forget that I know exactly what I'm going to see under those lights?' He stroked the curve of her waist. 'That's how I know you'll look beautiful. I look at the suit, and I picture your contours in it.'

The dressing room light was kinder than she expected, but not bedroom-low, and she winced at the puffs of flesh between the top and bottom of the suit. She wished her arms were firmer. But after examining herself from every side, she found the courage to leave the booth.

'Jesus,' Greg breathed hungrily, his eyes sweeping the length of her. He walked around her slowly. The saleswoman looked up from her busywork with the window display and winked at Lynn.

'You like it?' Lynn asked him.

'Like it?' He opened his mouth, stopped, shrugged. 'Everything I want to say is X-rated.'

'It's a funny time of year to buy a bathing suit.'

47

'You'll be coming back to LA. You always need a suit there.'

'I don't know. Business trips are too compressed for swimming.'

'Not *business*.' Careful to keep hands off, he spoke low in Lynn's ear. 'Pleasure. When you stay at my place.'

'Oh,' she said, surprised, excited.

'Take the suit,' he urged.

'Well. All right.'

'Star ...' he whispered. 'That's how I think of you.'

Greg took out his wallet and headed for the register.

'No,' Lynn said quickly. 'I'll pay.'

He turned. 'I wanted this to be my treat.'

'Thanks. But I'd rather.'

Back in front of the dressing room mirror, she made another appraisal. Amazing how admiration could change your self-perception. The body that had seemed pale and lumpy, she now saw as Greg had, all smooth curves.

She probably shouldn't have been so bossy about paying. He was just being nice. Susan Faludi wasn't going to pop out in a police hat and write her a ticket.

There was a knock on the door, and Greg came in holding another suit. 'I told the saleslady I was bringing this in for you to try,' he said. He put it down on a chair. 'I wanted the excuse to come in here. So now we have to waste some time.' He slipped down the straps of the jade suit.

'I'm letting you do this,' Lynn said into his neck. 'I don't believe I'm letting –'

He quieted her with his mouth. He pushed the suit all the way down, gripped her bare buttocks and pressed his own hips in close.

Lynn put her arms around him, and got a glimpse of the mirror, just a quick look at her own breast with Greg's fingers on it.

She forgot herself for a time as they moved hotly against

48

each other. He was fully dressed, she was half out of her suit, and his nubby jacket was sweetly rough on her skin.

He turned her so he could have the mirror view, and Lynn felt his body change as he watched them. He let go of her and opened his belt.

'We can't,' Lynn whispered, stepping back. She picked up her sweater and held it over herself.

'But –'

'We're in a *store*.'

He sighed. Lynn could see him gathering the threads of control. He smiled slightly. 'And you were worried about the light.'

They wandered through Quincy Market, sampling cheeses and chocolate, poking in shops.

'Look at all this,' Greg said. 'You can get a passport picture or a Movado watch or a diamond in your nostril.'

He picked up an aquamarine ear stud from a display and held it so it twinkled. He raised it to Lynn's ear. 'Perfect. It matches your new suit.'

'My ears aren't pierced.'

'No? They probably do it here. Uh-huh, there's the sign. "Free piercing with purchase."'

Lynn made a face.

'Let me treat you,' he coaxed.

But she wasn't interested in piercing. She had so many pretty clip earrings.

'Something else, then. You wouldn't let me buy the suit – so how about a gift to go with it?' He touched her cheek. 'You don't know what a good time I've had in the last' – he checked his watch – 'fifteen hours. A very special time. Maybe it's too bad we live in a society that expresses thanks by spending – but we do.' He grinned. 'So let me spend.'

They walked around some more. A silver-haired man pushing a twin stroller waved at Lynn; two college-age girls smiled shyly.

'People recognize you!' Greg said.

'Mm-hm.'

'That's *great*!' He squeezed her hand. 'Will I get to watch you sign an autograph?'

'That's what you want?'

'I can't wait.' Suddenly he stopped walking. 'Look.'

'What am I looking at?'

'The tattoo place.' He pulled her over to the shop. The window was full of sleek body parts in improbable colors, suspended at varying levels on glittering silver and purple ropes. Pink light from a revolving ball bounced off the shoulders and ankles, highlighting the small designs on them.

'Yes,' Greg said, 'yes.' He caressed Lynn's shoulder. 'Maybe right here. Or on your foot. Something delicate and ladylike.'

Lynn turned wide eyes on him.

He opened the shop door.

'I'm supposed to go in here?' she asked.

'You say no too much,' he said, pulling her inside.

They stepped into sinkingly plush silver-gray carpeting. Tattoo designs covered the walls. Music in a soft cascade, the 'Appassionata'; a fragrance like jasmine tea.

A pixielike woman in a pin-striped suit was working at a desk, a white coat on the back of her chair. She looked up and smiled at them, showing giant dimples. 'Good morning.'

'Good morning,' Greg said. 'My friend is interested in a tattoo.'

'I am not. I mean,' Lynn stammered, still smarting over his comment, searching for a way to be positively negative, 'I'm just, um, interested. No –'

'Let's see the designs,' Greg said.

The woman led them to a section of the wall that was clearly for feminine tastes, with discreet flowers and other shapes, artful and spare in flavor. There were initials, single and twined, some with just a suggestion of curlicue; a long-lashed eye; hearts, cats, stars, music notes.

'These are popular,' the woman said, indicating a group of single flowers: a lily, a tulip, a mum.

Greg scanned them as he moved along the wall. He reached out and tapped an inch-long pair of full pouty lips drawn in thin, delicate lines. 'I like this one,' he said.

The woman nodded. 'Very nice. A little daring, but reserved as well. Most distinctive.'

Greg turned to Lynn. 'Mm?'

'Well,' she said. She took a deep breath. She did say no a lot, actually.

The woman smiled. 'Would you like to ask some questions?'

'Yes.' At last. 'Is it completely safe? How long does it take? Will it hurt?'

Shocked at the *will*, Lynn missed the start of the answer, and had to ask for a repeat.

'It hurts a bit. There's an uncomfortable scratching sensation. People are generally relieved that it doesn't feel like needles. As for the safety,' she said, going back to her desk, 'here's the literature. I use my own safeguards in addition to the standard procedure.' She held out a pamphlet. 'This design will take about an hour.'

Lynn tried to restrain her relief. 'Oh, then I can't. I'm almost out of time.'

'We'll come back,' Greg said. 'What time do you close?'

'Six. Or I can do you a semi now. That's just five or ten minutes.'

'What exactly is a semi?' Lynn asked.

'The same design, but it doesn't penetrate as deeply. I use a stylus with vegetable dye.' She held up a pointed tool. 'It lasts for a few weeks, then wears off gradually.'

Greg said, 'Let's just come back later and get the real thing.'

'I really can't, after taking the whole morning off,' Lynn

51

said. She was into this now, savoring the adventure –
especially since it didn't involve a major life decision.
'Okay. I've decided. I want the semi.'

In Lynn's office, Kara hung up the phone and stood for a
minute smiling at it. Then she glanced at the clock, took a
hurried look around, and quickly decided what there was
still time to do. The piles of tapes on the floor by the couch
would have to stay; she'd wait until there was enough time
to file them, rather than just stash them out of the way. But
she could finish clearing Lynn's desktop and the tables.

What a pleasant surprise to get a whole morning alone
in here to excavate the rubble. She could only do it when
Lynn wasn't around to wring her hands and moan that she
couldn't find anything except in her own messes.

What a wonderful turn of luck for Lynn, Kara thought,
that she had someone to take the time for.

And most especially, what a joy it would be to pass on
the news Dennis Orrin had just called with: it was decided
– tomorrow's show would be the one test-marketed.

Lynn would jump and holler; every move forward made
the syndication deal more real for her. And Kara's smile
widened each time she pictured the credit that would be
seen next week in half a dozen cities: RECORDED AT
WDSE-TV, BOSTON. And, several lines later: PRODUCER:
KARA MILLET.

She checked the clock again. Twenty minutes before she
had to leave to meet Lynn and her new guy for lunch.
She'd finish the desk, shake the dust balls out of her hair,
change into the extra blouse she kept in the Green Room
closet. That should leave just enough time to phone her
sisters with the news – then her mother, so her mother
couldn't spill it first.

Kara lifted her wineglass. 'To the new national *Lynn
Marchette Show*.'

'I can do better,' Greg said, raising his. 'To the new nationally rated number-one host.'

Lynn smiled. 'Do I have to mumble something modest and self-effacing?'

'Are you kidding?' Kara said. 'I'd call a doctor.'

'When do you tape the pilot?' Greg asked. 'Have they set a date yet?'

Lynn shook her head. 'Not for a couple of months. QTV will run tomorrow's show in Chicago and Los Angeles and other places next week. They picked a good one – women doctors discussing the feminine health problems that male doctors are accused of blowing off.

'So they'll make a tape available to some of the major stations in exchange for ratings reports. Then they'll analyze and meet and diddle around and meet some more ...'

'You don't look happy.'

'It's frustrating. I know they need time to get their ducks lined up. They want to get the biggest affiliates interested. That's how I see it when I force myself to be professional.'

Kara said, 'But the truth is, we can't wait. We're panting to go.'

'I want them to have me on daily, nationwide, tomorrow. Today.'

Lynn's Caesar salad came, and she bit into a romaine leaf.

Kara was staring at her.

Lynn said, 'What's the matter?'

'That reeks of garlic. It's knocking me over from there.'

'Oh.' Lynn looked at Greg. Kara was right; her mouth burned with it just from the one bite. Did she date so few upright bipeds that the niceties like not having bear breath had to be written out for her?

In that way he had of getting everything before the second curve of the question mark, Greg solved the problem by taking a piece of her lettuce and popping it into his mouth. Chewing, he gazed from Lynn to Kara.

'I think,' Kara said, 'I'll go sit at some other table.'

'He's perfect.'

'He is, isn't he?'

Kara squinted at her. 'No bad news I didn't notice? No irritating habits?'

Lynn laughed. 'Not unless you count dropping Tums wrappers wherever he goes.'

'Is he as sexy as he looks?'

Lynn's face flushed as she was invaded by sensations of the night before – and this morning in the dressing room. 'He must have studied every article in every magazine about what women want.'

Kara smiled. Lynn watched in the ladies' room mirror as Kara smoothed her eyebrows with a toothbrush. It was an old grimy orange thing, and Lynn had been watching her do her eyebrows with it since they'd been production assistants together.

The homey comfort of it warmed her.

She'd done a show on that, the importance of friends to people without much family. The friends became the support system, and hence the family. Not a fact the average poodle couldn't have told you; but like a lot of seemingly elementary truths, having them demonstrated and articulated in the arena Lynn created brought them to vibrant credibility.

Lynn said, 'Do you notice anything different about me?'

'You mean the smile? The good mood? The fact that you've known a man for a week and he hasn't asked you for money yet?'

'I mean this.' Lynn lifted her foot. Under her sheer hose, several inches above her ankle, was a blue art-deco G. Beneath it was the outline of a pair of lush red lips.

Kara gasped. 'When did you get that?' She bent closer.

'This morning. Greg's idea. It was a present.' She

laughed. 'He picked the design. He calls it a portable kiss.'

'It's adorable. It doesn't look sore or anything. Did it hurt?'

'No. It's not the genuine needle kind of tattoo – they call it semi-permanent. It wears off in a few weeks.'

Kara straightened. 'What an unusual man. How long will he be in town?'

'Just two more days. He has business here pretty often. I don't remember his telling me that in California. But,' Lynn said, fluffing her curls so the long sides rippled down over her shoulders, 'Tom Brokaw could've invited me to sit in a hot tub with him and Bryant Gumbel that night, and I wouldn't remember it.'

'Think hard. If he did, they'll need a date for Bryant.'

'Let's go run over tomorrow's show again. I can't believe I took a morning off the day before such an important one.'

'You didn't know. But don't get obsessive, okay? The show is all set.'

'And I have to leave at six.'

'Let me guess,' Kara said. 'Dinner with the portable kisser.'

'Right. And guess who else?'

'Who else *is* there? Mary? Dennis?'

Lynn shook her head. 'Booboo.'

Kara stared at her. 'Already?'

'You think it's too soon?'

'I must have known you for a year before I met your brother. I guess I'm just – shocked that you're this serious, this soon.'

Lynn clicked her handbag shut. 'It's not that I'm bringing him to meet the family. My brother and I made the date the last time I was there, and I'd hate to cancel. You know Angela. If I didn't come tonight, she'd be upset at me for hurting Booboo.'

'Let her be upset.'

'I can't.'

Kara followed Lynn into her office. 'Your brother and sister-in-law have their life. You have yours. You're the busiest, especially now. Why should you pretzel yourself –'

Lynn shushed her with a gesture. 'You don't know how it is to have practically no family. You're surrounded by tribes of sisters and in-laws. All I have are my brother and his wife. I don't want to start trouble. Can you understand that?'

'Mm-hm.'

'Now you're mad.'

Kara smiled. 'I'm not mad. So finish. You decided to take Greg to Booboo and Angela's.'

'I was going to tell Greg I was busy for one night. Then I thought, Angela's always nudging me to bring someone. So – I'll bring someone.'

Angela came into the kitchen and wrinkled her nose. 'Awfully strong odor.'

Booboo grinned. 'Garlic. Finely chopped. Couple of big spoons of it. That's why my Mexican dishes always go over. *Gourmet* magazine will ask to do a photo shoot here any day now.'

'I'll spray,' she said, and went out.

Seconds later there was the hiss of her favorite Glade fragrance, Spring Rain. The sound stopped and started, stopped and started as she worked her way around the living and dining rooms and the front hall.

'Will Lynn and her friend be spending the night?'

'No,' Booboo said. 'She has a big show tomorrow.'

Angela came to the kitchen and spoke over the saloon doors. 'Then this is a bad night to be out late with a date.'

He shrugged, chopping chili peppers. 'She seems to have everything under control.'

'I don't know,' Angela said doubtfully.

'Well, we'll see. This man sounds like quite a gentleman.'

'He's from California.'

'Okay,' Booboo said. 'They have them there.'

'Should I put a water pitcher on the table? With all this spicy food –'

'Mm-hm. Dump some ice in, and lemon slices.'

She took a lemon from the refrigerator. 'Is this washed?'

'Yep.'

'Are you sure? The label is still on.'

'Then maybe not. What did she say his name is? George?'

'Greg.' She eyed his khakis and T-shirt. 'Are you going to change?'

'Soon as I do the dip.'

While he waited for his turn in the shower, Greg pressed a shirt. Lynn kept the iron in her bedroom, along with a handly little legless ironing board that rested on a marble trestle table. While he worked, he looked idly at the other items on it – a row of books in gargoyle bookends, a windowed jewelry box, a few framed photographs.

There were Kara and Lynn on a beach, palm trees behind them. Lynn's hair was a lot shorter. Kara's wasn't the same either. He had to look closer to identify the difference: cornrows, with those dangles on them.

A bigger picture showed a bunch of people at a banquet, Lynn and Kara among them, with a partially bald guy in a tux holding an award.

At the end of the marble table was a collage of photos, some black-and-white. He parked the iron, picked up the collage, and looked it over as he pressed the shirt.

All these seemed to be of Lynn and her brother. The cloudy oldest ones had what must have been their parents; some newer shots had another woman, maybe Lawrence's wife – what was her name? Angela.

Lawrence was huge, two heads taller than Lynn. Seemed to have been born that way; there was no picture of him small. Funny that this giant guy had such a kiddish nickname.

The childhood shots showed Lynn as a stem-thin girl in too-big pants and dresses. She rarely stood or sat straight; the camera always caught her slumped, in a sort of cringe.

Shaking out a sleeve, Greg thought about the contrast between that Lynn and the one he was getting to know.

This one sat confidently at a lunch table as people passed, aware that she was recognized, proud of the attention, owning it. She walked straight, head up and graceful, a presence.

Amazing, how some women evolved.

He wanted to watch her work, had urged her to let him see tomorrow's show. But no. She'd been definite. Not this show, with all the pressure.

Another time.

He unplugged the iron and put the shirt on a hanger.

There were no pictures of his own childhood. His parents hadn't owned a camera – or a home or land or a car or even a cooking pot. They had been grounds workers, what the higher-ranking estate-maintenance staff called 'brush slaves' – for brush was what the green grass became under the pitiless sun of south-central California if there were no workers to water it.

He had spent his early years on a series of luxurious estates around Aguanga, his family moving like the migrant workers they essentially were from one to the other to the next, as the owners' needs and fortunes fluctuated. Home was whatever ramshackle structure was assigned the outdoor staff; the brush slaves got the least space. It was not unusual for Greg and his parents and sisters to share one room with two other families.

That life had been gone for a long time. His apartment now was a palatial five rooms with chrome and black glass and all the cooking pots he wanted. But he never passed by a conventional family-style ranch house without thinking how odd it still looked to him.

Lynn was nervous, but Greg seemed not to be. He complimented Booboo's cooking and Angela's necklaces. He pretended not to notice that Angela was measuring him with everything but a slide rule. For all the nagging, now that Lynn had actually brought someone over, Angela seemed anxious and protective.

'You work?' she asked Greg as he helped himself to more of Booboo's guacamole.

'Of course he works,' Lynn said. 'He's in advertising.'

'No, I'm not,' Greg said.

Lynn blinked. 'But – you're here on business.'

'Yes. But not advertising business.'

Lynn spread spinach dip on a cracker slowly, tidying the strings that hung over.

'What *do* you do?' Booboo asked pleasantly.

'I'm a Texaco rep. I service our major station owners around the country.'

Booboo nodded. 'You troubleshoot.'

'Right. And build morale, listen to grievances ...'

Booboo shrugged at Lynn and smiled, as if to say, no big deal.

But she was mortified.

'Why didn't you tell me you worked for Texaco?' Lynn demanded as soon as they were back in her car.

He shifted and backed down the driveway. 'You didn't ask.'

Biting back peevish words, she made herself shut up and think.

What are you really angry at? Mary asked in her head, and she had to answer: At looking a fool in front of my family. *Is that all? What about the fact that Greg is right? You didn't ask him.*

'Oh, no,' Lynn groaned, sliding down in her seat.

'Is it that bad? I don't smell like gasoline, do I? No grease under –'

'Stop. It's me. I'm an idiot. How self-centered can I be? I'm so busy yapping about my show, my syndication deal, I never even asked a polite question, never mind drawing you out.'

Stretching to look for traffic before turning, Greg said, 'This is where I head south?'

'Oh, yes. Sorry, I wasn't watching.'

'Seems like the car should know. It does everything else.'

'Everything but make your lunch, the salesman said. So you like my car?'

'It's great. Thanks for letting me drive. Pretty suburbs Boston has. Nicer than Los Angeles. Hey, look at that raccoon on the grass there. I keep reading about your rabies problem in the East.'

Lynn glanced over. 'He seems healthy. You need to avoid them if they're wobbly and disoriented-looking. A rabid animal's saliva is fatal if it gets on you. If you don't have shots, you'll die.'

'Do you come from around here?'

'No. I didn't even know what a suburb was. Booboo and I grew up on a farm in East Tennessee. Our parents were so busy just trying to survive, that was their life.'

'And did they survive?'

'Only into their forties.'

Greg took his Tums from his shirt pocket and chewed one. 'They must have looked good sometime. Your brother is a nice-looking guy. And of course, you're a twelve. How did he get that nickname?'

'It was what he called himself. Lynn's booboo. Before he could say brother.' She smiled. 'I know it's dumb. I should call him Lawrence. But he's my only family. My booboo.'

'No wonder you know about animal disorders, with that background.'

'Growing up around animals, you learn a lot. Take this next exit. It'll bring us back to the bridge.'

'But you and Booboo managed to go to college?'

'He helped me out and then put himself through. He always said I was the more ambitious one.'

'And? Are you?'

'Yes.' It was so easy to admit things like that to Greg.

He squeezed her thigh. 'Sexy.'

'What is?'

'You. How you are.' He moved his hand up inside her coat, over her stomach, then down. His fingers pressed. 'So honest. A true star.'

He was exciting her, but she said, 'You'd better stop.'

'Why?'

'You're driving.'

'I can drive with one hand.'

'I still don't …'

He moved his hand insistently lower, and she couldn't subdue a shiver of pleasure.

'I only need one hand to –'

'Don't say it,' she said. 'Don't be crude.'

'If you were still being honest,' Greg said softly, 'you wouldn't be trying to stop me. I can feel you responding, Star. Just close your eyes and come.'

Later, in her bed, as Greg reached behind her to undo her bra, Lynn asked, 'How did you happen to be with those people from the agency if you don't work there?'

'Hm?'

'In LA. The night we met. I thought everyone at your table was from the Bailiss Agency.'

'Why did you think that?'

'It just seemed like it. A bunch of people from work out to dinner.'

He pulled off the bra. He stroked her back down to her waist and brought her close, pressing her to his naked chest. She could feel his hard, heavy cock against her. She began to breathe faster.

61

Before she could say anything else, he was kissing her, holding her head, using his tongue. He kept it up, barely stopping to breathe, leaving Lynn breathless too.

She knew there were more questions to ask, but they were rapidly losing importance.

'And we are *out*,' the director's voice boomed from the studio speakers.

The applause continued, even though the floor people had stopped leading it when they heard the outcue. Lynn threw the audience a kiss. She loved it when that happened.

Their mikes off, the doctors were filing out. Lynn shook hands with each.

'Just in case you need reminding,' Kara said, as they milled around in the Green Room, 'this tape is not for Boston only. Call your family and friends in Chicago, LA, Cleveland, Detroit, Baltimore, and Minneapolis. There are broadcast schedules on the table by the door.'

Ten minutes later the room was empty. Kara and Lynn collapsed on the couch. The production assistant moved around, straightening up.

'Sit, Pam,' Lynn said. 'Rest a minute.'

'As soon as I get the top layer of rubble. Wonderful show, you two.'

'Incredible,' Kara said for the fourth or fifth time. 'They were all excellent. *You* were your best, Lynn. Better than best. The challenge inspired you.'

'They applauded longer than they had to. Did you see?'

'Did I *see*? Does the Pope shit in the woods?'

Lynn got up and poked through the remains of the food for an intact Danish. She broke it and gave half to Kara.

'Aren't there any bran muffins left?' Kara asked.

'No,' Pam said. 'I'll send out.'

'The hell with it.' Kara bit right into the cheese filling. 'I'll run up the stairs a few times. Certain occasions just cry out for a cheese Danish.'

'Was there too much fat talk?' Lynn asked. 'Did we keep to the medical issues as faithfully as we planned?'

'I heard that,' Dennis Orrin said, striding in. He looked down at Lynn. 'Oy-veying already? Can't you graciously acknowledge the praise? The show was excellent.'

'I was afraid of superficiality,' Lynn said. 'Did you learn anything you didn't already know?'

'We all did,' Pam said. 'I didn't know there was a difference of opinion about menopausal women taking calcium. I've been pushing it on my mother.'

Kara said, 'I didn't know you could get so deformed by osteoporosis. That poor woman.'

Lynn frowned. 'Which woman?'

'The one who asked about magnesium. Remember? Around the third fade.'

'A short woman in yellow. Right? I didn't see a deformity.'

'You were facing her. You have to see the tape.' Kara went to the wall phone. 'Evan? I'm in the Green Room. Can we see a minute of the show we just did? A little back from the third fade.'

Lynn groaned when she saw the side shot. 'She's almost a hunchback. The poor thing.'

'Remember this?' Dennis asked as the shot changed. He pointed to one of the doctors on the panel. 'Cogent summation of the situation.' He turned up the sound.

'There isn't nearly enough research being done on menopause,' the woman said. 'If men got to fifty and stopped having erections, you can bet we'd know a hell of a lot more about the problems of aging.'

'Great,' Kara said. 'A panelist says something brilliant *and* funny *and* outrageous, and it happens to be on the show that's been scheduled for test-marketing. Isn't it wonderful how things work out sometimes?'

* * *

'I'm glad you called,' Lynn said. 'I've been talking to you in my head.'

'What have you been saying?' Mary Eli asked.

'I've been telling you all my exciting news.'

'Really!' Mary said. 'Work or social?'

'Don't faint. Both.'

'Great! Well, you know what I always say.'

Lynn chuckled. 'Do you know how many things you always say? Then you tell me. "You know what I always say." Which of your eight hundred sayings are you referring to?'

'"All the boats float when the tide comes in."'

'I swear I haven't heard that one.'

'No? Well, just enjoy the image. *So* tell me what's happening.'

'QTV wants to syndicate me. They flew me out to LA –'

'Fantastic!'

'– and I seem to have passed all their tests, whatever they were. We just taped a show they're going to test-market in a bunch of cities, to get some excitement going with their affiliates. The next stop is to make a pilot. If everything goes well, I could be on the air all over the country in a few months.'

'Lynn, that's just great! Will you relocate?'

'No. We'll tape in Boston. All I have to do is what I'm doing.'

'Kara too?'

'Of course Kara too.' Lynn leaned back in her desk chair and stretched her legs out. She let her shoes drop off. '*And* I met a guy in California, a wonderful man named Greg Alter.'

'Terrific!'

'He's here on business right now, and we're having a great time. He's met Kara and my brother and sister-in-law –'

'How did that go?'

'They're crazy about him.'

'Tell me more.'

'He's a Texaco rep. Travels all over, seeing station owners. He's around six feet, tanned – it's a state law out there – knows wine ... loves to go out ...'

'How old is he?'

'Maybe three or four years older than I am. Forty, forty-two.'

'You don't know?'

'I don't know much at all. We're still learning about each other. To tell you the truth,' Lynn said, eyeing her open office door and lowering her voice. 'I've spent the last five days either at work or in bed with him. All I know about his tastes is that he loves good coffee, and I only ever have Maxim. Other than that, there's barely been time to find out if he eats cornflakes.'

Mary's smoky laugh echoed through the phone. 'All this you've been telling me in your head? Well, I guess I should take my good news where I can. When people walk in here with a lot to tell me, it isn't usually about career break-throughs and what great sex they're having. Congratulations, Lynn.'

'Thanks. I'd love for you to meet him.'

'How about a week from Sunday? Gideon and I are barbecuing on the patio. Last of the season. That's why I called.'

'Greg won't be here. He's going back tomorrow.'

'Too bad. Find out when he's coming again, and we'll arrange something.'

For their last evening, Greg insisted on treating her to a special time.

'All the clichés,' he said from her living room as she changed in the bedroom. 'Candlelight, dancing, cham-pagne.'

'It sounds lovely. Where?'

65

'Surprise.'

Lynn appeared in the doorway, clipping her work skirt to a hanger. She still wore her blouse and panty hose. 'You have to tell me. How else will I know what to put on?'

Greg got up, went quickly over and touched Lynn through her hose.

'Greg.' She laughed and stepped away.

He said, 'You should get one of those catalogues that have the peekaboo underwear. Then I could go down on you even while you have these on.'

'But right now,' she said, moving farther away as he reached again, 'the problem is what to wear – not what not to wear.'

'Are you trying to sidetrack me?'

She laughed again. 'Yes.'

Abruptly he dropped his hands and flashed his splendid smile. 'Don't you want me to go down on you?'

Lynn winced. 'Don't say it that way.'

'I'm sorry. It's your fault for looking beautiful. I can't help being an animal.' He chastely kissed her forehead. 'I thought you liked me talking sexy.'

'Sometimes. But not – graphically.' She smiled. 'Anyway. Now I have to get dressed.'

'I'll help.' He went to her closet and started pushing the hangers around.

'You don't have to –'

'Let's find something dressy. We're going to the Ritz Roof.' He turned to catch her reaction.

'Wonderful.'

'I asked Kara to suggest the most romantic place. This. Wear this.' He held out a long, strappy black silk number.

'That's a *nightgown*!'

'But it's sexy. Your nipples will show right through.'

Lynn ground her teeth. Firmly she took the hanger from him and replaced it in the closet. She led him out to the living room, pushed him down on the couch, and, after closing the bedroom door, went back to her closet.

The Ritz Roof. She knew exactly what to wear.

She unzipped a garment bag and took out the white cocktail dress with the big mother-of-pearl sequins, the one she'd bought with Kara before her trip to Los Angeles. She stooped and moved shoe boxes, found her silver sandals, tried one on. Yes. Perfect with the dress, and the ankle strap sat just under her tattoo, highlighting it.

The tags were still on the dress. She'd been afraid it would meet the same end as the few other cocktail outfits she'd bought over the years. They'd hang in her closet until they went out of style; then she'd cut off the tags, because it was too embarrassing to explain, and give them to Goodwill.

She'd been to the Ritz Roof just once, with Booboo and Angela on her birthday. Booboo had insisted on going, and paying, even though he was still only an assistant branch manager then.

Toasting, Angela had wished her a boyfriend 'to take you places like this.'

Lynn had said what she always did when Angela expressed such sentiments – that she'd rather *be* a rich person than date one, which made Angela look at her as if she was speaking Urdu.

But in fact she'd been whistling in the dark, her brave response as true as always, but something she needed to hear herself say. Because what was to Angela a simple equation was like stilt-walking to Lynn. Economics aside, she couldn't seem to settle into a worthwhile relationship.

At the time of Angela's toast, Lynn was seeing Mark Manatay.

They met at a broadcasting convention in New York. Mark was program director of an all-jazz FM station in Portland, Maine.

'Boston,' he'd said musingly, looking at her name tag.

'What's the cliché? "Home of the bean and the cod"?'

'Yes. But I won't tease you about lobsters if you don't make Boston jokes.'

He laughed. It was a contagious laugh, the kind that comes from someone who does it frequently. He was talkative and cheerful, wore suspenders, brought her peanuts in a napkin when he went to replenish their club sodas.

They had dinner together that night. He asked intelligent questions about her work. He described his love of music, his Portland condo, his twelve-year-old daughter, the ex-wife he kept in touch with for the child's sake.

The following day was the last day of the convention. Lynn and Mark had gone to separate seminars, but they sat together at lunch and had dinner again. By then the talk flowed easily, as if they'd been going out for a while. She knew to pass him the salt right away; he poured it on everything. He ordered hot pepper flakes for her pizza.

Aside from excusing himself for lengthy calls to his daughter, he spent most of his time with Lynn, when she wasn't occupied with meetings and workshops. For her part, it felt so good to be in his company that she occasionally had to remind herself what she was really there for.

They shared a cab to LaGuardia. He walked her to her gate, gave her a hug and a soft kiss, and said he'd call.

When two weeks went by and he didn't, she decided she must have somehow given him the idea that a call wouldn't be welcome. So she phoned him at his station, got his secretary, left her name and both numbers.

He called back the next day. He'd been thinking about her. Could she come to Portland for the weekend? He hoped she could get away, had a hotel room on hold for her.

The two-week silence bothered her, but she put it out of her mind and accepted his invitation. She went out

Thursday night after work and bought a lovely coral sweater and a lipstick to match, and flew to Portland the next night in a rainstorm.

He met her flight and checked her in at the Radisson. While she changed into the new sweater, he went down for a newspaper – and returned an hour later full of apologies. He'd been on the phone with his ex-wife; there was a problem with their daughter that needed his attention; he was so sorry she had come all this way, but ...

There was a line, and Lynn drew it at that point. She went back to Boston and spent the weekend alone, doing paperwork, watching Chip and the birds feed on her wet terrace, too upset even to call Kara.

Mark apologized in a long message on her machine; it was waiting Monday night. The crisis was over, he hated ending the weekend before it began, but unfortunately children had to be put first. Could they start again? He so enjoyed her company.

She let him wait as she weighed the issue. Finally she decided to give him the benefit of the doubt. Parental problems created bizarre behavior.

They fell into a routine of visiting back and forth. They went to movies because Lynn liked them, and jazz clubs because Mark did. Always there were intermissions in whatever they were doing for the long phone calls, and cancellations occurred. But that seemed to be how it was when the person you were falling in love with was a parent.

Booboo and Angela knew she was seeing someone, and urged her to bring him to her birthday dinner.

Mark declined: a school event he couldn't miss.

Two weeks later he came to Boston and they went to the Parallel Bar, a dark club whose band played the screechy, unending clarinet music Mark enjoyed. He let her sit through an entire evening at a tiny table in a tambourine-size chair before leaning close and saying words she couldn't hear.

'What?' she asked, waving away smoke.

'I'm going back home,' he shouted.

Lynn thought he meant now, temporarily, and her disappointment was displaced by confusion, because there hadn't been a phone call immediately beforehand.

'Your daughter –'

'No.' He leaned in again. 'I don't have a child. I lied. I'm sorry. I'm going back with my wife. We were separated –'

'You don't have a child? Who do you call all the time?'

'My wife. You see why I couldn't say that. I didn't want you getting paranoid, thinking I might go back with her ...'

'But you *are* going back with her.'

'But I didn't know it then.'

At that moment Lynn thought of Angela's birthday toast, and the two pieces came together with a crash: the wish and the reality.

She sat there on the little hard chair, too frozen with fury and pain to cry or leave, while Mark talked on – until finally her brain kicked in and propelled her out of the Parallel Bar and into a taxi.

She and Greg had Dover sole, shared a bottle and a half of champagne, and got silly over the music, dancing to every single number.

He moved on the dance floor the way he did in bed, slow and deliberate, holding her close. Lynn sensed others watching them, not because she was Lynn Marchette, but because they exuded a connection people envied.

Still another activity she'd always dreamed of. Now she had someone to buy sweet cards for, to watch as he slept ... and to be the envied couple with.

When they got back to the apartment, Lynn went to the kitchen to see what she had before offering anything. It was ages since she'd been in a supermarket during this Cinderella period. She felt a little sad, looking around her

70

neglected kitchen, which she usually kept lab-neat and fully supplied: the disorder had happened because she'd been busy with Greg, and after tonight, who knew when he'd be there to preoccupy her again?

Greg came in and stood close behind her.

'You look far away,' he said. 'What are you thinking about?'

'About you going. I miss you already. When will you be back?'

'I don't know.' He reached over her shoulder and slid his hand inside the top of her dress. 'I've been waiting to do this all night. Looking and waiting.'

Lynn tipped her head back to nuzzle his chin. 'I guess you don't want a snack, then?'

Instead of answering, he squeezed her breast, not quite hard enough to hurt. 'Let's go inside, Star.'

In the bedroom he unzipped the dress and helped her step out of it, shielding her skin from the sequins. He stood holding it for a minute, looking back and forth from her body to the dress, as if savoring her release from it. Then he undressed himself.

He stood by the bed, looking down at Lynn under the covers.

'I'm thinking about you in those panty hose,' he said. 'Peekaboo ones. I could stick my tongue right in.' He got into bed, oblivious of her strained face. 'Wouldn't that be exciting? I could do it anywhere – in your office, in a taxi ... What's the matter?'

Her body had gone tight. 'I asked you not to talk like that.'

'I'm sorry. I forgot.'

'I told you I'm uncomfortable with graphic language –'

'Yes. You did.'

'Then why did you use it just now?'

He rose on an elbow and looked down at her. 'Lynn,' he said quietly, 'whatever I said, I meant lovingly. The last thing I want is to upset you.'

Above her his face was troubled. Her disgust was beginning to turn to embarrassment. Was she making an issue over nothing? Being picky and immature? Or worse, undermining a promising relationship?

So he liked to talk dirty. Sexy. She'd liked it too, at first. So now they had a little difference of taste, not quite the shock of the century. *That does tend to happen in real relationships, you neurotic idiot.* He merely liked to take the talk further than she did.

So she'd expressed her feelings, and he hadn't instant-aneously reversed his behavior. Again, not a titanic surprise. He *was* human. And wasn't that what she was supposed to want, a human?

So where did that leave her? On very familiar ground. 'If an appropriate date has a hangnail,' she'd told Mary when they first met, describing her dynamic for choosing men, 'I'll dump him. If a rotten guy is missing a foot, I'll say, "No problem – he'll grow another one."'

'I'm sorry,' Greg said again.

She sighed. 'So am I.'

'Can we forget it?'

Could she?

'Please?' He gave his wide grin, lay back and held his arms open.

Lynn tried her energetic best to get into the lovemaking. She recalled the dressing room in the waterfront store, his hands under her bathing suit. She thought back to the toe-curling desire she'd felt on the dance floor.

But it was hopeless.

'It's not working,' she whispered finally, when Greg had tried everything in his repertoire to satisfy her. 'I just can't.'

'Why not?'

'I don't know. Too much champagne, maybe.' She rested her head on his chest, and he put his arm around her, but Lynn could feel his tension.

She slept eventually. When she woke briefly two hours later, Greg was still holding her. She snuggled closer and closed her eyes.

CHAPTER THREE

Kara came to work with fresh onion bagels, Lynn's favorite. She brought one to Lynn's desk, buttered.

'No, thanks,' Lynn said. 'Just some coffee.'

Kara looked at the two empty cups on the desk. Lynn turned around in her swivel chair and started working at her keyboard.

Kara asked, 'What time did you get here?'

'Around seven,' Lynn said without turning back.

Kara walked around and stood by the screen. 'Do you want to talk?'

Lynn sighed. 'Not really.'

'Is it about Greg? How did last night go?'

'So-so.' Now she looked at Kara. 'You know what? I want to get to work. Let's forget I'm in a bad mood and just plunge right in.'

'Are you sure?'

'Yes. We have shows and a pilot to plan, and ... I need the distraction. What's come in? Anything good?'

'I made some notes yesterday.' Kara retrieved message slips and a looseleaf from a table that was fast returning to the mess she'd cleared. She pulled over a chair. 'We got a call from a volunteer at the Brighton Animal Rescue League. Carol Hirsh. Wanted to know if we can have some of the doggies and kitties on and let her explain their foster pet program.'

'Isn't that just a way to encourage people to keep the animals?'

'Probably, but –'

'But it's necessary. Okay. Not a whole show, or we'll all

be crying and dragging the animals home.'

'Christmas?'

'Perfect.'

Kara read her notes. 'Restraining orders. This judge out on the Cape someplace wants to come on and say how they can put teeth in those.'

Lynn shrugged. 'Great, if he really has material we haven't heard.'

'I'll call him and see. Okay, a man named, uh, Philip Tank – I swear – called to suggest an exposé on prescription drugs. He gets generic when he pays for brand name.'

'Not that again.'

'Says he has proof.'

'Well ... see what you think. But really lean on him, okay? You know I hate half-baked exposés.'

'I know.' She scanned her papers a last time. 'That's about it.'

'Where are we on the Parks Commission show?'

'I talked to the woman yesterday.' Kara reached for a folder. 'Pennina Russo. Her title used to be assistant commissioner – now they've got her answering phones. She says flat out it's because she raised hell when this commissioner, Allen Dray, kept pressuring her to date him.'

'So she'll come on?'

'She's hedging. She was willing until she found out we wanted to have all four commissioners too. She's only twenty-six.'

'Desiree Washington was eighteen.' Lynn took the folder, found the Parks Commission number, and dialed.

'Pennina Russo, please. Well, hi – this is Lynn Marchette. Sorry to hear you're still answering the phone. I'd like to try and change that.'

As she listened, Lynn retrieved the buttered bagel and ate it.

Finally she said, 'I don't blame you. But give me a

chance to explain why we want to do it this way. See, it *strengthens* your position when the other side is also allowed a forum. You're giving them rope ...'

Just before lunch there was a knock on the door.

'Come in,' Lynn shouted.

Pam brought in a wrapped oblong box. 'For you, Lynn.'

Lynn squinted at the label. 'It's from a place called Viviane. What's that?'

Pam watched her pull the wrapping off. 'I think it's near the Combat Zone.'

Lynn stopped. An odd feeling niggled. But Pam and Kara were still watching eagerly, so she pushed the paper aside and opened the box. She reached inside silvery pink tissue and held up the tumble of black silk by its rhinestone straps.

'What a dress,' Pam breathed.

There was a card lying in the box. Kara handed it to Lynn, who laid the dress over her arm to read it.

'It's from Greg. "For our next evening. I can't wait to see you in it."' She smiled.

'Did you say last night didn't go well?' Kara asked. 'I'd like to see what he sends when it does.'

'I'm ... flabbergasted. I thought he was mad.'

'Give me that.' Pam held the dress up. 'Look at the top.'

'The straps?'

'No.' Pam held it fitted to herself. The tips of her red-sweatered breasts protruded through.

Lynn's hand went to her throat.

'Dear God,' Kara said.

Pam whirled with the dress. 'A tattoo, the Ritz Roof, and now this. I am *so* impressed.'

Kara reached. 'Let me try it. Lynn, you are lucky. Nobody's ever been interested in seeing me in a peekaboo anything, let alone sending me one.'

It took Lynn a minute to realize she was the only one

76

whose surprise was anything but delighted.

'You wouldn't mind getting one of these?' she asked.

Kara and Pam stopped giggling over the dress.

'Mind?' Kara said. 'I'd propose to the man. I'd patent him.'

'Do *you* mind?' Pam asked.

'Kind of. Yes.'

'Why?' Pam asked, as if Lynn had just ordered mattress stuffing for lunch.

Lynn pulled apart the top of the dress as Kara held it. 'Is this sexy? Or is it demeaning? Two weeks ago I didn't even know Greg. To come on like this so fast –'

'Sometimes,' Kara said, 'love *is* fast. It's been very fast with you two. Greg didn't just meet you and have coffee with you and say, "I think I'll send a shockingly personal gift to this woman I've only shaken hands with." You've been sleeping together for a *week*.'

By the time he called her at work late that afternoon, Lynn had calmed down.

'Did you try it on?' Greg asked.

'Not yet.'

'You're going to look choice in it.' His voice was the baritone purr she remembered from the first night. 'I want you to wear it next time we go out.'

'Out? How could I?'

Across the office Kara smiled.

Greg said, 'You have to. That's the point. Don't worry. The top crosses over, so it's only open when we want it to be.' He whispered the last few words.

'How was your trip back?'

'Smooth. Just lonely. I hope I can get East again soon.'

'My friends Mary and Gideon Eli are having a barbecue a week from Sunday. You were invited to come with me.'

Again the whisper. 'I'd love to *come* with you.'

In spite of herself, Lynn felt a pang of excitement.

77

When she didn't answer, Greg asked, 'Is someone there with you?'

'Mm-hm.'

'Kara?'

'Yes.'

He chuckled. 'So you're at my mercy.'

'No,' she said, unwilling to play, 'I'm not – because I have to go. Did you mean that about the barbecue? Can you make it?' She heard the chuckle start again, and hurried to interrupt it with, 'Will you be there?'

'No. I can't get away that soon.'

'Too bad.'

'But I'm honored that you wanted to show me off.'

She hadn't said that, but it was true. 'Another time, then.'

He had always been beautiful to look at, a standout in the brush-slave families. Even when he was a small boy, his aura was sought after. People wanted to be in it. He would look up at someone, his gray eyes ringed by thick charcoal lashes, his lush little mouth curved in a smile, and that man or woman couldn't help but smile back and feel warmed by the glow of this perfect miniature person.

It wasn't usual for brush-slave children to get near the estate houses. But Greg was noticed. The owner family would see the precious boy and give him little jobs and errands, and sometimes reward him with outgrown shoes or bags of fruit.

Occasionally these jobs took Greg inside the house, where he saw the details of a life as foreign to his own as if he were an insect. He would come back to whatever enclosure was home that year and ask his parents why that was that and this was this.

Because, his father said.

Go wash for bed, his mother said.

* * *

In Lynn's home mailbox three days later she found a manila envelope, hand addressed, from Los Angeles. Inside was a lingerie catalogue with a note: *I was shopping in this for your next gift, and thought you might like to pick it yourself. Looking forward. All my love, Greg.*

Lynn flipped the pages. It wasn't what she'd thought – bare, lacy undies – but whorish, offensive getups with cutouts and tassels. There were open-tipped bras, harem-type outfits, the crotchless panty hose Greg had talked about. The models were in porn-magazine poses and wore the same dull, panting expressions.

She threw the book in the kitchen garbage and clamped the lid back on tight.

'What did you choose?'

'Pardon?'

'From the catalogue.'

Lynn decided to lie. But she hadn't expected Greg to call right away that night, or to hit her immediately with the question.

'What catalogue?'

He was quiet for a minute. 'I sent you a gift catalogue and told you to pick something. I don't believe you didn't get it.'

It's only an expression, Lynn told herself, feeling a little sick, taking comfort in the fact that the book was buried in fruit peels and eggshells. He doesn't mean he knows I'm lying.

She steered the conversation to fresher waters and they talked for a while longer. To her relief Greg seemed to forget about the catalogue; he didn't ask about it again.

The following week a big package came from Bullock's in Westwood, California. It was waiting with her mail when she got home after work. Uneasy and hopeful at once, she carted it into the kitchen and sliced the tape with a knife.

'Ha!' she said to no one when she saw the box inside the carton. Greg had sent her a coffee maker, a trendy, expensive Braun, and big bags of decaf and regular Italian roast. The card had blue flowers and the message: *Now you'll always have some for us.*

Smiling, Lynn pulled open the box and reached in to lift out the glossy white machine.

Her smile died and she dropped the Braun against the counter, denting the chrome trim.

Stuffed inside was another copy of the catalogue.

'Sorry you had to wait for me,' Kara said, buckling her seat belt. 'I wanted to take Nicky for a last walk before I left. What did you bring?'

Lynn pulled the Lexus away from the curb. 'I went to get wine, but I decided it was too boring. So I got sangria.'

'Good. I made a tomato-and-cucumber salad.'

'Mary will like that.'

They rode in silence for a while. Traffic was Sunday-light. A damp November wind flapped coats, but the sun gave some warmth.

'I'm glad it's not any colder,' Kara said. 'Remember their April cookout? Gideon was outside turning the chicken in a parka and ski hat.'

'Mm.'

'Too bad Greg couldn't make the party. This would be a nice bit of Easterniana to regale his tan friends with. How is he?'

'I haven't talked to him this week. He's been … sending me things.'

'That's nice.'

'I don't know if it is.'

'What did he send? Anything like that great dress?'

'A coffee maker and coffee. And a catalogue of gross underwear. He wanted me to pick something.'

'And did you?'

'No.' Lynn braked harder than necessary just past a parking space. 'They weren't pretty. They were disgusting.'

Lynn and Kara took their bags of food and sangria from the back and went up the walk of Mary and Gideon's town house. It was a triplex with a separate entrance for Mary's office, and a slate patio in back where the barbecuing was done. In summer the whole party took place out there, with cushions on the soft grass and Mary's raspberry margaritas.

Twenty or more people were already there, talking in knots in various rooms. 'How many are coming?' Kara asked Mary when they found her in the kitchen putting a pie in the oven.

'Just a few more. Twenty-eight in total. How *are* you?' Mary hugged them.

Kara surveyed the bowls and platters of food. 'Your usual spartan table. Everything looks great. Aren't *these* something?' She picked up a sparkling new set of grill tools, thick copper with black wood handles. 'Gideon's so well-supplied.'

'Those are a gift,' Mary said with a mischievous smile. 'We just got them.'

'Our gifts aren't as impressive,' Lynn said, putting two sangria bottles on the counter. Kara took out her salad.

'Everyone likes sangria. Mmm, those look like summer tomatoes.'

'Hothouse,' Kara said.

Mary set the timer for the pie and touched Lynn's hand. 'Follow me. I have a surprise.'

Her smooth blond hair moved like a shimmering curtain as she led Lynn into the crowded den, Kara following. Lynn saw Gideon in a group by the fireplace talking animatedly, gesturing with his beer bottle. He looked up as they approached. A man in the group turned. It was Greg.

Lynn was glad and confused, pleased and chilled.

81

Momentarily immobile, she stood passive as he spread his arms and wrapped her in a hug. She was conscious of Mary, Kara and Gideon beaming at them. Greg's scent settled over her.

When he let go, Lynn said, 'I thought you couldn't come.'

Greg winked at her. 'He called yesterday,' Mary explained. 'Said he'd arranged to get away and wanted to surprise you. So we gave him directions, and here he is. *With* that spectacular copper set. He came just an hour before you did.'

'Which was good,' Gideon said, 'because we had a chance to check him over.'

Greg grinned at them. 'Did I pass?'

Gideon grinned back under his bushy mustache. 'So far. Long as you take good care of our buddy.'

Mary squeezed Lynn's wrist. 'He's a love. *Excellent* choice,' she said meaningfully.

Lynn was still staring at Greg. 'How did you get their number?'

'Directory assistance. They aren't exactly Bob and Barbara Smith. What's the matter?' He took her hands. 'Aren't you happy to see me?'

'Of course I am.'

Mary broke away. 'I have to go put food out for all you savages.' Kara and Gideon went with her.

Greg was wearing a white cotton fisherman's sweater over a blue shirt. His tan was incandescent.

'I'm like a kid,' he said quietly. 'So glad to be with you, I can barely stand still. I kept waking up last night, waiting for it to be today.'

The room was warm from the fireplace, but Lynn felt cool sweat in her hair. She shivered slightly, and edged closer to the hearth.

'I'm flattered,' she said, wishing she could say, could feel, more. What the *hell* was the matter with her? Why should it throw her to have Greg appear at the Elis' when it didn't faze anyone else, least of all the Elis?

True, they didn't know about the catalogue. But Kara did. Of course, all Kara knew was the fact itself; she hadn't seen the sickening pictures, hadn't been the one asked to choose some perverted thing ...

Greg was talking about his trip from the airport, the Boston cab-drivers. She smiled and half listened, adrift in her thoughts. The fireplace threw reassuring heat.

But maybe the fact itself was all there was. Judging by Kara and Pam, at least, she seemed to be the only adult woman on the Eastern Seaboard who didn't find border-line-pornographic outfits exciting.

Seemed also to be the only person she knew here today who didn't instantly find Greg's surprise visit charming.

Maybe she should be ashamed of herself.

Lynn and Greg helped Gideon with the grilling, carrying out platters of ribs and pots of marinade. Greg was fearless at reaching across spitting flame to brush the liquid on the meat.

'Watch your sweater,' Gideon said, holding Greg's sleeve out of the way. 'It's great to have an assistant. And a scapegoat. Usually it's *me* getting nagged about what I put too close to the fire.'

'Nothing anatomical, I hope,' Greg said.

Lynn passed more marinade. 'His mustache.'

Greg brushed the goo on, then licked a drop off his finger. 'Mm. Tangy. What's in this?'

'Vinegar, apricot preserves, minced ginger ...'

Gideon went on, but Greg had stopped listening, the marinade brush still.

Lynn followed the direction of his frown to the tall, bushy evergreen shrubs at the end of the patio.

'What's wrong?' she asked.

Suddenly he ran for the shrubs, crossing the patio in leaping strides.

83

Gideon and Lynn followed as he disappeared around the hedging. 'What the hell?' Gideon said.

After a couple of minutes Greg came out, brushing himself off. 'I thought I saw someone.'

'You might well have,' Gideon said. 'We have neighbors.'

'Someone sneaking around, I mean.'

'The chicken can go out,' Mary called.

Gideon patted Greg's shoulder. 'Want to go get that? Unless you'd rather keep chasing prowlers with that marinade brush.'

Greg gave a last look at the greenery and grinned. 'Not a brilliant move, huh? I must be in love.'

They ate on laps, on furniture, on the floor. The sangria was a hit, so much so that they were running out while there was still plenty of food.

'I should have brought more,' Lynn said to Mary. 'I didn't think it would be so popular.'

'Do you have a couple of bottles of red wine and some citrus fruit?' Greg asked. 'We could make a batch real quick.'

Mary put down a rib. 'Great idea.'

'Let me.' Greg went to the kitchen. Lynn took the nearly empty sangria pitcher and followed.

'What should I get out?' she asked.

'The wine. Brandy, if there is some. Cinnamon.' Greg leaned into the big double refrigerator and brought out grapefruit, oranges, and a lime. 'Oh, club soda.'

Lynn watched as he mixed the wine with fruit juice, dolloped in brandy, added slices of fruit. He finished with club soda and cinnamon. He held a spoonful out to Lynn. 'Taste.'

'Mm. Better than the bottled.'

They brought it to the den.

'Fantastic,' Mary said, sipping. She turned to Lynn. 'Is there anything he can't do?'

Make me feel secure, Lynn thought, and then was genuinely ashamed.

84

Greg was being lovely to her, to her friends. Everyone liked him. He was attentive, gracious, articulate, attractive. He seemed to adore her.

What more could she want?

Later, handing around Mary's marshmallow brownies, Lynn found herself smiling extra warmly when she came to Greg. Whether it was the three glasses of sangria or just time passing, she felt more comfortable.

When she was done, she put the tray on a table, got coffee, and came back to sit with Greg.

'Delicious coffee,' he said.

'It always is here. Gideon's a maniac. By the way – thank you for the Braun.'

Greg drained his cup. 'I was wondering if you got it.'

'I tried to call. Your line is always busy.' She'd tried just twice, intending to state her feelings about the catalogue. But when she couldn't say her piece while she was geared up to, she'd simply put off calling again.

'But you like the machine?'

'I haven't tried it yet. I've been at the station thirty hours a day. The Italian-roast coffee smells wonderful, though.'

Lynn held her breath, hoping he wouldn't mention the catalogue. But all he did was take her hand and softly kiss it, and she relaxed.

He must have picked up on her distaste, realized he shouldn't push the underwear business.

She had just bitten into a brownie when Greg said, so only Lynn could hear, 'I have a present for you.'

'Another present?' she said without thinking, and then winced at her ungraciousness. 'I'm sorry. I just meant, you're so generous. It's a little embarrassing.'

'Come with me.' He stood.

'Where?' She took another bite.

Greg bent down and took the brownie. He put it on a table, out of her reach. Without answering, he clasped her

85

hand, pulled her up, and led her from the room.

He brought her to the guest bathroom. Another guest was just coming out, a tall model-like blonde. She looked Greg over admiringly, spotted Lynn, and grinned as they went inside together. Greg grinned back at her and shut the door.

Lynn fought the inexplicable urge to open it. 'Why are we in here?'

'You'll see.'

He reached inside his sweater and pulled out a small package wrapped in lavender tissue. 'Here.'

'What is it?'

He kissed her neck. 'Open it and look.'

Her skin tingling pleasantly from Greg's warm mouth, Lynn pulled off the paper and opened the box. Black fabric, rolled up.

Greg took the roll and let it fall open. He held up her present: crotchless panty hose.

The coffee lurched in her stomach.

Before she could speak, Greg said, 'Put them on now.'

She shook her head.

'Lynn –'

'No!'

He stared at her. He looked bewildered. 'I thought it would be fun. I thought it would help. Last time we were together, you didn't come. That bothered me.'

She was still shaking her head, but Greg went on. 'Please, Lynn – put them on. I'll go down on you right in here. Won't that be exciting?'

She took hold of the doorknob. Greg looked at her hand there, looked back at her face. 'I have to leave in an hour – I can't even stay the night. This is all the time we have together. Let's make it count.'

Lynn yanked open the door and ran out.

* * *

'I'm sorry,' Lynn said, the phone clutched to her ear, 'I'm really sorry.'

'But what happened? You and Greg both seemed to be having a great time. Then all of a sudden you go flying out of here –'

'I know. I feel awful. Sticking you with him ... leaving Kara without a ride home ...' On her living room sofa, Lynn rubbed her neck to loosen the tension collected there. 'The party isn't still going, is it? Did everyone leave?'

'The last one went just before you called. Ann Boden. The tall blonde in the olive jumpsuit? She was asking me about Greg, in fact. I told her he was taken. She saw you and Greg going into the bathroom together.'

Lynn hadn't wanted to tell Mary much. She was too confused herself to be able to make sense to someone else, especially a professional listener. She'd called only to apologize for racing out. She was going to fudge the rest for now.

But she was so unhappy. Her apartment, so recently filled with something other than herself and air, oppressed her. Yet again she had to confront the fact that this simple act of pairing, so effortless for everyone, for every*thing*, was confounding to her.

'Anyway,' Mary continued when Lynn didn't take the opening, 'you didn't stick me with anyone. Greg didn't stay long. He and Kara shared a cab.'

Lynn's neck was tighter than ever. She rubbed it some more. 'What did he say when I left?'

'Not much. He was upset. He'd offended you some-how, he said, he didn't really understand it himself. He said he hated to leave without making peace with you, but he was due back in LA. He thanked us for a lovely party.'

Lynn was quiet.

'So?' Mary prompted. 'Do you want to talk?'

She considered it, wondering where to begin, the lure of

letting out her anguish so seductive. But Mary wasn't done.

'Because, Lynn, I'd like to help. I know you don't want this relationship to get off on the wrong foot. Greg is … we all think he's dynamite.'

Lynn was tempted, but … no. Not if that was to be the starting point.

She made her excuses and got off the phone.

Gideon came into the kitchen with a bag of trash. 'Well?'

'I don't know. She was hedging.'

'Her privilege.'

'Of course.' Mary swiped gold hair out of her eyes. 'Where the hell is my headband? I'm dripping sweat.'

Gideon saw it behind the toaster and handed it to her. She used it to sweep her face free of hair, then blotted with a tissue.

'Hot flash?'

'Yup.'

'Did you ask Lynn to give you a tape of that show?'

'I forgot. I was so busy trying to glue her love life back together. How were they outdoors? Getting along?'

'Yes. And he did a lot of the work. Except when he was charging through the bushes.'

'Why?'

'He thought he saw someone sneaking around. Later he told me there was some woman awhile back who wouldn't leave him alone. A Letterman-type situation. Made him paranoid.'

'Understandable,' Mary said. 'A man that attractive … Aren't these something, though?' She touched the barbecue set.

'Yes.' Gideon put it back in its box, stuck the box in a cabinet, and started out of the kitchen.

'Why not keep it out in the shed with the grill?'

He stopped. 'I guess I can.'

'It's not an engagement gift. It doesn't have to be returned if they split.'

'Why don't I want to use it, though?'

Mary smiled. 'I give up.'

He pondered another minute. 'I'm being an asshole.' He got the set and took it out to the shed.

Kara was in another part of the building when Lynn got to work the next day. Lynn plunged eagerly into her routine, plowing through paper, returning calls. Always work, with its capacity to distract and anesthetize, had been therapeutic.

Around ten Dennis Orrin hurried into her office, waving a folder. 'The full ratings report on the test show. You're going to be happy.'

'Dennis! I am?'

'Very happy.' He leaned over the folder with her. 'Look at these shares. Excellent in Chicago –'

Lynn touched a number on the sheet. 'We *killed* in LA!'

'– and very nice in Cleveland, Baltimore, and Minneapolis. The only place we didn't win in the slot was Detroit, and there were two local football games running on cable there.'

Lynn sank into a chair. 'I love it.'

'You're launched, kid. The QTV affiliates will chow down these numbers. They'll be kicking doors in to see the pilot.' He bent and smacked a kiss on her forehead. 'Gotta go exploit the hell out of this.'

Lynn jumped up and paced the office, adrenaline thrumming. She replayed the numbers in her head, feeling jolts of proud excitement as she pictured the brass at each station reading them.

Greg came to mind. While the thought did nothing to dim her pleasure, it opened a hole in it. Even in so short a time, Greg's responses had become important to her.

She wished ... She wished she wanted to tell him.

* * *

She returned a message from Pennina Russo, and gave a silent cheer when someone else answered, 'Department of Parks.'

'No,' Pennina said when she came on the line, 'I don't have my title back – but I called to tell you I'm off the reception desk, and I'm getting a hearing. Probably a more honest one now that my grievances are so visible.'

After the goodbyes, the word stayed. *Visible*.

Lynn had driven home that concept on the Parks Department show. From some purposeful internal lockbox a closing monologue had sprung whole, as if scripted and rehearsed, so compellingly that Lynn had rattled her booth and floor staff by substituting it for the prepared closing that was rolling through the PrompTer.

'This is power we're talking about today,' Lynn had told the camera. 'Secret power fed by the dark – the dark where it happens, and the dark that results when we refuse to talk or see.

'It isn't just male against female. It's nowhere near that simple.

'We're starting to ask what we really think about sexual harassment and abuse and rape – what's actually going on, all the places where the power is in all this.

'What do we think now? What did we used to think? Is there a difference between how we *say* we feel and how we honestly do? Who's really doing the victim-bashing? Do women participate in their own victimization? Do we secretly believe they do? Do we *want* to believe it?

'We all owe thanks to the visibility of cases like Pennina Russo's – to Hill-Thomas, Bowman-Kennedy, Washington-Tyson. Once, all this injustice happened only in the dark. Too much of it still does. But we're starting to shine lights and open doors ... and that's the only way we can hope to blast the power away.'

The show had solidified Lynn's plan for the QTV pilot.

More and more her daily programs hewed to a theme – the theme she had so passionately stated in her spontaneous closing: the baffling web of questions about victimization.

So where better to base her pilot than at the beginning of victimization – childhood?

Among her messages this morning had been one for Kara from Oprah Winfrey's personal assistant returning her call. With luck Kara could pave the way for an invitation from Lynn to Oprah. They would try to have two or three more celebrities who had been abused as children. A small panel of child-abuse specialists would complete the lineup for a powerful pilot on the origins of the victim dynamic.

When Kara finally came into the office, she ran to Lynn and hugged her.

Disarmed, Lynn hugged back hard. 'Thank you,' she said into Kara's hair.

Kara moved away. 'You looked like you needed it. I heard about the ratings. Did it help?'

She smiled. 'What's that you always say about the Pope?'

'All *right*!'

'Dennis says the QTV affiliates will be kicking doors in to get the pilot. Speaking of which – Oprah's assistant left you a message.'

Kara grabbed the slip and dialed. 'Hell. Busy.'

'And I talked to Pennina. Someone else is on the phones, and she's having a hearing.'

'Thank God.' Kara began straightening the welter of paper on Lynn's desk. 'Did Mary tell you Greg and I shared a cab?'

Lynn nodded. 'I apologize for stranding you.'

'Lucky for you you did. So I got to be the one who listened to him, and not that Ann Whoever, or any one of the eleven other ladies who would have been delighted to do it. Have you made up with him yet? I'm guessing not.'

'What did he tell you?'

'That he came on too strong, and you were offended.'

Lynn gave a mirthless chuckle.

'He said he couldn't help it,' Kara said. 'He'd missed you so much, and then there you were, and he knew he had to leave soon ...'

'He makes it sound *sweet*.'

'But it is. I'd love to have a man like Greg find me so irresistible that he'd try to make love to me in someone's bathroom.'

'That's not what happened.'

Lynn longed for coffee. But if she didn't get the truth out now, she might not at all. She had to, because what was most infuriating was that no one was on her side. And how could they be, when they didn't know there was a side to be on?

'We were having dessert. All of a sudden he hauled me into the bathroom because he had a present for me. The present was ... was panty hose. With no crotch. He wanted me to put them on right there.'

Kara nodded.

'He wanted to go down on me. He said it in those words.'

With rising anxiety, Lynn saw that Kara didn't get it, truly didn't see what the fuss was about. Replaying her words, she realized that, without the background, it didn't sound like that big a deal.

'This has been an issue with us. He –'

'Sex? I thought it was really good.'

'It was. But then he started getting weird. Using crude language, even after I asked him not to. Even after it upset me enough so I couldn't do anything. Remember the morning he left, when I came in depressed? That was why.'

'But he talked like that from the start,' Kara said. 'You enjoyed it. You told me.'

'At first I did. But he kept pushing it, being more obscene. Then when he started sending things –'

'I remember the dress.'

'Not just the dress.' Shrill in her own ears, Lynn forced herself to stop, to sound more calm. She was about to describe the most damning part. Kara had to understand.

'He brought up the idea of those damn panty hose when he was still in Boston. "I could stick my tongue right in," he said. Then he sent me that catalogue. It wasn't sexy, it was pornographic. The panty hose were pictured in it. When I pretended it hadn't come, he – listen to this – he sent me another catalogue, but inside a nice gift, a coffee maker, so I couldn't say I didn't get it. When I *still* wouldn't play, he brought the hose to Mary's!'

Kara gazed at her.

Lynn reached out a hand. 'Now do you see?'

'I see a persistent guy who's a little lead-footed about taking hints.'

'*Hints?*'

'Did you ever actually say you didn't want the hose?'

'I made it clear!'

'Are you sure, Lynn? Are you sure he doesn't have ample reason to be confused? *I'm* confused. *I* remember you saying just a couple of weeks ago that Greg must have read every article on what women want.'

The ache in Lynn's neck was there again. She reached to rub it.

She wasn't getting anywhere. She couldn't make Kara see.

Her neck was loosening a bit, but it was going to knot up again, the way her teeth were grinding. Then there would be a miserable headache.

'Call him,' Kara said.

'I will. But only to tell him we need to cool down.'

'What do you mean? You had a misunderstanding. It'll

93

blow over. You sound as if you don't want to see Greg again.'

Lynn spotted a glass Channel 3 mug with an inch of cold coffee among the piles of paper on her desk. She picked it up, changed her mind, put it down. 'I don't know if I do.'

'But it was going so well. He seemed perfect. You thought he was perfect.' Kara spread her hands. 'How does something perfect turn into something this doubtful in just a few weeks?'

'It doesn't – if it was really perfect to start with.' Lynn went to the window.

Her back to Kara, she said, 'Greg and I met in the most artificial atmosphere. I was euphoric, queen for the day. We almost went to bed that night. Then I leave town, he arrives in a week, and we start this dizzying hot romance. Before the visit is even over, he's got me wondering.'

She turned around. 'Now I'm wondering more. And the smartest thing I can do is acknowledge that. The old me would have pined away for him without listening to my instincts. I –'

A knock on the door stopped her.

'It's open,' Lynn shouted.

Pam came in. 'There's a delivery for you. A humongous gift box. The man can barely carry it.'

Lynn sighed. 'You can send him in.'

It was a gigantic fluffy toy raccoon. Lynn stroked it absently in its box as she opened the card. "I'm sorry I got carried away,"' she read aloud. '"It was great to see you. I'll be calling."'

Kara touched an ear. 'This is an adorable present.'

Lynn lifted it out of the box. Its head lolled back and its legs dangled. She dropped it, but it missed the box and landed on the floor.

Kara moved to pick it up, but Lynn said, 'Don't.'

'Why not?'

'Look at it. The head and legs every which way, like it was … sick. Look at the eyes. They're crossed.'

Kara stared at her.

'*Look*,' Lynn said.

'I am looking. All I see is a cute stuffed animal.'

'It doesn't look sick to you?'

Kara picked up the animal and put it gently back in the box. 'Lynn, the man is bending over sideways to be nice. He admits he was out of line. He apologizes. He sends a present. What else do you want?'

She had to admit that, nestled back in the box, it no longer looked so revolting. But still, still …

'I want – I want … to do what my gut says is right. And my gut says, nip this affair in the bud.'

Kara started to interrupt, but Lynn went on. 'Listen, this is new for me. For a change, I'm doing my thinking from the right place – not from my hormones, or from the insecure little hogslopper inside.'

Again Kara began, and Lynn held up her hand. 'Let's go to work now. Let's get some hot coffee and go to work.'

Kara picked up a handful of message slips. 'If that's what you want.'

'We have five daily shows and a national pilot to plan. It's what I want. What's there? Anything good?'

Kara buzzed Pam for coffee and sat down with the slips. 'That judge who wants to strengthen restraining orders? He sounds very good. Thoughtful. But I didn't think we should just have another isn't-it-awful-about-women-with-orders-getting-killed show.'

'It is still awful, though. Just because we've done programs on it doesn't change the fact.'

'Sure it doesn't. But I thought it was time we added a dimension to the subject. So I called around. I spoke to a couple of matrimonial lawyers who are angry about how easy restraining orders are to get. They think some innocent guys are being shafted by *wife lawyers* – their term – who go for orders for the public relations value.'

'You mean – to make the man look dangerous.'

'Mm-hm.'

'That could be an important show.'

'I think so.'

'Thanks, Pam. This is terrific,' Lynn said as Pam set down a tray with coffee, plain cookies, and two apples. She turned back to Kara. 'This wife-lawyer business is worth following up too. *Are* some lawyers better for one or the other? Do they have biases going in?'

'You bet,' Pam said, opening the door to leave.

'How do you know?' Lynn asked.

'I only have about twenty-eight friends who're divorced.'

'Both sexes?'

'*All* sexes.'

Kara shrugged. 'Good sample.'

'Yell if you want refills,' Pam said, and went out.

'What else do we have?' Lynn asked.

'Osteoporosis. You wanted me to see what else we could do after the show with the doctors –'

'I remember. The woman with the deformed back. Go on.'

'It turns out hormone therapy isn't the only treatment that's controversial. Scads of doctors push massives doses of certain vitamins – and a whole other bunch hate them. Think they're harmful. It's shaking down as a vital issue.'

'I agree. Let's do it.' Lynn sliced one of the apples and gave Kara a chunk.

'Let's see. Exercise. Toning muscles and building bone mass by means of whole body tension, a new method using free weights ...'

'Is that a commercial enterprise?' Lynn asked, chewing.

'No. A woman named Elizabeth Vail developed it herself. She works at the Broome Club, but it's her own creation. She'll provide a tape that has real people, older ones, doing the routines, and bone-mass diagrams to show the effect.'

'I don't see it for an entire program.'

'I don't either, but we could use it on the osteoporosis one.'

'If she really addresses that.'

'She does. That's why she called – she saw the women's health show.'

'Okay. Anything else?'

'Sleep disorder. This –'

'We've done and done it.'

'I know that! Will you listen a minute?'

Lynn rubbed her eyes. 'Sure. I'm sorry.'

'Give me some credit, huh? You can jump on an idea after I pitch it, but let me pitch it.'

One of the few aspects of her job Kara disliked was the hierarchy that gave Lynn the last word on the content of every show. She and Lynn didn't disagree often, but when they did, Kara felt her underling status acutely. Lynn was the host, but her own experience and professional judgment were at least the equal of Lynn's.

Kara continued. 'Night terrors, this lady called about. Janet … Janet Drake. No, Drew. She wakes up at night and has to run from things.'

'Is she …?'

'A few cookies short of a pound? Yes. But I checked two sleep clinics, and there are many people like her. She called us because she's desperate. Medication doesn't help much. The doctors admit that. With this many question marks, I thought we should at least consider it.'

'You're right. See what some other patients have to say.'

'I will. Can I have the last piece of apple?'

'If I can finish the cookies.'

CHAPTER FOUR

Greg carried a cellular in his briefcase that he used in the car and wherever else he needed to. He could have just had a car phone – everyone else did – but their cars got broken into more. Car phones were so obvious, they asked to be stolen. And he truly hated having his car broken into. It was such an invasion.

He pulled into a Wendy's, thought of calling, but decided it was too early. He eased the car into the drive-up line and waited behind a white Saab convertible for his turn at the window. The Saab driver couldn't reach the window and had to step out of the car to get her order. Greg saw a long dark ponytail caught up with an orange ribbon. A lovely woman, sleek in bike tights. Strong quads; she must do distance pedaling.

He watched for another admiring minute while she paid, settled her bag of food, and rebuckled her seat belt. When she drove off, he pulled to the window and ordered a chicken fillet sandwich and an iced coffee.

He thought he saw the Saab again as he was parking on a scenic overlook to enjoy his meal. He looked for the flash of the orange ribbon, but without any real enthusiasm.

Beautiful jocks were crabgrass compared to a talk show star.

So. Nice for looking, but he was busy.

Busy with Lynn.

Too much coffee. Lynn had a good capacity, but the eight or nine cups she'd put away over this long day were pushing it even for her, and at dinnertime she found herself browsing in the kitchen with a stomach that turned down everything she thought of putting into it.

So she puttered for a while instead, tidying small messes. She hadn't been keeping up; the ups and downs with Greg kept her preoccupied. And the apartment was still full of emotional land mines. Each chore brought images: a glass like one he'd used, the whiff of his cologne on a pillowcase. She'd misplaced the running food-shopping list she always kept, and had to make a new one, recalling what had been on it that had to be written again, and what had been on it that didn't: cocktail snacks, shaving cream.

The few scraps of silver-and-blue paper she was still finding on the carpet were especially tough. Greg's Tums wrappers ... there were bits of them everywhere he went. She'd joked with him that he marked his territory that way, the way animals do by urinating on the ground.

As she moved around straightening up, the stabs of sadness got worse. For a brief time back there she'd been ecstatic; the pieces of her joy were all over the damn place. No wonder she wandered away from whatever chore she started.

It was so hard to stay focused on what she knew she had to do.

Eventually Lynn turned off the radio, put on her nightgown and robe, and heated a Lean Cuisine. She ate it slowly while watching *Murphy Brown* ... slowly because the toy raccoon kept coming to mind, wobbling through her thoughts – and because she'd promised herself she didn't have to make the call to Greg until after dinner.

She still had several bites left when the phone rang.

'Please don't.'

'I have to, Greg.'

'You don't have to. God, we were just getting started. We clicked. I know you felt that. You said so.'

'I was impulsive.'

99

'You know where I am? I'm in my car in Malibu. Near Geoffrey's restaurant. Where we met. Remember that night?'

She was silent.

'Talk to me, Lynn. You're not talking.'

On the hushed screen Miles Silverberg stomped across the newsroom, seething. Lynn watched, holding the phone with wet fingers. This was so much harder than she'd expected.

She was being brief and vague on purpose. Another lesson from a *Lynn Marchette Show*, one on keeping control of volatile situations: don't give the other person enough to engage you with.

'It isn't working out, Greg. It's best to nip this –'

'– in the bud. You said that. But it doesn't tell me anything. Let's talk about how I can make you happy again. What can I do?'

'Nothing,' she said softly, and listened to the sad silence that followed.

Greg lowered the car window to let the food smell out. Another car pulled into the overlook, its radio blaring, and he made a face and raised the window again.

'That's so cold,' he said.

'I guess it is. But –'

'I never thought you were cold.'

The disappointment and disgust in Greg's voice jabbed right through the shield of control she was fiercely struggling to maintain.

Defenses leaped to her lips, but she said only, 'Maybe I am.'

'No. Not underneath.' He began to whisper; his mouth must have touched the phone. It was as intimate as if Greg were right on the couch with his mouth touching her ear. 'With my tongue in you, you weren't cold. With my cock in –'

Lynn flung the receiver to the floor. She stared at it for

a shocked instant, then grabbed it and slammed it back on the phone. She cried into her wet hands.

He kept leaving messages. There were two or three on her machine every night when she got home.

They were normal-sounding, no sex talk, but they sickened her. The softly insistent voice that would not go away was maddening.

'Lynn, I really miss you. I'm sorry for whatever I did that upset you. I'd love to talk to you. Please call me.'

One evening when she dreaded getting into bed, and shifting restlessly while a burgeoning headache prevented sleep yet again, she decided to change her nonstrategy. If ignoring didn't work, she would do the precise opposite: bellow out her message loud and clear. She had never actually told Greg, I want no further contact with you, I will call the police if you don't leave me alone.

Heartened by her resolve, Lynn dialed the number he'd left. As always, it was busy. She tried a few more times, got the busy tone, and finally made chamomile tea and tried to sleep.

He began leaving messages at work. She'd find the pink While You Were Out slips after lunch or meetings, or when she got off the air.

'You haven't talked to him at *all*?' Kara asked, handing her one of the slips.

'Not since the night I freaked and hung up on him.'

'Shouldn't you spell it out, if you're determined that it's over?'

'I've tried. His number is always busy.'

'He's left so many messages,' Kara said reproachfully.

Lynn looked up from the program rundown she'd been reading. 'Am I hearing Poor Greg, Mean Lynn? I'm not avoiding the man. I want to settle this. If I could reach him, or if he ever called the office when I was here, I would. He knows my schedule. It's almost as if he purposely calls when I'm out or on the air.'

Pam stuck her head in. 'Delivery.'

'Not another present?' Lynn moaned. The others were all in the garbage – the raccoon, the dress, the coffee maker, dumped in the trash room of her building.

The delivery man wheeled in a crate like the one that had held the peaches.

Something fluttered in Lynn's stomach as she looked at it. The same Next-Day-Air sticker. Achingly she remembered the surprise and delight of the first time. All she felt now was nauseated.

She and Kara pried it open. Peaches again, but not cushioned and sectioned like before. They seemed to have been just piled in the box.

'They're bad,' Lynn said.

They gazed at the fruit. Rotten brown spots the size of quarters, mold on some.

'Now you'll have to reach him. He should get his money back,' Kara said. 'The box must have sat in some baking-hot terminal overnight.'

'Is it baking hot anywhere between here and Los Angeles in November?'

'Obviously. Give me his number. I'll see what the switchboard can do to use different routing.'

The veil of light snow around the Tobin Bridge was beautiful, but it made for slow going. Lynn's Lexus was better in weather than other sports cars, thanks to traction control and studded tires, and she usually enjoyed tackling snow in it, especially with one of Booboo's chive omelettes waiting for her in Salem. But everything she did now was grayed by the pall she couldn't dispel. She couldn't reach Greg, and he never reached her, despite the endless calls.

Her fingers moved on the radio buttons as she flipped back and forth between Bob Hemphill and Cleo Costello.

Cleo was an old-time Boston-Irish character with a thick Southie accent; Bob was more in Lynn's league, a thoughtful personality who dealt with social issues. Sometimes he was so good, she felt threatened. Now she could console herself with the fact that she was going to be on all over the country, while Bob's station barely reached Worcester.

She thought about that, trying to feel the excitement.

It was still snowing when she reached the house, but just the fat puffy flakes that never lasted. The browned-butter smell met her even before Angela opened the door.

'Your friend called,' Angela said.

Lynn stopped on the front walk.

'Well, come in.' Angela wore a fringed wool serape over her thick sweater. Her ubiquitous neck chains dangled over and under the shawl. 'Don't stand there letting the cold in.'

'Greg.' Lynn closed the door. She wiped her feet on the hooked mat.

'Very nice guy,' Booboo said, coming out of the kitchen, ducking under the doorway. He crushed her in a gorilla hug. It took a second for him to notice she was standing limply.

He drew back and questioned with his eyes.

'Greg called here?' Lynn asked.

Booboo nodded. 'Last night. He said you weren't home, and he thought you might be here.'

'I worked late. Kara and I went out for pizza. What else did he say?'

'He had a good time with us. Said my guacamole was better than Spago's, and he's sending me some special hot peppers to put in it. Let's see, what else? He misses you. He'll be in touch.'

'Come sit in here,' Angela called from the living room. 'The sun came out.'

'What's the matter?' Booboo asked Lynn, searching her face.

'This is – so bizarre. Look, I'm not going out with Greg. I'm not seeing him again. I told him that, but he … keeps calling around, leaving messages for me …'

Booboo brought her by the hand into the living room and deposited her on the couch next to Angela.

'He probably wants to talk you out of breaking it off,' Angela said.

Lynn shook her head. 'It's not that simple.' She told them what had happened: the unwanted gifts, the raccoon, her initial brave resolve to cut off a relationship that didn't feel right … the phone calls, the spoiled peaches. She stumbled over the sexual elements – Greg's vocabulary and the panty hose and catalogues.

'It was strange from the start,' she finished. 'It just took me a while to understand that.'

'And we thought he was great,' Angela said, her tone implying that she wasn't convinced they were the ones who were wrong.

Booboo scratched his chin. 'I don't really get what's bothering you. The man wants to see you again, so he keeps calling. You admitted you didn't give him the gate as plainly as you ought to have.'

'You two were pretty lovey-dovey here,' Angela put in.

'That business about where he works was an honest mistake – I heard it myself,' Booboo said. 'Are you suggesting that he tampered with a stuffed animal to upset you? You said he saw your chipmunk friend on the terrace; maybe a raccoon was the closest sort of animal he could find. And the peaches – well, you can't really think a person would purposely send you bad fruit.'

'He knew how to protect it,' Lynn replied. 'He did the first time. And we talked about raccoons right out here on the way back to Boston, how they seem when they're rabid …' Lynn ran down. She sounded unconvincing in her own ears. 'And the phone calls. So many calls, and he's never reached me. He leaves a number that's always busy …'

'Are you saying he doesn't *want* to reach you?' Booboo asked incredulously.

'*Yes!*'

There was no sound but the drip of melting snow. The sunlight made moving patterns on the pale gray carpet. Lynn felt chilly, though the room was Angela-warm. She rubbed her hands together.

Booboo came over and put his arm around her.

'Look,' he said, 'if the man calls again, I'll say whatever you want me to. What should I say? That you just absolutely don't care to hear from him anymore?'

Lynn shrugged under his arm. As well as she knew Greg wanted not to reach her, she knew he wouldn't call here again. 'Sure.'

'Fine. Then I'll do that.'

'Can we eat?' Angela said. 'I'm starving.'

'Me too,' Lynn lied.

Booboo got up. 'I'll have the omelettes done in three minutes. Then you can tell us all about how your pilot's coming.'

Lynn heard the phone as soon as she unlocked the apartment door.

'You're so hard to reach. I miss you,' Mary said. 'Now that you're almost a nationwide star, are you going to forget your loving friends?'

'Oh, Mary. Of course not.'

'What's new with the pilot? When do you tape?'

'QTV wants it in the can in six weeks. Marilyn Van Derbur and Sandra Dee have said yes tentatively. We're talking to some others. The one I'm dying to have is Oprah, but so far she won't do it.'

'And what else? How's Greg?'

Lynn gave an exhausted sigh and told her everything. 'I made my decision. I broke it off. But it didn't take. And everyone thinks I'm being an idiot.'

Mary said carefully. 'What everybody thinks shouldn't bother you if you're comfortable with your decision.'

'Oh, Mary,' Lynn said. She pulled off her boots. Her tattoo hadn't begun to fade yet; she kept it covered with corrector makeup from a surgical supply store and tried not to think about it. 'I'm not comfortable with any part of this.'

Mary was silent.

'But I felt even worse before. At least I took action.'

'So now what?' Mary prodded after a minute.

'I don't know. Don't you have any proverbs for me?'

'Like about babies and bathwater?'

'No. More on the line of ... being true to thine own self.'

'That's a good one,' Mary said. 'The bathwater isn't bad, though.'

'Don't say that. Don't be person number forty-seven who tries to convince me to stick with Greg. I was having more and more aversive feelings about him. What I just told you about was disgusting. The panty hose, the catalogues, all his dirty talk ...'

'Some people consider it *sexy* talk.'

'There's no difference. Not with Greg.' Lynn rubbed her aching head. 'You're not buying this, are you?'

'Are you?'

She slept even worse than usual Saturday night, her head throbbing. Tylenol Extra Strength didn't touch it. She rarely thought longingly of Valium anymore, but now she did.

By Sunday afternoon she was tormented, sitting out on her terrace in thermal sweats with hot tea, watching the gray harbor.

It was bad enough that Kara had no understanding. Booboo and Angela had stepped up the pressure. Not intentionally; but the fact that they too thought she was way off about Greg – and the added stab of Mary's gentle queries – had been enough to prompt further self-doubt.

Yes, she trusted her instincts; but what about the instincts of everyone close to her? It even seemed as if Greg had given up at last. The phone messages were dwindling.

All the indications that had made her back off were explainable.

Her backing off itself was especially explainable.

She sipped tea and then switched the mug to her other hand to warm the cold one in the steam. In the distance a tug pulled a long barge. If she went inside for her binoculars, she could see people and activity on the tug, but she didn't feel like using the glasses.

She didn't feel like doing much at all.

Four years ago she was going with a man who borrowed $1,500 from her to buy her an engagement ring. He spent the money on a Soloflex. She forgave him and lent him more. He spent that too, then broke up with her.

On the rebound she met a documentary film director. He rubbed her back every night after work and gave her a weekend in St Thomas for her birthday. When he complained that she seemed uncommitted, she lost interest in him.

Could she argue from any strength when Kara and Mary and her brother suggested her judgment of men was less than great?

She drank more of the cooling tea and huddled lower in her chair.

CHAPTER FIVE

Kara was a very careful person. When paying bills, she always read the reminders on the backs of the envelopes, and asked herself each question.

She was paying bills now, making a neat stack on the desk in her foyer.

In a little while she'd have to take the dog out. Nicky didn't know it was Saturday, never realized on weekends that he didn't have to wait till six or seven at night, and so never asked sooner.

Very sweet of her sweet beagle to be so predictable.

Pressing on a stamp, Kara thought about how she generally was at making decisions. She didn't fear them; she rather enjoyed them, in fact, for that reason. Some of her colleagues hated decisions, preferred her to make them, and so she got a chance to demonstrate a skill.

But occasionally she came to one she hated.

Like the one she was facing now.

No solution to this pleased her. She'd had to choose the one that disturbed her least.

And how she'd arrived at that was to ask herself: How would I want Lynn to handle this if our roles were reversed? What should Lynn do that would be best for me and for herself, and for the continuing welfare of the show?

The answer had come slowly as she wrote checks, stuffed envelopes, licked return labels and stamps. Mary called mindless work brain food; you made your best decisions over it.

Kara knew that if she was misreading a promising

relationship and was apt to damage it, and if Lynn had an opportunity to help, she would want Lynn to do just that.

To do what she was going to do: help keep Lynn's opportunity open. Buy her time to do some rethinking.

Saving Lynn from herself wasn't a brand-new project. Fortunately, it had grown less and less necessary over the last few years.

Her bond with Lynn was a profound one, as work partners and as friends. But she had evolved to her present position as producer of a major show by making careful choices – not by blindly following Lynn's star or anyone else's.

So while her efforts to keep Lynn on an even keel personally sprang from a genuine concern and wish for Lynn's happiness, realistically she had to acknowledge that she did have an investment.

She was invested in doing what was necessary to move the show ahead. To make a blockbuster pilot. To get the syndication going, and kill in every market.

To have continued success and fulfillment for Lynn and herself.

Lately those elements had been falling into place quite gratifyingly.

If sometimes it seemed as if she had to work harder than Lynn did for fewer rewards – well, that was life.

Not that Kara was jealous. Not directly, anyway; her objectives were so different.

She put away her checkbook and went to get a diet soda. She adored real Coke, but saved it for the sorts of occasions for which others hoarded Moët. She simply couldn't afford the calories.

Another way Lynn was lucky: she complained about her weight, but her stomach was flat as a Frisbee, and didn't need Diet Coke to stay that way.

If she were Lynn, she'd be doing more thinking and less whining.

And she certainly would be more careful about her own opportunities.

Everyone knew Lynn needed fifteen quiet minutes before a show. She was taking it now, sitting back in her desk chair, doing slow breathing.

It was a meditative technique that always helped. She would visualize the end of the program, feel the satisfaction of how she'd handled it. Then she'd mentally walk through it from the beginning, inserting any suggestions she needed that day: I'm balancing the speakers ... I'm not judgmental ... I don't seem nervous.

Today it was a chore to maintain her relaxed state even long enough for the meditation. She hurried through it. That would have to be enough. It was the best she could do.

She buzzed for Kara. She'd finally decided. She would accept the offer Kara had made several times: to get Greg on the phone so she could talk to him.

I'm sorry I've been hard to reach, she'd say. Thanks for everything you sent. Let's get together again.

She'd suggest they go slowly. She didn't want a mad, passionate, artificial relationship. But she'd be pleased if they could simply get to know each other some more. Assuming *he* still wanted to.

Then at least she'd be able to sleep, without agonizing over what her imagination was assigning to the poor man.

'Kara's not here. She's in the studio,' Pam said on the intercom. 'Should I call her to come up?'

'No. I'll go down. What I need we can't do until after the show anyway.'

Lynn walked down the three flights to Studio C. The audience was seated, watching the final details of the setup. Some people smiled as they saw her step in quietly through an aisle door. Most of the spectators had shaken her hand at the studio entrance on their way in earlier.

Kara was on the set, arranging chairs while a sound man ran mike cords to them. 'Six,' Kara said as Lynn climbed up. 'Right, Lynn? Three police detectives, the social worker, and the two rape crisis counselors. The professor isn't coming.'

'Right,' Lynn said. 'Make sure there's lot of water. Cops drink water. They have to be doing something.'

The sound man left, and Lynn touched Kara's arm. 'After we're done, I want to talk to you.'

She didn't see Kara's flash of alarm because she was looking down to edge a cord aside with her foot. As she did that, she saw some shiny objects on the blue rug of the set. She glanced up to suggest a quick vacuuming, saw Kara's face … and felt an almost physical sock in the belly as her subconscious put the puzzle together.

There was only an instant of merciful confusion before Lynn fully understood what the crumpled pieces of shiny paper were, what their presence meant, and how Kara's face fit the rest.

'Greg was here,' she whispered to Kara. 'Wasn't he?'

Kara swallowed.

The floor director called, 'Five minutes!'

'It was to help *you*,' Kara whispered back.

The production assistants were leading the guests onto the set. Lynn always made a point of being there to welcome them and talk a bit before going on the air, but now she pulled Kara to the side, out of earshot of the set and the control room.

'He called me at home yesterday and insisted on going to dinner. He was only in town for the day. He *begged* me, Lynn. He said he hadn't been able to reach you, and he needed my advice.'

'Go on,' Lynn said, her voice as cold as her hands.

Kara swallowed again. 'That's really all. We had dinner, and he talked about how he misses you. He kept asking me what he should do. He wanted to see the studio where you work, and I had my keys, so I opened up and showed it to him.'

A commotion from the set pulled Lynn's attention away. The guests were all in place and miked, but the floor people were fussing with the cords.

'What's wrong?' Lynn shouted.

'No sound on some of these. We're replacing them.'

Lynn shut her eyes.

Kara said, 'Don't jump to crazy conclusions, Lynn. Just don't. He only looked; he was barely in here for two minutes. You know the mikes conk out all the time.' She squeezed Lynn's shoulders. 'I'm sorry about all this. I'm sorry you're upset. Maybe it wasn't my best call. But we have to do the show. You have to be okay.'

Lynn nodded. She pressed her hands together hard. She made herself think about what she had to do now, right now, just now. She went into the control room.

'Sound yet?' she asked.

One of the technicians answered, but Lynn didn't hear. Something else had grabbed her notice.

A white Braun coffee maker was on the cabinet that held the sound gear. It was loaded with coffee and ready to perk.

Shakily she bent and looked closer. The little rupture in the chrome trim was there. The coffee had the Italian-roast smell.

She ran and got Kara. 'Where did this come from?'

Kara looked from the cabinet to Lynn. 'This what?'

'The coffee maker.'

'I don't know.'

Lynn left the control room before she could tell Kara that she knew the answer to her own question.

Greg had gone into the trash room of her building – she'd throw up for sure if she started thinking about *when* – and he had retrieved the Braun and the coffee. And had somehow, without Kara knowing, set it up in the control

112

room, to be found by Lynn the day after he'd been there, the day the mikes were bad.

Lynn walked carefully to the set.

Two years ago, when Hurricane Bob had roared up the coast toward Boston, she'd sat on her terrace, taking a last quiet moment before leaving for the safety of Booboo's. Gazing out over the strangely dark harbor, knowing it was out there and coming this way, she'd gathered her strength for whatever might happen.

Though she had no idea what Greg's objective was, she knew positively now that all her earlier feelings had been right. She could not treat him reasonably, any more than she could reason with a hurricane. He was at one end of something and she was at the other; and what was in between was unknown and frightening.

She had hosted shows with a high fever, with a tooth shooting root-canal pain. She did one the morning her gynecologist had insisted she go to the hospital after a week of abdominal pain; right after the show, she passed out, and an hour later underwent emergency surgery for an ovarian cyst.

She did very well with this one.

The topic was sex crime, thank God. She needed a provocative subject, because she was too shaken to do anything but hold herself in tight control as she moved through her dance steps, automatically listening for the places to break, to prod another guest, to ask a blunt question, to move into the audience.

She couldn't banish the image of Greg sneaking around, sneaking in everywhere, all her places … in her building, in here, in her *studio*. The fact that just this morning she'd finally decided to push aside her suspicions made it even more of an invasion.

Suspicions of *what*? That was the question that had tortured her all weekend … that had contributed to the

113

emotional cease-fire she'd reached this morning. Just what did she think he was after? There was no hypothesis that made sense, that fit the devilish acts he seemed to be perpetrating.

Something snagged her attention – not the counterfeit alertness that was running the show, but her real interest. One of the cops was speaking, a detective named Mike Delano.

'Mike, this is important. Say that one more time, slowly.'

She studied him in close-up on the monitor. He had ink-dark eyes under heavy brows, and a wide cleft chin. On the screen his gaze was pained and serious, not the media mask so many police wore.

He said, 'A sex criminal isn't just a guy who grabs a woman on a stairway, or who forces himself on a date or a child. He can be someone you have sex with willingly, who wears a three-piece suit and buys you caviar.'

Barely breathing, Lynn asked, 'Where does the crime part come in?'

'I was just getting to that,' he said irritably, mis-interpreting her question as a challenge. 'This is a path-ology we're learning more about all the time. He's often attractive, so he slips easily into your life. He has sex with you, showers you with attention. Everything seems rosy. But he's sick, and so eventually he gives himself away somehow, and you reject him. That's when the real violation begins. The public thinks of these as *stalker* cases. We call them pathological harassment – in other words, torture.'

The floor director was signaling her to break, but Lynn couldn't tear her eyes from the monitor.

Now she was starting to understand what Greg was after.

CHAPTER SIX

She was sitting in a chair by his desk, waiting for him when he came in with a lunch bag. On the show yesterday his plainclothes had been a suit and tie. Today he wore jeans and a gray hooded Tufts sweatshirt.

She watched him cross the big room, exchanging waves with the other detectives. When he saw her, he hesitated, then dropped into his desk chair and put the bag down.

'Thank you for appearing on the show,' Lynn said.

'That's not why I'm here, but thank you. You helped me personally.'

'Good. Why are you here?'

Lynn paused. 'Is there an office where we can talk?'

'This is it. Don't worry about them,' he said, gesturing at the roomful of closely positioned desks. 'We won't be discussing anything they don't hear about every day.'

'How can you know what we'll be discussing?' she asked, low.

Mike Delano let out his breath. 'Yesterday I talk about sex crime on your show. Today you're in my client chair before lunch, thanking me for helping you personally. If I can't hypothesize from there, I belong back at the academy. Want one?' he asked, taking two hot dogs out of his bag.

'No, thanks. What you said that helped was about the pathological harassment.'

Briefly she sketched what had happened with Greg.

'And everybody thinks it's you,' Mike finished for her, picking up sauerkraut from the waxed paper and adding it to his half-finished hot dog.

115

The threat of tears was palpable. 'Yes.'

Unconsciously she was eyeing the frank still on the desk. She hadn't even remembered to eat lunch in days, but suddenly she was starved.

'For God's sake,' Mike said, 'take it. I offered.'

'I'm not going to eat half your lunch.'

'Eat a quarter of it, then.' He gave her the frank he'd been working on and picked up the whole one. 'That's part of these guys' shtick. Their actions can be interpreted two ways. Your friends insist he's a garter snake; you know he's a copperhead. The really good ones can even make you doubt yourself. You said he gave you a phone number?'

Lynn nodded. 'But when I –'

'Let me guess. It was a 1288.'

She put down her frank. 'Right.'

'Any 1288 number with certain exchanges anywhere in the country is always busy. Scam artists use them. We use them.' He leaned toward her, his big dark eyes intense. 'That fact should take care of any doubt you still have that your guy is a wackball.'

Lynn had realized that just before Mike said it. She sat back in the hard chair, the hot dog a brick in her stomach. Sharp relief, sick fear – all at once.

She was right. She wasn't searching out the worm in the apple, beating herself up.

She was right. Greg, or whatever his name was, was after her, targeting her, torturing her.

'What else is going to happen?' she asked.

'How the hell do I know?'

'You were quick enough to call yourself an expert on the show!' Lynn snapped. No one at the other desks turned to look.

'I am an expert. I'm just not Kreskin. Look, it varies how far they take this. Their primary concern is control. They get their buzz from jerking you around – appearing and disappearing, being all over the place and yet not

116

reachable. Taunting you with how easily they can climb into your life and fuck it up. Some guys get tired of you and go on to the next lady; some keep hitting. How was he in bed?'

'We … He …'

'You did have sex with him?'

'Yes, but … he seemed to like talking about it as much as doing it. Maybe more. In gross language.'

'Ah,' Mike said. 'What else? Any weird requests?'

'The panty hose. The crotchless ones he was pushing on me? He kept asking me to wear them so he could … go down on me. Stick his tongue right in. Unquote. He wanted to do that in my friend's bathroom that time.'

She felt nausea start, and inhaled deeply.

'This dirty talk. You told him to knock it off?'

'*Yes.*'

'And he wouldn't.'

'Sometimes he did, a little. It seemed like I'd start to relax, and he'd get worse. I told a psychiatrist friend of mine about it. The one who gave the party. She said his language wasn't dirty, it was sexy. She intimated that I didn't understand the difference.'

Mike gathered up the lunch wrappings and threw them in the wastebasket. He fixed her with his dark gaze. 'I think you understand the difference.'

Lynn rubbed one cold hand with the other. It was steamy-warm in the room, and sweat trickled under her blouse. Divulging the other details – the phone calls and the raccoon and the peaches – kept her from dwelling on the intimate part. Being made to recall it now was revolting.

She swallowed. Was she going to have to get up and go to the john?

Mike said, 'This stuff fits with the rest of what you told me.'

'How?'

'Control.' He spread his hands. 'He gets his fun shifting your gears. Let 'er relax, rev 'er up. Throw 'er in reverse and gun 'er.'

Probably because she was so uncomfortable, she lashed out. 'They really teach you to turn a metaphor at Tufts.' She glared at his sweatshirt.

Mike shook his head. 'I didn't go to Tufts. Never *ever* assume that what's in front of your eyes is the truth.'

He took a notebook from a desk drawer. 'Let's get to work.'

As she unlocked her apartment door that evening, Lynn felt her customary exhaustion – though tempered with a drop of relief.

The inability to convince anyone around you that you weren't unbalanced was an enormous strain. Between the punishing tension of preparing for her pilot and agonizing over every word with those who were supposed to be her nearest and dearest – plus constantly wondering what torment lay in wait for her – she was drained.

Her lunchtime conversation with Mike Delano was her first speck of hope.

It was amazingly empowering to be believed.

Not that anything had really changed. Mike had warned her that since no crime had been committed, there was nothing he could do.

'These guys love knowing we can't touch them,' he'd said. 'A restraining order? Forget it. They laugh in our face. We have a stalking law in Massachusetts, but we can't even arrest them for that unless they threaten you.'

But the comfort of watching him nod when everyone else shook their heads in pity, the sensation of safety as he wrote down every detail, was a warm bath compared to the horrible confusion and uncertainty of the past weeks.

She set her grocery bag on the kitchen counter and glanced out the window at the lights of the harbor ships.

A late cardinal chirped its evening song somewhere. She put butter and yogurt in the refrigerator, set the flounder in a colander for washing, and pulled out her Cuisinart for the salad.

This was the first time in days she'd felt like having anything but tea. Tonight she could even dare hope that the most optimistic of the possibilities Mike had outlined might occur: Greg was growing tired of the game, would stop soon, might have already stopped.

She turned on the living room lamps and switched on the TV. She opened the long drapes and looked out again at the lights, their sparkling reflection on the water.

She went into the bedroom to change into her jeans. She sat on the edge of the bed and pulled off her shoes ...

... and stopped suddenly, still holding one black heel.

On the floor, right by the nightstand, was a scrap of a Tums wrapper.

Lynn fought down the urge to bolt from the apartment. It was only one scrap. It could have been under the bed. It might have escaped her vacuuming.

Like a frantic animal, she scurried around the bedroom, verifying that there were no more. She peered under furniture, raked her fingers through the pile of the carpet around the bed.

Finally, the shakes subsiding, she picked up the one scrap and went to the bathroom to flush it. She flipped on the light. And stood frozen, the scrap falling from her hand.

There were at least a dozen torn Tums wrappers on the bathroom floor.

'Didn't you hear anything I said this afternoon?'

'Didn't you just hear *me* say he got into my *apartment*?'

'But we don't *know* that,' Mike said. 'We only know there's garbage on the floor. I can't do a warrant because of garbage.'

119

Lynn leaned against the plastic wind guard of the pay phone. She'd raced out without her coat, and the wind was stiff and damp. She put the phone on her shoulder and crossed her arms.

'He knew exactly what I'd do. He didn't leave the papers where I'd see them right away. He knows I come in from work and putter before I change. He left the one paper where I'd find it first, and be scared but not certain, and then he *mapped out just what I'd do next*!'

'I can send a patrolman over to search your apartment and make sure there's no one there.'

'We know there's no one there. He accomplished his purpose. So you're telling me all I can do is change the lock and go back inside and wait for whatever this lunatic feels like doing to me next.'

'Don't take that attitude. Don't give up your power.'

'Can't you at least find out his real phone number and give him a warning? If he knows the police are aware of him ...'

Lynn rubbed Mike's card with her thumb as she listened to him explain again that Greg hadn't done anything criminal.

'This sounds strange,' he finished, 'but start hoping that if he isn't going to stop, he does the next best thing – some stunt that's threatening enough to put him over the line into a felony. Breaking in, instead of using a key you gave him. Then, if we know it's him, maybe we can do something.'

He could get in anywhere he wanted to.

It was his oldest skill.

No other brush slave would have dared in his whole life to create the adventures Greg was enjoying at twelve.

It had begun the way twelve-year-old adventures usually do, born of the ferocious curiosity natural to the age. He craved the chance to see the grand lives of the estate dwellers he kept hearing stories about.

But what wasn't natural was that the craving didn't end there. Seeing wasn't nearly enough. He had to experience the deeds and tastes and smells, every sensual piece of the mosaic of their lives.

Years before he knew there was such a thing as key duplication, before he'd ever seen a hardware store, Greg was an expert at entering, sneaking, and hiding. He learned to fix latches so they could be slipped from outside. He climbed like a squirrel. He used windows and ledges. He folded himself into cupboards and crawl spaces, under tablecloths and behind the ruffled skirts of vanities.

It was in the latter spot that he was discovered, for the first and last time.

Her name was Danita Colfax. She was fifteen and had chocolate hair cut short like a boy's, but was all female everywhere else – and she became his first conquest.

He was under her vanity one night at bedtime when she sat to file her nails. One bare foot touched him; she yelped and yanked back the table skirt, and he was caught.

He scrambled out. In his panic he thought to apologize, to beg her mercy by describing the horrific consequences that would befall him if she told. But before the words could start, he felt the current: she was afraid, definitely, but drawn to him also.

His next impulse was to use that, to threaten that if she told, he'd say she invited him in. He knew enough of the household, of her mother's railing against the girl's flirtatious ways, to be sure that would keep her quiet.

But then, feeling Danita's eyes on him like candle flames, remembering her in her bath, always touching herself, Greg felt another possibility dawn.

He understood only the edges of it, but that was enough.

Instead of bowing and cringing like a brush slave, he stood as tall as he could. He smiled at the girl, the smile that got grown-ups pressing goodies on him. He told her he was very sorry for hiding, but he couldn't help himself, he liked her so much.

He stayed an hour that night.

Danita began helping him hide in her room. She loved to kiss, and would happily sit with him half the night just doing that. But once the thrill of being in there with Danita's cooperation went stale, Greg needed new joy. Experimenting, trying to touch her the way he had seen her touch herself, he found that she soon stopped resisting and loved that too.

He pushed her further.

But each new boundary breached brought a letdown.

He was too young and untaught to understand the principle of enjoying the chase – and even if he had, wouldn't have realized that the quality in himself was, even at twelve, a compulsion.

He only knew that the kissing and touching and all were no longer fun. The only fun was in making Danita do things she didn't want to.

Finally the only fun was in refusing to do what *she* wanted to.

Mike Delano got off the T on Commonwealth. The wind hit his ears, and he reached inside his parka and pulled his sweatshirt hood over his head.

Sometimes he came in to work like that, and got hooted at. He looked, at best, like a dork. Beyond best, he was probably lucky he hadn't been shot yet; he wasn't that tall, and the covering hood was the uniform of the preteen criminal.

His apartment was on Newbury, a pleasant walk from the T stop when the weather was decent, an ice bath when it wasn't. Tonight definitely qualified as not decent, and it wasn't officially winter yet.

A lot of the guys at work wondered out loud, when the Boston freeze came around every year, what the fuck they were doing there instead of cruising a Crown Vic around West Palm or wherever.

But Mike never wondered, out loud or otherwise.

He'd been to Florida twice, Arizona and California once each. All that sun cooked your gray cells. More crimes, the worst kind, the crazy, vicious ones that were actually fun for some sick somebody ... and stupidity! The sun seemed to nurture that, just like the weird, dry thorny sticks they called plants there. A really amazing proportion of cretins.

He'd stay here, thanks.

Northeastern slimebags were like the cold weather – his hate for them was a reflex. They were familiar. The worst of them rivaled anything down in those bayous, but mostly they walked a pattern.

This asshole, now, this slug that was chasing Marchette, wasn't a Boston type. She hadn't had to tell him the guy was from Out There.

Maybe he'd just slither his way back and leave the lady be.

Maybe.

A gust of wind nearly pulled Mike's hood off, and he hurried to get off the wide avenue, around the corner toward Newbury. Halfway down the block an awning flapped above the door of Nancy Jean's. When he got there, he thought a second and went in.

Nancy Jean's was warm, schoolroom warm, half the reason he spent so much time in the place; it sure wasn't the beer, one of which, to be a good guy, he'd order and never finish. Or Nancy Jean's chili, which she probably made with old wristwatches.

'How do?' Nancy Jean greeted him. 'Shut the door tight, dear.'

'I always do.'

There were a dozen stools at the bar, half occupied. Beyond was a room with a very small dance floor and tables, more brightly lit than people liked, but Nancy Jean

123

was as profligate with light as with heat. Pairs and groups talked and ate. No one had ever mentioned to Nancy Jean that the law now required a nonsmoking section, and the ubiquitious haze hovered.

He hung up his jacket and took a stool.

Nancy Jean went behind the bar. She was way less than five feet tall, but the floor back there was built up with plants, so that everything from her nut-brown Dutch bob to her wattled chin to her large, low breasts showed above the counter.

'Miller, dear?'

'Sure.'

He'd eat when he got home, but meantime it was comfortable to hang here. The buzz of conversation would have been annoying to many people who worked all day or night in a giant loud room, but to Mike it was relaxing in comparison. He could get all the silence he wanted at home.

Idly he watched the small TV on the back of the bar. Nancy Jean had just plunked it there among the bottles at some past time. A commercial for a fiber supplement, then a weather minute, just what he wanted to watch – some twinkie who looked like she bit into a mouthful of teeth, jabbering cheerily about the cold.

Not Channel 3, the one he'd been on yesterday.

No twinkies there.

This Lynn Marchette had stripes. A good program, maybe a good lady ... kind of belligerent.

But so would he be in her situation.

Hell, so was he, period.

The locksmith Mike recommended had come fast, done his work, and left. Lynn kept glancing at the new hardware on her door as she made her calls.

Of course the Los Angeles Texaco headquarters had never heard of Greg Alter. The only other person Lynn could think of trying was Joanne Barbato, the Bailiss Agency woman.

She looked at the clock: eight-twenty. Subtract three hours. Joanne would still be at work if she wasn't a nine-to-fiver.

Lynn could smell the fish still in the colander in the kitchen as she dialed Los Angeles directory assistance again. As soon as she completed this call, she'd wrap the fish and put it away.

Don't give up your power.

'Of course I remember you, Lynn,' Joanne said. 'How could I forget meeting a TV star? I watched you just a few weeks ago. You were terrific.'

'Thanks. I'm calling about Greg Alter. He asked me to look around for a TV job for his cousin, and there's an opening here, but I lost his card. Do you know where I can reach him?'

'Gee, no. I didn't even remember his last name.'

'Isn't he a friend of yours?'

'No,' Joanne said. 'I just met him that night. I thought he was with one of the other girls. I could check and see if anyone has his number.'

While she waited to hear back from Joanne, Lynn worked on what she'd say to Greg if she could get someone to contact him, deliver a letter to him.

She could demand that he leave her alone, say she'd been to the police.

Or she could go for it. Try to make him furious, push him to be reckless.

Joanne called back to say that no one knew anything about Greg. Roger Massey had seen him around here and there. Did Lynn want Roger to pass on a message if he ran into Greg again?

Lynn bit her lip. Did she? She could mail Roger a sealed letter ... but who knew when or if Greg might receive it? And did she want a threatening note from herself floating around a Los Angeles agency? When she could be on TV screens all over the country in a few months?

'No thanks,' she told Joanne. 'I have that card somewhere. It'll turn up.'

She sat, drumming her fingers on the phone. She remembered the fish, went purposefully to the kitchen, wrapped it, and placed it in the refrigerator. She thought to close the curtains, but didn't.

Don't give up your power.

She burned to write Greg a letter. The phrases swarmed inside, begging to be voiced. But who could get it to him? And who could she trust not to read what would sound psychotic to anyone who didn't know the situation?

'Please don't involve me,' Kara begged. 'I haven't heard from him since that Sunday, and I still feel lousy about that.'

'Because it was hidden from me,' Lynn said. 'This would not only be with my knowledge, but it's a favor. Don't see him. All you have to do is talk to him long enough to get a mailing address, or arrange to leave the letter somewhere.'

'What if I just don't hear from him again?'

'Then you can't get the letter to him, of course. But if you *do* ...'

Kara was balancing a notebook, a clipboard, and a file folder. She put them on the floor and took a chair.

'I thought we were going to have a meeting now on the child psychiatrists for the pilot. That's why I came in here.'

'We are,' Lynn said, tapping her own file folder. 'So let's just settle this first. Here's the letter. I'm going to seal it in an envelope.'

Lynn scanned it a last time before folding it. In her small, roundish script, it read:

126

Greg – the things you're doing are stupid. You're no better at harassment than you are in bed. So cut out this game. All you're succeeding in doing to me is boring me to death.

Lynn licked the flap. 'Just see that this reaches him. That's all you need to do.'

'Can't you do it yourself?' Kara asked, taking it. Then, with uncharacteristic harshness, 'Sorry, I forgot. He's purposely avoiding you.'

Lynn swallowed her defensive retort and said quietly, 'I told you about the 1288 number.'

'You told me what you were *told*.'

'Kara, he went into my *apartment*. How can you make excuses for –'

'Not excuses. Explanations. You saw Tums papers. They could have blown out of the garbage. You gave him a key –'

'I forgot he had it. He had no right to use it.'

'Why *would* he go into your place? You said nothing was really disturbed, no harm was done. Listen, if he's so bad, why aren't you afraid for me?'

'Mike Delano says this type of person doesn't victimize indiscriminately. He picks one woman and hounds her.'

'What a relief.'

Lynn ground her teeth. 'Stop this. Please. Thank you for helping. There was no one else I wanted to ask.'

'You're welcome.' Kara picked up her folder from the floor. 'Let me just say one more thing before we start. You keep quoting this Mike Delano as if he wrote the Constitution. Aren't you wondering if he has an agenda?'

'Everyone has an agenda.' She opened her pilot folder.

Angela shivered as she leaned closer to Booboo. 'Is this the ticket holders' line or the ticket buying line? I never know.'

127

'I'll go find out. You two get in line.' Booboo strode off toward the theater entrance, his long red muffler flapping.

'I'm freezing,' Angela said. '*Already*. I should have worn my coyote.'

Lynn thought, as she often did, how Angela was one of those people whose conversation was completely impersonal. Everything Angela said to her would have been appropriate for a stranger.

'Your friend sent a nice package,' Angela said.

Lynn snapped around. 'Who?'

'Greg. Of course.'

'Ticket holders,' Booboo said, puffing from a quick sprint. 'I got the tickets. I always forget they're seven-*fifty*.'

'You don't want to remember,' Angela said.

He started to reply, but Lynn interrupted. 'What package did you get from Greg?'

Booboo blinked. 'Hot peppers. For my guacamole. Remember? He said –'

'Don't use them. Throw them out. Or, no – give them to me.'

They looked at her, Booboo sorrowful, Angela vexed.

Lynn held out her gloved hands. 'Please don't treat me like a mental patient. I told you what the detective said. This is a pattern of harassment –'

Booboo put his arm around her. 'Shh, shh. Let's just enjoy the movie.'

Lynn stayed over at Booboo and Angela's, then drove home after breakfast. She had a bit of banana pancake in her handbag for Chip.

The package from Greg was in her trunk. It could stay there until she took it to Mike tomorrow.

Nowadays she always opened her door fearfully when she got home. Even with the new lock, she had to walk the entire apartment to make certain it hadn't been invaded. On especially bad days she patrolled it over and over.

She filled the bird feeders and left the pancake scrap for Chip. She came back inside and was watching him investigate it when the phone rang.

'It's done,' Kara said.

'You sent Greg the letter?'

'Yes.'

'How did it go? Did he give you an address, or a place to leave it?'

'Lynn, I did what you wanted. I'm tired of the whole business. Can we skip the Q and A?'

'Yes. I'm sorry.'

'Don't be sorry. Just be …'

'What? I couldn't hear.'

'Never mind. I'll see you tomorrow. 'Bye.'

Lynn wasn't sure, but she thought Kara's words might have been: 'Be *you* again.'

Other than food and cooking, there was little Lawrence Marchette loved more than the Patriots, his adoptive team in his adoptive state. He'd been looking forward to this afternoon's game all week.

He was flopped on the couch now, a popcorn bowl in his lap, watching the second-quarter action. Angela was at her health club. He should have been having a wonderful time.

He wasn't.

Lynn had left a couple of hours ago. Hugging her goodbye, he'd almost asked her to call when she got home – would have, except that she was so edgy with his concern, he didn't want to upset her further.

But he was worried.

An explosive yell from the TV made him jump. For Pete's sake. A touchdown, and he'd missed it.

He got up and fetched an ale from a four-pack Angela had bought him at some Irish import shop. He drank a little and munched the popcorn, but still the game wasn't holding his attention.

He remembered the day Lynn had moved into her harbor apartment. He and Angela had helped, along with Lynn's friend Kara and two of Kara's sisters – a jolly group.

They'd all carried cartons and rolled out rugs and shifted furniture until it was dark, and then Lynn had taken them out for a feed and wouldn't let anyone contribute.

Fair enough. It was part of the fun for him, knowing his sister could afford the apartment and the supper, watching her enjoy it all.

But before they'd risen to leave, he'd seen the doubt slip into her face. She could hide this, but not from him, not from the one person who knew every flick of an eyelash. She was doing her number, looking for the worm. She couldn't just ease up and enjoy what she had.

But that had been awhile back, and he hadn't seen her do it much lately. He'd stopped watching for it.

Lawrence went to the kitchen and got a plate of deviled eggs from the fridge.

So now what the hell was going on? She brings a fellow to meet them, a smart, clean, articulate gentleman. Next thing, she's convinced herself he's some kind of creep. No, not herself; this other man convinced her, this detective. What was *he* all about?

The bottom line was that Lynn, who should have been ecstatic about her syndication deal, was agitated, more so every time Lawrence saw her.

With that thought, he sat up, catapulting the popcorn bowl from his lap.

The syndication deal.

That had to be it.

She was just plain nervous.

Once she mastered the routine of these big new programs, she'd be fine.

The fourth quarter was starting. He felt more like watching now.

He considered sharing his brainstorm with Angela when

she came in, but decided against it. Angela believed he squandered too much worry on his sister as it was.

He bent and picked up a few kernels of corn, then went and got the Dustbuster.

'Just hot peppers,' Mike said on the phone. 'No added substance. I didn't expect anything.'

'That's a relief. I guess.'

'You guess?'

Lynn leaned back in her desk chair, stretched her legs way out and rubbed her telephone ear. She'd been on the phone all day. The pilot was shaping up; thanks to Kara's favor-bartering in her offscreen buddy network, Lynn had spoken personally to Roseanne Arnold, who sounded sincerely interested in doing a guest shot.

They still had no answer on Oprah, the one guest whose presence could guarantee a knockout pilot.

Work was Lynn's only bromide, the focal point between pockets of depression and the dull, nagging anxiety of never being able to relax.

She was so tired.

'I was referring to what you said about hoping he'd break the law,' she said.

'And then what?'

'Then you'd have him.'

There was a tight silence, then: 'I keep telling you – it isn't that simple. First there has to be a clear threat. We have to know it's him. Then he has to be arrested and charged, which nobody is going to send officers to California for. Then, Jesus, there's any number of ways it could go. He'll have a lawyer, he has rights –'

'What *rights*? He's deliberately trying to scare me, degrade me, drive me nuts. Nobody believes what's happening to me. Even my best friend and my own brother think he's a sweet guy that I'm mistreating. If that isn't torture –'

'Yeah, but just don't pin your hopes –'

'*You* were the one who encouraged me to hope Greg goes too far.'

'I have another call. I have to go.'

'I also paid attention to what you said about not giving up my power,' Lynn said. 'And because I did, I don't think Greg will disappoint us.'

But he had clicked off.

Lynn was in the control room when Dennis Orrin poked his head in. 'Talk to you a minute?'

'Sure.'

'Bern would like to watch today,' he said when she'd stepped out. 'Do you mind?'

'Not at all. You didn't have to ask.'

'I told her that, but she –'

'I made him ask,' Bernadine Orrin said, walking over. 'I didn't want you to take me for the pushy princess wife that I am. So it's okay?'

'Of course. You might be bored, though. The topic is osteoporosis.'

Bernadine laughed. 'You sweetheart. Have you forgotten that I'm the oldest living mother of teenagers?'

'Yes,' Lynn said. 'It's easy to.'

'Ten minutes,' someone shouted from the set, and the Orrins said their goodbyes. Lynn watched Bernadine stroll off next to Dennis. Her navy slack suit was exquisitely tailored to show off her tight, narrow shape; she had small hands and feet, and she moved like a jazz dancer.

Fifteen years older, and Bernadine made her feel like a lumpy, lethargic canasta-playing relic.

Lynn had a pang of alarm, the same sensation as when she saw Angela in her leotard, or when she was dialing around on cable and found an aerobics show: What were these people doing that it was going to be too late if *she* didn't start doing too?

* * *

The Green Room was crowded with experts still arguing their vitamin therapies – although, Lynn noticed, they were gobbling doughnuts.

'Wonderful program,' Bernadine said, smiling at Lynn and Kara. 'Very well-balanced. And *this* young lady' – she waved at the producer of the exercise segment, standing near Kara – 'so knowledgeable.'

'Thank you,' the woman said.

'This is Mrs Orrin, the general manager's wife,' Kara said.

'Bernadine. And you're Elizabeth ...?'

'Elizabeth Vail.'

'Your body tension system is intriguing. Did I hear you say you work at the Broome Club?'

'I'm a trainer there.'

Lynn said, 'That's my sister-in-law's club. Angela Marchette.'

'I'll look out for her,' Elizabeth said. 'Are you a member?' she asked Bernardine.

Bernadine shook her sleek head. 'I belong to Harbor Sports. But I might change. Every time I start working with a trainer, they leave. I'm not making progress.'

Kara and Lynn exchanged looks. Kara touched Bernadine's slender arm. 'This is your idea of no progress?'

Dennis came in. 'Here you are,' he boomed at Bernadine. 'What did you think?'

'I'm glad I came. The show was excellent. I'm just asking Elizabeth about the Broome Club. Is the fee for the year, or can you sign up by the month?'

Elizabeth smiled. 'There's an introductory special right now. Three months for ninety-nine dollars. It's usually ninety-nine a month.'

'Good deal,' Bernadine said.

'It is. I wanted to let you all know.' She looked around the circle.

Does she mean me? Lynn stood straighter and pulled her stomach in. *Does she think I'm in bad shape?*

'I felt like such a whale yesterday,' Kara said. 'When that trainer was describing the Broome Club? She looked right at me. I wanted to go purge. I almost dug out our bulimia tapes to see how they do it.'

'Sick,' Lynn said.

'I know. But if I didn't laugh, I'd cry.'

'I meant me, not you. *I* thought she was looking right at *me*.'

The phone rang, and Kara answered. It was Bernadine Orrin, for Lynn.

'I'm in the utility room. I arranged to get a personal presentation on that workout method. Do you and Kara want to join me? Or are you swamped?'

'We have a pilot meeting in fifteen minutes.'

'Want us to come to your office?'

Lynn hesitated, then decided. 'Okay. Come on in.'

'Hold these,' Elizabeth Vail said, handing one barbell each to Lynn, Kara, Pam, and Bernadine.

'It's not very heavy,' Lynn said. 'But these are only for beginners, aren't they? You work up to much bigger ones. That's the part that puts me off. It's uncomfortable, and you can strain yourself –'

'No,' Bernadine said. 'That's what's different about this method.'

Elizabeth took the bells back and put others in their hands. 'These are twelve pounds, as high as I go with free weights. Later I have you bench press, but with a fifteen-pound curl bar – not the heavy one lifters use.'

'These aren't bad,' Kara said.

'Well, they're all a woman's body needs for toning and bone mass. You don't want to be Arnold Schwarzenegger – you just want to look good and stay healthy. I follow this method, and *I'm* not strong – but I'm in shape and I'm doing what's needed to prevent osteoporosis.'

Bernadine picked up another twelve-point barbell and hefted the two above her head. 'You *really* feel I'll be toned with these? Even though I've been benching seventy?'

'Yes. You'll see.'

Kara looked at Bernadine's calf-length slim skirt. 'Does this help you lose weight?'

'By itself, no,' Elizabeth said. 'Free-weight work is what we call anaerobic exercise. To lose pounds, you need to decrease your fat intake.'

'Do you have a card I can give my mom?' Pam asked.

Elizabeth handed her one. 'Three months for ninety-nine dollars, tell her. What do you think, ladies? Why not sign up just for that? If you aren't happy, you haven't lost. Except inches.'

Bernadine said, 'I'll give you a check.'

Dennis came into the conference room. 'Sorry. Yet another agent with yet another tape I had to look at this second. It took me ten minutes just to get her out. Let's see where we are here.'

There was a blackboard on an easel next to the table. Dennis leaned to read it.

CELEBRITY SEXUAL ABUSE, it said in block letters. Seated around the table, Lynn, Kara, Dennis, and two production assistants studied it.

Dennis rubbed his chin. 'I don't know. The wording is amorphous. It could mean the celebrities are the abusers.'

Kara said, 'How about "Sexually Abused Celebrities"?'

Lynn shook her head. 'That leaves out the childhood element.'

'"Childhood Sex Abuse of Celebrities,"' Dennis said.

'Hm,' Lynn said. 'Closer, but it lacks immediacy.'

'And it's wordy,' Kara said.

Dennis erased the blackboard and wrote CELEBRITIES WHO WERE SEXUALLY ABUSED CHILDREN.

Lynn squinted at it. 'It's even wordier. But I like it.'

'I do too,' Kara said. 'It leaves no room for confusion.'

Dennis asked, 'Where do we stand on the guests?'

'Two confirmed.' Kara patted her file. 'Sandra Dee and Marilyn Van Derbur will appear by satellite. Roseanne Arnold looks likely. We don't know about Oprah. We're hoping.'

'Who are the studio guests?'

'Child psychiatrists, maybe a social worker. We're not sure who else yet.'

Listening as Kara matter-of-factly described what was certain to be the most important show of her career, Lynn felt a feathery panic.

But then it faded, replaced by one concrete assurance: she was going to complete the pilot that would propel her to national syndication.

Greg had taken, was still taking, from her. But he couldn't take her job.

Pam opened the door. 'Lynn?'

'Is it really important, Pam? We didn't want to be interrupted.'

'This just came for you, FedEx.' She handed Lynn an envelope.

'He's signed out, ma'am.'

Lynn said, 'Can you contact him? *Please?*'

'If you'll tell me what this is in reference to, maybe someone else can –'

'No one else can help me.' Unable to sit, Lynn paced her office holding the phone. 'I have to talk to Mike Delano.'

'I'll see what I can do.'

Mike called back very fast. 'What's up, Lynn?'

'I just got a FedEx letter from Greg. A *threatening* letter. I hope it's enough for you to act on, because –'

'I didn't hear all that. Say it again.'

'I can hardly hear you either,' Lynn shouted.

'I'm in the car. Just talk loud and slow.'

'I got a very threatening letter from Greg. And Mike – it's in my handwriting! He copied my handwriting perfectly!'

For a minute she couldn't hear anything but static and her own heart banging. '*Mike?*'

'I'll be there in ten minutes.'

'"Dear Lynn,"' Mike read aloud, '"you made an idiotic mistake coming after me."' Mike looked up. '"Coming after me"? What the hell did you do?'

'I wrote him a note telling him to leave me alone.'

'How did you get it to him?'

'Kara did. I'm not sure how. I took a chance that he'd be in touch with her again, and I asked her to find out a mailing address or arrange where to leave it.'

'You handwrote it?'

'Yes.'

'Nice. You made this good and easy for him.'

'It served the purpose, didn't it? Isn't a threatening letter breaking the law?'

'That's what the hell you were going for? Sure rattled his ass.' Leaning back against her desk, Mike read, 'If you'd behaved yourself, I would have left you alone. I'm tired of you too, you see. But you want to pull. Now I'll just have to show you who's holding the strings.

'"Next time you have the ridiculous impulse to try to annoy me, remember who's in charge, Lynn. It would have been so easy to hurt you with the white dress. Think back. Remember me looking at it? Each of those circles could have been a razor on your flesh. But that's instant gratification ... and I'd rather take my pleasure with you for a long time. Let's see how bored you get now, Star. P.S. You were right – you do bulge out of that bathing suit."'

Mike looked up at Lynn. 'You're shaking.'

'But I accomplished something. You're here. What happens now?'

'Now we make inquiries.'

Lynn called Kara in. 'You remember Mike Delano.'

'Yes.' She looked warily at him.

'Let's sit down,' Mike said. 'I want to discuss this note. Lynn says it's the response to one she gave you for Greg.'

'Yes.'

'And he got in touch?'

'Yes.'

Lynn frowned at her. Kara was sitting tightly forward on the end of her chair, twisting her fingers together.

'Would you tell me how that went?'

'He called up.'

Mike nodded encouragingly, but Kara didn't say any more.

'Please, Kara, tell him all of it,' Lynn said gently.

Kara turned and glared at her. The fury in her face was shocking. 'You don't want me to do that.'

'But of course I do. Why –'

'Lynn.' Kara shook her head. 'Here's what I think we should do. I think we should go back into the conference room and continue our meeting. It was going so well –'

'What is the matter with you?' Lynn stared at her old friend. 'You can't be in any doubt now.' She got up and grabbed the letter out of Mike's hand. 'Here's the proof of what Greg is. You saw this part of the puzzle unfold with your own eyes. I send him a note through you telling him not to bother me. He carefully copies my writing from it, part of his campaign to make people think I'm imagining all this, and writes to me about razors on my flesh.'

She held the note out toward Kara, and the paper trembled. 'You were part of this. You saw each element. *You* know I'm not imagining it.'

Kara looked from the letter to Lynn and Mike. Finally

she let out an explosive breath. 'When Greg called,' she said, 'he was very upset. All he wanted was to talk to you, to make things right. You should have heard his voice, Lynn. The man is crazy about you.'

Watching her, listening, Lynn thought: This isn't happening.

'When I told him I had your letter, he couldn't wait. He insisted that I open it.'

Kara paused to gulp a breath. She wasn't looking at Lynn or Mike. 'I didn't know what to do. I wanted to get it done with. So I – so I opened the note and read it to him.'

She turned to Lynn. 'I'm not certain, but I think he was crying. I felt miserable, Lynn. Those things you wrote! How can you tell a man that he's boring you to death, he's no good in bed? I shouldn't have read your note. I'm sorry I did.'

She stood up. 'He didn't copy your writing, because he never saw the note!' she screamed at Lynn. 'I know your writing better than anyone on earth. I read it every day. Only one person can write exactly like you, and that's *you*, Lynn!'

With a furious swipe at the letter in Lynn's shaking hand, she ran from the office.

CHAPTER SEVEN

Lynn and Mike stared at the doorway. A paper on a table next to it still fluttered.

Lynn sniffed back shocked tears, went to her desk and carefully put the letter down. Mike took it and put it in his jacket pocket.

'Kara thinks I wrote it,' Lynn said incredulously. 'Wrote that letter and FedExed it to myself.'

Mike was shaking his head. 'Go easy. Look at it from her side.'

'I'm trying.' But she was numb.

'I think you should do what Kara said. Go back to the meeting.'

'Are you serious?'

'*Yeah*. You can't let this get a hold on you. Fight it.'

'You believe me, don't you?' she asked.

'Don't reduce it to those terms.'

She gasped. 'That's not an answer.'

'Don't baby out on me. You were doing all right –'

'How would you feel? *I* know I didn't FedEx myself a crazy letter. *I* know there's a sick bastard out there yanking my strings and loving that people think I'm the insane one. And *I'm* the person who has to watch everyone I trust stop trusting *me*.'

Lynn's throat ached. Rubbing it, she watched Mike's sad eyes watching her. Sad because of what was being done to her? Or because of what she was doing to herself?

Was that how it would be from now on? Would she always have to wonder whether her nearest and dearest *and* the police considered her a victim or a maniac?

Or wouldn't she have to, because Greg would succeed in erasing any doubt?

'What are you going to do now?' she asked.

'Go back out to Dorchester and try to find out why a seven-year-old has bruises in his groin and genital herpes.'

'Oh, God.'

'On the way I'll drop this at the station.' He tapped the pocket where Greg's letter was. 'And I need more information from you. Where will you be around six tonight?'

'Here, probably. If I'm not running naked and screaming around the city.'

'I'll meet you out front.'

'I did what you suggested. I went back into the meeting.'

Mike's eyebrows lifted. 'And?'

'And I ... played a part. I was perky old Lynn planning her pilot.'

'Good.'

'Is it? Now all my colleagues probably think I'm Sybil. I tried to talk to Kara afterward. She avoided me the rest of the afternoon.'

Mike saw Nancy Jean approaching the table. 'Hungry?' he asked Lynn. 'Or do you just want coffee or a beer?'

'I should probably eat.'

'Chili tonight,' Nancy Jean said, dropping small plastic menus.

'I'll have that, please,' Lynn said. 'And tea.'

Mike ordered hot dogs and sauerkraut. When his food arrived, the smell made Lynn recall her visit to the police station.

She'd left there feeling hopeful and protected: this wasn't her imagination, her neurosis, her anything. Greg was a freak and the police were going to catch him.

'How's the chili?'

'A little ... chewy.'

'Here even the beer is chewy.'

For a while they ate in silence. Then Mike said, 'The letter was routed from West Los Angeles to the FedEx office on Morrissey Boulevard. Other than that, we didn't get anything.'

Lynn looked up. 'I wasn't even hoping. If he was that careless, we wouldn't still be at this.'

Mike wrapped sauerkraut around his fork like spaghetti. 'You don't understand police work. Most cases, we just wait patiently for the bad guy to step on his dick.'

'And if he doesn't?'

'We wait some more.'

Lynn had had enough of the chili. She put down her spoon.

Mike looked at it. 'I should have warned you. Want dessert? The Indian pudding is good. Everything else is terrible.'

'Just more tea.'

A cloud of smoke wafted over the table and settled. Lynn waved at it.

'Tell me about Kara,' Mike said. 'She's your assistant and your friend, right? Close friend?'

'Very close. She's the sister I don't have. I'm the – the sister who encourages her to succeed. She has hot and cold running sisters, but none who do that.'

'She's single?'

'Yes.'

'Guys?'

'She was engaged once, to a Channel 7 publicist. She's had a few other relationships. No one right now.'

'She seems to like Greg.'

'Everybody does.' Lynn felt queasy as she remembered again how simple and solvable it had begun to seem that day at the police station. 'As you pointed out, they all think it's me.'

He leaned the wooden chair back and watched her. The

room's strong light made his eyes a gleaming black. He was frowning, but he almost always frowned. It was impossible to tell what he was thinking.

This time Lynn broke the silence. 'Are you still convinced it's *not* me?'

'You mean, do I think he's a wackball? Yeah.'

'So as far as you're concerned,' Lynn began, searching for words to make a net, the way she did to trap answers on camera, 'nothing has changed because of this letter. There is no doubt in your mind that everything I'm saying is true.'

Mike stayed tipped back in the chair. Nothing moved. But the pause sliced through Lynn like an ice dagger.

He said, 'I told you before, don't reduce it to those terms –'

'Is that why we're here, instead of in your office or mine? You wanted to catch me after a miserable day, when I'm tired and upset, and who knows what I might admit?'

He brought the chair upright. 'We're here because there was no room in my shift, and I get hungry at dinnertime. The rest I won't bother answering.'

'But you –'

'And I wasn't finished with my questions. Is Kara jealous of you?'

Another stab. 'You're trying to rechannel my attention.'

'I'm trying to see what's going on here,' he said tightly. 'Is she jealous?'

'Because of Greg?'

'Greg, your job, your jewelry, anything.'

'She could be,' Lynn said hesitantly. 'I've wondered about it.'

'I don't know how she couldn't be.'

'What are you getting at?'

He shrugged. 'Kara wrote the letter?'

'*No.*'

143

'She lied about not giving yours to him? To make you look bad? Or maybe it was true, but she didn't at all mind leaping to the conclusion that you wrote this one?'

Lynn was vehemently shaking her head. 'She might be a bit jealous, but Kara would never – She's not capable of that.'

Mike said quietly, 'Too bad she doesn't have the same confidence in you.'

Fighting back the hurt, Lynn said just as quietly, 'She does.'

He didn't respond, just fed out coils of silence for her to hang herself with.

Lynn said, 'Sometimes, in a crisis, Kara loses it. She gets terribly upset and she strikes out. It's happened before.'

'Dessert, dear?' Nancy Jean asked. 'I have custard pie, Indian pudding, pineapple cheesecake, and chocolate roll.'

Suddenly the notion of chocolate felt wonderful, and she ordered it.

'Indian pudding,' Mike said.

'Ice cream on top?'

'Yeah. Two scoops.'

Nancy Jean left. Mike said, 'You'll be sorry.'

The place was starting to empty out. Lynn checked her watch: almost eight. Her car was still back at the Channel 3 garage. She thought about driving home alone, going in alone, and shivered.

'Chocolate roll,' Nancy Jean said, serving it. 'Indian pudding.'

Lynn tasted her dessert. Mike was right: a dry brown sponge with shaving cream inside. She put her fork down.

He pushed her dish aside and slid another in front of her with half his pudding and a scoop of ice cream melting on it.

'Oh,' she said. 'Thanks.'

'Welcome. Listen next time.'

* * *

144

By lunchtime the next day Lynn still hadn't been able to pin Kara down. She hadn't been around much since the morning's show, and seemed busy and distracted when she was.

Bernadine called.

'I really can't talk now,' Lynn said.

'You sound terrible. What's wrong?'

'It's … complicated.' Lynn realized she was gripping the phone, and relaxed her fingers.

'I won't keep you. I'm at the Broome Club – I only called to ask if you're going to join with me. Kara doesn't seem interested –'

'You spoke to her? Today?'

'Just a minute ago. She was very negative. Oh, hold on. All right. Lynn? Elizabeth says to tell you these workouts are excellent for stress.'

'I think we should go now. Together,' Lynn said, trying not to be put off by Kara's stubbornly set face. 'We need to talk, and I can't seem to get you to do it here. We don't even have to exercise if you don't want to. They have a steam room. There's a snack bar –'

'Stop pushing me.' Kara folded her arms. 'And stop treating this as a sandbox spat. I'm very upset.'

'I am too,' Lynn said quietly, retreating a step. In her eagerness to open the lines of communication with Kara, she had nearly backed her into the Green Room refreshments table.

Kara said, 'You've pulled me into a situation I want out of. *Out.* I don't know who to believe –'

'How can you say that, Kara? I've been your friend and work partner for ten years, you barely know Greg, and you'd even think of trusting him over me?'

'All I can trust is what I heard and saw –'

'But Greg manipulated that!'

'He didn't manipulate what *you* wrote to *him*!'

145

'It was crude, I know. To anyone but a – a freak, it would have been an awful letter. But the police keep telling me they're powerless unless Greg does more. I was trying to force his hand, just to get him to *stop*!'

They were quiet for a minute, looking at each other, unknowingly sharing a thought: *I was so sure I knew her a hundred percent.*

'So,' Lynn began, afraid to force the point but more afraid not to, 'you really believe I wrote a threatening letter to myself.'

Kara looked away, her lips compressed, as Lynn waited in pain.

Finally Kara said, 'I don't know what to think. I go around and around with the pieces, and I just don't know. I keep asking myself why you would do that. But then I remember the writing, your writing, I know it so well ...'

'He copied it, Kara. He can do weird things, he –'

'He's not a magician, Lynn!'

Lynn's hurt was turning to anger. Bitter words boiled just beyond speech. She could accept Kara's first reaction as shock, but this was a day later, and she was entitled to some understanding.

But before Lynn could respond angrily or otherwise, there were voices in the corridor: a touring school group about to see the Green Room.

Lynn ground her teeth and hurried out before she had to force an impossible smile for the visitors.

Greg's landlady disliked loud music or too much TV volume. That was a Mrs Minot word, *dislike*, and she was precise about demonstrating her *dislike*; he knew the exact pitch that would bring her to the phone.

In fact, he didn't care for high volume himself, but it was a handy device that served several purposes.

It drove home the impression that the worst sin her

upstairs tenant was going to commit was to be noisy.

It kept her focus away from other quirks of his, such as his lack of guests, personal mail, and phone calls – though he faked the latter two occasionally, careful man that he was.

And it gave Mrs Minot a reason to be in touch with her handsome, well-spoken renter, something no one knew better than Greg how much she needed, it being his primary business to create those needs.

Not that he had any plans for the dear lady. He wanted her just where she was. There was nothing like having an ultrarespectable landlady to cast that same mantle over you.

He could hear her now, stepping about below him. She was coloring her hair; he smelled the chemicals. He kept track of such matters. It was useful to know when she'd want to stay away from windows and doors.

He put on another lamp, then changed his mind and turned it off. The moonlight was warm vanilla tonight. It lightened the whole sky and glinted off the Christmas lights he kept on the palm tree all year.

Soon it would be time to turn them on.

He knew Lynn loved Christmas. She'd told him.

She wasn't going to love this one.

He snuggled down into his favorite chair.

Where would Lynn be right this minute? He loved picturing his Star all shaky and agitated. She must be quite paranoid by now, watching her friends and colleagues step out of her way.

It just thrilled him, knowing what other plans he had for her. She wouldn't even know to fear them, since she had no idea how wide-ranging his skills were.

He so enjoyed that, pushing out the limits a crumb at a time.

He'd learned that process as painstakingly as a glass blower learns his trade – but with no mentor, of course. Just his own trial and error.

Starting way back with little Danita.

He hadn't known then what he liked, had thought each part of the affair was the object ... until he stumbled to the next part.

In that way he learned what the best part was – the dessert, the mountaintop.

It was making them scramble like the grubs did when you raked their rock aside. No haven. Slaves to your direction.

With Danita he'd been clumsy. Forgivable; how can you know where you're going when you've never been there? But he'd created a wonderful result anyway, just by following his instinct. By the end of that one, she was dangling on his invisible string, cursed as a tramp, her young beauty ruined by the misery that ate at her.

He'd changed her.

'He copped the label from an office mailroom on Hollywood Boulevard,' Mike said, neatening the notes on his desk while he talked to Lynn on the phone. 'The mailroom belongs to an accounting firm. They keep their preprinted FedEx air bills on a counter. Our man probably just walked in, took one, and walked out. There was only one unaccounted for.'

They talked awhile longer. He took her back over some of the early details again.

'I've described everything so many times,' she said. 'There's never anything new.'

'Don't assume that. Significant details come out without you realizing.'

'I can tell you one significant detail. I know how he copied my writing.'

Mike hadn't called on one of the automatic-record lines, but he pressed a button now to start his personal tape rolling. Hearing the barely audible *wssh* as the cartridge turned, he asked, 'How?'

'My grocery list. I missed it awhile back. I kept it on the refrigerator door with a magnet, a running list, and one day it was gone. He probably took other papers too. There's enough paper in my life to make trees. Lots of it I'd never miss.'

'How do you figure he got so good at that?'

'I don't know,' Lynn said. 'One of his many talents, I suppose.'

He didn't like the challenging note in his own voice. He switched topics. 'How's your assistant today? Are you communicating?'

'Not much,' Lynn said, and he could tell she had that face on, the defiant look he'd seen at Nancy Jean's when he'd baited her with the no-confidence crack.

He finished with a promise to call if there was any news, and hung up.

He killed the tape switch and reached down for the cartridge. He held it for a second in his palm, and then stuck his pen in and deliberately broke the thing.

Lynn felt excruciatingly self-conscious, parading around the gym floor in the tights and scoop-neck leotard Bernardine had helped her choose in the Broome Club's shop. But she was kept busy, and the sweating became her distraction from the sensation of being in a living monsters-in-the-closet dream.

'Two programs for two days,' the trainer had said a week ago, sketching out a stick-figure diagram of a leg lift. 'People burn out if they start too fast. You can come two days a week, can't you?'

'I'll try.'

Now, starting her third early morning workout, Lynn was surprised to find she wasn't dreading the ten-minute StairMaster stint.

'Your body gets used to its fix,' Elizabeth explained. 'There are chemicals released during cardiovascular activity, and your system learns to look forward to them.'

Whatever works, Lynn thought.

Later, showing Lynn how to do biceps curls, the trainer said, 'It shouldn't take too long for you to start seeing muscle tone.'

'You think so?' Lynn asked.

'Sure. You're starting from a trim, healthy place. Most of the members have overweight to work off and habits to realign.'

'I thought I'd be the only mushy one.'

'Mushy?' Elizabeth tapped Lynn's upper arm with her pencil. 'Women in their thirties usually start to get saggy here. You have a decently developed triceps.'

'That's encouraging. I had nobody to compare myself with but my sister-in-law and Bernadine Orrin.'

The woman smiled. 'Bernadine's in a class by herself. I haven't met your sister-in-law. But if you want a realistic comparison, just look around.' She checked her watch. 'Seven-thirty. Are you out of time?'

'God, yes. I have to go to work.'

'Let me stretch you first, or you'll hate me tomorrow. You will anyway, but this will help.'

Toweling after her quick shower, Lynn thought about whether to make another pitch to Kara about the club. Maybe, in the pampering atmosphere, with all those natural chemicals flowing, they could ease back on track. Lynn badly missed the closeness, for which their wobbly truce, composed mainly of silence and avoidance, was no substitute.

Leaving the club, Lynn met Angela coming in. She tried to get away with a quick hello, but Angela said, 'I have to tell you something.'

'What?'

'Lawrence's blood pressure was elevated when he had a physical yesterday.'

'He didn't tell me. How bad is it?'

'Not terrible, but ... you could help, Lynn. I know he's awfully worried about you. Maybe if you kind of soft-pedal what you tell him ...'

The fun with Danita had taught Greg how much more satisfying it was to *do* than just to look. And so he had started applying to the people in the house some of the techniques he had been playing with outdoors.

In the vegetable and flower gardens the brush slaves spent their endless days caring for, there was abundant opportunity to experiment. He had learned that by tying a seedling in a certain way, he could produce a misshapen adult plant: twisted asparagus; sunflowers with half their petals missing; stunted, miniature cilantro leaves. Stones strategically placed made plants fight for growth and light, and look wondrously weird.

He began adding bits of herb to items in the house that the people ate, drank, and put on themselves. He knew generally which plants to pick, as the outdoor staff were the ones who used them as treatments and thus knew their properties, and he refined his knowledge by carefully observing the results of his acts.

And the results were many. He learned to tell who in the family had ingested or absorbed this or that by their behavior, the look of their skin, the odor of their urine. Licu root, mashed and dried and added to tea, created high energy and a flushed face. Irisbane kept you running to the bathroom. Greg's favorite was white chili, tiny cute flowers that, when mixed into food, swelled the lips with red bumps.

As he got older, though, the limitations of estate life bored him, and he began to contemplate leaving his family, such as it was. The death of his parents within months of each other from Valley Fever facilitated the decision. There were only his sisters left, and he felt no more kinship to them than he had to his parents. They had all seemed on one plane and he on another, these people for whom life was what it was and that was that.

So he made his way to San Diego, leaving behind his pharmaceutical games and his affluent victims, and began the process of learning how easy and rewarding it was to make changes in people by using nothing more artificial than his own personal resources: his magnetism and intelligence and ingenuity.

After her workout, Lynn was the first to get to work on the twelfth floor. The mail was there already, stacked by the glass door to the reception area. Distracted by her concern for Booboo and her annoyance at her sister-in-law's protectiveness, Lynn was just going to leave the mail, but changed her mind.

Reaching for her keys, she flicked through the envelopes and noticed several identical oversized ones with typed address labels. She used a key to slit the envelope with her name on it and pulled out the object inside: a photo.

A glance at the nude woman in the legs-apart pornographic pose was enough to make Lynn head right for the reception desk, heart pounding as she crumpled the picture tight in her fist, her other hand already reaching for the trash basket under the desk.

But then she stopped, hand still extended, as the afterimage crashed in.

The bluebell-patterned pillow under the nude hips was *her own pillow*.

She smoothed out the picture and stared at it – and it *was*. It was the pillow from her bed. It was her bed. And the woman, dear God, was her.

Greg had been especially loving that night, stroking her back over and over, his warm hands contrasting with the bite of fall breeze through her open bedroom window. He'd put a pillow under her head and shoulders, and another beneath her hips, murmuring how sweet and soft her skin was down there. Elton John and a geyser of piano, Lynn remembered, the richly rising notes in rhythm with their bodies.

And the intimacy they had already, so soon, more profound than she could ever remember. Marveling over her comfort with this man who saw wrinkles as badges ...

So at ease, it had not even occurred to her to prettify her pose, though the bedroom was only semidark, when Greg had risen to find a fresh condom ...

He must have done it then. Fetched not only the condom – she recalled the *snick* of the latex as sharply as the rest of the tableau – but a night-vision camera. And aimed and focused and framed her body at the most degrading possible angle, a schematic of bunched flesh, of hair and membranes and even moisture.

The picture was all over the station. A security guard named Jaime Cortez made it his business to collect and destroy every one he could find, even, in two cases according to Kara, demanding them from technical personnel who wanted to keep them.

'I'm sorry,' Kara said as Lynn sat determinedly straight in her desk chair twenty-five minutes before air, waiting for the Tylenol to work on her headache. She had to take herself down to the studio, she had to do a fine show, she had to build an iron wall against the churning humiliation, the outrage. 'I'm sorry for you about this, and for being a brat all week.'

Lynn looked at her, the first time she had been able to meet anyone's eyes directly all morning.

'I talked to Mary,' Kara continued. 'She helped me figure out that I was mad because you seemed to be screwing up. I was afraid you'd lose this syndication

153

opportunity for both of us. So ... I was lumping my own fear in with other issues, where it didn't belong, and I'm sorry. I wasn't here for you. But I am now.'

CHAPTER EIGHT

Greg wasn't usually attracted to redheads. But the woman had beautiful little fine-edged features, a pointy mouth, pink stones in her pink ears ... and he liked the whole package enough to follow her into B. Dalton.

He didn't watch many women these days; he had plenty on his plate right now. Ever since the beginning of Lynn, he hadn't needed much else to keep him happy.

Quite a distinction for Lynn, one she could add to her other awards. He should have a plaque made.

The woman stopped at a shelf. He stood a rack behind her and craned to see what book she picked up.

Adolescent Modalities of Learning. She must be a specialized teacher of some sort. He felt a quickening in his primary parts. Again, Lynn's distinction. She was spoiling him for workaday women. The challenge was so choice.

Sun poured in from the front window, making a fiery gloss of the woman's hair. Greg watched her flip pages, her fingers surprisingly wide, with big unpolished nails. She seemed to be able to scan complex diagrams in a single bound.

He had to cover his mouth to keep from chuckling.

But that was one of his most endearing characteristics – his sense of humor. Lynn had told him that often.

It would be amusing to know what she thought of his sense of humor now.

He remembered another time with the night-vision lens: Marti, the Calistoga beautician. By then he'd begun his love-name tradition, and his love name for her was Pony, inspired by the long auburn hair she wore caught up with a ribbon.

He'd gotten several shots of her bending over a chair with the hair hanging down and her butt in the air – a nice butt, worth double-rubbering for, his genuine excuse for leaving her for the minute needed to grab the camera.

The next night, Sunday, he'd slipped into her hair-dressing shop, taped the pictures inside the window, facing out, all ready for when she came to open the place at the start of the week, and jammed the door on his way out.

GDIM.

Only a single shot for Lynn. She had a reporter's senses; he'd feared she might hear the lens whir even just the one time.

But she hadn't, and now he had leaped from a one-horse beauty shop to a TV station for his stage.

God, she was inspiring.

It delighted him to picture her wondering and worrying what would be next. He enjoyed thinking about the police or whoever skipping along the paper trail, if they were, checking out Federal Express and post office nonsense. Probably even Lynn Marchette wouldn't rate public-service time for these little tricks.

Maybe later.

The woman went to the cashier and paid for two books. As he followed her to the exit, Greg caught sight of their reflection in the glass door. She was so delicate; he towered over her in the most appealing way. He could get her in a wink.

But once again he found that he didn't care to.

The real action was with Lynn. He could only think of Lynn.

'I've been trying to reach you,' Mike said. He stood in Lynn's apartment doorway in black jeans, a turtle-green parka, and his ubiquitous sweatshirt. This one said *BC*. 'I left a message at your office an hour ago.'

156

Lynn stepped back to let him in. 'I came home early. I haven't collected my messages yet.'

She'd given up feeding her headache Tylenol when the pain had ballooned through the pills. Getting through a demanding show despite the knowledge that every person on the set, in the booth, had just finished looking at her vagina, had used up her resources for the day.

Mike said, 'The pictures were mailed in two bunches – from West LA and from Studio City. Just dropped in the boxes.'

Lynn went back to the couch. An ice pack sat on the coffee table. Her dentist had given her a prescription for Percodan after her last root canal, but she hadn't dared fill it. 'Was that what you called about?'

'No. I called to get your okay to feed LA more details.'

'Which details?'

'Who you are,' he said.

'*No*.'

Lynn's phone rang. She went to the kitchen to answer.

'It's me,' Dennis said. 'Kara says you went home sick.'

'A bad headache.'

'Understandable. How are you now? Can we talk about what's going on?'

'Let't talk tomorrow.'

Lynn went back to the living room. She really needed the ice pack, visitor or no. She lifted it to her forehead.

'That was my boss. Look, I don't mean to be negative, but I don't want the LA police to know it's me.'

'Think this through,' Mike said. 'If anybody has records on the guy, it's them. Plus, they have the only antistalking unit in the country. They sit up and do tricks for celebrities; they're *LA*.'

'But why do they need my identity to give you information?'

'They need a reason to go looking harder for it. And I have no other chip. There's no felony, not even a –'

'He humiliated me with a disgusting, invasive picture taken secretly. He threatened me in a letter –'

Mike was shaking his head. 'It's not a crime to take your picture, even secretly, or to send it to people. As far as the letter goes, he told you what he *wasn't* going to do. "It would have been so easy to hurt you ... but that's instant gratification." Look, Lynn, the guy has been, I hate to say it, brilliant. He hasn't even committed the crime of stalking, technically. I can't justify spending much shift time on this, and if he's found, all we can do is have a talk with him at this point. What did your boss want?'

The abrupt question made her blink. 'To talk about this. He's nervous. We have our pilot coming up – and an especially important daily show.'

Mike nodded, studying her. She kept noticing how he watched people mercilessly, never looking away, never breaking that cord of tension. 'What's the deal with this particular show?'

'It's being picked up live by twenty-two stations. We'll be taking phone calls from all over the country.'

A cracking noise came from the kitchen, and Lynn jumped. Mike ran in there.

'Ice,' he called. 'There's a bowl of it, settling.'

'I'm a wreck,' Lynn said. 'Every sound scares me.'

'Who's on this show?'

She was getting used to his sudden changes of subject. She just followed along. Why not, when she had nothing to hide?

She said, 'Parents whose daughters died after self-induced abortions.'

'Good topic. You should do more on child-related issues. Foster care – I can give you more information than you can stomach.'

'I'll take you up on that.' She put down the ice pack and tipped her head back to ease the increasing pressure in her forehead.

'Are you taking anything decent?' Mike asked.

'Tylenol, this morning. It didn't help.'

'Real aspirin's the best. Do you have any?'

'I'm not sure.'

He located the bathroom without needing to ask. Lynn heard him opening cabinets. She stood up to go in there – but instead went tightly still, the pain pounding through her whole head, as the significance of one of Mike's remarks fell on her.

'*I can't justify much shift time on this.*'

What was he doing here, then?

Why was he pursuing the case?

To solve a noncrime committed by an invisible non-criminal? *Or because he thought he might have a delusional, pathological TV personality on his hands?*

Lynn stood. A hollow panic was building. With that and the pain, she was unsteady on her feet, but she headed purposefully for the bathroom.

Mike was crouched at the under-sink cupboard, poking through bottles of cosmetics and vitamins. He found the aspirin bottle.

Lynn stood over him. 'If you can't justify spending time on my case, why are you here?'

He looked up at her, an assessing flick of his eyes, as if checking a thermometer. He stood.

She was in her stocking feet and he wore boots, but they were nearly eye to eye. She was trembling with pain, fear, and fury, but she gripped a countertop and met his stare. 'You think I'm a psycho,' she said. The words hurt, as if each sound wave was battering her head. 'You're letting me think you're on my side, but you're not. You're digging a pit around me and waiting for me to fall into it!'

She expected him to yell back, craved it, needed the reality of sentences and answers and yeses and noes. Whatever came out would be better than this formless drifting between terrors.

But instead he moved past her into the living room, getting a glass of water from the kitchen on the way.

'Come in here,' he said over his shoulder. 'Sit down.'

She stayed right where she was. 'Don't patronize me. I'm waiting for your answer.' Her head hurt so, she had to hold it.

He opened the aspirin bottle and handed her three, with the water.

''I'll give you all the answers you want. But first swallow these.'

She returned to the couch. She did as he'd said; it was the easiest way.

Mike sat in the chair and pulled it closer to the table, cutting the distance between them. He leaned forward. Fleetingly Lynn recalled how he'd sat this way on her show. All that aggressive intensity had radiated right through the camera.

'I was thrown at first, I admit that,' he said. 'Your assistant accusing you – your friend ...' He shook his head. 'It didn't freeze. The damn *letter* didn't freeze. Copying your writing ... nah.'

He leaned forward another bit. His eyes were almost black. 'Yeah, I considered you. You could have wanted to fan the attention. Make a story out of it. You maybe were a wackball yourself.'

As much as she'd wanted to flush the idea into the air, Lynn cringed from it now, hearing the words.

'After a day,' he went on, 'I decided it wasn't you. You would never have put in that crack about bulging out of the bathing suit.'

'That was the only reason?' she asked.

'No. It's just the only one I can articulate. And those pictures today ...' He shook his head again. 'Is that enough answers for you?'

She said, 'No. I still don't·see why you're staying with this.'

He sighed. 'Because we're dealing with a different kind of freak than I thought. A whole other level of wackball. Forging your writing so even your assistant can't spot any difference ... sneaking a night-vision photo and mailing it around ...'

'What? Finish.'

'I don't *know* what. That's the point.' He paused. 'Before the note, all his shit fit the usual pattern. Unique, some of it, but it fit. You could have expected he might get bored and move on, leave you alone. Now ...' He shrugged. 'That probably won't happen. This'll all probably get worse.'

Dennis pulled over a chair for her. 'How's your head today?'

Better than my dignity, Lynn thought to say, and didn't. In the long night, she had reached the understanding that the picture was supposed to have that effect precisely: to make her shrink and cower from all those who'd seen it.

Don't give up your power.

'I could waffle around with small talk,' Dennis said, 'but you don't want to, and I don't. Let me just say this: with all the attention you've given to obsession and stalking on the show, it's goddamned ironic that you have to go through it yourself.'

Lynn sat straighter in the luxurious chair. 'Thank you for understanding, Dennis.'

'It's an epidemic in Hollywood now. I keep reading about it. Never thought I'd get to see it firsthand.'

'Neither did I,' Lynn said.

'Seems like we always have to be reminded there's a flipside to celebrity. You put yourself out there, you can't control who you draw. Some nut gets fixated, thinks he has a claim on you ... What are the police doing? I'm going to put some pressure on.'

'One detective has been working on it when he can – he

was a guest on a show. But there isn't much they can do. There's no crime.'

'Bull. How did the man get into your apartment to take the picture?'

Lynn realized then that Dennis didn't know anything about Greg. She'd assumed versions of the story would be all over the station by now.

'The man isn't a stranger,' she said. 'We had a relationship. But it got weird, and I broke it off. That's when he began sending me things, hounding me. He wrote me a threatening letter in my own handwriting –'

'That was the matter that postponed the pilot meeting?'

'Yes.'

'Did you say in your *handwriting*?'

'He imitated it so well, even Kara ... couldn't tell.'

'When did he take the picture?'

'He took it secretly, when we were still dating.'

Dennis looked at her without speaking for a minute. 'How long were you dating?'

'Just a couple of weeks. He lives in Los Angeles. We met there when I went to talk with QTV.'

There was a knock on Dennis's door, and Kara came in. 'I just got off the phone with Oprah's assistant. They're definitely considering the pilot. She thinks you should call Oprah.'

'Now?'

'Now.'

CHAPTER NINE

Greg had never had so much fun planning his surprises.

Usually he had just one person to surprise. In Lynn's case, he had an audience, should he elect to exercise his potential access to it. And he would, he would. Just today he had secured the essentials, which he would put in place on his next visit to her turf.

He was nowhere near done with Lynn.

As a rule, he was through with them by now. He had his souvenir and there wasn't enough still happening to hold his interest.

Occasionally, in fact, he was through before they were, proving, if he needed proof, that there were crazier people in the world. Sometimes one of them got it into his or her useless head that his gifts and tricks constituted a bona fide relationship ... like dogs too stupid to realize sirloin has gone maggoty.

These were some of the few times Greg regretted being, as it were, self-employed in the business of love, and thus having no one with whom to share the joke.

He remembered the dark-eyed doe: long legs, the small face that inspired her love name, Tina. Sweet and eager to please. He had first met Tina as if hearing a radio play, with his back to her at a little hanging-plants café in Studio City.

Eating his grilled salmon, he'd been listening for just idle entertainment as she talked to her husband. As the husband talked, actually: he did all of it, with Tina injecting admiring and attentive noises.

But as he waited for coffee, Greg had begun listening

more carefully, aware of a current. Tina's husband – Jeremy was his name – was three or four vodkas in, and playing a game. Jeremy was making it impossible for Tina to get out of this dinner without committing some verbal crime that he could pounce on her for. Jeremy was doing a most creditable job of herding her into a box.

Greg had never needed to stoop to such tactics. That was for the average guy, carrying on an honorable tradition, as his father and grandfather had before him. But that didn't mean he couldn't appreciate the routine when he happened on to it, the way a gourmet occasionally enjoys a nice burger.

So Greg eavesdropped for his dessert as Jeremy neatly set Tina up. The man told her a confusing, disjointed story, then accused her, when she asked questions, of not paying attention ... then moved in for the coup de grace.

'You weren't listening. You *never* listen,' Jeremy had hissed.

'I was. I always do.'

'You're so fucking self-centered. It always has to be about *you*. I'm sick of your bullshit.'

'Stop yelling –'

'*Don't you fucking tell me what to do!*'

Suddenly Greg had an inspiration. He could turn this little play into living theater.

He put money on the table and got up out of his booth. He stepped to theirs, looked down on them: Jeremy half out of his seat and red-faced, Tina with arms valiantly folded but chin trembling.

Gently Greg said to Tina, 'I couldn't help overhearing. Let me call you a taxi.'

Jeremy sputtered, 'Who the fuck –'

'Shut up,' Greg said. 'You're bullying this woman. Go find a real fight if you're such a macho guy.' Greg patted Tina's shoulder. 'You don't have to put up with this. Come on outside with me.'

She hadn't wanted to go home to the house she shared with Jeremy, so Greg had paid for a motel room and sat with her half the night, just holding her hand, watching old movies until she fell asleep against his chest.

It had been ridiculously easy to win her. Tina had divorced Jeremy, rented her own place, then solicited his advice on every aspect of furnishing and decoration. To complete Act Three, Greg, after building Tina up, had gradually bullied her right back down into the same box as Jeremy had, much more subtly, of course; but that was so effortless, it was more boring for him than fun.

He could sympathize with Jeremy.

She hadn't seemed to miss Jeremy, but she sure held on like a limpet to him, Greg recalled. Not matter what he did to turn her off, she only tried harder to please. She loved her tattoo, would have gotten one on her pancreas if he'd asked. There was no demand too unreasonable, no sex act too demeaning. She would scrub floors three times, replace every outfit in her closet, blow him under the table in a Chinese restaurant.

Even after he bailed out, he couldn't get a rise out of her. Whatever he sent or wrote or made happen, she wouldn't back off. Wouldn't let *him* go; spent her evenings and weekends driving around Los Angeles looking for him.

A couple of times she found him, making an interesting experience. Never before had *he* been the object of such activity.

But that was the hallmark of a true adventurer, wasn't it? To welcome and savor the complexity added by the unexpected.

Then there had been Abel, his seatmate on a Sacramento–San Diego run – so named by Greg for his impressive endurance.

Greg had flown first-class, that particular job carrying the perk, and had, in the spirit of celebration, indulged in the champagne that flowed like –

'Champagne,' the balding man next to him had supplied, causing them both to laugh gustily.

They had introduced themselves, Greg providing one of his collection of business cards, for an Ethan Richards of Sacramento – the card newly acquired from the real Ethan, a block trader he'd met in the Marriott lounge.

Abel wore a Hugo Boss sport coat, and eyeliner. When, after lobster Mornay and still more champagne, he had suggested they repair to the lavatory to share a joint, Greg agreed ... and had watched with interest as Abel disarmed the smoke detector, fired up the doobie, and, after they'd finished it, shucked the sport coat and everything below.

Greg had spent evenings with Abel for a week. Then, his own job nearly completed, he'd squeezed in some quick fun, sending gifts to Abel at work: the raunchiest muscle magazines, a magnum of champagne with a dildo twisted around the neck.

But Abel, like Tina, was undumpable.

Back home in LA, Greg kept seeing classified ads in the papers: 'ETHAN' – 'ABEL' MISSES YOU. GET IN TOUCH. On the next job that took him through Sacramento, he'd been pounced on at the Marriott, Abel having seen him use a matchbook from there.

So once again Greg had bent with the breeze, utilizing the situation. He'd let Abel think they were cozy again, pumped him up – then had all that sweet leverage for another barrage of truly devilish tricks.

Never let it be said that he couldn't be spontaneous.

The Tuesday after Thanksgiving was overcast and blustery, with traffic lights shaking overhead and grit blowing; invisible, but you crunched it in your teeth.

Lynn unlocked her apartment door. She was struggling

to keep on top of her tension. Each day seemed to bring a new pressure, without the old ones going away. She was always wondering about Greg, what he'd do next. Wondering what those around her were thinking.

Angela's prescription was more exercise. She seemed pleased to have Lynn at her club, but was bossy about what she felt Lynn should be doing there. Between that and her vigil over Lawrence's worry index, Lynn tended to avoid her.

But she had done what Angela asked. Booboo didn't know about the picture. His blood pressure was all right.

Lynn closed the door behind her, dropped her armload of mail on the coffee table, and sank down on the sofa.

The wind huffed against her terrace door.

She was drawn to go out there; weather always made her want to meet it close up, to see how it felt on her skin, what it did to the harbor.

But she was too tired.

She sat up and looked through the mail. Among the letters and circulars was a stiff manila envelope. She brought it into the kitchen and slit it with a knife.

And stood there at the kitchen counter, frozen in place.

It was the same awful photo mailed to everyone at Channel 3 – but this one was altered. There were bloody red holes where her nipples had been. A steak knife protruded from the vagina, with blood dripping from the bluebell sheets onto the carpet.

Something was wrong with her muscles. She wanted to drop the loathsome picture, but couldn't. She just held it up, transfixed by it, touching the blood drops …

Suddenly her hands were back in working order. She threw the picture to the floor and stepped on it, grinding it with her gritty boots.

A practical voice asked whether she should be destroying what could be evidence. A more practical one answered that she should be so lucky.

167

Outside, the wind was louder, whistling along the terraces. It was no longer an alluring, friendly sound.

She forced down her alarm. If she didn't make that supreme effort, she'd be screaming.

But the panic was threatening to get away from her.

She had better call Mike.

She brought the phone to the couch, dialed the police station, got a busy signal.

A busy signal?

She must have dialed wrong.

She tried again, then two more times. Now it was circuits-busy.

The panic fluttered. She could feel it in odd places: beneath her tongue, under her arms.

She dialed the number again. Got the busy, kept pushing redial.

The lights went out.

She screamed and jumped up, banging her knee on the coffee table. She ran to the door, yanked it open, started out into the dark hall, then ran back for her coat, moving as fast as she could while using her hands as antennae.

No elevator. She ducked back in a last time to grab her umbrella. She felt her way down the dark stairs waving the umbrella in front of her like a blind person's cane, the only defense she could think of.

Pushing open the door from the stairway into the lobby, she saw a blessed glow – streetlights! She raced to the door and threw herself against it, stumbling out into the wind and the normalcy.

'It's the weather,' Mike said. 'There are outages all over the place. Where are you? What's the number I called?'

'Kara's. I took a cab here. Mike, I couldn't even get the police station on the phone!'

'Well, everyone calls on a night like this. You aren't the only one who panicked.'

'But I *am* the only one whose lights went out on the night she got a – a malignant thing in the mail from a sick, vicious –'

'*Lynn!*' he interrupted. 'You have to take it easy. When you get rattled, you're helping him.' A beep sounded. 'My chicken's done. Hold on a second.'

Nicky was looking up at Lynn. She reached to rub his head.

Mike came back on. 'I'm going to eat now. I worked seven to seven today; I'm starving.'

Lynn said, 'Can an officer check my building?'

'Tonight? Are you kidding?'

'No, I'm not kidding. I want to be sure the electricity wasn't tampered with.'

'The electricity only did what everyone else's did tonight. There are scattered pockets of darkness all over the city. It's too bad that damn thing arrived on the same night, but it's just a coincidence. Let me give you some advice.'

'What?'

'Pretend this isn't bothering you. Sleep at Kara's tonight if you need to, but starting tomorrow, act as if nothing terrible is happening in your life.'

Nicky nudged her with his nose, but Lynn was concentrating on Mike's words. 'Isn't that just denial?'

'It's method acting. It empowers you instead of him. It's what we tell all our victims. You can't control what he does, but you are in charge of your reaction to it. The more you can take control that way, the better. And taking control is what you need to do now, Lynn. You can't go fantasizing that your freak is running to the East Coast to shut your power off.'

'I must not be doing this right,' Lynn said to Elizabeth Vail. 'One of the main reasons I joined the club is for stress reduction. But it doesn't seem to be working.'

They were sitting across from each other at the desk in the fitness oficce. Elizabeth got up and wheeled over the sphygmomanometer and cuffed Lynn's arm.

'One ten over seventy. Perfect,' Elizabeth said. 'When was your last physical?'

'About a year go. I'm not sick. I get wound up, and I can't wind down. I have horrendous headaches ...'

'Do you stretch before and after working out?'

'I usually forget.'

Elizabeth got up. 'Come on downstairs.'

She led Lynn into the massage room. It was softly lighted, with peach walls and lush carpeting. There was a padded table with a fresh sheet on it; the air smelled of perfumed soap.

Elizabeth adjusted dials on a speaker to mute the elevator music. 'Spring forest? No, waterfall, I think,' she said, and the sound of gentle splashing filled the room.

She had Lynn lie on the table. For the next half hour, Elizabeth pulled and pressed and rotated every limb. She worked on Lynn's neck where the headaches began, and gave extra attention to the upper back and shoulders.

'You feel the pain in your head and neck, but it germinates here,' Elizabeth said in her quiet voice. 'A bad day at work floods this upper-back triangle with tension. The tension makes knots as it collects. For many people, the next step is a back spasm; you get a headache instead.'

Hearing the explanation softly through the splashing, Lynn thought how she wished bad days at work were the only cause of her tension.

At the end, she actually felt better.

'This is the first time in days I don't feel like I have a backpack on.'

'Should I show you movements to do in your office to keep the tension from building?'

'Yes. Too bad you don't make house calls.'

'I do, sometimes.'

'Really?'

'For certain clients.'

'So,' Lynn said, 'if a person couldn't get here, you might go to their home or office?'

'I would for you or Bernadine.'

'Thank you.'

Elizabeth shrugged. 'You've both been helpful to me. You make me look good. Let's face it, the two of you are high-profile, and you both look fit, and everyone knows I designed your exercise routines. When the day comes that I open my own place, I want women like you and Bernadine to be the ones signing up – and bringing your friends.'

The dead girls' pictures were pinned to a corkboard in Lynn's office.

A shot of the montage had been used in the promos for the show. The faces were haunting: five cute teenagers, all button noses and moussed hair, who had become pregnant, didn't want to tell, and died.

Lynn sat back in her desk chair and looked at each in turn. She'd been studying them for weeks. She knew who had the eyebrow mole, whose smile showed the overbite.

Five girls; five mothers and five fathers, each of whom would sacrifice limbs for the chance to give their daughters the advice and reassurance it was way too late for.

In two hours all the parents would be in her studio, telling their stories to a national audience.

'Nervous?' Kara asked, coming in with two coffees.

'Yes.'

Kara touched Lynn's sleeve. 'You look great.'

'Do I?' Lynn stood to show the whole dress, winter-white wool crepe with a high collar that framed her face. 'I was saving this for today. I hope the show goes well. It should. The topic is vital, and irresistible. The parents are eloquent. You can't not feel for these girls. We got

171

twenty-two cities. I haven't yet spilled coffee on myself.'

Thirteen minutes into the show, watching from the control room, Dennis said, 'What the hell is that?'

Kara looked at Lynn, walking across the set with her mike. Kara's eyes went wide. The back of Lynn's white dress was soaked with what seemed like blood.

'Break!' Kara told the director.

'But –'

'Break now! Cut her off!'

The monitor jumped to a commercial, and Kara ran out to the set. Floor people were crowded around Lynn, who was just realizing the reason for the commotion. Kara hurried her toward an empty dressing room.

'This is unbelievable!' Lynn said. 'How could I – I don't even have my period!'

'Where is it coming from, then? Should I get an ambulance?'

'No! I want to go back to the set. I need another dress, quick.'

Kara ran out, met Pam, sent her up to Lynn's office for fresh clothes, and started to run back to Lynn. But Dennis stopped her.

'No,' he said when she'd filled him in. 'Lynn's not moving until a doctor sees her. This show is canceled. Have them run a Best Of, and say it's being joined in progress.'

Greg had the TV on ahead of time. Asinine commercials – new, improved Tide and brownie mix. Housewife stuff.

It reminded him just exactly what a different league his Star was for him.

They ran the abortion-show promo – 'That's on Lynn Marchette, fifteen minutes from now!' – he'd been seeing right along.

He remembered very well how proudly Lynn and Kara had discussed this program, how delighted they were to be going on in Chicago and LA and Miami and blah blah blah.

He sat in his living room swivel chair, his attention riveted to the TV screen. He didn't want to miss a second of the program.

The show started. The parents were introduced; pictures of the girls were shown.

Greg's mouth was dry. He wanted a drink of water. He wouldn't see anything until Lynn took her seat, and she never did that until the first segment was under way, but he boosted the volume and ran to and from the kitchen, just in case.

Back in the chair, he drank his water. When Lynn sat, he tensed.

Nothing.

Could his trick have failed?

The phone rang, and he jumped a foot.

He considered letting the machine answer, but decided to pick it up.

'Mr Sellinger? It's awfully noisy up there.'

He winced at the squeaky old voice, always annoying, right now maddening. 'Sorry, Mrs Minot. I'll take care of it.'

She was replying, but he hung up. He'd smooth her over later.

He lowered the sound again, then looked at the VCR clock. They were nine minutes in.

If he didn't see anything soon, he'd have to start assuming they'd caught the trick in time.

But how? It had been goof proof. No one ever sat in the host seat but Lynn. The capsules were as good as invisible.

Eleven minutes. He clutched the chair arms.

He realized he was holding his breath, then released it slowly.

He got up out of the chair, paced the carpet, his Weejunned feet leaving tracks in the buttery gold pile. He

173

walked quietly and stayed off the bare floor; the last thing he needed was Mrs Minot ringing him right at the golden moment. Red moment.

Finally he settled on the carpet smack by the screen, so close the tiny lines that comprised the picture were clear to see. The brightness hurt his eyes, like staring into a sun haze.

Lynn pointed the mike, pulled it back, went striding across the set, her back to the camera – and suddenly there it was. He'd forgotten the dye took a few minutes to bloom. Her whole dress was crimson in back!

The audio clicked off, then the picture. The Marchette show logo appeared. They went to a commercial.

Two more spots, then three station promos. Then the live announcer's voice: 'The program scheduled for this time has been postponed. Please stay tuned for "The Best of Lynn Marchette," already in progress.'

'*Choice!*' Greg shouted, leaping up. He drumrolled his fists on the TV. He danced on the carpet, applauding himself, danced to the kitchen and back.

He pictured the Channel 3 control room. He exploded into laughter as he envisioned Lynn and Kara and the rest of them.

He was still laughing as he danced to the ringing phone to smooth Mrs Minot down.

'How can it not be against the law?' Lynn asked. 'He destroyed an important, expensive live broadcast!'

'Your boss only made that point about fifteen times,' Mike said, glancing at Lynn's office door, through which Dennis and Kara had just departed. 'I'll tell you once more. I don't know how he got the money-marking capsules, but even if he stole them, it wouldn't be a big deal legally. This stunt is a civil matter, not one for the police.'

Lynn rubbed her eyes.

Mike watched her. Tension showed in the curl of her

shoulders under her blouse. Her skin was like skim milk.

He was surprised to realize that a part of him wanted to touch the shoulders, squeeze her hand, make it better.

'Dennis was talking about hiring private investigators,' Lynn said.

'To do *what*? There's nothing to go on.'

'He knows that. He decided not to. And he wants to keep it in the family for now. But he's going to bring in a lot more security.'

Mike asked, 'How did Greg know this show was the one to trash?'

'Oh, I gave him that. He drew me out, and I fed him everything he needed about what shows are important to me, and which are being carried on the West Coast. I described this one in detail. I was so proud that the parents trusted me.'

'How do you think he got in here?'

'I agree with Kara. He must have copied her keys when she let him into the studio – or copied mine earlier. I was a big help to him there too. My keys are all labeled.'

Mike moved toward the door. 'He seems bent on screwing up your career. Could he be a TV professional?'

'I think I would have known. But maybe not. There's so much I didn't know.'

CHAPTER TEN

'Why didn't you tell me?' Booboo demanded.

'I should have. I should have known you'd find out.'

'That isn't the reason!' Lynn held the phone away, but her brother's voice boomed through. 'My sister gets doused with blood, and I don't happen to see the show that day, so I have to hear about it from one of my tellers –'

'Not blood. Money-marking dye.'

'He got hold of that stuff? How?'

'I don't *know*!'

'You should have told me.'

'I didn't want to worry you.'

'I worry more, knowing you held out. I wonder what else you aren't telling me. You were right about that guy. I wish I'd listened while I could still get my hands on him.'

Lynn closed her eyes, thinking hollowly of the secret she still kept: the night-vision picture that had apparently not reached the rumor circuit.

Lynn knew before they were off the air on the foster care show that it was one of the most powerful they'd ever done.

Every day that went by with no harm to herself or to the show was a reason to be thankful.

As the credits rolled, there was a standing ovation from the studio audience.

Dennis shook hands with Mike Delano, the social workers, and the two young teenage guests as they left the set. Mary Eli gave Lynn a quick hug and hurried out.

Kara came running down the hall. 'I just returned a call from Oprah's office. She said yes. She'll do a live satellite appearance on the pilot!'

Lynn closed her eyes. 'Thank God. I was so afraid she'd turn us down.'

At six Bernadine came up with champagne, and they gathered in Dennis's office to celebrate.

'How do you feel?' Bernadine asked Lynn.

'Great,' Lynn lied. Her pleasure over the news had faded fast, beaten back by her fears.

She kept trying to draw courage by concentrating on how she was fortunate. She was a strong, public person; her victimizer was far away, not hounding her physically, like those poor women who had to see their torturers every day, feel their presence with every action they took.

But the courage never lasted.

No sooner would she finish a good show than the questions battered her.

What would Greg do to her between now and the pilot taping? His usual tricks that drove her crazy? New and devastating ploys? Would he somehow tamper with another show, and would Dennis decide not to tape the pilot because of sabotage potential?

How much chance was there of the police identifying Greg? If they did, could he even be stopped?

Would she be able to keep QTV from finding out all this?

'You haven't had your champagne,' Bernadine said softly.

Lynn drank some, tried to smile, thought she succeeded, but Bernadine said, 'Is everything all right? No, I can see it isn't.'

'I'm ... kind of pressured.'

Her voice still low, Bernadine asked, 'Is it about the man who's been harassing you? Dennis told me a little.'

Lynn looked at the compact, elegant person who did not at all embody the brittle cliché of boss's wife. Her light-lashed eyes were sympathetic and intelligent. Bernadine seemed to invite her burden.

'This is hell,' Lynn said. Her eyes stung. She didn't dare continue.

'What can I do?' Bernadine asked. 'I can listen. Do you want to tell me about it?'

Lynn hesitated, and Bernadine said, 'This isn't the time. But, hon, you need to buck up. You're going to be the hit of the dial. Try to focus on that.'

Greg hit the Pause button on the VCR as the credits finished. Interesting show; Lynn held it together well. He only wished he'd seen it live. But tape was better than not seeing it. It was too bad he couldn't see her live more often.

It was too bad the rest of the nation wasn't going to either.

Now was study time.

Postponing the choice moment, he went to the window and drank in the view, the lights of the city in their jewel clusters. Then he drew the drapes, the better to see details on the screen, and rewound.

Now for the mood score.

He skipped around in the tape, freezing close-ups of Lynn's face and long full-body shots. He concentrated on the beginning and end of the show, when, he'd noticed, she was less *on*.

His heart jumped in delight. Definitely a progression.

He could see the strain in the tight little pockets around her lower face. The signals of body language he felt rather than gauged visually, keying them to the memory of what her body had done when it was his to play with. But her movements were a tiny bit stiffer, he was sure. That loose way she galloped around the set wasn't quite the same now.

Well. Well.

Excitedly he hunted back through the tape, this time looking for the tattoo. There were few shots tight enough on her lower legs in this one to see, but he picked up a trace through her hose. It wasn't all gone yet.

He was still sorry he hadn't been able to get her to go for the permanent kind, like the others.

But that was more than made up for by this incredible ongoing opportunity to track her.

Always before, he'd had to hide and sneak to get a glimpse – a quick live-action peek, nothing like the glorious treat of videotape to study.

None of the others was a TV star.

He remembered his first look at Lynn in person.

It was in the bar at Geoffrey's, as she stood in the knot of QTV people. Her aura had nearly sung to him. Compared to the picture that still lay secreted in his crawl space, that publicity shot of her from *Broadcasting*, she was a shimmering, vibrating vision.

That skin. Those hands.

The delicacy of her, the candy coating of it that barely gilded the delicious sinews within.

You could feel the vitality in there, the unbreakable, unshakable wire-tautness of who Lynn Marchette was.

He'd had to build his way next to her that night with great care, so that later, no one would ever be quite sure whose friend he was.

It had gone surprisingly well. A surprising night all around – possibly his finest opening performance ever.

A lot of effort.

But he was having such a splendid time.

He still fell down laughing every time he thought of Kara and Lynn explaining satellite broadcasting to him.

Mike clanged another twenty pounds onto the bar and slid

under it. That made one hundred and seventy, his max; he should have a spotter, but he didn't want one. If you had no spotter, you had to get it up there yourself.

He lifted the bar off its hooks, brought it down, felt the challenge in his arms, his pecs and shoulders readying to assist. Slowly he struggled it up, up, focusing on evening the push ... pressing, pressing through the impossible point, *passing* it.

He rested on the bench. The air was on in the gym; sweat rolled from his chest and torso, and he felt chilled. He reached down for his towel.

Way at the end of the weight room was an alcove with treadmills. Mike disliked them, preferred the free weights and, when he felt lazy, the Cybex machines. But the other reason he avoided the alcove was that a TV set hung in there.

He obsessed about Lynn Marchette a little too much as it was. He didn't need to see her on the screen and obsess more. Even this late at night there were commercials for her show.

That night at her apartment, he'd had a shock. The kind you have when you're being a self-deluding asshole about something.

There Lynn was, yelling at him in the bathroom, demanding to know what he really thought. The screaming hurt her head, and he'd given her aspirin.

What he really thought, he'd realized with a crash of chagrin, was that he wanted to hold her.

Which had of course made him immediately detach. Back right off.

Spend the next few days convincing himself he had felt no such impulse.

He'd done such a good job that when the feeling came again, after her lost program, he'd actually been surprised.

Then came the show he was on, and it was all back once more. He couldn't stop looking at her. Even one of the uniformed playcops they had guarding the place now picked up on it, shot Mike a look.

He did two sets at lower weight, pushing the last one to fatigue, and went in to shower.

Soaping up, he thought of her with the young kids on the show. The pain in her face.

He stepped out of the spray, grabbed a clean towel.

He was going to have to get better at not thinking this way.

For a thousand reasons, it was out of the question to have any relationship with Lynn other than the professional one.

He left his locker key at the front desk and went out into the damp night, waving goodbye to a couple of other cops.

Maybe he didn't really want one anyway. Maybe it was just the new experience of being around a celebrity.

Maybe he felt sorry for her. For the whole crappy situation. Maybe he'd get some handle on it and be able to help her out of it, and his feelings would fade away.

That must be it.

'Shit,' Dennis said.

'What's the matter?' Bernadine called.

Dennis was standing in his closet, surrounded by a pile of sweaters. 'Damn it. I can't find my brown V-neck. Did you take it to the cleaners?'

'No.'

He shoved hangers around furiously.

'Do you want to tell me what's on your mind?' she asked.

'Just that my station is going to hell.'

'It's not going to hell.' Bernadine went into her bathroom and opened the porthole, a small window between their two baths, which they'd had constructed so they could talk without shouting as they went about their

181

routines. 'What bothers you most?' she asked.

'Murder. Mayhem. Homelessness. Drug crime –'

'Seriously.'

'The anchor spot. Every audition tape is the same: a vapid face with eyes that only see from there out. And the Marchette show is on my mind.'

'The show? Or Lynn?'

'Both.'

'I know she's got her troubles. You can see the strain. But the show looks as good as ever.'

'Does it?' Dennis asked. 'You don't see a difference?'

'Not really.'

'She looks frazzled to me,' Dennis said around a toothbrush. 'We need to get her pilot in the can. I want her to be at her best.'

'I hope the police can hunt down this terrible man who's after her.'

'I didn't realize it was someone she had an affair with.'

'She *did*?'

'She told me herself.'

'How sickening,' Bernadine said. 'How could she – Well, who knows? I'm turning on the shower.'

'Close the porthole,' Dennis said, but she had already started. Steam billowed through, and he closed his side.

'She should go public,' Detective Howard Landrau said. 'Make noise. Scare the shithead off.'

'She wants to keep it quiet. Besides, that could backfire. He might love it,' Mike said.

Landrau shrugged. 'Nothing else is working, am I right?'

'Nothing else is being tried.' Mike looked over at his own desk, next to Landrau's, where the Marchette file sat. There was practically nothing in it. 'The guy's been careful not to cross into the stalking law. California's is the same as ours – there has to be a credible physical threat. I don't have enough to take to the DA, so I'm not even officially looking for him. And officially or no, I can't find his dust. He's a ghost.'

'Talk to her. See if she'll come out with it. Bet you anything she'd get more publicity than she can handle.'

'Detective Delano,' Kara said to Lynn, who picked up her phone.

'Hi, Mike. Is something new?'

'No. I called to put the idea of going public in your head one more time. Someone else here was talking about it.'

Lynn leaned way back in her chair and stared at the acoustical tiles on the ceiling. Kara had left the office, and she was alone.

It was a frightening thought. But she hated the helplessness she felt, the terrified-kid way she acted.

'I still don't see how I can. But what would happen if I did? Walk through it with me,' she said.

In his own office, Mike was sitting straight up, the receiver cradled in his forearm, his mouth right on top of it. Years of making and taking calls surrounded by other cops had taught him how to use his normal voice and not have every syllable overheard.

'Best case, he's flushed out of the woods, doesn't like the light, and runs back in and stays there. These jerkoffs love to play hide and seek, but not to be found.'

'So this whole mess could end. He might really leave me alone.'

'Might.'

'Or?'

'The publicity might turn him on. You'd have to issue a statement, sit still for interviews – am I right? This is a big story, a TV personality being stalked.'

'Yes.'

'So that's the worst case. He doesn't hate the light, he loves it and wants to stay in it.'

183

She was shaking her head as she listened, picturing herself hounded everywhere, phones ringing, notes in a blizzard, obscene gifts piling up, burying her.

Making use of the time as she waited for Lynn to finish her call, Kara looked through mail. Lynn's new Broome Club membership card was there. Kara put it on Lynn's pile and glanced at the brochure that had come in the envelope.

Where did they get the people to pose for these things? The bodies exercising couldn't be more perfect. It discouraged you.

She put the leaflet with the card and went on, but the images of solid thighs stayed.

She'd promised and promised herself to do something about her own oatmeal legs, her impossible rear. She'd ordered literature from two clubs and never even read it.

Now here was Lynn, size nothing-minus, with more going on in her life than the President, starting an exercise program.

It made Kara a little crazy.

Lynn hung up and paced the office. She looked out at the boulevard traffic. The time-wasting zigzagging down there had always been a motivating contrast to the momentum up here.

Not now.

Each of those vehicles contained at least one person to whom, if she released the story of how she was being tortured by a sadistic monster, she would be presenting the right to examine and judge it.

Twenty or thirty vehicles in sight right now. Multiply that by an hour, by a day, and then a week. Add on for passengers.

Thousands of Bostonians, then hundreds of thousands of others as the story was picked up. Other media: *People* magazine, the tabloid papers, and TV shows.

And what exactly were the facts of this victimization she was inviting them all to judge?

Though she'd been hurt many times by making poor relationship choices, she'd let herself be picked up while on a business trip by an attractive man. She'd spent the evening with him, then invited him to stay in her apartment a week later. She'd slept with him every night, introduced him to her friends and family, all of whom adored him. He'd given her, and them, lovely gifts.

Then she ended the brief relationship because of behavior that she thought was weird and everyone else thought was fine.

Then he urged her to reconsider.

Then he started to make things happen that never hurt anyone, and that couldn't be proven his doing anyway … and that some of those closest to her felt she was misinterpreting.

For her sanity, Lynn had kept that part in a mental closet. But she had to open the door now, to put herself in the place of these hundreds and thousands of people who would see the facts with no investment in pain-postponing closets.

If her own loved ones weren't sure they believed that a situation she had danced enthusiastically into had turned rancid, just what did she expect those hundreds of thousands to think?

What did they think of Patricia Bowman?

What did they think of Anita Hill?

What would QTV think of a personality they were grooming starring in a drama like Patricia's or Anita's?

Lynn's breath had made a circle of fog on the window. With her fingertip she drew a face with eyes and nose but no mouth.

The irony was beyond unspeakable. She who insisted on shining the light had to choose to stay in the dark.

* * *

'I brought some bands and hand weights,' Elizabeth said. 'Or did you just want a stretching session?'

Lynn rubbed the back of her head. 'Both, I guess.'

'Headache?'

'Working on one. Thank you for coming to the office.'

'No problem. You sounded hassled when you called. Bernadine Orrin says you're having a rough time.'

Kara came in with papers while Lynn was working her arms with a stretch band.

'Want to join in?' Lynn asked.

'No,' Kara said curtly.

'It's not that hard –'

'*No*. I just came in to get your signature on these.'

When Kara was gone, Lynn thought how she missed the freedom of being able to discuss anything at all with her. She understood Kara's worries about the show and the syndication; Kara had been honest about that. But, selfishly, Lynn hated the wedge it drove between them.

'I am having a rough time,' she answered Elizabeth. She was starting to understand the popularity of the personal trainer relationship, a trend she had considered shallow and self-indulgent. It wasn't hard to appreciate a person who could relax you, improve your health and serve the bartender/hairdresser function of impartial sounding board.

Especially when no one else around you was impartial anymore.

'We might have to put off the pilot,' Dennis said. 'We can't risk having that sabotaged.'

Lynn clenched her hands under her desk. 'There hasn't been a problem with a show since the one time.'

'But look at what that one time was. Our national hookup. Not a random choice.'

Kara said, 'Let's not rush to decide about the pilot. I'm checking out special security. Wait until I know more.'

'Another thing,' Dennis said. 'You are not in top form,

186

Lynn. You're under fire, and it shows.'

'I'm trying, Dennis. You can't deny the shows are strong. It could be a lot worse.'

'Yeah, but is could-be-worse where we want to be for a national tryout?'

When Dennis had gone, Kara said, 'I don't want us to lose the pilot. We've killed ourselves to get it set.'

'I don't either. But I'd rather lose it because *we* changed our timing than because Greg destroyed it.' Lynn tried to smile, but her lips wouldn't. 'Isn't this ironic? I used to destroy opportunities for myself. Now I'm not doing it – but Greg is! So what's the difference? They're still being destroyed!'

Ten days till Christmas Eve; then he'd turn on the lights of his Christmas palm.

A lot of joy this year.

His rhythm was perfect.

He'd never had anyone at this stage at holiday time. It offered so many delightful refinements.

Like the one he'd just prepared.

Greg sat for a few minutes gazing at the phone, the instrument of his latest treat for Lynn.

A technically sophisticated treat, seemingly – but he hadn't needed any technology to arrange it except touch tones.

To a satellite consulting engineer who installed uplink and downlink systems as routinely as other people ran their dishwashers, technology was a yawn.

He'd known the first time he saw Lynn's picture that she would be special.

A big upper-body shot in *Broadcasting*. She was holding an award her show had won. The glory of it was in her eyes, in the proud way she sat for the camera.

He'd actually been halfway up a satellite tower drinking

coffee and flipping through the magazine when he'd seen it.

Greg liked having coffee that way; he could count on being left alone. Even the fabled Indians weren't as at ease with high places as he was. It was part of the reason he earned so much in the field.

And he had just found another reason to be thankful he'd kept up with his professional reading.

Later, of course, he would have that sense again, when he read about the progress of her forthcoming syndication. All kinds of information that fit his needs like a sock, right there for the using.

So there Lynn was, smiling out at him from the page. He'd never picked anyone from a picture before, but this one ...

He could see enough of her body in the shot to know what was under the conservative blouse. Narrow shoulders, a bit bony, a long midriff. Sizable breasts. Smallish virginal nipples.

And that sparkle, that pride, that strength ...

What a difference he could make!

It was all nearly his already.

This one he had to have.

The goodie he'd just arranged was a true surprise, since there was no way of telling how soon it would befall her. Soon enough, though, it being ho-ho-ho time.

And after that would come Lynn's Christmas present.

By Saturday the nineteenth, Lynn couldn't put off her shopping any longer. The stores would be zoos as it was on the last weekend before Christmas; her only other choice was to wait for Christmas Eve, with the other procrastinators, and that was a more depressing thought than doing it today.

She got up early and spent an hour at the Broome Club.

Angela was there, watching and clucking and correcting her form on the StairMaster. Finally Lynn had hidden away in the steam room, where two women her age were fretting about how to throw together a New Year's Eve party without taking time off from work to cook.

Lynn tried to recall the last time she'd had the luxury of classifying such an issue as a problem.

From the club she drove to Quincy Market. She hadn't been there since the day with Greg. The tattoo was almost gone now. She could only make out a trace. But the experience jumped back as soon as she went inside: the scratch/poke of the stylus; the prom-night bliss.

She passed a sporting goods store and remembered that she hadn't yet bought the protection Mike kept advising, for the psychological benefit. She had her gift list in her hand; she'd intended to start on it immediately and not stop until it was done. But this was a worthwhile detour.

She bought a tear gas spray from a hefty, bearded man who smiled at her as he counted out change from her twenty.

'Hope you never need it,' he said.

'Me too.'

Back out in the mall, she looked at her list. She went to a directory and mentally plotted a course. She could probably get the whole chore knocked out in three to four hours.

She headed toward Crabtree & Evelyn. Angela like their bayberry fragrance; one of the gifts Lynn had planned for her was a basket of bayberry-scented shampoo, room spray, sachets, and soap. She'd shop there for Kara too. Then she'd go over to Eddie Bauer for Booboo and Dennis.

Quincy Market was crowded but festive. Christmas carols played, not blaringly loud, thank goodness. Everyone smiled.

Crabtree & Evelyn was packed. Tiny store, polite but harried clerks, lines of shoppers.

It was hard to examine the merchandise; she had to give up on making choices for Kara. She'd do that in one of the larger stores.

But in twenty minutes she'd filled a big pale green basket with bayberry products, including an unexpected bundle of lingerie hangers; and in another twenty it was her turn at the cashier. She handed over her Visa.

The clerk inserted it, pushed keys, stopped, whispered to another cashier. She turned back to Lynn and extended her hand, with the card cut in half.

Lynn snapped her attention back from a display of candles. 'What are you –'

'We got a retrieve-card prompt, ma'am. That means Visa is instructing us to destroy it.'

'That's impossible!'

'I tried it three times.'

'This is ridiculous. There must be something wrong with your system.' Lynn took the pieces and gave the clerk her AmEx.

This time she saw the message herself on the machine: 'Retrieve card.'

Again the clerk handed her two pieces. 'Do you want to give me cash, ma'am? I can't take a check without a valid major –'

'How much is it, again?'

The explanation was starting to form, like the hum of a train in the distance, and she was getting all cold inside.

'Sixty-two eight,' the clerk said.

'I don't have that much cash.'

Thrashing around for what to do, battling the ballooning horror, she thought of returning the tear gas, adding the cash to what she had to buy the basket.

But that didn't really help anything.

And what she needed most was not to buy the basket, but to know.

So she took out her two other cards, her MasterCard

and Optima, and told the clerk, 'Try these.'

Behind her people in line were losing their smiling patience. She could hear sighs and groans. Someone back there called to her, 'They get a reward for this. The credit card company gives the cashier money.'

Someone else said, 'That's Lynn Marchette.'

More whispers now. They were explaining the situation to one another. She should just turn around and get out of there.

But she had to know.

'These are retrieves too, ma'am.' The clerk gave her four more pieces.

'What does that mean, exactly? That the system was informed I haven't paid my bills?'

'Yes, ma'am.'

Now she knew.

Waiting for Lynn to come to the door, Mary admired the view out the hall window. There was something so calming about water, with its eternal motion.

'Hi,' Lynn said.

'Hi. I hope you don't mind that I came over.'

Lynn shook her head and opened the door all the way.

Mary followed her into the living room. From long years of evaluating patients as succinctly and yet accurately as possible, her mind scanned for the right descriptor, and produced *listless*.

'You sounded so upset on the phone,' Mary said. She draped her coat over a chair.

'You called at a ... You caught me at a horrible time.' Lynn rubbed her eyes, which were already red. Makeup was smeared.

As if it was midnight after a very long day, Mary thought, but it was only noon.

'I came to hold your hand, and ... see what we can think of to do.'

191

'Thank you,' Lynn said.

'What have you done since I called?'

'Talked to Mike Delano. Called the credit card companies. Of course, there's no proof Greg did this.'

Mary went and sat next to Lynn on the couch and took her hand. She held the chilled fingers.

Usually Lynn had such presence. You didn't notice until it was gone.

Mary said, 'You're too quiet. I know I've been nagging you because you were tense, but I'd rather have you tense than apathetic.'

'You're impossible to please,' Lynn said, with what Mary hoped was a glint of a smile.

'What can we do to jump-start you?'

Her fingers still resting limply in Mary's, Lynn said with frightening calm, 'Find Greg and cut him up with a dull knife.'

Mary said, 'I was thinking of something more like, let's go shopping and you can do your list on my card and give me a check.'

'No –'

'Don't say no. It's better than sitting here glooming and gloming. Look, we have to separate these issues. The general issue of Greg harassing you is one thing; that is overwhelming if you think about it in one bite. So we break it down. The part that's important right now is you getting your Christmas list done. I know you don't feel much like it –'

'I don't.'

'That's the best reason to do it.'

Lynn sighed and stood up.

'Good,' Mary said. 'I want to see you moving and doing. You worry me when you don't react enough. Aren't you *ripped* at the sonofabitch?'

'Yes,' Lynn said. 'I told you. I'd like to stab him. But I try to follow Mike's advice about acting as if I'm in control.'

Mary took out her car keys. She groped for tactful phrasing. 'I know Mike is well-versed in this type of experience. And I agree that feeling in control is vital. But you want to avoid engaging in denial behavior.'

'I'm not denying anything, Mary. I'm standing in a spotlight with my emotions in shreds, holding them up and trying to cover myself. No one can protect me, it seems, but at least Mike is trying.'

Following Lynn out, Mary thought about this warning bell.

Was that a new note in Lynn's view of Mike? Could something be developing between them?

Mary winced. She was Lynn's friend, not her therapist, and wholesale judgments were inappropriate. *But* her wholesale judgment, based on personal impression and on what Kara had confided, was that Mike Delano was a rude, dictatorial manipulator. Just the sort of personality to pray Lynn wouldn't pick.

Lynn had explained to Mary and Gideon why the police couldn't be more aggressive in trying to stop the harassment.

But wasn't it possible that Mike had an investment in keeping the harassment going? Mary wondered. Keeping Lynn needing him?

Where else could he get an open media window? How else could he hook up to so much genuine power?

Later, over dinner, Mary told Gideon, 'I don't know if I did her any good at all.'

'How much can we do? She's trying to be brave, and we're supporting her. That's what it's about. She's dealing with a maniac.'

'He is a maniac. But she picked him.'

'You're blaming the victim.'

'I'm blaming her choices.'

Gideon kept quiet, letting his wife do what she let her

patients do in her better moments, mentally reduce a feeling to its bottom line.

'I'm casting around for why it can't happen to me,' Mary said, thinking of some of her own past choices in men.

'That's human.'

'How do you see it?'

Gideon smiled sadly. 'What I think is what I tell at least five eighth-graders a week. The past doesn't equal the present. Who cares what choices she made before? The reality is, she's in trouble now.'

'True.'

'Why can't they do something, find the guy, cut his balls off? To think we had him in our house ...'

'She's lost weight,' Mary said gloomily. 'And her hands shake. I hope she's not taking anything. I suggested she stay with us for a while, but she won't.'

Gideon raised his eyebrows. 'You're *that* worried? You think the man might hurt her?'

Mary shook her head. 'I doubt it. Usually the type of personality who likes to stay in the background and let his actions make his statements doesn't come *out* of the background. But how reliable is *usually* when someone's a psychopath? He hasn't taken any oath that he'll adhere only to what the text says weirdos do. Even that detective person told her they can't be sure what to expect, the way he's acting.'

'You really respect the detective, don't you?'

Mary made a sound of disgust. 'Don't get me started.'

'Eyewitnesses claim all of your credit cards were cut in half by the store personnel. Eight or ten cards, including a platinum AmEx.'

Lynn knew that trick, but might have bitten anyway if she hadn't expected a call like this and prepared for it.

'We're researching a credit card topic for a show. That's all I can tell you.'

'You're doing the research yourself? Just you?' The *Herald American* reporter asked.

'Of course not just me. But people don't recognize my staff and call newspapers.'

'Then,' the reporter said, 'this wouldn't have anything at all to do with the program you heavily promoted, then dumped out of. Or the rumors about embarrassing pictures circulating around the station.'

'No.'

'Technical difficulties, hot rumors, and unpaid bills … one could wonder if we're looking at personal problems.'

The phone was wet with sweat against Lynn's ear, but the reporter couldn't see her ear. So she fed all her strength into her voice.

'Not at all.'

Lynn finished the conversation and hung up. She wiped her ear with a Kleenex and blotted her face carefully so as not to smear the makeup, and went down to the studio.

'The police keep insisting they can't do anything. But I'm being worn down and humiliated, and I'm constantly afraid. Every time I start to hope it's over, he does something else, something new and sickening.'

Helene Skolnik nodded. She was a private investigator who wore Anne Klein skirt suits and loved opportunities to demonstrate her superiority over the police. But this wasn't going to be one.

'They're right,' Helene said. 'There's nothing to start with. It would cost you a pile for me just to go out to Los Angeles and come back with what I'm telling you right now for nothing.' Helene leaned across her desk. 'He never made calls from your phone? Left a credit card slip around?'

Lynn shook her head.

'And you don't want me pushing your business contacts in LA.'

'I already pushed as much as I dared.'

'If you'd grabbed a look at his wallet –'

'I didn't. And I'm sick of being told *if*.' Lynn got up.

Helene held out her hand. 'I wish I could help.'

'I wish you could too. I wish somebody could.'

On her way back to the office, Lynn stopped at the police station to tell Mike she'd made no progress with the investigator.

'I'm a mouse in a cage, and a lion is slapping the cage with his paw,' she said. 'He can smash it any time he wants to, but he just keeps slapping it. And I shiver in the corner, throwing up.' She grabbed Mike's wrist. 'This isn't going to be over. He'll just keep destroying every shred of my life. He knows he can do that without putting a finger on me. I showed him all the parts. I helped him.'

Hours later that same night, Mike was sitting up in bed, looking at his hand where Lynn's fingers had been.

He'd sat there, listening to her agony, smelling the powdery sweetness of her cologne.

He'd waited till she ran down, and then given her more of his method-acting advice.

And all along he'd been focused on her touch, the rest working on cruise control.

He shut out the light and moved down under the electric blanket. It was a dual control, and he kept both sides on. For over two years now the filaments had provided the only heat the double bed had seen.

Before that there had been Renata for a year – Renata who had taught him why he should never again have a relationship with another cop. Before her there was Dee, into whose Allston apartment he'd moved his bed and a few other possessions. Dee was pleasant and loved him, but eight months later, when he finally understood that he was never going to love her as much, he'd rented this place and brought the bed. He bequeathed her the other stuff, which was in much better shape.

In the time since Renata, who was five years closer to retirement than he was and had, thank Christ, taken her pension to the sun someplace, his passion had gone to the pummeled and bruised people he encountered each shift. What fire he possessed seemed to express itself there, anyway; he'd never felt the consuming emotion for a woman that could funnel up for a bloody baby in a Dorchester tenement or a dirty traumatized rape victim.

He was still grateful that the bed was empty but for himself and the filaments.

He slept fine in it. His night's rest was his salvation, the circuit-interrupt that fixed him to do it again the next day.

He didn't know why he was having trouble tonight.

After a half hour he got up and made a salami sandwich and ate half of it. He wrapped the rest, went back to bed, and slept, waking as usual at six. He had a sense of having dreamed actively, but could remember nothing.

CHAPTER ELEVEN

The annual Channel 3 party was held in the studio on the Tuesday before Christmas. It was a wide-open event, not limited to staff. Dennis liked to support the family spirit, and there were wrapped toys under the big tree for everyone's children and pets.

Lynn had holly in her hair, which had seemed a ridiculous idea at first, but was really no worse than the other accoutrements of the role she struggled to maintain.

She watched Bernadine, serene and elegant as always, circulating among the crowd. She should be doing that too, she thought. But it was a strain this year. She never knew who, returning her handshake, was envisioning her on the bluebell pillow …

Two men from the catering staff that supplied the Green Room were chatting with some Broome Club people. Lynn headed in their direction, but spotted Booboo and Angela coming in, and went that way instead.

'Dennis wants you to make the rounds,' Kara whispered. 'I'll keep your family company.'

Lynn arranged her face and posture and moved through the studio, saying her hellos. When she finally made her way back, Booboo was talking to Elizabeth Vail.

'Did you wave a magic wand?' he asked her. 'My wife has been trying for years to talk my sister into exercising.'

Lynn didn't hear the answer, and her brother apparently didn't either; he leaned closer to Elizabeth. As if tugged by a magnetic field, Angela, several groups away, turned sharply. She watched them for a second, then began threading her way back.

But by the time she got there, Elizabeth was occupied with the caterers again. Angela gripped her husband's arm.

'Where did you disappear on Saturday?' she asked Lynn. 'I was going to ask you to lunch.'

'I had to do my shopping,' Lynn said. She groped for a way out of the topic. But her brother, her dear brother who was always on her wavelength whether it was convenient or not, chose that moment to say, 'No more problems since the red dye?' and she had to confess the credit card fiasco.

'Why didn't you call me right away?' Booboo asked angrily. 'What's being done? Are the police taking this seriously, or is it still just that one goddamn detective who wants to be a TV star?'

Defensive anger rose in her like a bad lunch. 'Mike doesn't –'

'Maybe it's Lynn he's interested in,' Angela said.

'That's stupid,' Lynn said, 'and an insult!'

In the car on the way back to Salem, Angela said, 'She shouldn't have snapped at me.'

'She felt demeaned.'

'Well, she overreacted.'

'She's uptight. Try to understand. You're not the one who's got to look over your shoulder all the time.'

'*I'm* not the one who got into bed with a crazy person!'

Though he kept the lights strung on the palm all year round, Greg only turned them on on Christmas Eve.

He had done that just a short while ago. Now he sat admiring the scene.

He thought he probably should have a glass of eggnog. But he disliked eggnog, the slippery thick stuff, and besides, anything alcoholic would be inappropriate on a night when he had so important a mission.

199

There was much to be done to arrange Lynn's Christmas surprise.

It was dark now. The colored lights were vivid. Against the dark green fronds the contrast was attractive.

He so enjoyed contrasts.

Craving a Christmassy taste treat, he went in to the kitchen. The star cookies Mrs Minot had left by his door were on the counter. He put two on a plate. He measured coffee into the pot, shook in some cinnamon, and inhaled appreciatively as the fragrance filled the room.

When the coffee was done, he brought everything into the living room. He sat back contentedly in his TV chair.

A deliberate choice, that chair, given the object of his holiday preparations. The giftee, as it were.

He finished his coffee. Done once in a while, the cinnamon was a refreshing touch. He liked it late on moonlit evenings, with liqueur, and at a festive time like tonight.

And what could be more festive than this night, with the lights and the holiday mood and his plans?

He had one errand to accomplish: buy Mrs Minot's gift. He'd do that someplace where he could watch people paying with their credit cards, and savor once again the mental picture of Lynn being shamed at a cash register.

Then it would be time to begin his work.

Kara took a Fig Newton from the box, turned away, and pushed a pill into the soft filling. She stooped and fed it to Nicky.

'I don't believe I saw you do that,' Lynn said.

'He has to have his diuretic. I can wrestle it into his mouth and make us both miserable, or I can hide it. What can I get you? Coffee?'

'Nothing. I'm not staying. I just came to bring you your present.'

She'd given Kara dangly earrings in a coppery finish

that matched her hair. Kara had given her three gifts: leather gloves, a crystal pendant, and Chanel soap.

No, her sister Theresa was right, Kara thought. Guilt didn't play any part in gift giving, not at all.

Theresa also believed homosexuals shouldn't be allowed to vote.

But three nice presents or no, Kara still felt edgy around Lynn, couldn't help constantly gauging her.

And she wasn't reassured by what she saw.

'Where are you going now?' she asked Lynn.

'Home.'

'You're spending Christmas Eve alone?'

She should have lied. 'Yes,' Lynn said.

Kara watched Lynn pack her presents in a shopping bag. Her hands were trembling.

'Are you okay?'

'*Yes.* I'm sick of people asking me that.'

Kara kept backing away from asking the next question. But the signs were alarming. 'You're not – taking anything. Are you?'

Lynn nearly lashed out. But she was finding that too tempting lately, and Kara of all people could be forgiven for bringing it up, under the circumstances.

Lynn signed. 'Nothing. Nothing but aspirin or Tylenol. I'm not addicted to a thing – except maybe exercise. It seems to be all that keeps me from jumping out the window sometimes.'

Rub it in, Kara thought, and then felt more guilty than ever.

Last year, Lynn had put up a tree on the terrace, a tiny real one that smelled right. On Christmas Eve she and Kara had made mulled cider. Mary and Gideon and Booboo and Angela had decorated the tree with them, each person contributing only two ornaments, since there was so little room.

Standing out there now, Lynn remembered how they

201

had laughed at the miniaturization of the whole business. Gideon and Booboo had harmonized on carols, their voices floating off on the cold wind.

There was no tree on her terrace tonight. She'd thought of getting a fake, just so she wouldn't not have any.

But she'd decided that forcing a tree on herself would be the height of fakery.

Out in the harbor a buoy clanged sweetly, like the wind chimes at Booboo and Angela's.

She'd never been alone on Christmas Eve before.

She could have avoided being alone on this one. Probably she should have.

The radio was saying snow, but so far the night was clear.

Lynn pulled her parka tighter around her neck and leaned over to see the adjacent buildings. Lights all over, and an occasional laugh. Quiet family sounds; tonight was preparty time for most people.

She could have gone to Salem, stayed over at Booboo and Angela's, since she was going there tomorrow anyway. Kara had tried to talk her into staying this afternoon. Mary and Gideon were having dinner out, their Christmas Eve tradition; Gideon insisted on lobster. They'd coaxed her to join them.

But she just hadn't felt she could pretend tonight. And she needed to rest up for all the pretending she'd need to do tomorrow.

Her shopping had been completed as Mary urged, the gifts distributed. The family ones would go with her; they were packed and ready.

The light was shrinking, Lynn looked up and saw clouds covering the stars and moon, skipping along fast.

She opened the terrace door. If there was really going to be snow, she had to leave a good pile of seed.

She took a fresh bag from the kitchen and poked around for the jar of dry roasted peanuts she'd bought for a holiday treat for Chip and the birds and went back out. In just those few minutes the snow had started.

Already it was coming down fast. The harbor resembled a shake-up toy.

She pulled her hood up and tucked seed and nuts in the terrace corner, where they'd be safe from the wind. Then she squeezed back inside fast to keep the carpet dry, but the drips from her jacket dampened it anyway.

In Angela's family, they had always exchanged presents on Christmas Eve. She would have preferred to continue that tradition; it was a cozy, adult time to be sharing gifts. Christmas Day was a time of food smells and unkind bright light.

But the Marchette family, for what celebration they had – Lawrence and Lynn had talked of the one year there was no tree and just a small goose for dinner – opened gifts on Christmas Day. There were so few Marchette traditions, Lawrence felt, that it was important to preserve them.

So this Christmas Eve they were spending trimming the tree and wrapping presents.

'Do we have any more replacement bulbs?' Booboo asked, clipping wires to the tree.

'Here.' Angela gave him a pack. 'This is all.'

'It'll do.' He inserted the new bulbs and ducked out from between the branches, scattering needles.

'I poured brandy.' Angela passed him a glass.

'Ah.' Booboo sank into a chair and sipped it.

After a minute Angela said, 'You look unhappy.'

'Do I?'

'You do. No Christmas spirit.'

Booboo looked into his glass. He twirled it slowly. 'I was recalling last Christmas Eve. Remember? We went to Lynn's. It was fun.' He looked at the brandy some more. 'She's not having any fun now. It's the prime of her work life, and she can't enjoy it.'

He put the glass down, got a pile of unwrapped boxes, and stacked them on the table.

'I bought all this stuff for her – a pin, a cashmere muffler, a Bean's bird feeder, on and on. You saw. But what I really want my sister to have is the ability to enjoy and have peace, and I can't give her that.'

To Angela's enormous consternation, two big tears spilled down her husband's face.

He rubbed his eyes and sat back down. 'I feel helpless.'

'I know.' Angela patted his hand. 'What can I do?'

Booboo shrugged. 'That's what I keep asking myself. What can I do?'

'Well,' Angela said, 'probably all we can do right at this time is give her the best possible Christmas.'

Booboo loved his wife very much, but there were times when she left him open-mouthed, unsure what planet either of them was communicating from or to. He looked at her now and wished this wasn't one of those times. He wished that, by sharing his apprehensions, he could divest himself of this boulder of despair.

But the welcoming openness he sought wasn't to be found on Angela's face. It wore its usual expression of baseline emotion: nothing too complicated, please; tokens only.

Booboo stood up. 'Yes,' he said. 'That's what we can do.' He passed Angela a box of ornaments and opened one himself.

Bernadine closed her locker. She zipped her gym bag, put on her coat, and went upstairs. She found Elizabeth in the fitness office.

'Have a good Christmas,' Bernadine said.

'Oh, you too. Nice coat. Is it fox?'

'Thanks,' Bernadine said. 'It's fitch.'

'Present?'

'Not this year.'

204

Elizabeth smiled. 'Wonder what this year'll be?'

'I'll be happy if it's just my husband. He's due home from a trip tonight. But they're saying snow. Listen, has Lynn been in?'

'Yesterday.'

'How does she seem to you?'

'Holding her own,' Elizabeth said. 'It can't be easy. She told me about the big show she's trying to get ready for, and about this old boyfriend who keeps doing things to her.'

'I worry about her,' Bernadine said. 'She looks worse and worse.'

She went out to her car. It wasn't very cold; she was a little warm in the fur. Maybe there would be rain instead.

Backing out of the Broome Club lot, she thought of turning on the radio, but decided not to. She wouldn't be happy no matter what; if it said snow, she'd assume Dennis wouldn't get home, and if it didn't, she'd assume it wasn't a current forecast.

Bernadine got onto the highway. A few water spots appeared on her windshield.

When she exited at her turnoff, there was enough coming down so that she needed the wipers, and it was clearly snow.

The rest of the way home she kept an eye on the sky. Looking for planes, she saw two and felt optimistic.

But by the time she turned into her driveway, the flakes were fat puffs, billions of them, covering everything. The front walk was buried already.

'God*damn* it,' Bernadine said, thumping the steering wheel.

Fifteen thousand feet above Boston, Dennis Orrin unwrapped the wheat crackers left from the USAir 'dinner' and looked glumly out the window at the rapidly thickening black clouds.

He'd read that effective executives like himself always selected aisle seats on planes. But he *liked* a window seat, damn it. He enjoyed seeing the lights of his city rise up to welcome him home as his plane settled into Logan.

This time he probably should have sat, not even on the aisle, but in the goddamn middle of the 747, so he wouldn't have to look at his chances of getting home for Christmas Eve diminishing as fast as the cardboardy crackers.

They'd been circling for forty minutes.

Dennis was sufficiently versed in airline euphemisms to understand something many of his fellow passengers did not – that despite Captain Hooha's cheery talk of what number in line they were for landing, the weather was moving faster than the control tower, and they were going to close the goddamn field to arrivals while this flight and five or six others were still yanking their yinks up here.

A loss, totally: the trip had been as productive as the circling.

For two days he'd scouted newscasters in LA and San Francisco. Armies of excellent-looking, interested-sounding, eye-contact-keeping men and women of numerous sizes and colors, all of whom could have come out of Anchors R Us.

He finished the last cracker and stuffed the cellophane in his empty coffee cup.

Snow was flying. It came on suddenly, growing from uneven swirls to pelting clusters in moments. As if in response, the big plane lifted, and Dennis craned to see the city receding. A minute ago there had been moving traffic and ships in the harbor; now he could see nothing but white.

He felt trapped.

It wasn't the plane. It wasn't even the plane seat, though those seemed to get smaller every year, gripping his hips and impeding elbows.

It was the teeth-grinding impossibility of his situation.

Not even three more months, and Les would be gone, and if he, Dennis, didn't hire a replacement, there would be nothing but an empty chair on the set come six and eleven every night.

Filling in with an interim substitute like Vanessa or Irving from noon wasn't an option; ratings plunged if you didn't begin immediately to rebuild viewer loyalty to your night anchor.

He'd seen tape after tape. He'd studied candidates on their own broadcasts. He'd look at pictures and résumés and agents' grinning faces until they all blended together into one montage face with a mustache and earrings and lipstick.

Was it him?

Was he such an old fart that *he* was the one not getting it?

Would he remain unsatisfied until Chet Huntley reincarnated himself right into the anchor chair of Channel 3?

He gave a deep sigh, louder than he thought; the woman next to him frowned sidelong.

He looked out again. Solid snow now. Down below, Bernadine would be home, he hoped to Christ, and not out in this. The tree would be a blaze of color in the warm den, presents heaped underneath, including the pearl-and-diamond bracelet watch Pam had helped him pick for Bernadine. She and the girls would be working in the kitchen, and there would be edibles on the counters that smelled a hell of a lot better than the garbage in his coffee cup that was flattened inside the seat pocket.

Would he get to share any of that tonight? Or would they circle for another couple of hours until the ceiling lifted, and he'd get home after everyone was in bed?

Trapped, trapped.

He took another deep breath and let it groaningly out, and the woman on his left shifted and rubbed her forehead.

His news ratings were great, and they were going to dive, and he had to find a way to prevent that. And what about the rest of his lineup? The center of his galaxy, the Marchette show – would it come to a point where he had to replace that too?

He watched every second of every show of hers on his office monitor now. Like keeping an intercom near a sleeping baby.

She looked lousy, but she plugged along, pulling the elements together with an invisible string that ran from herself to the set to the audience. You didn't even need to have the sound up to feel it.

He hoped she was all right.

That satellite disaster ... what a hell of a lot of money and time wasted, not to mention the fancy dancing he'd had to do with all those pissed-off stations.

The very idea of the pilot taping being tampered with was unimaginably awful.

He wished there was more the police could do, he or anyone could do – besides keeping a monitor on and employing some high school dropouts in uniforms.

No wonder he was making scary noises. He was walking on sand, and the waves were breaking around his ankles and carrying off his surface as he stood on it.

And he was up in the sky while his family missed him on the ground, and they all might have to spend most of Christmas Eve that way ...

Ding, chimed the PA system.

Or worse ...

'Folks, we've been waiting here, hoping to get y'all home to Boston tonight. But, ah, we've just been informed by air traffic control that, due to unacceptable landing conditions, we are being diverted to New York ...'

'This isn't ringing any bells. Sorry.'

Mike hunched over his desk. Someone had hung ribbon

candy from the light fixtures, and the sugary smell was all over.

He put the phone to his other ear. 'How about trying your MO computer?'

'Soon as I get a chance to fill out the form,' the Los Angeles detective said. Her name was Abigail Stern, and she sounded like she had a lot better things to do on a Christmas Eve shift than help this Boston cop track an LA freak who hadn't jumped right out of her files or her head. 'You've called here before, haven't you?'

'Once or twice.'

He'd actually called several times – after each new episode of harassment, and sometimes just to pick a fresh brain. He guessed that subconsciously he was always hoping some veteran would jump up and say, 'You're describing the crotchless underwear nut! Hold on while I pull his file!'

He probed Detective Stern's limited resources with another few questions, but accomplished nothing. He hung up, tipped back in his desk chair and told himself to go home.

His shift had ended two hours ago. A couple of groups of cops, on their way out to do some Christmas Eve partying, had invited him along, but he'd declined, early evening being a good time to phone California.

But he'd been at his desk long enough. He was starting to feel cemented to the goddamn chair.

For the twentieth time he wished he could justify the time and expense of a trip out there. There was only so much you could do on the phone, even with more cooperative and facile minds to mine than Detective Stern's, of which he'd lucked into a few.

If he could be there in person, then the part of his technique that operated on its own power might give him data he couldn't reach now. He'd ask better questions and maximize what he did best, which was to look and listen and let details feed in and make a picture.

But to secure permission for such a trip, much more of a crime would have to be at the bottom of this puzzle.

And in a thousand ways he was glad it wasn't.

That thought was enough to propel him out of the chair. He got his jacket. Close to the door, he saw the wet floor, and then the snow. He pulled his hood up, cursing. Wet cold stuff hitting his face was not his idea of pleasant on Christmas Eve or any other time. But at least it was light snow. It didn't seem to be sticking.

He headed toward the T station.

He wondered what Lynn was doing tonight.

Was she alone, moping around that incredible apartment? Was she out Christmas shopping? He himself had been done before the end of November. There was a stack of carefully wrapped boxes in his coat closet for his parents and brothers and in-laws and nieces and nephews, but the most surprising people were last-minuters.

In fact, he didn't imagine she was shopping or visiting or hanging her stockings by the chimney with care.

He thought she was probably alone, feeling like crap.

There was a pay phone on the next corner, and he looked hard at it as he reached that block.

But if he called her, he'd be setting what an illiterate commander of his used to call a president. He had not yet made any gesture that was clearly social.

In recent days he had caught himself thinking about her a lot. One night he had dreamed they were making love in his bed. He woke fiercely aroused, the feel of her thigh a velvety imprint on his hand. All that day he'd kept being revisited by the erotic haze of the memory.

The phone was just another half block.

He could fill pages with reasons for passing right by it.

But, Jesus, he wanted to call.

Then he was there and the receiver was in his hand, and the dial tone demanded his response.

But his procedural brain followed the action through

for him. It showed him the twin scenarios of every prospective deed: what was hoped for, and what would probably happen.

He hoped, to be honest, that they would live the dream in some form. Then at least the barrier would be broken.

What would probably happen was that no signal would come from her, and he would do what he always did, maintain the stance of the caring, uninvolved professional. So it would be all about her, and not in the slightest about them, and he'd wish he'd hung up the phone.

But still he held the receiver – and he took off his glove, put in a quarter, and started to punch up her number. As he watched his finger on the buttons, he saw the snowflakes start to pelt down faster. In a second his sleeve was covered. He turned and saw that the sidewalk and street were suddenly white.

He made a face and hung up the phone and kept walking.

A slight miscalculation, Greg realized: he'd thought the stores would be open late on Christmas Eve. But the gift shop where he'd intended to pick up something for Mrs Minot was shut tight.

He window-shopped a few other stores. He was just about to go into Leaves 'n' Loaves for a set of English jams and biscuits he'd spotted in their display when that closed too.

Rather than draw attention to himself, he turned away as if his plans hadn't been interrupted, and strolled off.

Only a tiny error, and fixable, but this was no time for mistakes and misfortunes. Not when he had such an important job ahead of him.

He made himself slow his pace. Discipline was salutary; discipline helped him to think.

So. What was the immediate problem?

A present for Mrs M.

Not a detail to be skipped. It was wise to stay in her good graces.

He kept walking. All he needed was to find an open store where he could get a suitable gift. Then he'd hustle right home, wrap it, and present it to her, and go on to the next phase of the night.

He came to the B. Dalton where he'd followed the woman with the taste for texts and the pink earrings. It was open. He went in.

He wasn't sure what his landlady liked to read. The few times he'd been in her apartment, he'd seen only magazines.

He let his sense of her lead him through the store.

He found himself in the back, where a table was piled high with large, tasteful-looking coffee-table books. His eyes went to one with a castle on the jacket. He picked it up. A history of royal architecture.

He looked through it. A lot of space, plenty of pictures. Thick, ostentatious pages.

Perfect.

A PA system came to life with a *scree* of feedback. A voice said, 'Attention, shoppers. The time is now seven-fifty PM. B. Dalton will close in ten minutes. Please bring your purchases to the front.'

He went to the cashier and waited in line and paid, enjoying once again the memory of Lynn's horror in such a line.

He tucked the bag under his arm and walked out into the steadily falling snow.

Nearing his building, he was pleased to see the palm with its tiara of colored lights through the window. It made a delightful spectacle.

Not nearly as unique as the spectacle that was to be Lynn's gift tomorrow, but amusing enough in its way.

He went up to his apartment, noting as he passed Mrs Minot's door that she was home. Doing her dinner dishes.

Tuna something. Casserole.

He got out paper and wrapped the book. The receipt fell out of the bag as he was cleaning up, and he looked fondly at it, thinking back again to Lynn at the cashier in Crabtree & Evelyn.

He'd stood not fifty feet from the scene, watching as she loaded up with her selections. He'd wandered off for a bit, so as not to spend too much time in the same spot, then returned at the choice moment: she was gratefully unloading her armful onto the counter and pulling out her credit card.

Credit cards.

A third and a fourth.

His heart had pounded from the pure theater of it. Not as subtle as shutting off her building's electricity in a windstorm, but wondrously showy.

He savored the body language, hers and the clerk's and the line of shoppers behind her. The indefinable signal going to the other clerks of something off, their attention turning Lynn's way.

The scissors. The pieces.

And Lynn's face, the unfolding of emotions, from one to the other to the next ... climaxing in the total hopeless collapse of her power.

Greg had homed in on that, freeze-framing it for himself, to return and enjoy again and again.

He finished cleaning up and checked his watch. He'd go downstairs with the present, charmingly decline Mrs Minot's offer of tea or sherry, or whatever pseudo-aristocratic refreshment she thought de rigueur for Christmas Eve, and get to sleep.

Santa was coming to town.

213

CHAPTER TWELVE

The lobby of Lynn's building was Christmas Day empty.

Riding up to her floor, she rested her bag of presents on the elevator carpet, avoiding the muddy bits of melted snow. Her new scarf and bird book and pin were in there, plus a pack of leftover food Booboo had made her take: thick slices of roast beef, horseradish sauce, baked onions, and cheesecake.

There was a wreath on her door, the same jolly one as on her neighbors' doors. It brushed her face as she inserted her key. She couldn't wait to get rid of the thing, had made herself put it up. One minute after New Year's she was going to yank it off. That was about all the method acting she could expect of herself.

Balancing the shopping bag, she pushed her door open and went in ...

... and knew immediately that something was different.

The light was on in the foyer, the one she always left on. The rest of the apartment was dark.

She stood still, just inside the foyer, holding the doorknob. She listened hard, but heard nothing but her blood booming through her veins. She looked around, turning her head slowly, alert for any sign of what had triggered her personal alarm.

There was nothing.

Still holding the door open, she replayed the moments that had preceded this sense of disturbance.

Up in the elevator. Out at her floor. Bag in her hand, heavy, onion smell. Key in lock, door open, the usual series of little sounds ... any new ones? No.

214

What should she do now? Go back out and call the police, and ask for someone to come over and go in with her?

She stood for another minute. From the kitchen she heard the refrigerator hum. Some lights moved outside a window; the VCR display moved from 6:57 to 6:58.

Nothing out of the ordinary.

She propped the door open with the shopping bag and went to the light switches on the foyer wall where the living room began, and flicked them on.

Much more light now. Warm, reassuring, friendly light, shining on her neat apartment.

She was being a ditz.

She let out her breath, did one last scan of the living room and foyer, and went back and brought the bag inside and locked the door behind her.

She went to the kitchen and set the bag on the counter and was about to take a self-humoring walk through the other rooms before putting the food away when she realized her hands were wet.

She made a sound of annoyance. She must not have been as careful in the muddy elevator as she thought.

She took a dish towel and started to wipe the bag and countertop.

The first thing she noticed was that the wet stuff was clear, not muddy. The second thing was the feel of it: thick. Not watery. Slimy.

She froze.

Now a sound came from the bedroom, a scraping, clicking sound. Fear shot up her legs and closed her throat.

She dropped the towel and ran back to the front door, yanking at the bolt, her wet fingers slipping. Now she could see the big wet spots on the rug, shining in the light.

She heard another sound above her own gasping breaths, and had to turn and look, and the sight froze her for another agonizing moment.

An enormous raccoon, stumbling out of her bedroom, its head wobbling. Saliva trailing in bubbly strings.

Sobbing with her terror, Lynn gripped the bolt with both hands, shoved it back, leaped out, and slammed the door behind her.

Two uniformed policemen were following animal control officers up to the apartment when Mike rushed into the lobby.

'Where the fuck are the paramedics? Weren't you examined yet?'

'No,' Lynn said. 'Will I –'

'What's that on your face? Did the saliva –'

'It's me. Mine. I was crying. *Don't!*' she yelled as he reached for her hands. 'Don't touch me! It's on there!'

'*Quiet.*' He gripped her hands in one of his and shone his flashlight on them.

'You're crazy,' she said. Her voice was uneven, threatening to blink out, like a flickering lamp in a storm. 'It's on you now.' She was sobbing again.

A few people were in the lobby, drawn by the hoopla.

'Everything is okay,' another policeman told them loudly, coming in with a man in overalls who carried a head cover and a pole with a snare on the end. 'Something flew into an apartment, and we're removing it.'

'Something like what?' a woman in tight jeans and bunny slippers asked, but no one answered.

'I can't see well enough,' Mike growled. He looked quickly around. Still holding Lynn's hands, he pulled her into the dark mail alcove and flicked on the light switches. In the new brightness, he bent to her hands, his nose nearly touching a palm. Slowly he shone the flash over every bit of skin. He peered at the cuticles and under the nails.

'Thank God,' he said finally. He looked up at Lynn, meeting her eyes. His were raw-looking. 'There's nothing.'

'But I know the saliva is on me. It got all over my hands –'

'Just your hands. Nowhere else. And you weren't bitten. Right?' Mike demanded.

'No, but what's the difference? I don't need any test to tell me that animal is infected. All you need is the saliva. I have rabies now. You do too.' Tears dripped from her chin. She looked down, and saw one fall on his hand, still gripping her two.

'No, we do not. Not if there are no cuts or sores. The virus doesn't penetrate unbroken human skin.'

'It doesn't?'

'No. You'll be checked out, but I think you're okay. What exactly happened? I only got a brief message.'

While she told him, he tried very hard to listen but he couldn't. He was too aware of her small, dirty, hot hands in his big sweaty one. He absolutely could not let go.

He was catching enough of what she said to put the fiendish picture together, but the horror of what he heard was nearly swamped by the horror of his inertia.

Any second someone, another cop, would wander into the alcove and see this. It would be insane to be found standing here the way he was, clutching her hands, inhaling her scent like a bum at a bakery door.

He had to let go.

He couldn't.

He wanted to clean her up himself, soap and dry the hands.

Put his arms around her and hold her very close. Snake his fingers in her hair.

Kiss the still trembling mouth.

Light a big match to the monster who kept slamming at her, drilling her, reducing her.

'It is a fragile virus,' the emergency room doctor said. She

217

was Korean, and Lynn had trouble following all the words; *fragile* came out *fraja*.

The doctor took off her gloves and dropped them in a waste can. 'Virus is neutralized as soon as saliva dries. You are lucky; no open wounds. Twenty-four hours, you are safe to be back home. You have other place to stay for tonight?'

'Yes,' Lynn said. She had called Kara, who had just come home, and was on the way to the hospital with clean clothes.

The doctor bent to her clipboard and began writing additions to what the intake clerk had already noted. She paused, paged back, and scanned the information.

'Does not state when this happened,' the doctor said.

Lynn started to answer, and then didn't. The missing part was too enormous.

In order to select a *when*, you had to identify the *this*. The vital event in question.

And just which vital event should she focus on? There were so many, they simply kept happening, they made their own gravy, and Lynn was too tired, too wired and too tired, to pluck one from the heap.

But she had to, the doctor was waiting.

She leaned back against the stretcher they'd sat her on, and stared up at the round light in the ceiling.

Was *this* the slime on her hands that she'd thought would kill her?

Or was *this* simply Greg himself?

Maybe *this* was all the ways Greg was torturing her. Because of course it was torture, you wouldn't call it anything else. Lynn shivered, her logical mind leaping to the obvious, what you had to see if you faced the concept: where does torture ever lead but to more torture and death? But she couldn't stop there, she'd be run over if she did, so she kept going.

This might be her trip to Los Angeles, her meeting Greg.

218

Or his visit to Boston. Her red-hot welcome. Maybe *this* was their sleeping together.

She shivered again.

Maybe *this* had nothing directly to do with Greg.

It could be her syndication.

Or more basic, her show itself.

Her eyes hurt from staring at the light. She rubbed them, but didn't drop her hands.

What about her hands, what *this* about her hands? Not the gunk on them, she'd enumerated that, and they were clean now anyway.

But they weren't when Mike grabbed them.

And that had agonized her.

She sat up straight and brought her hands down and looked away from the light, and now it was the hands she stared at.

His face came back to her, the look as he'd rushed to make sure she had no cuts. Not the stoic detective. Not the careful public servant.

And what about herself? Her desolation when he ignored her effort to protect him. Her anguish, thinking he'd be infected.

But she couldn't stop there either, or she'd be run over from the other direction.

The doctor's expectant look was changing, she was concerned. Lynn watched her level features move, then the mouth, as it asked something, probably whether she was all right.

But she wasn't, unless it was all right to watch someone talk and be able to hear nothing but the word *this* repeated louder and faster, and then faster and softer as you stopped hearing anything at all.

'I made tea,' Kara said. 'Or would you prefer wine? If it was me, I'd be stuffing in cookies. Lie back, will you?'

Lynn obeyed, then started to feel dizzy and sat up. At

219

the hospital they had insisted on giving her a tranquilizer when she was brought in, and she still had the artificial pillowy sensation, a feather barrier holding back the reality.

The phone rang. Kara went to answer.

'Mike Delano,' Kara said, bringing Lynn the cordless.

'I heard you passed out in the ER,' Mike said.

'Yes. But they said I was okay to leave. Mike, what *happened*? It was Greg, it had to be, wasn't it? How did he get in? Where did the raccoon come from? My apartment —'

'The apartment is a mess. But there's no danger once the saliva dries. He got in,' Mike went on, his tone heavier, 'by breaking your lock. Obviously you failed to notice when you opened the door.'

'I didn't see. I thought something was strange —'

'When?'

'After I opened the door.'

'And you went *in*? What the hell is the matter with you?'

'I wasn't sure! I'm so paranoid all the time now, if I paid attention to every suspicion, I'd have to sit in a playpen and never come out!'

'Being jumpy is one thing. Instinct is another. You have to learn to differentiate. Your survival depends —'

'It seems to me that what my survival depends on is getting more action from the police! *Now* can't you go after him officially? This is a criminal act —'

'I can try for a warrant for breaking and entering. But I might not get it. Nothing was taken. There's no proof of who broke in.'

'He set up an ambush for me. A rabid animal —'

'That's not a crime.'

'It's a *deadly weapon*!'

'Yeah? You find the statute that says so!'

'I'm not the one who should be researching statutes!' Lynn yelled.

But he had hung up.

* * *

220

Greg sipped cinnamon coffee and decided he would keep the tree lights on until tomorrow.

What a Christmas.

He'd been up since four-thirty and he was tired, but it was the relaxed weariness that follows a productive effort.

By now the police would have collected the details of what he'd done – the empty cage of the Kemp Park wildlife lab, the missing gloves and all, the broken locks at the lab and on Lynn's door.

Purposefully, clumsily broken; he wanted them to assume he hadn't been able to get in with a key since she'd changed the first lock, the one she'd given him the key to.

He still had that key. It was in the crawl space behind the dresser in the bedroom, along with his mischief toys, postmarking gear, infinity bugs, photographic stuff, key copying equipment, and his current copies. But that one he kept in a lacquered box that contained only the keys lovingly volunteered to him over the years.

A hundred eighty-seven now.

He took a Tums roll from his pocket and popped one.

Lynn was uninfected. He'd found out from the police, an exercise that had served another purpose besides producing that information: he'd proved he could be police to police.

That would come in most handy.

He finished his coffee, washed the cup, and put on music. A hot beat, not Mrs Minot's taste, but she had gone to bed an hour ago. He was familiar enough by now with her nightly routine to hear and smell it. He no longer had to let himself into her apartment and listen for snores.

He boogied across the carpet to the window and leaned on the sill to watch the Christmas night traffic on Morrissey Boulevard.

* * *

He kept his senses oiled because they fed him data, but the joy of gaming with them had been outgrown long ago.

He still loved to make changes. Still had to have that souvenir – the pierced ears or nose, or tattoo, that she, or he, had to look at every day for the rest of their lives, and remember who had changed them.

But the changes themselves had evolved since his Aguanga days. His old tricks with roots and seeds were childish by comparison. Drop-and-run techniques; only by hiding or peeking could he be around for the rest of the process.

What satisfaction to progress to where his persona, not his anonymous actions, was the instrument of change.

To where his direct participation wasn't just added to the process.

It *was* the process.

There weren't many cars out. Morrissey Boulevard was relatively quiet. Two blocks south, where the residential part blended into the start of the commercial portion of the street, there was a 7-Eleven open, and nothing else that Greg could see from the window. Even the print shop that ran all shifts was dark.

He'd had a print shop girl once, a typesetter, in Cincinnati. Very thin, ashy brown hair pulled tight in a bun on top of her head. When he'd gotten her clothes off, which had taken, if memory served, an unusually lengthy five days, she'd been actually bony.

Pierced ears, that souvenir had been.

She'd switched apartments at least twice before he was done with her.

He didn't care for thin ones, they were less vulnerable to his more subtle tactics. But still there were a few after the print girl who were fun, and changed as nicely. The third-grade teacher he'd called Miss Chips; she tattooed her shoulder for him. Later he'd trotted her around to the

222

grossest strip clubs Vegas had to offer, and convinced her it would turn him on big-time if she did an act like that privately, for him.

She never saw the video camera inside the lamp. She did see an assembly of freaked-out school kids when he substituted the tape for one on bird migration.

The dance music was over, and a slow song was playing. He was quite sleepy now, yawning; it really was time to get to bed.

He turned off the radio and undressed and went contentedly to sleep.

Mike Delano sat hunched over his desk, brooding into an empty cup.

He had paperwork stacked eye-high, and was trying to bite through it a piece at a time.

Chewing gum for the mind; you could think while you knocked the shit off – which he had to do by tomorrow, the last day of 1992.

The only problem was, they expected you to write stuff on the papers that made sense.

He came to the report about the raccoon they'd taken out of Marchette's apartment. It had tested rabid, of course. The lab knew it would. He thought of calling Lynn to tell her that, but their last couple of conversations had been official, brief, and formal after the Christmas night fight.

Two weeks ago he'd watched his sister Claire scream at her son after the kid ran out in front of a car. Not smart of Claire, but human, terror released at the wrong target: *Now that I know he's not dead, I want to kill him.*

It was exactly what he'd done to Lynn.

His phone rang.

'Delano.'

'Happy New Year,' a woman said.

'Who's this?' he growled.

223

'Detective Abigail Stern. LAPD. You might want to give me your fax number.'

He sat up. 'For what?'

'A motor vehicles head shot of Gerard John Sellinger. Male, Cauc, black/brown, six-one, one ninety, DOB eleven/eight/'fifty-three. Plus a complaint filed seven/two/'eighty-eight by one Barbara Alice Hysmith. Harassment following dating relationship, possible illegal entry, da-da-da, no proven felony. Harassing phone calls, da-da-da, on and on, and then we come to the *last* paragraph, where we learn that Barbara Alice received several sets of unwanted pornographic-type lingerie from the gentleman, *and* had her thigh tattooed at his request.'

'Really,' Mike said, his heart pounding. 'Really.'

'That's not all. The MO computer came up with this after I had the analyst feed it details in five or six different configurations and the picture was included because it had been located for ID at the time of the complaint. But the complaint wasn't filed against Gerard Sellinger. The name the complainant knew him by was Greg Walter.'

'Holy shit.'

'And you thought I was an airhead.'

Driving to Channel 3, Mike was so conscious of the fax on the seat beside him that it might as well have glowed like the crucifix in his grandmother's dining room.

He'd gone running to the fax machine to see the picture as it came out, and had stood glaring ferociously at each feature as it appeared: hairline, eyebrows, nose, on down to lips and chin … then back up to lips.

Narrow upper, very wide lower, the whole mouth broad, movie-star-ish.

He stared at it for a long time.

It pained him more than he would have thought possible to reflect on where that mouth had been.

Howard Landrau had wandered over to see what was absorbing him.

'Alec Baldwin?' Howard said.

'In your ass.'

'So who is it?'

'A freak by the name of Gerard Sellinger. Known to us as Greg Alter. The jerkoff who's after Lynn Marchette.'

'She ID'd him?'

'She's about to.'

Landrau paused, then said carefully, 'You're putting a lot into this case.'

Mike shrugged. 'Big TV show. Pressure from the front office.'

Now, alone behind the wheel, threading his way through the late afternoon Morrissey Boulevard traffic, he gave himself the same challenge.

He hadn't needed to defend the fact that he was personally taking the picture to Lynn. It was procedure to observe the victim's reaction and speed of identification.

But that was the only thing he could let go by. For the rest, he might not owe Landrau any answers, but he owed himself some.

He *was* putting considerable time into Lynn's case. And energy: he thought about it at work, and not at work, in the shower, at the supermarket.

In fact, he was doing just what he kept insisting to Lynn he couldn't do – chasing a noncriminal who was committing noncrimes.

Even this picture, this trophy. Now that he had it, what was he going to do with it? He'd gone barking down the street chasing a car and had caught it. But what use could he make of it? The DA had gone for the threat-to-safety argument after the rabies scare and had agreed to a warrant for stalking, but a crummy little felony didn't let him go out to LA and try to make an arrest. Even if the asshole presented himself at his door and said, Hello

225

there, I'm Gerard Sellinger, a.k.a. Greg Alter, arrest me ...
he still had to docilely show up and stand trial.

Sure.

Mike braked for a light, watched his fingers drumming
the wheel. There was a 7-Eleven on the corner; maybe he
should stop a minute, get a soda, level out before
continuing the half mile to Channel 3.

The light changed, and his mind did too. He accelerated
and proceeded along with the traffic.

He knew what he was going to do. He was going to
scatter that picture around like snow, to airports, hotels,
taxi and car rental companies, and every avenue of travel
the guy could be using for his trips between Boston and
LA. He was going to lean on LA some more to comb their
turf. And one way or another he was going to locate
Sellinger/Alter/Shitbrain – and go to LA.

There was nothing in that he needed to justify to himself
or anyone else. He'd take the time off and pay for the trip.
He'd continue to work his full schedule of other cases.

And he was finally going to take the responsibility for
why he was doing all this.

'I hate lower abs,' Lynn said.

Elizabeth laid a towel on the padded exercise bench.
'Everyone hates them. But we have to do them. The lower
ab muscles make a hammock for the rest of your trunk
muscles.'

'Nature's girdle,' Bernadine said from the next bench,
where she was barely puffing after 150 crunches.

Elizabeth laughed, but Lynn didn't. She didn't remember the last time her face had formed a positive expression
without her consciously producing it.

The strain of not knowing when or how Greg would
depth-charge her again – plus the pressure of having to
appear the ever-bright personality – produced explosive
headaches and vibrating tension.

226

On the wall nearby right now, Oprah spoke from the fitness room TV. Oprah had her pressures; but Oprah wasn't living in someone else's sickness.

'– forty-eight, -nine, fifty,' Elizabeth finished. 'You can rest now. Good sweat there. You're working, Lynn. How's the headache?'

'A little better.'

'Really? Or are you humoring the trainer?'

'It's really better. But it'll be worse in half an hour. I'm going back to work.'

Elizabeth sat down on the bench Bernadine had vacated. 'I don't like to mess in my clients' medical business. But maybe you should ask your doctor about your headaches.'

'I've had them all my life. They come from dental problems, and from tension. Right now my tension level is in the stratosphere.'

'From that big taping coming up?'

'Partly ...'

'I'm trying to imagine what that's like,' Elizabeth said. 'I understand the responsibility of having to appear in charge and *up* all the time. I have to in my job. But in front of hundreds of thousands of people? I'd be a wreck.'

Lynn wiped her face with her towel. Remains of the on-camera makeup dotted it.

'That's not it,' Lynn said. 'I asked for that responsibility. It's a privilege. I'd never be so arrogant as to complain about it.'

Lynn tried not to unload on people about Greg. Nobody wanted to hear it, no matter what they said. It was demented, and it tainted her, and they were afraid it would taint them.

How many times had she heard guests complain on her show about people edging away from their need for support – and had to beat back her own involuntary impulse to retreat?

227

But sometimes she felt as if the feelings would blow her open if she didn't let them out.

'I told you,' Lynn said, 'about the man who wouldn't leave me alone –'

'Is that still going on?'

'It's worse. He broke into my apartment and put a rabid raccoon in there –'

'Good God, Lynn!'

Telling the story, she watched Elizabeth's face for the wariness, the urge to be away from the bile, but saw only horrified sympathy.

Elizabeth clasped Lynn's hands. 'No one should have to live with such a thing. No wonder you're in pain. I'm so sorry.'

Taking strength from her grip, Lynn swallowed a push of emotion. 'Thank you.'

In the steam room, Bernadine shoved a dangling strand of hair back into her cap and stretched her legs out on the plank benching.

Angela Marchette came in. They said hello.

Bernadine wondered how much Angela knew of Lynn's situation. Lynn and her brother were close, but Bernadine detected some distance between Lynn and Angela.

She was worried about Lynn, though, and couldn't freely share her concern with Dennis; the subject of Lynn's problem seemed to drive him crazy.

Before Bernadine could find a way to feel her out on the topic, Angela said, 'How well do you know this Elizabeth?'

Bernadine turned, startled. 'She trains me. She's very good.'

'I mean personally. Is she married?'

'No.'

'She goes to the station to train Lynn. Did you know that?'

228

'Yes,' Bernadine said. 'She trains me there too.'

Angela shook her head.

Bernadine waited, but Angela didn't go on. Finally she asked, 'What's wrong with that?'

'Well,' Angela said, 'I just think you want to keep in mind that she seems to like other women's husbands.'

The day-people were gone when Lynn got back to the Channel 3 building. The reception area outside her office was half dark. It took her a moment, when she stepped off the elevator, to realize Mike Delano was sitting in a chair there.

He stood when she approached. 'They said you were at the gym and you'd be back. I decided to wait.'

'What's up?' Lynn asked coolly.

He held up the folder. 'Something to show you. Let's go in your office.'

She led him in, turned on the lights. The exhaustion that passed for relaxation had vanished suddenly; her headache was throbbing back in. It was difficult to look at him. She was very conscious of the still unprocessed moment of awareness she'd had Christmas night, after he'd examined her hands; and she was still angry at him for attacking her at such a vulnerable time.

She supposed those emotions magnified each other, but didn't care to analyze that, any more than she was willing to probe her confusing hangover of feelings for him.

Watching her, Mike waited for her to stop moving and give him her attention. When she did, he opened the folder and held out the picture.

'Oh!' she shouted, grabbing it. She gaped, then held it away from herself in a reflexive gesture of revulsion.

Mike squinted. Bingo.

'Before you get too worked up,' he said, 'this isn't as significant as it looks.'

'Why not? Now we have all kinds of information we didn't before. His *address* –'

'A dead end. There've been two other tenants since he lived there. And as I've told you, we can't go around the country arresting people and bringing them to another coast on cases like this, so –'

'But if you find out his real address, and you start to see his movements, it'll help you get him when he's *here*. You can catch him in action, and maybe charge him with something worse than stalking. And if he sees you moving in, that inhibits him. Right? What about this Barbara Alice Hysmith? Did you call her? Can *I* call her?'

'I haven't found her yet.'

Lynn went to the window. She still held the picture. Mike watched her looking out at the lighted buildings, the zooming commuters.

Her hair was a wild tangle that two ivory combs barely held off her face. The ends were still wet from her shower. A soft-looking light blue sweater pulled a little across her back; either it had shrunk, or her workouts were building her lats.

She was tight with tension beneath it.

His hands wanted to ease that. To give them something to do, he clutched the folder tight, creasing it.

'We're going to spread the picture around,' Mike said. 'Copies will be given to Kemp Park, the security men here at the station, your building –'

Lynn turned. 'Not my building. My neighbors are jumpy as it is. I don't want the *Herald* to get interested again. It's already taken a lot of effort to convince them there's no story.'

He stepped closer to her. 'Are you sure you don't? Rethink it. I know you're avoiding public attention to the case, but that's one goddamn good way to get a bigger commitment from us. If the papers are full of the TV star in danger, what do you bet my captain won't be quite so quick to blow this off?'

'I've considered that. But no. QTV would be out of my life so fast, they wouldn't leave a breeze. They want a vibrant, healthy, together host. Not some victim.' She laughed without smiling. 'Are you leaving me to wince at the irony of that all by myself?'

Instead of answering, he switched topics. 'Did you decide whether you want to move back to your apartment?'

He saw her take a slow breath and let it out. 'I've considered that too. Kara says I can keep living there as long as I need to, but this is long enough. I want that Stanley Door you told me about. Then I'll go back.'

Three different security guards checked his ID on his way out, and they made him sign out anyway.

That heartened him.

It drove him crazy how unprotected she was. He didn't love that she had chosen to go back to her place. But he'd known she would. Her bravery was his favorite quality of hers.

He'd have to be brave too.

Greg slipped easily out of Kara's building, his prize safe in his jacket pocket.

That dog was annoying, but not dangerous. He'd known it wouldn't bite him, but he could have done without the noise.

In any case, he had what he'd gone in for, and he hadn't needed to do anything to the dog.

Most of his affairs had been pet-free. He remembered a couple of birds, including one that talked, and several cats. Women in the Midwest tended not to have any animals; Californians accounted for ten or twelve of the dogs he recalled. One of his male lovers had had a dog, a yappy little fluffball.

Had he put an end to the yapping? He couldn't quite fine-tune that memory. But he remembered the human quite clearly: Buddy, a big guy who loved to be called Big Guy. Buddy had tumbled for him like a hill of sand, pierced both ears, colored his pubic hair. Much easier to convince than a lot of the women. Did better later too; he'd howled and squealed when Greg put the pressure on, flitted from one rental to another until Greg got bored with Buddy and Wisconsin and took the chance to work on a downlink system in Minneapolis.

The moving around was one of the advantages of both his profession and his avocation. Aside from the sheer fun of it, Greg loved the extra tang it added to his affairs, affording him the ability to keep people off balance about where he really lived – since he didn't live anywhere for long, and could use legitimate travel to, say, snatch real FedEx air bills – and to make a fast change when the situation dictated. Plus, the pickings were ever fresh.

Not that he had quite intended for the Lynn episode to be so far-flung. How was he to know, when he'd begun following her around Boston, that he'd have occasion to follow her all the way to LA? And to Geoffrey's, of all places?

But the California trip had ended up providing an unexpected advantage. More than one great laugh had come out of the fiction he'd so easily perpetrated on them all, the phantom fact of his West Coast location. What brilliance to grab that opportunity and make the meeting happen there.

He passed a knot of people waiting for a WALK sign, cheerily wishing one another Happy New Year. He smiled at them, and they smiled back.

Everyone was happy on New Year's Eve.

A time of change, a new year, a clean strip to plant.

Back in his brush-slave days, they'd thought he was loony for saying such things. His family had treated the start of the year as a nonevent, a night on which to try to sleep through the noise from whatever big house before awakening to more of how it always was.

Well. He'd proven the idiocy of that – on many New

Year's Eves, and at countless other times.

He continued to prove it with every delicious affair, every delicious trick.

Kara watched Lynn tie her apron. 'You're so thin.'

Lynn took a bowl of shrimp from Kara's refrigerator. 'I know,' she said unhappily.

Nicky jumped around at their feet.

'Don't moan about it. I'd love to weigh what you do. Nicky, chill out. He's so nudgy tonight.'

Lynn put down the shrimp. 'No. No, you wouldn't. The hell I'm trapped in ... it isn't worth being thin or anything else.'

'I didn't mean that. I was only saying you look good. That Mike Delano can't take his eyes off you.'

Lynn's cheeks heated, but she said, 'That's just how he operates. He watches everyone.'

'If he watched everyone the way he watches you, he'd get hit. Anyway, self-disgust is part of being a victim, remember?'

They worked in silence for a while, making scampi for dinner.

'We used to cook together a lot,' Lynn said.

Kara nodded.

Lynn reached for the garlic. 'How come we got out of that?'

'Too busy. And too much crap. Mostly mine.'

'You don't have to –'

'I don't mean only about Greg. I still feel guilty for doubting you. I meant – well, it sounds awful, with what you're going through, but ... I'm jealous. You and Bernadine and everyone have this exclusive thin society of exercise fanatics; I'm the invisible fat person. You all talk as if I'm not there –'

'I'm sorry. I didn't –'

'I plug away on the phone, you're successful and

233

powerful and killing on live TV. I feel – I feel like you're the movie and I'm just sitting in the audience.'

Tears rolled. Shocked, Lynn dropped her cutting board and put her arms around Kara. 'Don't cry. You never cry.'

'I know.'

'You always say you don't want to be on the air.'

'I don't. I just want to be as outstanding at what I'm doing as you are at what you're doing.'

'But you are. You're the whole reason the programs have the integrity they do. I can only run with what you give me. Everyone knows that. If it wasn't for you, we wouldn't have our pilot.' Lynn made a face. 'If we do.'

'We do.'

Lynn rubbed her eyes. She used to wake up in the morning impatient to get to work, all her senses focused on the thrilling challenge of what was going to happen in the studio. Unpredictable elements, when they arose, made her better. In her extraordinary connection with the audience, they knew, and grew tense with her, and were beside themselves applauding afterward.

Now those same surprises, in her work and her personal life, were being used to weaken her.

The qualities she relied on for the shows, the acrobatic bundle of skills she had honed, were wobbly, less dependable.

Was she selfish to insist on doing the pilot regardless? Did she have what she needed, what she owed everyone concerned?

'I'm not sure. I've started to wonder if we should postpone –'

'Lynn, listen. You have to make this pilot. If you don't, you're giving in. We'll take whatever measures are necessary to make it tamper-proof. We'll change studios, hire ten times more security, keep all the communications secret. But don't let Greg take your pilot away.'

* * *

234

Later, stepping from the shower, Lynn looked at the bathroom clock. Twelve forty-five. The horns had stopped blowing in the street.

She took off her shower cap and let her hair tumble down around her shoulders.

'*That Mike Delano can't take his eyes off you.*'

What was Mike doing tonight?

Her imagination immediately produced a party. Racy and raunchy, men and women cops. Plenty of alcohol and hot, throbbing music.

Or maybe not. Maybe he was having an intimate night with one woman.

'Want some frozen yogurt?' Kara called, and Lynn gratefully gave up the fantasy and grabbed her night-gown.

'One in *three*,' Mike repeated, holding up fingers.

'One in three what?' another cop asked, joining Mike's group.

'One in three women treated at emergency rooms nationwide is there because of domestic violence.'

'You're kidding. Is this a new figure?'

'What I want to know,' someone else said, 'is whether this was always so bad. Is domestic violence worse? Or are we recognizing it and quantifying it more now?'

'Lasagna's ready,' Grace Landrau yelled from the dining alcove.

The others moved that way, and Mike followed, taking a plate and filling it. But he'd been nibbling chips the whole evening, and he wasn't very hungry. He ate some of the so-so lasagna and pushed the rest around.

The party broke up not long after the food.

The T was full of the expected looped college kids. He supposed he should be glad they were on the thing and not driving. But he hadn't felt festive this whole holiday season, and his patience with other people's joy was limited.

Walking home, he hesitated outside Nancy Jean's, then went in. It was jumping, and he almost walked out. But Nancy Jean spotted him and reached up short arms for a hug. Then, taking quick notice of his expression, she led him to an empty table in as shadowy a nook as existed in the train-depot lighting, away from the dance area.

He'd thought the revelry might infect him, but it didn't. He didn't feel sad, but rather restive and in abeyance, as if he were shifting around in bed and couldn't get comfortable.

'Saw your friend on the TV,' Nancy Jean said. She set down a beer and a plastic dish of pretzels. 'She had nutrition people talking about fat. All the things that have it. So now I put these out instead of peanuts. Tell her.'

'Okay,' Mike said.

'Even better, bring her back here and I'll tell her myself.'

Watching her inch her way through the crowd, Mike was aware that his discomfort index had just jumped way up.

He ate pretzels, first one at a time, idly, then stuffing them in.

He had not yet kept his promise to himself.

He'd only had a couple of sips of beer, but the pretzel dish was empty. He got up to go fill it, but understood halfway out of his chair that this was merely another delaying ploy.

He sat back down.

He had promised he would take the responsibility for why he was dedicating himself so earnestly to Lynn's case.

To keep playing games with himself about this was dumb. It wasn't going to go away because he ignored it. At least, if he let it out into the air, he could get on to the next part of the process of dealing with it, however miserable that might be.

So. Why was he doing this?
Because he was in love with her.
He covered his head with his arms and groaned.

CHAPTER THIRTEEN

'Do you want me to go in with you?' Mike asked.

Lynn looked at the new keys in her hand, then up at him. 'Would you?'

He held her office door open for her.

She drove home, Mike following. He showed her how to operate her new door, the seven bars on the inside, the standard-looking outside locks that each required a different key and series of turns.

'Give yourself an extra five minutes when you leave for work or anywhere,' Mike said, 'because you have to secure them from outside.'

When it was open, she stood uncertainly, and then walked in.

'It smells medicinal,' she said.

'The disinfectant. You'll have your scent back on it soon enough. Did you know that about cats?'

'What?' She looked around the foyer, walked to the living room.

Mike rolled his eyes at himself. He was babbling like a dork with a necklace in a singles bar. He kept quiet, hoping she'd let it drop, but she turned to him. 'Did I know what about cats?'

'They have to scent foreign objects in order to feel comfortable in their environment. If you bring a paper bag into your place and leave it around, and the cat paws it all up, that's to scent it.'

'You'd never leave a paper bag around,' she said, surprising him.

She prowled the living room, peered at the rug. Walked

through the kitchen. Mike followed a ways behind, letting her get the new feel of her place.

She went into the bedroom. He wanted to hang back, and he wanted to see it. He settled for a compromise, standing at the door and looking around as if he couldn't give less of a shit.

Where the rest of the apartment was airy and stylish, the bedroom seemed to be her nook. Family pictures, an ironing board that looked like she didn't usually bother to collapse it. Soft-looking big bed.

Once his glance hit that, it locked on.

The bed was tightly made, but his imagination immediately mussed it, put her in there with Whatshisass, on the flowered sheets. Again, as when the freak's photo had come through the fax, his whole body vibrated with the desire to smash.

He watched Lynn wander around the room. She opened her closet, and he thought he saw a sleeve of the dress Greg had taunted her about, with the sharp stuff.

She came out, passing him, and he took a fast step back as her perfume reached him.

He realized that, even with the medicinal smell, her scent hung in the bedroom, came wafting out after her, as if she'd reactivated it by being in there.

His chest hurt.

She went to the kitchen again, poked around in there. Her answering machine sat under the phone. She pushed the Play button.

'Hi, there,' a male voice said.

Mike looked questioningly at Lynn, and she said, 'My brother.'

The message continued, 'Just wanted to welcome you home. Hope you're okay.' He sounded worried.

Then, 'Ms Marchette, this is Dr Gurian's office. Your crown is ready. Please call for an appointment.'

Then a squeaky child's voice: 'Don't, please don't hurt

me! No, no, noooooo! Oh, that hurts!'

Mike saw Lynn's face go from confusion to alarm, and then to horror as the voice continued: 'Please, I'm only a little chipmunk, don't kill me!' Then a choking sound.

'No. No,' Lynn said, and ran to the terrace door and yanked it open. Mike ran after her, felt her scream ripple right through him.

Out on the terrace, surrounded by sprinkles of seed, was Chip, his neck broken, with one of the Liz Taylor napkin rings around him.

She cried in Mike's arms. His sweatshirt was soaked. He was overwhelmed by the tickle of her hair on his chin, the feel of her under his hands, bones and muscle and wrenching sobs that came from somewhere he couldn't reach.

Eventually, when she quieted enough so he could sit her down, he got a bag from the kitchen and went back out to the terrace and put the poor little thing in it.

He knew how she loved it, she'd talked of it a couple of times, how she fed the birds and this one brave chipmunk.

So now there was yet another dimension to this psycho. Because it was clear from the signs that he'd somehow scaled the terraces from outside.

Was the fuck a mountain climber?

Whatever he was, one thing was clear: he'd crossed the country twice in the last week, and this second time his picture was all over the airports and car rental agencies.

'You should move,' Mike said.

'I'm not moving. He'll have to blow up the building to get me out.'

She rubbed her neck. A headache was climbing up the back of her skull, drilling, showing no mercy.

Tonight she'd have to take something.

Her heart hurt for Chip, and the sickening knowledge

that she'd been invaded from yet another direction filled her.

'That *is* the man's voice on the tape?'

'I guess. Who else would it be?' she asked.

'I just want you to ID it if you can. So we'll know.'

'We know.'

'Yeah.'

They were quiet for several minutes. Finally Lynn said, 'Thank God you were here tonight.'

Mike looked at her. Dried tears crusted her face, and her eyes showed desperation, desolation, the haunted look he saw on older kids, the ones who were aware enough to start realizing things were never going to get any better for them.

He wanted to take her in his arms again.

He had to get the hell out of here.

'I have to go,' he said.

She turned to him. She didn't say anything.

He pointed to the terrace door. 'I don't like you being vulnerable to that. Why don't you go back to Kara's for tonight?'

'*No*. I want to stay in my home. I won't just lie back and let him take it away from me bit by bit.'

He shook his head.

She said, 'What did you do with the body?'

'Left it out there, in a bag. I'm taking it with me.'

She started to cry again. 'I can't believe I won't be seeing him anymore. Feeding him.'

She bent her head into her hands. Her shoulders trembled.

He remembered their angles.

He really had to get out of here.

But then he stopped thinking and went to her and pulled her up from the couch and held her, and this time it was different.

This time she wasn't just leaning on him but was with him, hugging him back, holding tight.

She moved in closer to him. Their bodies met full-length.

He held his breath, not daring to feel her, to allow in the realization of how close they were.

But she pulled him nearer. Buried her face in his shoulder. And then drew back to look at him, and he saw her grieving eyes and her open mouth and the dried misery on her skin.

Without conscious thought he held her head and kissed her.

He hadn't know he'd been imagining the taste of her mouth until he did taste it.

He felt as if he were in a film he was directing himself, jumping back and forth from participant to viewer.

His back burned where her hands were.

His own fingers held bunches of her hair, squeezing it, as if by taming that he could tame the situation.

But it was ridiculous, he was lost here, and getting more lost every second.

Mike's back moved under Lynn's hands. She had the impulse to go under his sweatshirt and feel the warm skin, but she didn't obey it.

In a way, she felt as if they belonged there together, bodies fused along their length. And in another way, she was in a bad dream.

His tongue was in her mouth, his hands in her hair. She could feel his pulse pounding in his chest. His face was rough with growth. She touched his neck. The hair there was surprisingly soft. She found herself pulling him into a deeper kiss, and willing that to block out her pain.

She was crying again, kissing him and crying.

Mike heard her whimper, felt the vibration in his mouth. He could have answered with noise of his own, but he held it back. He had to hold back whatever he could. With

242

every second, every touch, he was sliding further down the chute.

She whimpered again, and he felt tears on his face that became part of this endless kiss. He stopped, and wiped her face with his thumbs.

She reached for him again. Her thighs were pressing his through her wool skirt. She moved a little against his groin.

He was going out of his mind.

He gripped her buttocks with one hand and pressed, and now he couldn't keep the noise back. If he'd been at all alert, he'd have picked up her slight retreat, but he was past noticing anything short of a bomb blast.

And so he continued to press her in closer, kiss her harder, until, with a gasping cry, Lynn wrenched away.

She stood looking past him, breathing raggedly. His own breaths were heavy and furnace-hot and came from deep in his chest.

'What's the matter?' he asked finally, needing to hear it.

She shook her head. 'I feel crazy.'

Mike wiped his mouth. 'You were with me. Then what happened?'

'I suddenly felt ... like you do in a nightmare. When you're stuck in some trap and you struggle and can't get free.' More tears came, and she angrily wiped them away.

Mike went to the terrace door, slid it open, and came back with the bag. He picked up his jacket.

'I'm sorry,' Lynn said.

He waved it away. 'Are you sure you want to stay here tonight? You don't want to go to Kara's?'

'No.'

He waved again and went out.

Lynn listened to the elevator door open and close and started to cry again, and stopped herself.

She didn't dream but kept waking up. The images of Chip that didn't come in her sleep met her each time she woke.

243

She couldn't stop running the film, seeing Greg ambushing the animal, capturing it, killing it. Getting up to her terrace and setting it there for her to find, with the seed around it.

Maybe she should have gone back to Kara's. But there was an anchoring feeling in staying put. The more pieces of her life Greg bit into, the more she needed to hang on to what was left.

Thank God Mike had been there.

She missed him, and at the same time welcomed her aloneness.

The fear for her safety and sanity was a constant now. There was no room for a new set of flickering, frightening reactions and urges.

She didn't know her way here, and she certainly didn't know Mike's. *Was* he taking advantage, in more ways than one now?

Part of her remembered the warm fit of their bodies. Another part was revolted and terrified.

That voice was louder.

January 5, 1993
Too bad Lynn didn't have a happy New Year.
I love that she never knows where her next surprise is coming from.
I love watching her shrink under the blows.

'I don't remember if the napkin rings were packaged so we would have noticed one was missing when I first gave them to you,' Lynn said.

Kara shook her head. 'It was probably missing then.'

'He knew from the start the napkin rings were for my best friend. That's why he held on to it. He knew there would be a way to use it to create doubt between us.'

Pam came in. 'I've been talking to the studios on the list Kara gave me for the pilot. I've narrowed it to two. Both are set up for satellite transmission. But the Revere Studio is best from the security standpoint.'

The phone rang, and Pam answered. 'Detective Delano,' she told Lynn.

Lynn felt her face flush, and turned so Kara wouldn't see. 'Hi. Not too bad, thanks. February 14, but there's a meeting here a week from Friday at three to run over the format with you and the other resource people. No, the taping isn't definite. Dennis is leaving it up to me, and I just haven't decided for sure yet. But we're proceeding with the planning in case. Okay. 'Bye.'

'I can't talk you out of having him on?' Kara asked.

'No.'

'He's taking advantage. He wants the glory.'

'He's a child abuse professional. He has expertise to contribute. And *I* certainly feel more secure having a detective there.'

Dennis had the flu. His hands were hot, his eyes were heavy, and his mind took detours.

He lay in bed watching Dan Rather do his plodding job on the evening news. Dan read every story as if it were a tragedy with worldwide consequences, even the kickers.

As he lay there, an odd thing happened. He became Dan. He, Dennis Orrin, was doing the network news.

He watched himself lean into the camera with just the right mixture of authority and sympathy. Watched the tape footage intercut with his own face.

Bernadine came in, snapping the fantasy.

'How do you feel?' she asked.

'Somewhere between terrible and dead.'

'Can I get you anything?'

'No, goddamn it! I throw up anything you bring in here.'

'Don't be mean.'

'Sorry,' he said unconvincingly.

* * *

245

'What the hell is this?' Mike asked Lynn.

He had picked up a child's bike license plate that said 'Sean' from a table.

'It's mine,' Kara said. 'For my nephew's birthday.'

'Buy him something else. Destroy this. Unless you *want* some pervert to get him.'

'I really don't think –'

'Weren't you listening to your own meeting? I specifically said, don't give kids clothing or license plates or anything with their name on it.'

They were in Lynn's office following the pilot meeting, which had been held in the Channel 3 conference room. Kara had run down the format for the noncelebrity guests: Mike and a woman officer, a social worker, the administrator of a New York child abuse hotline, a hypnotherapist specializing in adult incest survivors, and Mary Eli.

'All *right*,' Kara said.

'This stuff isn't pretend, okay? There are monsters out there.'

Kara departed, leaving Mike and Lynn alone. To fill the silence before it could form, Lynn said, 'Are you trying to alienate all my friends? Kara said you yelled at Mary.'

'The blond shrink? Yeah, I yelled. She started quizzing me about what we were doing to protect you –'

'And you defended yourself.'

'I was defending *you*. Those questions weren't as simple as they looked. She doesn't take your situation seriously enough.'

'What gives you the right –'

'You ought to be damn glad –'

Lynn's phone rang. It was for Mike. When he finished, he said, 'That was my office. I'm off duty tomorrow through Monday. The reason I came in here after the meeting in the first place is to tell you I'm going to LA to talk to Barbara Hysmith.'

Lynn gasped. 'You found her!'

246

'LA did.'

'I want to go.'

He hadn't expected that. 'No.'

'I'll pay.'

'It's not the money.'

The idea of being with her for three days at all, let alone in the forced intimacy of travel, was ludicrous. It had been his mental project since that night at her apartment to separate himself from her, from his feelings about her. To drag himself inch by excruciating inch back to his initial resolve to keep his interactions with her professional and friendly. Period.

But she pleaded incessantly. He watched her face, thinner and paler even in the week and a half since he'd seen her last. This was the most animation she'd shown in weeks. He couldn't even confess that the trip wasn't official.

Finally he couldn't not let her have this.

Barbara Hysmith's apartment was in a beige three-story building on Crescenta Boulevard in Glendale. There was a courtyard with lemon trees, a tricycle, and three picnic tables.

Barbara was around thirty-five, quite tall, with long legs that were a shade heavy. She had straight brown hair that she wore in a braid, and lovely fresh skin. She had on a denim skirt and an olive peasant blouse.

'You're on TV. I've seen you,' Barbara said to Lynn when she opened the door. 'I thought this was about finding Greg Walter. If this is supposed to be an interview –'

'No, no, no,' Lynn said. 'I'm here because I'm a victim of his too. I know him as Greg Alter.'

The conversation had proceeded from there. She had met Greg at a beach club in Monterey and they had started going out.

'It was great at first,' Barbara said. 'He was so good-looking and nice. He bought me expensive clothes. He was wonderful to my friends. After a while it got raunchy. He wanted to videotape us in bed. He wanted all kinds of stuff, and he thought I was uptight for not going along.'

Mike asked, 'How did it end?'

'It didn't. Not when I wanted it to.' Her eyes were hollow. 'He wouldn't leave me be. He sent me porno stuff. Underwear I'd refused to put on before. A dildo with blood on it. Looked like real blood. He kept calling me and hanging up, all night sometimes. But if I tried to call him, the line was always busy.'

'Remember the number?'

'I'll never forget it – 543–1288.' She turned to Lynn. 'The police told me you have a tattoo also.'

'I did. It was only semipermanent. It's gone now.'

Barbara lifted her skirt. On her thigh was the familiar pair of lips and the letter G. This time the letter was square.

Barbara said, 'I wanted to take a knife and cut this right out. I still want to.'

'I'm sure there were a lot of others,' Detective Abigail Stern said. 'She never sees his apartment; his car turns out to be a rental in a dead-end name. What he says he does for work, he doesn't. That's a practiced act. And a man that crazy doesn't just do a woman or two and then say, "Well, I'm satisfied." Most of the women probably never reported it.'

'He made sure of it,' Mike said. 'He's very shrewd at instilling shame and guilt. Christ, you have a lot of these wackballs out here.'

'Don't tell my commander. He's just here for the surfing.'

Lynn listened to them spar. Detective Stern was a petite, shapely twenty-eight-year-old who looked at Mike appreciatively, though he appeared not to notice. Some impulse in

Lynn resented the woman's interest, but she subdued that and reminded herself that she had much to be grateful to Detective Stern for.

'What are the chances,' Lynn asked her, 'of finding more of his victims? I want to know what makes him stop.'

She shrugged. 'We're hamstrung, like Detective Delano. More so, because we don't have the pressure of a prominent current victim. That might be why he hasn't stopped with you, to be honest. Even though you're not making your situation public, *you* are public. Your visibility is a tightrope walk for him.'

'She probably is right,' Mike said. 'But she's also right that the more famous you get, the more he'll back off. He may be crazy, but he has to protect himself. How much chance would some freak have coming after Oprah Winfrey?'

'Barbara Hysmith had to move twice. *Twice.*'

'At least then he dropped it,' Mike said.

'Maybe he just couldn't find her the second time.'

'He found her once, he could find her again if he wanted to. He just had enough jollies. Went on to the next stop.'

They were in a rented Buick, driving away from the police station, both sorting out reams of input, alternating between long silences and bursts of conversation.

'She was so open. Barbara. I appreciated that,' Lynn said. 'Thank God I didn't get a real tattoo. Imagine having to live with that forever.' She laughed without humor, the only way she seemed able to lately. 'Listen to me. As if I don't have to live with *him* forever.'

'Don't say that,' Mike said angrily. 'Keep doing what you were doing. Take what she had to give you.'

They drove on along wide streets of low pastel buildings and exotic trees and shrubs. Sadly, Lynn remembered her first look at the phenomenon of Los Angeles. It was her personal magic carpet then.

They turned a corner, and Lynn caught her reflection in

the car window. She looked bent and cowed. Self-consciously she straightened, lifted her head.

'Did you hear what Barbara said about her self-image?' Lynn asked.

'She said she can't look at herself with no clothes on.'

Lynn nodded. 'I can't either.'

He glanced at her.

'When you were in the bathroom,' Lynn went on, 'I told her about Greg buying me that bathing suit and then saying I bulged out of it. She said once he called to her to come into the living room naked. He knew she was just out of the shower. She thought he was joking around, being, you know, sexy and playful, and she did it. Turned out the cable TV repairman was there.'

'Jesus.'

'That's not the end. After he started sending her things, she got a letter, supposedly from the repairman, telling her how ugly and lumpy she was. Detail by detail.'

'Psychotic.'

'He climbs inside your subconscious and taints your messages to yourself. That poor woman.'

Mike glanced over again, at the shape he knew very well now. Lean arms and legs, flat stomach. It was impossible that the possessor of such a body could regard it as garbage. But all these years wading through the dregs of sex criminals and picking up the physical and emotional pieces of their prey had taught him more than anyone could stand to know about what the mind does with their effects.

They were passing a small shopping center. Abruptly he pulled in. 'There,' he said, pointing.

'There what? Where are we?'

'Go into that clothing store. Buy a bathing suit. *Don't* give me any shit. I said yes to your coming to LA with me ...'

It took another several minutes of leaning on her, but

she did it, and meanwhile he ducked into a drugstore and bought a disposable camera.

'Exposure therapy,' was all he would say as he drove on.

He parked across from a public beach near Malibu. He made her go into the bathhouse and put on the suit.

'Walk down the beach,' he said when she came out. 'I'm going to follow you.' Then, ridiculously, 'I won't look.'

Again he had to convince her, but she went walking off, barefoot in the sand, pale as hell beside the natives. He kept his promise, didn't watch her any more than he had to for focusing, congratulated himself on that for his own protection as well as honoring the promise.

He used almost all the film in the camera – pictures not only of her, but of men watching her.

He wasn't sure how much good it would do.

But it kept him busy too many miles from home with this woman. And it just might help stanch the slow but consistent outflow of life from her that alarmed him more all the time.

CHAPTER FOURTEEN

'She's where?' Dennis asked.

'Los Angeles. She'll be back tonight,' Kara said. 'Are you feeling any better?'

'It comes and goes.' Dennis had showered and dressed, meaning to go to work, then had to reconsider when nausea overcame him as he went out to the garage. 'Ask her to call me if you hear from her, please.'

Bernadine heard him hang up in the den. 'Should you go back to bed?' she called.

'*No.*'

She came in and picked up an empty glass, her movements anger-stiff, and he told himself he'd make it better; she was much, much nicer than he deserved. But then his mind wandered, and his problems were over-whelming him again. The anchor, the Marchette show, the QTV pilot.

'How is Lynn at the gym?' he asked suddenly.

'Lynn?' Bernadine frowned. 'How do you mean?'

'What does she do there?'

'What I do, more or less. Weight work, treadmill, floor exercises.'

'Does she act erratic at all? Seem out of it?'

'What you'd expect. She's hassled and anxious. She has a lot of headaches.'

Bernadine waited, and when he didn't continue, she asked, 'Why?' But he didn't answer.

Somewhere over Indiana, Mike said, 'Tell me again about the night you met him.'

'We've been through that fifty times.'

'Tell me anyway. We were just there; your memory is stimulated. Something new might fall out.'

So she leaned back in the narrow seat and described it again, the restaurant and the Pacific and the Farmers Market. Mike took her through Greg's visit to Boston. As his good deed for the day to himself, he glossed over the sex and went on to the Elis' party and the packages and calls.

The pilot had just announced that Lake Erie was below, for whoever cared to lean over and look, when Mike said, 'Okay, *Murphy Brown* is on; he calls, you think from his car.'

'I know he was in his car. He said he was.'

'Run through the conversation.'

'I said I wanted to nip this in the bud. He said I shouldn't. He asked me if I remembered the night we met, and said he was calling from Malibu, near the same restaurant. He insisted I should tell him how to make me happy again. That this was cold –'

'Put yourself back there. Hear all the noises,' Mike said. 'He might have deliberately misled you about where he was calling from. Does anything sound like a service station? A factory? Do you hear the ocean?'

She tried to breathe slowly and feel it all. 'Cars are whizzing by. It sounds like a highway.'

'He's driving along a highway.'

'I think so.'

'So his voice is vibrating a little. Maybe the connection fades.'

'No.'

'Does it sound like he's stopped?'

'Yes.'

'Go on.'

'I said maybe I *was* cold. And he – and he –'

Lynn sprang upright in her seat.

Mike tensed. 'What?'

'That's how I know he's stopped. A car radio, someone else's, comes and goes, like another car stopping for a second. But listen, I never realized this before, but it's the Bob Hemphill show!'

'Meaning?'

'Bob Hemphill is local. You can only hear him in eastern Massachusetts. Greg couldn't have been in California! He was in Boston! He was calling me from Boston!'

Mike called himself an asshole for a day and a half.

Who else but an asshole has to go from one end of the country to the other to discover he was probably at the right end to start with?

Then he began reassembling his jigsaw pieces.

Don't place the freak where he tells you to. Don't keep buying into that.

Place the freak right here at home.

Don't scatter his picture around and then wonder why nobody saw him pass Go.

Think of the times he supposedly came East to do his shtick. Think how it might have been instead.

And don't just look in the other direction. *Think* in the other direction. Climb inside the freak and look out from there and find him that way.

He looks as bad as I do, Lynn thought, taking in Dennis's unusually prominent cheekbones and chalky skin. His suit seemed half a size too large, and there was a sprinkling of sweat on his brow.

'Kara told me you were upset that I wasn't here on Monday,' she said.

Dennis wiped his forehead. 'It wasn't your not being here. God knows you practically live in the ceiling. And I've been out myself. It's more that … I feel I'm losing touch with you.'

'Oh, Dennis.'

'Are you all right, Lynn? How worried should I be?'

Lynn hesitated. They looked at each other across the enormous VIP desk with its carafe and tapes and terribly important papers.

She wasn't sure precisely what he was asking, and guessed she wasn't supposed to be. Dennis had always been her friend and ally, but he was also the man who sat on the other side of this ocean liner of a desk, and if he needed to be deliberately murky to get clarity, he would be.

Then again, given no direction, she could elect to choose her own.

She was lucky to sleep three hours at a stretch now, but she wouldn't tell him that.

She didn't get on the scale anymore because the drop was too alarming, but why mention it?

Out on the street, any street, she looked eight ways and still felt hounded. She couldn't walk from her car to her door, or a cab to her office, without imagining hidden eyes trained on her. But she wouldn't trouble Dennis.

Her headaches were meteor showers under her scalp. She dreamed, when she did sleep, of Valium in a caviar jar. But that certainly wasn't what Dennis needed to hear.

'If you mean how am I leaning in terms of the pilot,' she said, sitting back, 'I'm still formulating that decision. I'll get back to you Monday.'

After work Lynn went to the Broome Club. In her briefcase were five Tylenol-with-codeines wrapped in a Kleenex.

She was at minute twenty-three on the StairMaster when Bernadine climbed onto the next one.

'How are you doing? Did you have a good trip?'

Lynn was tempted to really answer. To let some of her misery out. Bernadine had a knack for offering a valve just when Lynn needed one. And she desperately needed it now.

But she couldn't put on a brave professional front for

255

Dennis and then dump all her fears on his wife. So she answered, 'That's any essay question. Why don't you tell me how *you* are?'

'I'm all right.'

But she wasn't, anyone could see the taut nonsmile, the frozen motions. Even Lynn.

'How does Dennis seem to you?' Bernadine asked.

'Not too good. But this flu is supposed to be a killer.'

'I mean his mood. He's so different lately.'

'He's under a lot of pressure.' That I'm adding to, Lynn thought guiltily.

'Maybe I'm just being the paranoid wife, but, you know, he travels, and he's at the station more and more, and when he's home he stomps around like a dragon ...' She paused. 'Could Dennis be having an affair?'

Lynn turned to Bernadine, stumbled, then caught the handrail. 'Are you serious?'

'Yes. I am.'

Lynn thought about how to answer. Dennis would be the last man she'd suspect of playing around. Besides that, he couldn't possibly have the time.

She decided to simply say what she thought. 'You and Dennis are very close. Couples who are close have periods when they drift apart for a while.' Now listen to *me*, she thought; the maimed guiding the whole. 'I think he's in a tight situation that he's maybe taking out on whoever is handy. I *don't* believe there's a woman. God, Bernadine, between you and me, one or the other of us is with him every second of the day.'

Lynn finished her first set of bench presses, and Elizabeth took the curl bar away. She sat up to rest and saw Mike Delano coming into the fitness room, holding an envelope.

'Your office said you were here. I have the copies of the statutes you wanted for the taping. I wasn't going to leave them around that hurricane rubble you call your desk.'

Elizabeth held out the bar. 'Don't stop for too long.'

Self-consciously, Lynn lay back and did her reps. She could feel Mike's critical gaze.

'That's too light for her,' Mike said.

'It's … intentional,' Lynn said between presses.

'The most I give her is the curl bar with nickels,' Elizabeth said, adding a five-pound ring to each end of the bar.

Mike looked around the fitness room, went and got a straight lifting bar. 'This weighs forty-five. You could press it easily.'

'I don't want to get too big.'

Elizabeth said, 'Women need multiple reps at lighter weight. Those heavy weights are for strength training, not tone and bone mass. I don't use them, and my clients don't.'

'She could use them for negatives.'

'Negatives put too much strain on the elbows.'

'Not if you –'

'*Mike*,' Lynn said.

Later, stretching her, Elizabeth said, 'A lot of knots in your back.'

Lynn closed her eyes. 'I'm having a rough time.'

'Things aren't any better?'

'No. It just gets worse.'

'Bernadine was asking me about your situation with that man. I wasn't sure how much to say – what you want your boss to know. So I sort of changed the subject.'

'Thank you.'

'Lean your shoulder left. I thought it might be your boyfriend making you tense. He seems quite argumentative.'

'He is argumentative. But he's not my boyfriend.'

'Could have fooled me,' Elizabeth said. 'But I'm glad he's not. From what you've been telling me, you already have more man problems than you need.'

'That's for sure. You sound like you know what you're talking about.'

Elizabeth's hands slowed on her shoulder blades. 'I ... It's ...'

Lynn waited for her to go on, and when she didn't, Lynn said, 'Sorry. The questions fall out of my mouth sometimes. You don't have to answer.'

'It's just ... a very long story.' Elizabeth's hands resumed their soothing work.

'Do you have someone better now?'

Elizabeth smiled. 'I'm working on it.'

Lynn stretched her arms out in front of her as Elizabeth worked on the biceps. 'I know what I'm talking about myself.'

'You?'

'That's one of the reasons I was attracted to Greg, the man who's making me so miserable now,' Lynn said. 'He was sweet and supportive when I met him. He seemed so different from the pigs I used to end up with. How little I knew ...'

Lynn closed her eyes again and listened to the waterfall hiss. She imagined herself in a green oasis with the cool drops on her face.

She could feel her back loosening. She cherished the temporary calm of the grayed lighting, the sweet woodland sounds, and the hands freeing her banded muscles.

It was all she was going to have.

Lynn sat in the steam room for a while, and when the heat ebbed, she sprayed the thermostat with the powerful wall-mounted hose to bring a few more minutes of hot steam. She thought how her own emotional thermostat had become as reactive, but plunging instead of rising as it got each new blast from Greg.

Dressing, she pulled her makeup bag from her briefcase. She looked at the Kleenex-wrapped pills, and touched them, but didn't take any. She saw the pack of California pictures Mike had given her a few days ago, and took them out for a longer look.

The walk on the beach had been one weird experience in a three-day marathon of them.

She thumbed through the photos. She looked scrawny and flabby in the black suit.

But Mike had been right: the looks that followed her said otherwise.

She scoured each shot for another woman or a dog or an ice cream stand that might be the focus of the attention. But there was nothing.

Lynn was four blocks from home, waiting for a red light to change, when the passenger side door of the Lexus opened, and Greg jumped into the seat.

Her mouth opened in a silent gasp. The blood pounded in her veins.

Reflexively she grabbed for the door handle, but Greg was quicker. He hit the power lock.

Lynn leaned on the horn.

Greg laughed. 'Don't bother. No one will pay any attention. How've you been?'

The deep chuckle, the tan, the beautiful smile ... like a living-dead creature that looks real just before it putrefies in front of your eyes.

Her whole body was shaking, but suddenly Lynn felt an infusion of the superalert courage that sped to her rescue when she had just seconds to avert a catastrophe on the show.

'You sick bastard,' she said, the words raspy with her terror and hate, hurting her throat. 'Don't you have what you want yet? Haven't you made me miserable enough?'

Greg smiled wider and reached for her crotch.

Her courage disappeared. She screamed, and was still screaming as she watched him thread his way on foot through the traffic, until she could no longer see him.

Lynn took the pills, of course; not all five, but two before she was even home, and then another.

She couldn't reach Kara or Mike.

She thought about her brother. Calling Booboo would mean changing her policy of downplaying, which Angela was still leaning on her to do, making ominous predictions about his blood pressure. But keeping the extent of the danger from her brother had also given Lynn some control. If Booboo didn't know how serious the threat was, he was less likely to force the issue by insisting, instead of suggesting, she stay in Salem, or let him stay in Boston, or even, if it was possible, not be on the air.

Now, finally, these possibilities weren't nearly as frightening as what *was* happening.

But while she was debating, Mike called back.

She met him at Nancy Jean's, jumping at the chance to leave her apartment.

Another frightening first.

Sitting on the hard chair, she could still feel Greg's fingers digging into her crotch, the pressure of the palm.

She should have showered again.

But that was ludicrous.

'I keep thinking about Barbara Hysmith moving twice,' she said. 'Is that what he's trying to get me to do? But if I'm on TV, it doesn't matter where I live; I can always be found. Unless *that's* it. Maybe he wants me to give up the program.'

'You'd do that?'

'I never thought I would. But maybe I shouldn't make the pilot.'

Mike shook his head. 'I think you should go for it. You make this program and you're the Goodyear blimp. You're hanging up there in the sky, visible as hell. It's hard to pull

260

commando tricks on something big and shiny that everybody's watching.'

Beneath the reasonable, analytical words, Mike burned with fury over Greg's latest invasion. To try to restrain the feelings, he stared at the little TV way over on the bar. A network newscast showed a shaggy, waiflike child climbing into a police cruiser.

'Katie Beers,' Lynn said. 'That's some story.'

'Yeah. And no. There are a million like her. One kid is rescued, everyone gets their fairy story ending, and the country breathes a sigh of relief. They think someone is taking care of the child abuse problem.'

Lynn met his eyes. 'Say that on the pilot.'

'I will.' He stared back. 'So you're going to do it?'

'I want to. But I'm terrified. What if Greg destroys it? He has just the instinct for homing in on exactly what's important to me. He knows this pilot is a life achievement. He knows that there's no way he could hurt and humiliate me more than to take that away. And he's coming closer, and getting bolder and more dangerous.'

'I agree.'

'But you think I should go ahead anyway.'

Mike tipped his chair back. 'We have an advantage now. We know he either lives in the area or spends a lot more time here than he wants us to be aware of. We're not all looking West while he sneaks in between our legs. And he doesn't know we know. So we concentrate on securing the Revere Studio and the technological arrangements. We assign a guard to every person vital to the operation. And maybe, because this one time we have a lot of sets of eyes, we spot him and we let him lead us to the rock he lives under. And maybe we catch him pulling something that helps us put him away for a good chunk of time, more than just for stalking.'

Mike took a handful of pretzels and broke them all at once.

'And one more thing,' he said. 'It's an important program. It should be done. People should see it.'

For a while Lynn had shrunk from going out on the terrace, unable to stop thinking of Chip. But she made herself do it. She had to hold tight to what was left, as more and more pieces of her life were carried off by the human tsunami that Greg had become.

It was freezing out there tonight.

His presence hovered, the invasion of his fingers. The obscenity of her intimate connection to the monster/man, and his to her.

Back in Greeneville they'd always said hot tea kept your blood warm, but she'd downed two cups at Nancy Jean's, and her blood was as cold as the rest of her.

Her phone sounded inside, and she hurried in. It was her brother.

'I wish you'd think some more about staying here for a while,' he said.

'I did think about it. I love you for offering. But –'

'I'm not offering, honey. I'm … pleading.'

'Oh, Boo.'

'You can commute from here. Angela does, and quadrillions of other people. You'd have all the comforts. Your own bathroom. Breakfast in bed. Free morning *Globe*.'

'I don't –'

'Okay, okay. I'll throw in *USA Today*.'

'Look, I got out of here for a week. I have this whole new Fort Knox door. I simply want to stay in my apartment. Is that so terrible?' Lynn rubbed the back of her neck. 'I'm sorry for snapping –'

'It's all right. We're all scared.'

* * *

262

It stayed frigid all week. The wind snatched debris from the gutters and threw it in your eyes. It dirtied your hair and chapped your skin.

Three days before the pilot taping, Greg put on a fur hat and a heavy coat and his favorite Storm Trooper boots and took a constitutional down Morrissey Boulevard, right past Channel 3.

He knew the taping was at the Revere Studio. He knew, of course, precisely where that facility was. He knew the location of every entrance, the size of the ceiling tiles, the number of stalls in the men's and women's johns, and the brand of deodorant in the dressing rooms.

But that was in three days, and today was today, and ever since he'd begun planning his affair with Lynn, he had loved walking this street, just wrapping up in some bulky outfit, altering his posture and his stride, and joining the crowd of businesspeople hurrying along.

It was the opposite of hiding, and yet the best hiding of all.

He watched the show every single day now, live when he could, taping it when he was working.

Lynn tried to hide it, but there was a definite change in her. Comparing current tapes to those of three months ago, he could chart a weight loss of about eleven pounds. There were puckers along her upper lip line. Sometimes her hands shook; you could see it when she switched her mike from one hand to the other. In the car he'd noticed how her hair was dulling.

He didn't care a damn now that he'd only gotten her to do that semipermanent tattoo. He had progressed way beyond such artifice. To be able to follow profound systemic change like the ones he could see on the tapes – that was a reward beyond any he'd ever had.

Passing him, a plumpish, mittened woman with very white teeth flashed them at him and winked. He smiled slightly and left it at that.

He was nowhere near done with Lynn.

No one had ever held his fancy this long. It was amazing.

To keep him pumping all this time and be only more exciting each day … the prize went to Lynn. His Star. The treasure of the VCR.

His dream date.

'They're begging us for demos. Big markets too,' Vicky Belinski said. 'As soon as they hear Oprah *and* Roseanne, they just can't get a tape fast enough.'

Lynn was thrilled and sickened. Big stations all across the country waiting to see her pilot. Big stations all across the country poised to see her screw up.

'You're becoming very well known, my dear,' Vicky went on. 'I rarely have to explain who you are. Len and I are very, very excited.'

She wished she could say to Vicky Belinski, A crazy man has been hounding me and has destroyed one of my shows. I'm terrified I won't come across well on the pilot. I'm terrified it will be sabotaged.

There was a chance she could say that and get a compassionate response. QTV wanted her because she *was* human and genuine, and it was possible Vicky would say, Why didn't you tell me, we understand, how can we help?

But QTV was also a successful, profit-conscious corporation accustomed to skimming the rich top layer of television talent. They didn't have to work with anyone who wasn't pristine and perfect.

They were human too. And it was human to want to feel comfortable with the health and integrity of your investment.

'Three more days,' Vicky said.

Lynn clasped her hands tight and answered, 'I can't wait!'

* * *

*I knew Lynn would be different. I knew she
would be the most challenging conquest.*

*Some of the others were better-looking, younger,
sweeter. But no one has been as powerful, so
admired, as she is.*

*She's very nervous now. She doesn't know what
to expect.*

I love the way she shakes.

*Nationally respected? Nationally famous?
We'll see.*

On February 13, Lynn and Kara and Dennis were given a
security tour of the Revere Studio by Bernard Stricker of
Stricker Protective Services. He was very tall and thin, with
a gentle voice.

'Here is your only audience entrance,' Stricker said.
'Two of my most senior people will be in place as your
staff processes the audience members. Of course, they will
have pictures of the subject. No other entrance to the
building will be unlocked or unbarred.'

He led them to the control room and set. There were
guards in each area.

'Have all the security codes been explained to your
satisfaction? The arrangements for communication with
your satellite guests, the backup power sources, all the
passwords?'

'They have,' Dennis said. 'But I still want guards at all
times.'

'My people are assigned here in shifts around the clock.
I also have three men assigned to guard the three of you,
from ten tonight until after the taping tomorrow.'

'My commander cleared a man to guard you,' Mike told
Lynn. 'Tonight through the taping.'

Lynn had taken the call in the reception area, where she

was reading a fax from Vicky Belinski listing the interested markets.

'But I have someone. Stricker people are assigned to all of us.'

'I want a real cop there with you.'

'All right,' Lynn said. 'Thank you.' She wished they could both be there, with a few more in a helicopter following her everywhere she went. She never felt protected enough.

'Going to sleep?' Lynn's guard asked. His name was Norman Lee, and he was a wide-shouldered uniformed policeman with short light hair. He sat on her couch reading the *Globe*. A thick sandwich and a can of Coke were on the glass coffee table in front of him.

She smiled weakly. 'I'm going to try.'

'All right, then.'

Lynn washed and put on her nightgown. Mercifully, there was no headache tonight. Not that she would have taken anything if there had been; the Tylenol-with-codeines she'd been allowing herself when the pain was too much to stand were out of the question when she was going on the air within hours.

She got into bed and read a text Mary had lent her called *The Narcissistic Parent and the Sexually Abnormal Female Child*. She'd assumed she'd either fall asleep or learn something, and she did both. She slept until her alarm went off at six-forty.

She had grapefruit and a bagel, and gave one to Officer Lee. She drank a cup of coffee, poured another, and took it into the shower with her.

She was surprised that she had slept. There was a patina of calm over her anxiety. It must be her program persona kicking in, thank God. Mentally she had moved into position with her mike and her brain and her mouth all on.

Greg hadn't been able to rob her of that. She was ready.

She was tuned to do the show. Her eyes and ears and hands and mind were going to pull the best out of her audience, herself, and her guests.

She sipped coffee and let the hot water course down her back.

She was on their frequency already, and they were on hers.

Officer Lee washed his plate and mug. The coffeepot was empty, and he washed that too, and wiped the counter.

The phone rang.

'Marchette residence, Lee speaking.'

'Norman? Mike Delano. I need you here at the Revere Studio. Fellman is on the way up there to relieve you.'

'Shouldn't I wait –'

'*No*, goddamn it. Move! This is bad!'

Lee hung up and grabbed his jacket. He rapped on the bathroom door, but she couldn't hear it over the running water. He waited a moment, rapped again, considered opening the door a crack and shouting; but that would scare the hell out of the poor woman.

When Detective Delano said to move, it was not a good idea to do otherwise. He'd better get going.

He went out, frowning at the Stanley locks. He hesitated another second, thinking he maybe ought to wait for the lady to bolt up behind him. Give Fellman a minute to get here too.

But again he remembered the urgency in Detective Delano's voice, and he made up his mind and hurried out.

Lynn toweled her hair and worked in mousse. She turned on the blow dryer.

When done, she pinned back the wild tumble of curls with two combs. Her outfit was laid out on her bed; she wrapped herself in a towel and opened the bathroom door.

267

Movement off to the side caught her eye. Instinctively, before her brain even had the message, she began to turn. Then there was a huge, numbing blow to the side of her head, and she fell.

CHAPTER FIFTEEN

At eight-ten Kara was escorted into the Revere Studio by her Stricker guard. She went to the set, where Pam was arranging Danish around a coffee maker. Sound people were setting up in the control room.

At eight-fifteen Kara looked at her watch, went to the phone by the control room and dialed Lynn. When there was no answer after seven rings, she ran through cues with the engineers and watched while they tested the satellite hookups. Then she called the office of each celebrity guest, supposedly just to touch base.

By eight-thirty Kara was relieved that the technical arrangements seemed fine, but uneasy about Lynn. They'd agreed on eight o'clock. She phoned twice more.

It wasn't like Lynn to be more than five or ten minutes late. Or to forget to turn her answering machine on.

Then again, there was a policeman with her, bringing her here. Maybe he had his reasons for taking some unusual route.

By 8:45 the entire audience was seated. Mary arrived, and the three other studio guests, and then Dennis, Vicky, and Len.

Mike Delano came in just half a minute ahead of Norman Lee.

Lynn came awake suddenly. Her head hurt unbearably. She was lying in a heap on her side, in the dark, on a cold hard surface.

She lifted her head, and then cried out at the rush of

agonizing pain to her left cheek and eye. She touched it and felt blood.

The pain was limiting her ability to think, so she put pressure there and concentrated hard.

As she did, her heart raced, equaling the internal noise of the throbbing in her temple.

So she pressed with both hands and let the pictures come back.

Shower. Hair dryer. Phone. No; that was the phone *ringing* faintly now, not a memory.

Lynn swept an arm in an arc.

Wool. Coats. A familiar smell: lavender, her lavender sachets.

She was in her coat closet.

The phone stopped, then started again.

What about the taping? Had she missed the taping?

She tried to get up, felt horribly dizzy. And cold. She was naked.

She reached for the inside knob. The door was locked. Someone had banged her with something and then closed her in here.

The phone rang again.

Lynn pulled herself up by holding on to coats. She leaned her weight against the door and pushed.

Nothing – and it hurt.

She tried to get leverage to throw more weight against it, but there was no room. The coats crowded her.

She started pulling them down.

Her heart was thundering. Her head hurt. The wool and hangers scraped and poked her naked body.

Again she threw herself against the door, hard this time. It didn't even rattle.

Tears came, adding to the mess on her face. Her hands were wet and sticky. She kicked the door, but succeeded only in killing her toes, then her heel.

She dropped to the floor and scrabbled around in the

270

coats and hangers for anything she could use to break out of there, and found her old bowling ball.

Mike, Norman Lee, Kara, and Dennis ran to Lynn's door. Mike pushed it right open.

Lynn was leaning against the wall near the coat closet. Her hair was matted in a bloody mess to the side of her eye. She held a towel around herself. There were smears of blood all over her. A bowling ball sat in the hallway.

Kara screamed. Mike probed her wound quickly while Lee ran to look in the other rooms.

Kara grabbed a coat, put it on Lynn, and helped her to the couch.

Mike shot questions at her. She answered as best she could.

'That's all I can tell you,' Lynn finished. 'Officer Lee was here when I went into the shower, and that was the last I saw of him.'

'He went to the studio,' Mike said. 'He got a call, supposedly from me, that there was an emergency situation. He was told a man was on the way up here to take over for him.'

'And,' Dennis said, 'it wasn't you who called.'

'No, it wasn't *me*.'

'It was Greg,' Lynn said hopelessly.

'But you didn't see him at all,' Dennis said.

'No.'

Mike said, 'You have to go to the emergency room. That cut's not deep, but it needs stitching.'

Lynn pulled the coat tight around herself. She was pale and dazed. 'What will you tell Vicky and Len?' she asked Dennis.

'God knows.'

'I'll talk to them,' Kara said. 'You're a crime victim. Period. They were in the control room when Officer Lee came in. They didn't hear.'

271

'Before you do anything,' Mike said, 'help Lynn get some clothes on. I'm taking her to the hospital now.'

In the taxi on their way back to the Revere Studio, Dennis asked Kara, 'Did you buy all that?'

'You mean, do I think it happened like Lynn said? Why wouldn't I?'

Dennis sat straight and tense on the hard seat. 'Call me skeptical, but when I find a person with a history of a drug problem groggy and depressed and nursing a head wound the morning they're supposed to tape their breakthrough show, my first assumption is not that they got cold-cocked by a mysterious stranger. Maybe she got blitzed and took a header.'

'And locked herself in the closet?'

'We never saw her in the closet.'

'She doesn't use drugs. She only took pills for her teeth. Any problem she had was years ago.'

Dennis said, 'How can you know that?'

Lynn lay on her side while the doctor stitched her temple. The Lidocaine they had injected into her face must have numbed her feelings too. She didn't seem to have a single one; just a flat colorless nonmood.

There were questions she needed to ask Mike, and Kara and Dennis. She supposed she should call Booboo.

But she couldn't think where to start.

She didn't really want to ask, or hear, anything.

She wasn't even up to dealing with the basic problem of where to sleep tonight. She wasn't worried and she wasn't scared.

That scared her.

'I've been told,' the doctor said conversationally as he snipped something out of her sight, 'that I'm not supposed to question you about what happened.'

'I got hit,' Lynn said. 'I didn't see the person or the weapon, if there was one.'

272

'Random attack on the street?'

'No. It's ... complicated.'

'Am I also not supposed to acknowledge who you are?'

'Not to any media,' Mike said, coming in with his notebook open.

The doctor stopped what he was doing and turned to Mike. 'Look, is this a domestic situation? Was she hit by someone she knows? Because you'd have to be certifiable to go back to violence like this. And covering it up doesn't help anything.'

'Hold it,' Mike said. 'That's not the explanation. She was hit by a character who has been harassing her.' He faced Lynn. 'I just talked to one of the men who went over the apartment and the building. There's no sign of anyone having been there. As usual, the freak is invisible.'

After Greg left Lynn's building, it was too soon to start watching the fun at the Revere Studio. He was due for a visit to the tanning place, but he was too excited to bother right now. So he moseyed over to the Muffin Hut on Demeter, around the corner from the studio, and had a leisurely breakfast.

He kept thinking of the hefty light-haired policeman jumping on his steed and galloping away from his guardee.

This was a new refinement.

He, Greg had impersonated people on the phone many a time; his mimic skills didn't stop at handwriting. But being a policeman to a policeman – that was choice.

He really, really liked playing in this league.

The explosion of inspiration that had come when he'd first seen Lynn's *Broadcasting* picture, and put that together with the combination of his current home address and her business address, was more than fulfilling its promise.

He took his Tums out and chewed two.

There was a twenty-year-old girl once in Seattle whose

father was a retired cop working as a limo driver. The old man had gone all protective when his baby complained about what was happening to her; it was Greg's opinion that he wanted to keep the girl for himself and had probably been having her for years. In fact, Greg thought, he had most likely done the man a favor by giving him an excuse to crowd her.

In any case, what Greg did for fun was to call her at work and pretend to be her daddy, and tell her to meet him places. Then he'd call the father and be Officer so-and-so of the highway patrol and report dispassionately that she'd been in an accident.

He did that four or five times. The old man knew it was bullshit, but do you ever really know, where your kid is concerned? So Greg would have him leaping up and down and blowing smoke out of his ears until the girl turned up, and it got funnier each time …

He finished eating, paid the cashier, put on his coat and muffler and hat, and went out. There would be enough confusion at the studio entrance, with the audience leaving and all the honchos running around like a Chinese fire drill, so that he could soak up the scene without taking any chances.

'No wonder you didn't want to come in the front way,' Elizabeth Vail said, tucking a fresh sheet around the massage table mattress. 'Does that feel as bad as it looks?'

'It hurts,' Lynn admitted.

Gently, Elizabeth helped her onto the table.

'I'm hurting everywhere, if you want to know the truth.'

Elizabeth shook her head. 'I'm sorry. I asked Bernadine why she was calling to make the appointment for you. She said you were mugged.'

Lynn looked at the ceiling. She was so sick of hearing herself whine.

'The mugging story is the official one. But that's not

what happened. Greg got into my apartment this morning and knocked me out.'

'Oh, Lynn!' Elizabeth bent to hug her.

'He did it. He stopped the pilot. We were supposed to be safe, but we weren't. Now I don't know what will happen. To the pilot or … to me.'

Lynn's damaged eye started to burn under the bandage, and she tried to hold the tears back. But they had to come out sometime, as embarrassing as it was.

At least she wasn't breaking down in front of Bernadine or Dennis or Vicky.

Or Kara, who was insecure enough about the immediate future as it was.

Or Booboo, who would be crazed.

Mike hadn't had dinner, and he wasn't hungry.

He sat on his made bed, still dressed. The TV was on. Larry King questioning some yuppie about the economy.

Sometimes he could think better with background noise.

His day was over, and he was burning to make headway on this fiasco that wouldn't release its grip on him.

As Larry droned low, Mike grabbed a pen and made nonsensical shapes in his notebook.

What was Greg doing right now?

As good a place to start as any.

Celebrating his hosing of the Boston police.

Mike threw the pen at the wall. No, you asshole, it is not the Boston police he's so fascinated with. So, again. What is he doing right now?

Looking for Lynn? Does he want to get at her again?

Mike dropped the notebook and put his hands behind his head and followed that possibility backward and forward. How does it fit into the freak's thinking? How would he try it?

Nothing clicked in.

He decided to start earlier.

Six o'clock this morning. The freak knows about the taping, and knows we know he knows. He must know about all the sabotage precautions.

He's in Lynn's building. He has a cellular. He knows our whole setup, Lee's name, my name.

He has to wait for the shower to run. Does he have some way of identifying her shower from pipe noise? Or does he just listen right by her door?

So. She's in the shower, he phones Lee, doing my voice well enough to convince. Lee takes off, the freak walks right in, waits for Lynn to come out of the bathroom, clubs her with a fist or some object.

At the memory of the blood and the swelling and Lynn in near-naked confusion, Mike felt his empty stomach curl. But he was getting somewhere, he really thought so, and he kept on.

So he clubs her and locks her in the closet and scoots out, and then does what? Sits back somewhere and wishes he could see the effects of what he did.

Then what? He's already hurt her, set a precedent. Is he going to back down and start doing anonymous stuff again?

What pleasure is that when he's advanced this far?

So he'll hurt her again. Worse this time. He waits for night, now that they'd be watching for him; or he waits a week or a month and lets her sweat, and then gets her good.

Mike sat up. That didn't taste right.

Larry had stopped for a commercial. Mike wasn't sure what the advertised product was, but the picture showed a fat sandwich, and suddenly he was hungry.

He went to the kitchen and made a tuna melt with Swiss cheese, brought it back to the bed, and let his mind go again as his mouth worked.

He pictured the freak following her, put different

weapons in his hands, had him take her down in various places: an apartment, a garage, the TV station, the street.

It didn't freeze. He knew he was off the trail.

Okay. Try it from another direction. Humiliation. Where does he go now? Another ambush, but a rape this time? Rape and injury?

They'd caught a rapist a couple of years ago in Roslindale who punched victims in both eyes before screwing them. Cute; business before pleasure.

That didn't feel right for the freak either.

Why not?

Because violence didn't seem to be his thing.

Good, Mike. Watch her get her face sewn back together, and then proclaim that violence isn't her attacker's thing.

He let out his breath. Finished the sandwich and thought some more.

Another commercial. Mouthwash. A couple dancing to moony music. Talking and kissing at once, fresh minty mouths tasting each other.

Then the memory sneaked up on him.

Mike and Lynn in her living room. Her body under his hands. The feel of her, leg to leg; the taste of her skin.

The life in her, coursing through her, his for a moment.

Now, on his bed, he rubbed his face to erase the memory, but stubbornly it stayed.

She had been right there with him at first. They were two heat-seeking missiles. She held him tight, molded against him. Her kiss was as hungry as his.

For the first time since this morning he let himself recall the scene as she'd dropped her towel to get into the coat Kara was holding.

Her skin, her pale soft skin, ribs showing; long, strong thighs. Her smooth chest, round breasts with a little weight.

He had to stop this, it was against all his training to regard a naked victim with anything other than

277

professional detachment and dignified sympathy.

The picture of her injury intruded then, and he remembered that with the same intense clarity as he had just done his forbidden tour of her body. The half-dried blood and caked hair, the dazed and helpless expression.

Of course, the freak would have had a second for a good look before he brained her. A look at remembered territory, at what had been freely given to him.

Mike was getting angrier.

But that wasn't a good way to feel either. To take this attack, this case, personally, helped nothing. Feelings colored and covered facts and processes, gummed them up like rubber cement in an engine.

Was her nakedness part of the game for Greg? Had he relished the image of her in the shower, coming out to dress, wearing a robe or a towel because she thought Lee was there, but bare under it?

For that matter, *were* the police part of his routine? Was he flipping the finger at Norman and him and the other cops and guards? Was that why he had grabbed Lynn that way, right in their faces?

Probably not. Like the violence, the police element seemed separate from whatever Greg's objective had been.

So. Back to basics. What *was* Greg's objective today?

More basic. Why *pick* today?

Because of the pilot. He wanted to use the pilot.

Larry King was addressing the econo-yup on a screen. A satellite interview.

No.

Greg wasn't using the pilot. He was using Lynn. Lynn as equipment.

He burned to fuck up that pilot. He knew we were watching for him to try. So while we were roadblocking and securing, he ran in early and fast and in a new MO, and damaged the once piece of equipment the pilot couldn't survive without.

278

That did freeze.

Larry was talking. There were close-ups of him, his big teeth.

Something Detective Stern in LA had said came back just then: 'Your visibility could be what turns him on.'

Did the freak prey on women in television? Or was Lynn a new taste treat? Either way, seeing her up there on a screen right in his cave must be incredible for him.

Mike remembered something else: Barbara Hysmith's tattoo. Lynn's tattoo. The porno lingerie Greg had wanted to see them in, the cutout dress.

The man liked Show and Tell. Without the Tell. He seemed especially to like it when he arranged the Show himself.

Had he gotten off on that, looking at Lynn's tattoo up there on TV for as long as it had lasted?

Mike sat up suddenly, spilling sandwich crumbs to the floor.

He had an idea.

'Hi, this is Lynn Marchette. We're on hiatus right now, working on some unique new programs that we will be bringing you in the coming weeks. Keep watching for information on the start of our new schedule of shows, and meanwhile, here's one of my favorites.'

Lynn hit the Pause button on the videotape monitor, freezing the *Lynn Marchette Show* graphic that had accompanied her voice, with no image of her. 'Well?'

Mike nodded. 'That should drive him up the wall.'

'I don't like doing this. Kara and Dennis don't like it either. They want the copy to give a date. They're worried about losing too much of our audience.'

'It might work fast. He's going to want to get a look at what he did to your face. Once he knows he can't see you on TV for a while, he'll try to eyeball you in person.'

'I can't stand to think about that.'

'Don't think about it. Think about not having him anywhere around you at all anymore.'

Across from WDSE-TV, at 330 Morrissey Boulevard, there was an office building with three suites vacant. In the second-floor one that faced the street, Mike stood with binoculars morning, evening, and lunchtime, as Lynn went in and out of the Channel 3 building, watching for who would watch her.

He had a clear view of her apartment house from another empty suite, a vacant shop in a condo development across and one down from hers.

He had taken a week of vacation.

It tore at him that he had promised her a real cop, and he hadn't been real enough.

He hoped to make up for that now.

If he was right, then one of these times very soon the freak would be there.

Then he could track the sonofabitch to where he lived or stayed, where there should be very helpful evidence, where he could be arrested and charged.

Then, Mike told himself, he could finally start to back away from all this. And work at getting it, and Lynn, off his mind.

Greg was very accustomed to seeing without being seen. But he wasn't accustomed to being stalked with the precision he used himself.

It only took two days.

At five-twenty on the afternoon of February 16, Mike was standing in the dark office. The window grime that helped hide him in daylight got in his way when it was this dark out. He squinted into the glasses as he scanned the passersby around WDSE-TV.

He remembered some of the people from the night before: Channel 3 employees, and workers from offices in the surrounding buildings. An Airborne guy making a last pickup.

A man came into view who Mike thought had just passed five minutes ago. Returning from an errand? Where was he going now? He was pausing near the Channel 3 building, checking his watch, as if waiting for someone. Good overcoat, shiny shoes. Why wait outside, though, when it was cold out?

Mike turned to the picture of Greg Alter, taped to the window frame. He knew every whisker of that goddamned face, but he looked anyway, and a second later in his binoculars was the same nose and chin, in profile.

He jammed the binoculars in his jacket.

He wanted to run downstairs and across the street. He wanted to jump on the man and beat the heart right out of him. He wanted to smash the face, the entire face, not just the side, and let's see how lovely the ladies think you are now, prick.

But he had known he'd want all that, and he'd rehearsed and rehearsed in his head what he would do instead, and he did that now.

He grabbed his cellular and phoned Lynn in her office. Then he left the empty suite and walked quickly and deliberately down to the street, and slid behind a parked van to wait for the animal to lead him to its cave.

The overcoat wasn't Greg's favorite attire. It felt long and awkward, and he'd have been more comfortable in a casual zipper jacket. But at this hour he'd stand out if he wasn't in business clothes.

He'd kept to himself for a couple of days, considering his observations of the Revere Studio his dessert. He'd even had a look at Kara Millet, turning before she could see him; not that she would have realized who he was, all bundled up like that. Blustery days were just wonderful for watching.

And today wasn't cold enough to provide the measure of safety he liked, but he'd kind of been forced to come here.

He so wanted to see the decorated Lynn.

He'd combed the newspapers, thinking the WDSE people might not have been able to keep her injury secret, but there was nothing. He'd thought she'd be back on the air pretty soon, nothing he did seemed to keep her off, but then there was the announcement that it would be awhile.

He didn't want to wait until she looked normal again.

So here he was, and all he wanted was a glimpse, which he should have within a half hour.

He checked his watch. More like twenty-five minutes. She generally left around quarter to six.

He kept his eye on the people streaming out of the building. He watched them through the glass of the facade, so he could see anyone coming before they were outside.

And suddenly, electrically, there was Lynn, taking off dark glasses as she approached the door.

He didn't see the bandage at first, just a fleshy mound on her face, but as she came closer, he saw that it was a flesh-colored dressing. Her temple and cheekbone area were discolored around it. And, oh my: that eye was a big fat darkened acorn, an acorn with a slit across it where the thing was forcibly closed. Closed by him.

He bit his cheeks to keep from breaking into a grin.

Lynn was hurrying, she didn't usually move this fast, he had to step back in the flow of people to be part of the background when she reached the sidewalk. She stepped into the street and waved for a cab.

She was pale where she wasn't bruised. He liked that. Her carriage was a bit different, not as ... energized. Was it his imagination, or was her unswollen cheekbone a touch more prominent, signaling another couple of pounds down?

A cab stopped and she got in. Greg watched it fight its

way into the rush-hour stream. He kept watching until he couldn't see it anymore.

February 16, 1993

> *Hiatus, hell. She can't do it. She's not up to it.*
> *Her face looks like she fell into a lawn mower.*
> *I love that.*

The whole adventure was simply, absolutely wonderful. He had never made so many waves in his life. Waves upon waves, the full effect rippling on and on.

Greg turned on the Channel 7 news to see if there was anything yet about the attack on Lynn. He understood why her own station might not carry it, but the competition should be eager to. If they knew.

They probably didn't know.

Maybe he should see that they did.

Not for the first time, he felt a charge of delight over his ingenuity in bringing along a camera the other morning.

He was trying to cut down on his camera use. They were fun, but a picture was a solid thing that could eventually be used against him. He much preferred the invisible data he so enjoyed collecting.

Once in a while, though, who could resist? You could always burn what shouldn't be saved.

The news was over. There had been nothing but the usual boring drivel.

But he was growing attached to the whole TV arena. So far he'd just enjoyed watching Lynn, but it would be *so* choice to hear them talk about *him*.

Greg tipped his head back musingly on his TV chair. What would he have to do to achieve that? He would have to start really hurting people. Branch out from his current activities, let his work show.

He frowned. That was risky. He hadn't spent all these years stopping short of major crime for nothing.

Then again, *with* all his experience, he was slicker and better than ever. If there was an uncatchable criminal, he was it.

He turned the set back on, found another news show, watched the news team reading their banal stories, and inserted himself as the star of the day, the reason for their grave expressions and leaden voices.

This could mean an enormous growth opportunity.

It was the second floor. Mike had watched Greg enter the small building, go up to his apartment, and turn on the lights. He could see the bluish flicker of a TV reflection. It went off for a while, then on again.

There were Christmas lights in the window, not on, draping what looked like a palm tree.

He couldn't get over the outrageous fact of where the apartment was. Couldn't stop pounding himself for going along all that time buying the California shit when the freak was right down the goddamn street from Channel 3.

His blood hammered with the fury of it.

He had to move on his plan. Get men over here and go in.

But he stood there, something telling him no.

There was stuff in there, stuff that would help them fry the guy; he knew it. And he knew he had to go in right now, or it would be gone.

He waited another minute, asking himself if he really believed that, or just couldn't wait.

But whichever, he couldn't.

Greg was surprised to hear the bell. Mrs Minot always used the phone, and no one else would be out there.

He walked to the door and looked through the peephole and went icy, sickly cold.

'Open it,' Mike said.

This couldn't be.

284

'*Open the fucking door.*'

Greg willed the sick feeling away. He'd always known this could happen. It actually didn't matter. They couldn't prove he'd broken any law. Even if they hung that stupid little stalking statute on him, he'd be out of it in a breeze.

He was safe. He was fine. This Detective Delano couldn't touch him. It might even be amusing to welcome the man in his own voice.

Smiling, he opened the door.

Mike looked hard at the freak.

What a package. Movie-actor face, shiny black hair, hard toned shape.

But something coming from him like an invisible fog, like a bad smell, only neither.

He wanted to smash the grin with a rock.

'How can I help you?' the freak said.

Mike stepped in, his eyes working. There was the TV on a stand against the wall, the palm tree in a huge pot with the string of Christmas lights. A table and a few chairs, soft, expensive pieces.

'I'm going to search this apartment.'

Greg's smile widened. 'Oh, I hardly think –'

Mike pulled his pistol from his hip. 'Shut up before I kill you.' He took the search warrant from his pocket.

Greg started to speak, and Mike said, 'Don't play with me. Don't pretend you don't know who I am.' He moved closer to Greg, into his fog. It was more like a smell now, so strong Mike had to fight to stand his ground against it. 'And don't for one second make the mistake of thinking you aren't in very deep shit.'

Greg folded his arms and stared back. Before he could speak, Mike turned and walked away, toward the bedroom.

'Where the hell do you think you're going?' Greg yelled. He leaped after Mike. All his belongings were shut up in the bedroom crawl space, but the dresser covering the opening to it was only sufficient to keep Mrs Minot out.

Mike dodged, pointed the gun at his chest. 'Hands off, asshole,' he growled and kept going.

Greg felt his first jolt of real alarm. How far would Delano go? What did they have? Probably not much, or the man wouldn't be here by himself making threats.

He would leave tonight, Greg thought, and just settle as he always did in his next spot, and beyond that no one could control what he did or who he contacted. He could still have plenty of fun with Lynn long distance, and these morons wouldn't have a hope of locating him.

But would Delano find the crawl space? If that happened, this all could get quite inconvenient.

Suddenly Greg stopped still.

He had just remembered. The pictures of Lynn were on top of the armoire, to his left. He resisted the impulse to turn and look that way.

Goddamn the pictures. He never should have taken them. They were practically proof of the assault.

He had to grab them and hide them.

He felt energy bubble up and course through him, the way it did on his most important missions. This was serious.

He made himself smile again and retrieve the uncaring, insolent tone of voice.

'You might as well give up,' he said. 'I have nothing to interest you. Whoever you are.'

As he'd hoped, the taunt fired Mike to move around faster, look harder, opening drawers, checking under them. He waited until Mike was turned completely away from him, bending over a drawer. Quick as a snake, Greg reached left and grabbed the pictures.

Mike turned back toward him just as he tucked them in his pants pocket.

'What did you just do?'

Greg made himself smile and shrug.

Mike covered the distance between them in a jump and lunged for the pocket.

'Get away from me!' Greg yelled, and pushed with all his strength.

Mike was thrown against the dresser, hitting with a crash. The pistol flew from his grip. He felt a screeching pain in his back. For a moment he couldn't remember how to move, and horror filled him.

Greg ran into the living room.

With a yell that came from deep in his chest, Mike heaved himself up and ran, stumbling, after him. Greg was doing something at the back of the TV. There was a flash of white in his hand, the flash that Mike had seen disappearing into the pocket.

Greg froze and Mike did too. Both chests heaved. Their breathing resounded in the room.

Mike wanted to rush him again, but he was out-weighed. Every move sliced his back like a laser. One more blow and he could be down for good. He had no clue where his pistol was. His eyes raked the room, searching for a way to delay, to immobilize, and fastened on the Christmas lights draped on the palm tree.

Moving like a bullet, Mike dived for the string of lights. He yanked the length of cord off and in the same motion looped it around Greg.

Cursing, Greg tried to fight free. Mike pulled on the ends, toppling him to the floor with a yell. Bulbs snapped and shattered under Greg's weight, spraying them both with the glass.

Oblivious to the gashes in his hands from the wire and the bulbs, bending away from the ballooning pain in his back, Mike tightened the wires and tied them, imprisoning Greg's arms against his upper body. Then he hurried as best he could around to the back of the TV, spotted the white, saw the pictures that Greg had stuffed inside the set.

Mike had them in his hand and was trying to ease them

287

out without leaving pieces in the TV when Greg threw himself off the floor and at Mike.

But Mike jumped sideways.

The giant loop he had tied in the string of lights caught the corner of the TV. Seeing what was about to happen, Greg screamed, tried to twist away, and lost his balance. An instant after he hit the floor, the TV crashed down on his head.

The phone rang and rang and rang.

CHAPTER SIXTEEN

Lynn slept badly. Mary called it a post-traumatic effect. She'd dream about Greg, bloody and dead, or Greg in her apartment. Sometimes she would switch places with him, and be the broken corpse herself.

Sometimes he wouldn't be in the dream at all, not as himself; but Lynn would know he was in there in some form, because she would snap awake, sweaty and queasy, just as she did with the more obvious dreams.

Then she would lie there waiting for her heart to slow. Eventually she would start to relax, as her mind and body remembered they no longer had to be on guard.

Generally she would fall back to sleep after ten or fifteen minutes, but when she didn't, she got up.

If it was after five, she got into her sweats, drove to the Broome Club, and let the hypnotic pumping of the fake stairs lull her ... then lay in the quiet lighting of the massage room as Elizabeth stretched her, before she stepped under a hot shower.

If it was still night, she put on a coat over her nightgown and went out on her terrace.

It calmed her to feel the sharp chill on her face. To look out at the water and the lights and know she had her home back. And her career; just this week the show was back on the air live, her face presentable with concealer and makeup. Soon she'd be talking to QTV about a new pilot-taping date.

When she was out here in the dark, it was hard not to think of Mike Delano.

She pictured him as he had been the last time she'd seen

him, just before he got out of the hospital. He'd been moving with difficulty, his trunk taped and corseted for his broken ribs. His hands and face were healing, but scabs and bruises lingered.

That day when she'd gone to visit, bringing apples and hard candy, another policeman had been there, making awkward jokes about hospital gowns. The man had appeared intimidated by her, and they had both more or less ignored her. She'd stayed twenty minutes, then left, feeling oddly annoyed.

Her reasons for seeing Mike seemed to be over. But she kept remembering.

She remembered with aching clarity that horrible night she'd come out here and found Chip.

Her grief, her crying.

She remembered her body and Mike's finding meeting places automatically, as if every motion and breath had occurred before, often. She could taste his lips still. She could feel herself straining to be closer.

And she could recall just as acutely the flickering impulses like a defective headlight, the frantic push-pull of her feelings.

In the weeks since Greg's death, as her world had begun to knit, she had confronted that memory and asked herself the same merciless questions she asked others on camera.

Was she genuinely attracted to Mike? Was she in love with him, or getting close? Or had she reacted out of need, so devastated emotionally that she simply craved the connection?

Why had she short-circuited whatever might have happened that night? Because of her stress, the long-term or that night's? Or were those her honest feelings surfacing, yanking her back from a mistake, from being false to Mike and to herself?

She truly had no answers.

How did Mike feel? Did he care for her? Or had he just

rolled with the moment, needing release or escape himself?

She didn't have any answers for him either.

Once the news of what had happened had reached her at Booboo and Angela's, she had hurried to the hospital, and had visited him there every few days. But aside from an occasional card or call, there seemed no justification to continue the contact; and Mike himself hadn't seemed to want her to.

So she could only conclude, when his face or voice or, for God's sake, his hands or mouth surfaced in her recollections, that it was because of gratitude.

He had almost died protecting her.

She owed him her survival.

How could she expect *not* to be haunted by a jungle of emotions over such a person?

And after all she had been through, invaded intimately in so many ways, did she have any love to give now that wasn't a shriveled parody of the real thing?

It was only right to protect Mike, as he had protected her. Protect him from herself.

Mike couldn't work anything like a full shift yet – couldn't sit that long, for one thing, in a car or a desk chair, or even over a bowl of tool-chest chili at Nancy Jean's.

But he couldn't stand to do nothing either. He saw too many people who did that, and they ended up crawling back inside themselves and getting crazy.

The administrative investigation into Greg's death had cleared him of any fault. But when you were a cop and someone had died, and you had been the only one there, it didn't matter what else had or hadn't happened, or who anointed you blame-free. The ghosts were there waiting for you if you invited them in.

So every afternoon, when the boredom got past intense and into frightening, he'd pull himself painfully into a clean sweatshirt and take the T to work. He'd nod and wave off the what-the-hell-are-you-doing-heres, and prowl around his desk and the files.

He'd done that today, and made what had become his nightly trip to Nancy Jean's, as he seemed to need to sit in the midst of lights and conversation. He was home now, checking his mailbox, and among the usual bills and flyers was another card from Lynn, this one with a preprinted Thank You on the front instead of Get Well.

I owe you a debt of gratitude for your dedicated help, she had written inside. *I hope you're continuing to feel better.* It was signed, *Best, Lynn.*

That made him briefly furious. *Best, Lynn?* Best what?

He went up and opened his door and gingerly collapsed on the made bed and went through the rest of the mail.

He had kept his promise to himself. He had made it his main mental project to move away from this case, and from Lynn and his feelings about her. With every painful day, he was reminded of why he should not have let it get this far; he hurt in his heart as much as in his side and shoulder and every other goddamn place that was either bruised or cut or cracked.

He didn't know what Lynn thought or wanted, only that she'd had plenty of opportunity to respond to the overture he'd plainly put out there. Since she hadn't, since she was dutifully showing her deep thanks and nothing more, he would be an asshole to stand around waiting for more. Whether the problem was indifference or psychic injury or empty spaces, he didn't need it.

People said cops were a different breed from humans. Maybe that was true, but celebrities ... you just couldn't goddamn tell what was down there, what was real and what was missing.

He glared at the card. He opened it and read the message again, the neat handwriting, the antiseptic two sentences.

Best, Lynn.

He spun it toward the wastebasket, and didn't look to see if it had gone in.

On the second Tuesday in March, just before three-thirty in the afternoon, Pam brought an envelope to Lynn in her office.

Kara came in as she was opening it.

'I'm reorganizing the tape library,' Kara said. 'Do you want me to – What's the matter?'

Lynn's face had gone bluish pale. Kara hurried to look at the note she was still staring at.

She read the typewritten lines aloud over Lynn's shoulder: *You thought this was over, didn't you? Go look in your car.*

The Lexus was just as Lynn had left it that morning, locked, in its spot in the parking garage.

Her fingers trembling, Lynn pressed the knob on the key, and heard the dull click as the doors unlocked. She opened the driver's side; Kara went to the passenger side.

They peered at the seats, the floor. They looked under the seats, in the glove box, the console box, and the door pockets.

Nothing.

Lynn popped the trunk switch and ran around and raised the lid. There was a towel inside, not hers, covering something, and she lifted it.

Nicky lay there, dead, his tongue out, the angle of his head showing the broken neck.

She screamed and screamed, and heard Kara's screams too, and couldn't separate them, and couldn't stop.

When the police came, Kara was in the bathroom being sick. Lynn met them in her office, two men she hadn't seen before.

Her hair was wet with sweat and tears. She was chilled and shaky and couldn't quite focus.

She didn't know where to start, so she simply answered their questions.

Yes, she was certain she'd left her car locked. Nobody else had a key. No, she didn't know who could have written the note.

Yes, these kinds of things had happened before.

The two men waited for her to continue.

'It was a man I went out with briefly last fall. He was sending me stuff, harassing me at work. He killed a wild chipmunk that used to climb up on my terrace and eat the bird seed. He canceled my credit cards. He broke in and knocked me out. It went on and on.'

She stopped, drew a shaky breath. 'There were security guards here all the time. Mike Delano was working on it too, when he could. I tried to call him an hour ago –'

'He's on disability leave,' one of the policemen said.

'I know. He was hurt in a fight with the man I'm talking about –'

'The one who injured Detective Delano? But he was killed.'

Lynn could only nod.

Kara wouldn't talk to her or anyone.

Finally Lynn left her in the ladies' room and poured a glass of water from her office carafe and went into her briefcase for her pills.

But Tylenol-with-codeine wasn't what she needed. She stuffed them back.

She sat in her desk chair and hugged herself. Her insides burned and rolled. She shivered as if with flu. The tremors came and went, came and went.

She went down to the drugstore and bought an over-the-counter tranquilizer and took four.

* * *

When she'd called the police station, she'd been told Mike usually came in afternoons. His machine had answered his home phone.

She got a cab and went over there to wait for Mike to come in.

Taking the side chair by Mike's desk, Lynn was swamped with sudden emotion. Not a rarity on this day; it had been a monsoon so far. But this was a new one, this ache of recollection.

She could almost smell the hot dogs. She remembered watching Mike stride to this desk, swinging past the others with a practiced grace, carrying the lunch in a small brown bag. She saw the Tufts sweatshirt. Recalled the startling difference after the suit and tie of the day before.

She remembered his intensity, the perpetual frown, the dark hair falling over his eyes. The crowded and yet impersonal desktop, as if there never had been time to fill it with his own favorites. Nor time to *have* favorites.

He'd been argumentative that day. Not that day; he was contentious all the time, she just hadn't known it yet. He'd challenged and prodded her; she remembered them spitting anger at each other a couple of times. But in the end she'd felt something in his office that had been long gone: safe.

She yearned to feel that again.

Mike was there in the flesh suddenly, coming over. He had seen her. His face didn't change at all; she might have been sitting there every day of his life.

His body bent slightly to the side, but he moved well.

He had another little brown bag, wet in spots, and the hot dog smell became real.

'What's up?' he asked, lowering himself carefully into his chair.

The tears that had been swallowed back all day burst forth. The question was enough. Or not just the question; was that it? The police station, the chair, the stupid steaming wet bag of hot dogs. Her shrieking awareness of the journey from then to now.

'It's Greg,' she said. 'He's alive.'

Mike shook his head. 'No, he's not.'

'He must be, Mike. He's after me again.'

A change occurred as Mike listened to her recite the details that had slightly lost their power to sicken her, only because she had to keep repeating them. His face lost something, or gained something; she couldn't pinpoint it, and didn't really try. She was concentrating on choking out her story.

He let her finish. He never looked away from her eyes.

When she was done, she asked, 'What was the exact cause of Greg's death? I don't think I ever knew.'

Mike blinked. 'How about brains leaking out of skull?'

She looked away. 'So there's no doubt in your mind that he was killed.'

'None.'

'Then –'

'Who has a key to your car?'

'Nobody. I keep the extra in my desk at work. There's a small one in my purse. Lexus calls it a purse key. There's also a valet key. That's kept in the car, in the console box.'

'What about Kara's apartment? You have a key?'

'Yes,' Lynn said.

'Who else does?'

'A couple of her sisters, I think.'

His lunch bag was still on the desk, unopened. He looked at it, then turned back to Lynn without touching it.

'Who knows about what was happening to you before?'

'A lot of people.'

'Name them,' he said, pulling over a legal pad.

'Kara. Mary and Gideon Eli. My boss and his wife. My brother and sister-in-law. A lot of the Channel 3 people. Some of the QTV people.'

'That's the list?'

Lynn shrugged. 'Police and security guards. People at my health club. Some of my neighbors know a bit.'

She watched him write. 'Why do you want to know? You think it's someone copying what Greg did?'

He didn't look up. 'I know it is.'

'Oh, do you?' Lynn snapped, suddenly furious.

Now he did look up, and his eyes were their most opaque black. 'You aren't seriously going to try to tell me I don't know a dead man when I see one.'

'You probably do. But –'

'Not probably. I haven't been doing this job all these years so I can look down at a stretcher case and think it's a stiff. The freak was *dead*, Lynn, dead as road kill. His brains were watering his carpet.'

Mike pulled himself out of his chair, went to a cabinet, and brought back two folders. He slid pictures and forms out onto the desk.

'Coroner's report. Crime scene shots. Pathology shot. Cremation certificate.'

Lynn concentrated on what wasn't bloodied and tried not to dwell on the rest. She held her stomach. It was Greg; there was no doubt. She even knew the shirt.

'If someone is doing that stuff to you again,' Mike said, 'I don't know what the answer is, but it *isn't* that the same shithead jumped out of the morgue drawer and put his pants on and came after you.'

He ripped the page off the legal pad and spun it around for her to see. 'Your answer's here.'

The gesture said, And don't count on me helping you find it.

Not knowing what else to do, Lynn read the sheet over.

She wanted to run out of there, away from the rows of desks and the seemingly uninterested rows of detectives.

But at the same time, something held her – the remembered balm of safety, or the plain fact of the police station?

No; it was simply, really.

She put the sheet back on the desk.

She had just been shocked into immobility by the fact that she was now stranded.

Outside, she stood uncertainly on the sidewalk. She felt like a lighted target.

She wasn't sure whether it was Mike himself she had depended on, or what he represented: the official designation of what was happening to her as a crime with a villain, and not some shadowy problem of hers.

But it didn't matter, because she didn't seem to have either anymore.

'Your answer's here...'

'If someone is doing that stuff to you again...'

If.

Kara's apartment was more empty than it could have been if there was nothing in it at all.

No paw clicks on the floor. No snuffling nose at her feet.

She'd been home for an hour, just long enough to answer calls and deal with the mess the locksmith had left, and wonder what to do with Nicky's things.

She went to the living room window and watched the early evening traffic without seeing it.

Her bell rang. It was Lynn. Kara buzzed her in.

'How are you doing?' Lynn asked.

'Not too bad.'

'You don't have to –'

'Okay. I feel like shit.'

'I know,' Lynn said quietly. 'I'm so, so sorry. He was the best dog in the world.'

'What are you going to do?'

'I don't know. Leave the country? I don't know what to do, or even what to think.'

Kara asked, 'Is Greg really dead?'

'Yes. I saw the pictures of his body.'

Kara's observational instinct, dulled by grief, prodded her. Lynn's eyes were foggy. Her gestures were a drop out of synch.

Kara knew those signs. She had seen them years ago, watched them escalate at the time.

'Then what is going on?' Kara asked.

'I don't *know*. Mike Delano says someone has to be copying what Greg did.'

Kara turned away. Sick anger boiled. Her work, her dog, her *life* ... and she had to sit helpless while Lynn parroted a power-happy detective, and gobbled God knew what drugs, and screwed things up still more.

She spun back to Lynn. 'We were all done with this! Greg was hounding you and beating you up, and then he wasn't because he was dead! *Isn't that right?*'

'Yes.'

'I've been in your corner a lot of years. Haven't I? Lynn and Kara, the team. I did everything you wanted, abided by your decisions whether I agreed with them or not, and we helped each other look good.'

Lynn started to respond, but Kara stopped her. 'It's time to be honest. Are you in some trouble nobody knows about? Who and what are you involved with? Are you an addict, Lynn?'

'*No!*'

'We always tiptoe around this, but we can't now!' Kara shouted. 'Is there extortion going on? Does someone know you're on drugs, and are they doing this to you?'

Lynn was shaking, but she faced Kara. 'I'm not involved in anything I haven't long since told you about. I'm a professional trying to do her job.'

'Then how do you explain –'

'I have no explanation!'

* * *

Mike usually stayed at work for the whole afternoon; it was better than anything else he was currently able to do. But after Lynn left, he found he hadn't the tolerance for the noise and activity.

He went outside and, without knowing it, paused on the sidewalk in roughly the same spot Lynn had stood earlier as she counted her rapidly disappearing choices.

The day was ironically, mockingly, lovely.

He wanted to put his fist through something.

He began walking. It wasn't easy, but neither was it as tough as it had been, when every step hacked at his side. Eventually he got on the T and rode awhile.

In midafternoon he found himself at the waterfront.

It was active for a weekday. Gulls swooped for treats kids offered. There were strollers and bikes, and a couple of ice cream carts. He saw a hot dog vendor and thought briefly of the untouched bag in the trash back at the station, but still didn't feel like having anything.

He stopped by a bench and leaned on it. He was very aware of Lynn's building down the street. Her apartment practically emitted a magnetic signal.

He had thought he was dealing with the relatively simple matter of deciding not to pursue a personal relationship.

But as of today, the situation had taken on layers and corners and hidden places.

He almost didn't want to know which of the possible explanations of what might or might not be happening was correct.

He wasn't sure he had a choice.

He straightened and walked some more, consciously heading away from Lynn's building. He strolled along past shops, taking it slowly, the only way he could keep moving after all this now-unaccustomed exercise.

He thought of the list he'd made for Lynn. She'd left it on his desk.

He stopped and faced his reflection in the window of a T-shirt place. What did you expect her to do? he asked it. After everything that's gone down, is she supposed to nod and grab a pencil and hunker down and analyze this list of her closest friends and relatives and decide which one has elected to replace her tormentor?

He made himself stand there and continue to face himself as he posed the next question, the one that had been festering all afternoon.

Is it her? Has she replaced the freak herself?

Does she need attention – from her friends and coworkers and family? From the police, from him?

Is it some crazy big-time celebrity behavior?

Could she be disturbed enough not to realize she's doing it?

He stayed there for a long time, watching his own impassive face.

'Take some time off,' Vicky Belinski said. 'Get a good rest.'

Lynn tightened her grip on the phone. 'And then?'

'Then we'll see.'

Lynn was way beyond polite games. 'Please spell that out, Vicky. I want to know what QTV's intentions are. Do you foresee a pilot in the next couple of months? Or are you postponing it indefinitely?'

There was silence, then a Californian sigh. 'Indefinitely.'

In the following days, Kara came to work and did her job, and Lynn did the same, and that was the sum total of their communication.

Lynn got through it by slipping on her public persona like a raincoat. Smile, shake hands. Take the on-air demeanor and wear it. Let it help her pretend to be all right.

She didn't dare *not* pretend. Didn't dare be vulnerable.

Dennis called her in for a talk that echoed some of what Kara had thrown at her: Was Lynn in some kind of drug trouble? Why Kara's dog? Was this a vendetta involving her *and* Kara?

Only at night, alone, could she slump into the depressed, frightened, suspicious woman that was the true core of the amazing inflatable television talker.

She kept taking the drugstore tranquilizers, as few as she could.

On Friday she had to go to the dentist. She considered canceling the appointment, but didn't; she had put off this root canal far too long.

Physical discomfort was a sort of relief. It replaced the other kind. And she knew how to deal with the physical, knew its aspects and finiteness.

She had to take her relief where she could.

'You'll have pain tonight,' the dentist said when he was done. He was a compassionate man who hated to hurt anyone, and tended to have an even more exaggerated idea of people's pain thresholds than they did. 'I'm giving you some Percodan samples, and a prescription for more.'

'No, thanks,' Lynn said.

'Take them. You'll need them.'

'I made this appointment for a Friday on purpose,' she said, half her face not moving well. 'I don't have to work till Monday. I'll be okay by then.'

Dr Gurian shook his balding head. 'By eight tonight I'll be eating lobster in Wellfleet. I won't even be back on call until Monday morning. Are you going to ruin my weekend by making me worry about your pain?'

Lynn said, 'You don't need to worry.'

'I'll worry. Take the pills home.'

The dentist was right. By the time he was cracking open his

302

lobster, Lynn was on her couch with an ice pack. That didn't do anything except numb her jaw only as long as she kept the bag pressed painfully to her cheek. After a while she gave that up and took more aspirin, remembering how Mike had forced it on her during one of her headaches.

Like the hot dog smell, the acrid taste brought him starkly to life.

It was strange how many things did.

She didn't know if it was Mike himself she missed, or the mock comfort of having a person to call when something happened, a procedure to follow.

But every time she thought of Mike, she had to think of his list. And that was so hard. She would scan it mentally, and try to picture those on it taking pleasure in her pain, and give up.

The only bearable part of the list was that hazy possibility of some unbalanced person at Channel 3 she barely knew, acting out resentment. The tabloid shows were full of such cases: some poor ill person with a scenario and an agenda, and a scapegoat.

She kept thinking of the video and sound people, the floor staff, the telephone operators, and wondering who might be Greg's imitator.

Or it could be someone in the police department. Plenty of police had access to the necessary information.

She had called Helene Skolnik, the private investigator, and left a message. She had thought about getting Stricker guards again, on her own this time, to personally protect her; but how much did she dare increase the visibility of her nightmare at the station?

The aspirin wasn't helping.

She thought of the Percodans in her purse.

Her mouth really hurt.

Sleep would help, but she was sleeping so restlessly. Her pain would make the night still more of an ordeal.

Percodan would have a relaxing effect as well as helping the pain, making sleep more attainable.

She found her purse, broke open one of the sample packs, took two pills with water, then one more.

At a few minutes past ten she was getting ready for bed, her mouth a little less hellish, when Helene Skolnik called back.

'Sorry about the hour, but you said it was important.'

Lynn told her about Nicky.

'But the man is dead?'

'Yes. The police think someone is copying him.' Between her impeded tongue and the medication, her speech was indistinct.

'I'm having trouble understanding you.'

'I had dental work today.'

'I don't think I can help you,' Helene said after a pause. 'There's still nothing for me to work with, if the police already did what I'd do and came up empty. And the situation is … bizarre, to say the least.'

'Yes. That's why I need help,' Lynn said, refusing to respond to yet one more implication that it wasn't just the situation that was bizarre.

CHAPTER SEVENTEEN

Pam came into Lynn's office to collect lunch money from Kara and Lynn.

Lynn got her handbag, found just two singles in her wallet, and remembered she'd put the envelope of cash she'd withdrawn from the bank machine into her brief-case. She leaned across her desk to get the case and reached in for the envelope.

Something raked her hand ferociously. She screamed, yanked it out. Blood bubbled out, so much blood, all over everything in seconds.

For an instant Pam and Kara were frozen, staring. Then Pam yelled, and Kara grabbed a wad of Kleenex, ran to Lynn and pressed it to her hand.

'What *happened*?' Pam cried.

With her free hand Lynn grabbed the bloody briefcase and threw it down. She lifted it by the bottom, dumping out the contents.

A book, folder, papers, a clothes brush, pens ... and something metal with white plastic ...

'Isn't that a Cuisinart blade?' Pam said. 'God, Lynn, it's as sharp as a razor!'

'You're lucky,' the emergency room doctor said as a nurse cleaned Lynn's arm.

Lynn felt unbalanced laughter rise in her throat. Whatever diabolical act she survived, there was always someone telling her she was lucky. She amended the laugh to a cough.

'Another inch,' the doctor went on, 'and we're in artery country. This is something to thank God for. You could

305

have exsanguinated faster than you could get here.'

His name was Turco, and he was the same big-chested, open and cheery man who had treated her when she'd been punched. He looked curiously down at her as he prepared to stitch the jagged line that crossed half her palm.

'Run this through for me one more time,' he said.

Lynn had been shaking off and on, and now her teeth had begun to chatter. She said, 'Could it w-wait until you're d-done?'

'No. The distraction will help. Lidocaine, please. Easy, Ms Marchette. So. You got cut with what? A sickle?'

'The blade from a C-Cuisinart.'

'Sorry for the stupid jokes,' the doctor said. 'I tend to do that when I don't know what to say. And I sure don't right now, having Lynn Marchette back here again with another violent type of injury.'

Lynn watched her hand as he worked on it, not really focusing, as numb throughout as in her anesthetized palm. She knew the blessed cold frozenness would pass soon, but for now all she wanted was not to think too much.

'The police brought you last time,' the doctor said. 'Now it was your assistant. We're all supposed to not talk about the fact that it's you.'

He put the black-threaded needle through the skin next to the cut.

'What does that all add up to? I'll tell you what,' he said. 'A domestic violence situation.'

Now the laughter did come out. Lynn couldn't stop it, and hardly cared. But it quickly became crying. The nurse turned sad dark eyes to her, and held out a tissue box.

'You want to lay off?' the nurse said to the doctor.

'I'm sorry.' He looked genuinely upset. 'I guess I'm only making this worse. I just hate to fix women up so they can go back to whoever's breaking them and get broken again. It's that simple.'

* * *

306

Booboo came to the hospital and insisted on bringing her back to Salem, which Lynn agreed to on the condition that they stop at her apartment first.

She packed clothes for a couple of days, and her remaining sample Percodans.

Riding next to her brother across the Tobin Bridge, Lynn felt very helpless. She always drove this bridge herself, went to her brother and sister-in-law's and left when she wished. Now she was the person being driven. The feeling added to her panic.

Booboo said, 'Was the blade from your Cuisinart?'

'Yes. I looked as soon as I walked in.'

Her brother cursed. 'Then they got into your apartment.'

'I don't think so. The blade could have been taken a long time ago.'

'But we don't know. I can't deal with you being so unprotected. You can't keep changing locks. What are you going to do? You won't leave the area. You won't stay with me and Angela. You won't move to another –'

'I don't want to just sit and wait to be hurt again either. I'm convinced. I'm going to arrange for someone to protect me.'

'Not that damn detective!'

'No. I'll hire someone. I want an investigator. I want someone who can find out what in God's name is going on, and stop it.'

They were turning into the driveway of the house. The crocuses were up, fat clusters of Easter colors.

Booboo lifted her overnight bag out of his trunk. 'There's some people I think we should talk to,' he said.

Arbor Investigations had their offices in a smoked-glass building in Worcester. Lynn and Booboo waited in expensive wing chairs in the reception room. There were original oils of Parisian street scenes on two walls, and an arrangement of award plaques on a third. The fourth was clear glass. Behind it was a receptionist, and behind her three women and a man worked at terminals in front of several closed office doors.

The receptionist's phone buzzed. She led Lynn and Booboo into one of the offices, where two men stood by a desk.

'Mr Craig Reeb and Mr Dominick Speranza,' she said.

'I'm Lawrence Marchette. This is my sister, Lynn.'

The men eyed Lynn's bandaged left hand and shook her right.

'Of course, I've seen your program many times,' Reeb, the older man, said. He was about sixty, with graying brown hair and military posture. Speranza had the deceptively relaxed air Lynn had grown used to seeing in police officers. No wasted talk, a gaze that missed nothing.

They seemed to be just as her brother had said, the kind of discreet professional investigators banks put their trust in, his bank and many others.

She was starting to feel a tiny bit less helpless.

'Our understanding is that you're experiencing a harassment problem,' Reeb said. 'Why don't you fill us in?'

Lynn pointed to her injured hand. 'This happened today. Twenty stitches. I cut it on the blade from a food processor. Someone put it in my briefcase, right where I'd hit it when I reached in.'

'Where were you?' Speranza asked.

'In my office at the station.'

He wrote in a small lined notebook.

'Former policeman?' Lynn asked him.

'Retired six months ago.' He looked at her with respect.

Reeb asked, 'What else?'

'A week ago a note was delivered to me in my office. A security guard had found it. The note said to look in my car. My assistant and I ran down to the station garage.

308

What we found was – was the dead body of her little dog, in the trunk.'

All the horror washed in. She had to make a fierce effort not to break down.

Reeb asked gently, 'You live alone?'

'Yes.'

Booboo cleared his throat. 'I've nagged her and nagged her to come stay with me and my wife, or let me stay at her place. She's stubborn as a goat. But something's got to be done now.'

'I would say so.' Reeb had been sitting at the desk, but now he stood and came around.

'Have you handled situations like this before?' Lynn asked.

'Yes, ma'am.'

'Then you think you can help me?'

'Oh, we probably can help you quite a bit.'

'Thank God,' Lynn breathed.

Booboo put his arm around her. 'What did I tell you?'

Reeb pushed a buzzer and the receptionist opened the door. 'What would you like?' she asked. 'Coffee? Soda?'

'Nothing, thanks,' Lynn said.

'Have something,' the investigator urged. 'We have a lot of information to get from you. It'll take awhile. Wet your whistle.'

'All right. Thank you. Coffee with just milk, please.'

When the receptionist left, Speranza began writing again. 'I'm noting the events you described, and the times and dates.' He turned the notebook for Lynn to see. 'Is this correct?'

She read it. 'Yes.'

'Any other acts?'

'Not in this series.'

'You were harassed before?' the former policeman asked.

Lynn turned to Booboo. 'Didn't you tell them?'

309

'Not about the stopping and starting again, not precisely.'

The receptionist came in with the drinks, and Lynn sipped gratefully at the coffee.

Speranza went to a new page. 'When were these other acts?'

Lynn massaged her aching wrist, strained from trying to keep pressure off her hand.

'They started in October and ended in February. The man who had been harassing me was killed on February 16.'

There was a beat of quiet. Speranza said, 'So we're talking about harassment from two different people.'

'Yes,' Lynn said.

'You've been to the police?'

She sighed and began to answer, but Booboo did it for her.

'The police have been useless. We only have their word that they've made any effort at all –'

'You *only* have the word of the Boston Police Department?'

Booboo shook his head. 'Hear me out. This fellow, this detective, was taking advantage of my sister's position –'

Lynn put a restraining hand on her brother's shoulder. 'That's what you feel. I don't agree. Mike doesn't even know about what happened today. But it's not our opinions they want to hear.' She turned to the investigators. 'I guess I should start at the beginning.'

'Wouldn't hurt,' Speranza said.

Her hand was a burning, hurting weight in her lap. She was exhausted and dizzy from hunger, and the hot coffee had made the unhealed surgical site in her mouth come alive, sending darts through to the back of her skull.

But she made herself tell it all, in order, her professional persona working to clearly display all the puzzle pieces despite her turmoil.

She stumbled over the sexual details in a way that she never would have if Booboo hadn't been there.

At some point as she talked, the disturbing fact penetrated that Speranza had stopped taking notes. But she kept on, just as she did when a show wasn't going the way she'd planned it but had to go somewhere.

When she finished, there was quiet for a full minute.

Reeb said, 'This is very mysterious. This pattern of harassment beginning again when the perpetrator is dead. I must ask: What's your gut feeling about what's going on?'

Lynn rubbed her arm. 'The only answer is that someone who knows what was happening is imitating it.'

'Someone close to you.' It wasn't a question.

'I don't want it to be,' she said. 'I want it to be some anonymous somebody who's unbalanced and has a grudge. But, yes, the logical conclusion is that it's someone close.'

'What do your coworkers think?'

'Those *are* the people close to me.'

There was another minute of silence, and then Reeb asked, 'Who's your immediate boss there at Channel 3?'

'The general manager, Dennis Orrin.'

'What's his evaluation?'

Lynn's stomach turned over. She had to be honest. 'He ... suggested that because of some past personal problems of mine, this could be a vendetta.'

Speranza leaned toward her. 'Personal problems such as what?'

'Drugs. I *don't* have that problem now, but he –'

'Why would he say that, then?'

Lynn sighed. 'A long time ago, I sometimes had to depend on medication for severe pain from dental problems. Dennis knew about it. I guess it would come to his mind now ...'

Speranza and Reeb looked at each other.

Reeb said, 'Pardon us just a second.'

* * *

In the next office, the two investigators leaned against an empty desk.

'What do you think?' the older man asked.

'I'm not positive. But if I had to guess –'

'You do.'

'Then my guess is, the first set of acts was real, and now that the guy's dead, she's stringing it out herself.'

'That's what I get too.'

'So what is she? A celebrity nut case? Needs the sympathy? What?'

'She seems distraught,' Reeb said, 'but not psycho. Could she be pulling something to get a program out of it?'

Speranza nodded slowly. 'Maybe. Maybe the real threat ended before it was convenient for her. Before the cameras could get there.'

'Can't see her killing her friend's dog, though.'

'Who knows what she really thinks of the friend?'

'True.'

'I mean, Christ, she has nothing to show us that points away from her. She has all the keys involved, and the blade that cut her came from her own apartment. Doesn't sound like the Channel 3 brass buys it. My only question is, why did she come to us?'

Reeb straightened. 'Her brother is beside himself worrying. He probably forced her hand.'

'Hold your horses,' Booboo said. 'An hour ago you said you could help. Now all of a sudden you're not available.'

'Not for a job this complicated. We were given to understand it was a simple matter of harassment. We aren't set up to –'

Booboo's face and neck were flushed. 'It *is* a simple matter of harassment.'

The older man said placatingly, 'I know it seems that way to you and Ms Marchette. But after hearing all the circumstances, we have to conclude that the case is too diffuse –'

'A much longer-term project than we thought,' Speranza said. 'Impossible to schedule into our workload now.'

Booboo started to argue more, but Lynn interrupted. 'Don't waste your energy.'

'Well, this is an insult. The bank gives these guys a lot of business –'

'And it still will. They're obviously good. But they don't want to work on my case. They don't believe me. Come on, Boo. We're leaving.'

In the car, headed back to Booboo and Angela's house, she finally broke down.

'It's the same as before,' she sobbed. 'Someone is after me, and nobody can help.'

'Those bastards,' Booboo said. 'I shouldn't have let you drag me out there. Where the hell do they get the gall to treat a famous television personality like slop?'

'It's not just them. It's everyone. There's no explanation, nothing is believable, so they don't believe anything. They back away.'

She was out of Kleenex, and her nose and eyes were streaming. She raked through her bag for more, and there wasn't any, and she cried harder, big howling sobs.

Her brother's own eyes were filling. He draped a huge arm around her shoulders and pulled her sideways and held her tight there as he drove.

Lynn lay awake in the guest room. Night sounds wafted through the screen.

Angela had worked her magic with the room decoration. The bed was a fluffy tumble of daisy print; the sheer yellow curtains lifted in the breeze. The nightstand held every lotion and potion.

313

But Lynn was barely aware of any of it. Sleep was miserably distant. Her hand felt like a catcher's mitt. Her arm and shoulder muscles ached as if she'd been in a car accident. Two Percodans had made no difference.

Her mind rolled with the events and words of the day. She needed strength so badly now, and it wasn't there for her. It was dribbling away as if through a pinhole.

'Nothing is believable, so they don't believe anything.'

Her own words.

'What's your gut feeling?'

She remembered the expression on the investigator's face: You probably can't convince me, but just for the hell of it, try.

'Someone close to you ...'

'Yes ...'

Lynn shifted onto her side and rested her hand on the high, hard pillow Angela had given her for elevation.

She'd been over and over that ground. Was she supposed to actually consider whether people like Kara and Dennis were trying to make her bleed to death?

But she had to consider it.

It almost made more sense to think what the investigators obviously did: that nobody was doing anything to Lynn but Lynn.

The window was at the foot of the bed. She heard a rustling just outside, the soft squeak of an animal, and she sat up and eased down to see. But there was nothing, not even sounds of it going away.

She sat at the bottom of the bed and breathed deeply, trying to calm the tremors that had seized her all this awful night as she groped and struggled with the jumble in her head.

But the sweet earthy air couldn't chase the poison that was at the bottom of this: the idea that the investigators were right.

Her new torturer was a phantom.

A being no more tangible than the animal she'd thought was outside the window just now.

She lay back down as the tears came again.

Could that possibly, possibly be? Was she delusional?

Was it remotely conceivable that *she* could have done these things after Greg died?

Cut herself?

Killed Nicky?

She'd aired shows on rape victims and murder witnesses who suddenly remembered decades later the crime they'd totally blocked. Would she herself do that, wake up in ten years and remember these acts? Did that happen to doers as well as victims?

Maybe she should find out.

Hello, Mary? Is it possible to torture yourself and attempt suicide and murder a dog without knowing you did it? Oh, no reason, I just wondered. Have a good day.

Lying there, Lynn began to laugh. It was the same crazy noise that had erupted in the emergency room, and it turned as fast to crying.

The tears ran down sideways and soaked the daisy comforter.

'I don't know what to do,' Kara told Mary on the phone. 'I'm terrified for Lynn and me, and for the show. I even had to convince Dennis *I* wasn't involved in whatever this is.'

'What are your options?' Mary asked.

'I could look for another job, I guess. But even though I'm furious at her, I don't want to abandon Lynn. And it's not as if great producing jobs are out there waiting.'

'I'm not hearing that you want another job,' Mary said, lowering the phone to check the clock. She had five minutes before her next patient. 'You've always loved this one. But you seem to feel the show is being jeopardized by Lynn's situation.'

'It is. Look what's happened already. We were right on the brink of making the pilot, and we lost it. We're hoping QTV will reschedule the taping at some point, but they won't if Lynn doesn't shape up. Dennis is very nervous about Lynn's judgment right now. And Lynn *is* the show.'

'Can you assume more of the responsibility for making the decisions and organizing the shows? Separate yourself from Lynn's trouble? Sometimes you have to do that with people. Their problems become overwhelming. You can't let them overwhelm you as well.'

'I've thought of making a case to Dennis. Right now Lynn has the last word on program decisions, except for him. I was going to ask to share that.'

'Makes sense,' Mary said.

'It's a slap in Lynn's face.'

'Is it, Kara? Or are you just doing what you must?'

March 21, 1993

Too bad it was her left hand.

I should have allowed for that. I wanted her to be immobile, unable to work or function.

I want to take away pieces of her, force her to live with less and less ... as she has done to me.

I watch her on the screen. She parades around like she owns the world.

She has no sense of what other people have to go through just to make it from one day to the next.

But I am making sure she understands that better and better.

Understands that what she takes away can be taken from her too.

After two days at the house, Lynn told Booboo, 'I'm going back to my apartment.'

'Lynn, you are in danger there!'

'I could be in danger anywhere.'

'In your apartment you're alone and vulnerable. Someone got in.'

'We don't know that,' Lynn said. 'I haven't used my Cuisinart in forever. I wouldn't have noticed the blade missing. And that door is supposed to be impenetrable. I have to go home. I can't work from Salem.'

Booboo said, 'Work isn't the most important –'

'It's important to me. It's practically all I have. And it's protection. If I didn't have the show, I'd be a stationary target in a dark alley.'

'There are other detective agencies.'

Lynn shook her head. 'I'm not going through that humiliation again.'

'Could you work from another apartment?'

Lynn looked at him. 'Another apartment in Boston? I can barely manage just to exist and do the show, and hope QTV doesn't give up completely on the syndication. I can't go looking for an apartment.'

Booboo tapped the coffee table. 'What if I found you one? And moved all your clothes and gear? A safer apartment, with no terrace, no glass door. No lock that every Tom, Dick, and Harry has a key to. Let me try. Just let me give it a shot.'

March 22, 1993

I'm going to get her off the air.

Then I'll have my scrap of peace. I won't have to see her, hear her, either near me or on television. I won't have to watch everyone fawning over this creature, this thief who steals what you treasure and then goes on, flapping it in your face.

She asks for sympathy because she is alone.

She doesn't know what alone is.

I know.

317

I am among people all the time, but I am truly alone.

Soon Lynn will know what alone is. People are staying away from her. I am making sure that continues.

No one knows how I feel. They think I'm fond of Lynn.

I can't go on much longer being who I have to be as well as who I am. Some days it is so hard to keep them separate.

Pilgrim Trust kept a furnished one-bedroom on Gloucester Street. It happened to be unused at the moment, and wasn't committed until the end of June.

Booboo had hired the bank's lock consultant to work on the apartment and her car and the new keys went only to Lynn and himself. He insisted they each carry the keys on them at all times. Her home phone was set to forward calls to the new place. He'd gotten wardrobe boxes and moved all her clothes. By Sunday the switch was almost done. There was nothing still to go over but her plants, and she loaded those into a carton herself, having sent her brother back to Salem after repeated calls from Angela.

Mike Delano arrived just as she was locking up, balancing the carton.

He pointed to her bandaged hand. 'Why didn't you tell me?'

Lynn said, 'That's an idiotic question. What good was it to tell you when Kara's dog was killed?'

Instead of answering, he said, 'I was just at the hospital for physical therapy. I ran into Frank Turco. He asked me what the hell was with you.'

Lynn shifted the carton to drop her keys in her sweater pocket. She started toward the elevator.

'When you find out,' she said, 'would you let me know?'

* * *

'There's no place to park around here,' Mike complained. 'It just took me ten minutes to find a space. Where did you park?'

'The garage on the corner. A space in there comes with the apartment.'

He looked around the small living room. It was airy, with a triple window facing the street, but nothing like her waterside showplace. The furniture was hotel-room utilitarian, not cheap, but boring.

She was half turned from him, hanging dish towels, and he took the opportunity to study her. She was definitely a few pounds down even from two weeks ago. Her color was off. The strain of what was happening now showed in new ways that hadn't been there even at the height of the Greg shit. He could see it in the way she held herself and spoke and didn't smile. She looked terribly tired. There was a lot of makeup around her eyes, the hiding kind.

'You don't look good,' Mike said.

She faced him. 'I'm not good. I'm a wreck.'

He was afraid she might ask him to go, so he said, 'Let's go over to Nancy Jean's. She keeps bugging me to bring you back there.'

'Dr Turco said I could have bled to death. That day, I went to see a firm of investigators.'

'And?'

Lynn leaned back in her chair and crossed her arms. She was cold in the hot restaurant. 'First they said they could help. Then they said they couldn't.'

'Why not?'

'It was too complicated, they couldn't fit it into their schedule, and so on. But it was easy to see what they thought. They thought I was nuts. Pretending, or hallucinating.'

'Who were these clowns?'

'Arbor Investigations. They're not clowns. They just weren't convinced.'

Later the music got slow and dreamy. Refilling their coffee cups, Nancy Jean looked from one to the other and said, 'Get up and dance, will you, dears? You're not at a wake, you know.'

'No,' Mike said.

Nancy Jean smiled. 'Do I have to tip over your chair?'

Mike wasn't sure how it had happened, but his arms were around Lynn and they were moving to some very gooey music.

It brought back every day- and night dream that had plagued him these last months. The planes and curves of Lynn's shape were as familiar to him as if she lay beside him every night, though he'd only held her the one time.

He had tried every way not to think of her. When that proved impossible, he had tried to funnel his feelings into his usual role: if it was unacceptable to him to abandon her to her nightmare, the nightmare that it had not taken more than a day for him to understand was real, then he would do what he could to help. Within his current limitations. And without personal involvement.

Now, that resolve seemed to be disappearing with the others.

There was a tremor in his hands. He didn't want her to feel it, so he touched her only lightly. That seemed to make it worse, so he tightened his hold.

The song wasn't ending, didn't sound like it was anywhere near done. He wanted it to be over this second.

And he wanted it never to end.

'Good work,' Mike said, looking at the lock on the door of her new apartment.

'My brother used someone who does a lot of work for

the bank. Booboo and I have the only two keys, and we'll keep them with us. I don't carry mine in my purse anymore.'

'Your brother's too far away to be the only other person who can get in here. You'd better give me one too.'

'I promised him I wouldn't give one to anybody.'

'Tell him what I said. Are you going to talk to another investigator?'

'No.' Lynn took off her sweater. 'You can't imagine how humiliating that was. My brother nearly hit one of them.'

'Well, what the hell *are* you going to do? If you insist on staying in the city –'

'There's no choice. I have to be here for the show. Not doing it isn't an option, so don't even start. QTV already postponed the pilot taping indefinitely.'

'I'm sorry.'

'So am I.'

'I could help you find another investigator.'

She sighed. 'Why would another one believe me when they didn't?' She looked straight at him. 'And you didn't.'

He went into the kitchenette, took a glass, and drank water.

'I didn't know what to think,' he said finally.

Lynn gave a choked laugh. 'That's very supportive, relatively speaking.' Then she heard herself ask: 'What do you think now? Do you believe me now?'

They were several feet apart. Mike took two wide steps and put his arms around her.

'I believe you,' he said, his voice unsteady.

He held her as he had on the dance floor. But they weren't dancing and they weren't in public and she was so sick of playing parts and holding back.

She held him. His lips came down on hers. They were warm and eager, and his breathing was rough.

His hands moved over her. Hers were in his thick hair. She dropped them to his back. There were still some

321

bandages. Her fingers found the spinal furrow and traced it.

He made a sound and pulled her tight against him, and she felt the hard heat of his erection.

It had grown dark in the apartment. The only light came from the kitchenette and the lamplight outside. Lynn watched his shadowed face, and didn't quite know what she was seeing in it.

He held her shoulders. He kissed her again, more restrained, but she felt his hands shaking.

'You're not safe. You shouldn't be alone. I think I should stay with you.'

'You mean,' Lynn said, 'live here?'

'I didn't plan to say that. I haven't thought it through. But, yeah, more or less. Until we find a way out of this.'

He was still holding her shoulders, but suddenly Lynn wasn't sure she liked it.

A chorus was rising in her ears. Booboo and Angela and Kara ...

'*He's taking advantage* ...'

'*You're very useful to him* ...'

'*Aren't you wondering if he has an agenda?*'

Watching her, Mike dropped his hands.

He was so in tune. He could read her, feel her; she'd had that sense from the first conversation at his desk.

An expert at hearing what wasn't said, knowing un-expressed needs.

Had he done that tonight?

Was he pouncing at her most vulnerable moment – her unfamiliar home, her exhausted personal resources, her loneliness, her fear – to utilize a window in her time and emotions and create a need for himself?

Was this all just a way of inserting himself into a very advantageous situation?

The phone rang.

'I was ready to come and look for you,' Booboo said. 'I left three messages.'

322

'I'm sorry. I haven't checked the machine. I went out to eat.'

Listening to her brother, Lynn watched Mike get his jacket and put it on. As she hung up, he was opening the door.

'Lock this behind me right now,' he told her.

CHAPTER EIGHTEEN

Mike resolved to watch her show every day now. If he couldn't be at her place, he could do this. He'd know she was okay for that long, at least.

He didn't want to watch at home, and he didn't want to at Nancy Jean's either, Mike had realized as he headed there Monday morning. Seeing Lynn on TV with that grimy little dance floor right there would make him nuts. His body's memories were torturing him as it was. He didn't need the scene of the crime to add to it.

So he'd changed course and walked to another neighborhood dive, and watched his ladylove's program at the bar with a silent, gray old man smoking Camels, and a catatonic bartender.

He sat mesmerized for the entire hour. Even though her personal stress was etched in every move, she was unbelievably good, wholly in charge, running the program like the master she was.

He was crazy about her.

For the twentieth time since last night, he told himself he should have said so. Then maybe she would have let him stay with her, and he could be doing a decent job of protecting her, and figuring this out and stopping it.

And again he argued the other side: she wasn't ready to hear it. It wouldn't clear up her doubts about him, but would merely exacerbate them. She would become even more internally defensive, push him further away.

For he knew about her doubts; he was good at reading feelings anyway, and with this much a chunk of his own invested, he was nearly psychic at it.

He couldn't blame her. Why should she be anything but ambivalent, considering? She was in no place to trust a man not to cause her pain. Had she been his sister, he would have advised her to stay away from involvement now, even if she wanted it.

So he'd wait, and try not to end up with his hands on her again.

And try to make his choices from someplace higher than his dick.

March 23, 1993

I won't have to endure the ordeal of watching her for much longer. I will make sure she can't be on TV.

I have to hang on and still be who they expect me to be.

But only until I make my chance.

My Greg, I miss you more every day.

My tattoo no longer gives me comfort. Not when I know you are gone forever.

That night, our last night together, you told me to wait for you, because you would come to me. I should have know you didn't mean it. You were touching me, but only when no one was looking. You wanted Lynn. You were looking at her the way you used to look at me.

I should have made a stand. I shouldn't have kept our love secret. I shouldn't have let her have you.

It was bad enough that I lost you to her. Then she made sure I'd never have you back.

You are dead, and it is her fault.

But I still have to look at her – not only face-to-face but on the damn screen all the time.

Everyone watches Lynn.

I can't abide you, Lynn.

*You spoiled it all for me. I should have been in
your place.*

Lynn dragged herself to the Broome Club after work on
Thursday.

She had no energy for the StairMaster, so she tried the
free weights for a while, but soon lost interest.

She saw Angela working on the Gravitron, and considered going over. But as always now, anytime she
thought of seeking someone out, Mike's list appeared like
a lighted frame of tape behind her eyes.

She had started to dial Mary's number last night, and
seen the list, and stopped.

Mary knew what she was going through. If Mary
was such a trustworthy friend, why wasn't Mary calling
her?

Elizabeth was working one-to-one with another client,
but finished as Lynn was going down to shower. Lynn said
goodbye.

'Didn't you just come in?' Elizabeth asked.

'Yes. But I'm not up to this.'

Elizabeth studied her a minute. 'You looked so much
better the last time I saw you. What's happened?'

It was the first sympathetic face Lynn had seen since
hugging her brother goodbye. She began to cry.

'Come on,' Elizabeth said, leading the way down to the
massage room. 'I have a few minutes free. I hope it's
empty.'

For once the quiet lighting and bucolic sound effects
didn't help. Elizabeth worked on her taut arms and legs,
but she remained wired. She hadn't expected anything
else.

She didn't want to pour out her misery yet again. But
the words just seemed to flow of their own accord.

'No wonder you haven't been in,' Elizabeth said when
she was done. 'You should have called me; I would have

come to you. Can't the police do *anything*?'

Lynn started to answer, but the door opened. It was Angela.

'There you are. Sorry to interrupt,' Angela said. 'But I knew you were in the building, and you weren't answering the page. Bernadine called here looking for you.'

Lynn tried Bernadine's home number from the pay phone, but there was no answer. She showered and dressed and tried again with the same result, then left the club and headed for Gloucester Street.

Approaching her building, Lynn heard her name called.

Bernadine's Lincoln was parked at the curb, and Bernadine got out.

She was putty-faced. Her fine light hair hung in wet strings, and tears shone in the dusky light.

'God,' Lynn said, 'what's wrong? What is it?'

'This,' Bernadine said hoarsely, and slapped something into her hand.

It was the packet of pictures of Lynn in her bathing suit at the beach in California.

Lynn was mystified. 'I don't understand.'

'Neither do I,' Bernadine said. 'I don't understand what these were doing in my husband's drawer in our bedroom.'

'But that's impossible. They're mine. How could –'

'*You tell me!* Are you and Dennis sleeping together?'

'*No!*'

There were pinch lines around Bernadine's nose. She was breathing as if in great pain, her chest moving under her silvery sweater.

Bernadine began to sob. 'Just what the hell am I supposed to believe?'

Lynn felt the blast of Bernadine's anguish. And something else, something painfully familiar: the hopeless knowledge that this was out of her control. She was to be carried along by a terrible current, and nobody wanted to hear that she didn't belong.

She reached for Bernadine's hand, but it was snatched away.

Lynn said, 'These were taken in California. They were kind of a therapeutic project. The detective I went out there with was trying to help bolster my self-confidence.'

The explanation sounded stupid in her own ears, and Bernadine was glaring furiously, but she went on.

'After what happened with Greg, I ... well, you know, I never have a good image of how I look. And he made it much worse. Mike, the detective, was trying to help, by showing me I was admired.'

'Lynn.' Bernadine shook her head. 'I'm supposed to believe that? Do you think the whole world buys whatever you sell? How about this? Yes, you were feeling insecure, so you had to seduce your general manager. Maybe then he might overlook the fact that *he* isn't sure about *you*! He might ignore what a Calamity Jane you are!'

Bernadine leaned closer, screaming. 'I stood up for you! I defended you when Dennis thought you were on drugs! I said we should stick with you when he said you have too many problems and too many disasters!

'Well,' the woman said, shaking her head, scattering tears, 'thank you, Bernadine!' She patted her own shoulder. 'Thank you for being a moron!'

People were passing, entering and leaving the building, parking and pulling out, but Bernadine was beyond caring. She pointed to Lynn. 'I bet that's why you moved! To be closer to the station! Your sister-in-law tried to tell me Elizabeth was after Dennis, but it was you! You even let me confide in you, and *you're sleeping with my husband!* This is your place to meet Dennis. *Isn't it?*'

'No. No. Please, *please* listen. I'd never do that. Ask him! He'll tell you! We've barely even had much to say to each other these last few weeks!'

'I did. He denied it. He said he'd never seen the pictures before.'

'He's telling the truth. Somebody put those pictures there. Somebody took them from me –'

'We're back to the mysterious *somebody* now? I've had enough of this.' Bernadine rubbed furiously at her wet cheeks. Without her precise makeup, she looked older and thinner. She grabbed the pictures back from Lynn, changed her mind and threw them to the ground. She ran to her car, started it with a ferocious grinding, and drove off.

Lynn wanted to follow her, but forced herself to wait. She went inside. To fill the crashing quiet, she turned on the news, and was astonished to see Dennis anchoring.

She watched him finish the cast, picked up the phone to call him at the station, but didn't.

She got her light jacket and went down the street to the garage.

Mike's list flashed in her head, and she squeezed it back.

She had a long connection with Bernadine and Dennis. They were almost family. Dennis appeared in more of her favorite keepsake pictures than any man but Booboo.

She had to fight this.

Dennis opened the front door of their house and frowned.

'Please. Let me talk to the two of you,' Lynn said.

'I don't know if –'

'Lynn?' Bernadine shouted from behind him. 'What are you doing here? I guess I know what.'

'Tell her, Dennis,' Lynn said.

'I did.'

'We barely see each other, except for short business discussions,' Lynn said. 'I didn't even know he was going to do the news tonight.' Out here in the suburbs, it was chilly for what she was wearing. Lynn shivered. 'Can I come in?'

'You'd better not,' Dennis said. He saw her face crumple. 'Everything's all screwed up. We need a chance to fix it.'

'I'm part of that. I want to fix it.'

Dennis answered as kindly as he could, but his eyes were hard. 'You'd better do your fixing and let us do ours.'

Lynn had used up the sample Percodans, and had filled the prescription, but hadn't taken any.

Tonight, back from the Orrins', her head screaming for help, she took two.

Mike's list glowed silver-bright in her mind, the names beaming out one by one, like the guests at the start of one of her shows.

She pulled the curtains against the street lamps and lay on her bed and waited for the calming threads of the medicine to ease the thumping in her head and help her think.

She tried to remember what had happened to the pictures when she moved here.

Had they been left at the apartment?

Had they been packed in with the rest of her belongings?

Her head was no better. She got up and drank some water and lay back down, and finally had to take two more pills.

A thought came.

What if they weren't the same pictures? What if there was another set?

She stood and began rifling through drawers and closets and envelopes. Then she started over methodically, searching each room in turn.

Back to the bed.

What had she just tried to prove? That there *was* another set? She hadn't. But she didn't know that there wasn't one either.

330

And what if there was?

Mike could have a second set. No one else could.

She must have dozed, because the bedside digital clock said 2:50.

But whether asleep or half awake, her brain had been very productive.

Like a View-Master, it had run tape backward and located pieces to show her.

'You'd better give me a key ...'

'I should stay here ...'

She could have encouraged Mike to stay longer Sunday night. But she hadn't, because she was being careful.

Because she had begun to wonder if her friends and family were right about Mike being an opportunist.

What if they were more right than that?

Could Mike be one of her old-style miserable mistakes? As bad as Greg? Worse?

Mike was the one who believed her from the start ... and who found all the evidence against Greg. He was the expert who interpreted it for her. He was the one who kept telling her how helpless the system was against this masterful noncrime.

It was Mike who wanted the real cop, instead of a security guard, keeping her safe for the pilot ... and the one whose voice was imitated to lure her protector away.

Mike was the one fighting with Greg when Greg died.

Dear God in heaven, could Mike be the one doing this to her all along?

Was he using his uncanny instincts to manipulate the situation, and her, for his psychotic reasons?

Could Greg have been the scapegoat? Could she be responsible for the death of an innocent man?

The pain was returning in rolls, squeezing her skull. The pill bottle was on the nightstand. But it was four-forty. If she took another pill now, she wouldn't be alert for the show.

She knew she wasn't going to be able to sleep any more either.

She made a pot of coffee and turned on the TV, and switched from channel to channel to channel, using the cacophony to drown out the voices in her mind.

CHAPTER NINETEEN

The show was nearly over. Lynn's headache had subsided to a dull pressure. The pills didn't seem to have affected her acuity, but she was glad she'd resisted that last one after four o'clock. As soon as the credits rolled, though, she'd be drained. The misery of last night, plus the nearly total lack of sleep, had left her with no more resources than she could muster to get through the show.

That was all she was going to do. Get through the show. Then she would go home and take a damn pill and pull the drapes and shut her eyes and lie there the whole weekend if she had to.

'Dennis?'

'Hello, Vicky.'

'How are things there?'

He didn't even consider massaging her. God knew what she had heard, and would.

'Not great,' Dennis said.

'I've seen a couple of the shows. Lynn looks like hell.'

'Yep.'

'Stations are bugging us about rescheduling the pilot taping. I'm going to have to tell them we're dropping the project.'

He was silent, and Vicky said, 'I'm sorry.'

'So am I.'

Kara asked Dennis, 'Does Lynn know?'

'Not yet. I'll talk to her after the weekend.'

'Did you think about what I asked you?'

Dennis rubbed his eyes. 'I did. And you're right. We'll make you executive producer. You and Lynn will vet each other's decisions.'

'I feel ghoulish doing this now. But it's not personal. All I want is to save our show.'

'I'm sure Lynn will understand that,' Dennis said.

March 26, 1993

> *I want you to die as I am dying.*
> *Everything is ready now.*
> *Nobody can get into your new apartment. But I*
> *can ...*

Lynn unlocked her apartment and went straight to the bedroom and took two Percodans.

She hadn't eaten since ... was it lunch yesterday? She still wasn't hungry, but the medication could make her nauseated on an empty stomach.

She toasted an English muffin and ate as much of it as she could.

She got undressed and turned the shower on.

Bernadine's wet face kept appearing in her thoughts. A portrait of pain.

Lynn's fault. Her responsibility. Bernadine suffering, because of her.

Not true, and not right. But not fixable.

Kara too had to suffer an awful personal tragedy because of her.

Her poor brother, worried to distraction, his health affected ...

Dennis, his personal and work lives turned upside down ...

She thought of Mike, and her stomach lurched.

She'd buried the repulsive notion of Mike's real role in her nightmare, because she had to function this morning. But her personal bargain with herself had now run its course, and the questions flooded back.

Finally, she turned off the taps and dried herself. She wrapped her wet hair in a towel and squeezed toothpaste onto her brush.

Leaning over the sink to do her teeth, she saw in the mirror that a piece of towel lint was stuck to her lip, and she reached to flick it off with the toothbrush.

Suddenly her lip was burning.

Lynn rubbed at it, not understanding that it was the drop of toothpaste her gesture had left that was the problem. The burning became instantly unbearable, agony as searing as flame.

Her eyes opened in horror as the skin at the corner of her mouth bubbled and whitened and the odor of burning flesh rose.

She screamed at her terrified face in the mirror, screamed over and over and over, otherworldly shrieks that were deafening in her own ears.

It was a different hospital emergency room, but the experience was sickeningly the same.

She only vaguely remembered the banging on her door, and opening it for yet another couple of police she'd never seen.

The city seemed to have an unending supply.

But not for any way she needed them.

'Something was apparently injected into the tube. I would guess drain cleaner,' the doctor said. 'There seems to be just external damage. If you'd swallowed it, your esophagus would have been eaten away.'

He had recognized Lynn Marchette, and raised an eyebrow, and she hadn't even tried to explain or defend anything.

There was no point.

She only wanted to go home and cover herself in her bed and forget about everything.

The burn was the least of what hurt.

It was the thought pictures that hurt most, that had to be shut off somehow.

The image of what a toothbrush full of the paste would have done to her tongue and the inside of her mouth.

The pictures of the other almosts: the raccoon and the blade ...

'Are you sure you don't want someone called? Family or a friend?' a nurse asked.

Lynn shook her battered head.

She knew that by going back to the apartment, she was leaving herself wide open.

It was hard to care.

She slept for several hours without dreaming, and when she woke, it was dark. She got out of bed to go to the bathroom, but felt dizzy and sick.

The ointment had worn off her burn. It was raw and oozy. Again she thought of how her whole mouth and throat could have been destroyed.

Vaguely she wondered why she wasn't more terrified.

More anything.

But she wasn't.

She thought of the LSD kids who had leaped off buildings, sure they could fly. She felt kind of like that. Harm was irrelevant. She was too far beyond it.

The difference was that they felt powerful. She just felt ... already dead.

There was no reason to stay up, so she got back under the covers.

She fell asleep again, but the doorbell woke her. She didn't answer. After two more rings, she got up.

'Who is it?' she asked through the intercom.

'Mike.'

'I'm ... not feeling well.'

'I heard. Buzz me in, will you?'

Again she found herself unemotionally following the path of least resistance. She pushed the buzzer.

When she opened the door, he was standing there in his Tufts sweatshirt. His brow furrowed at the sight of her in her nightgown, an oversize T-shirt with kittens on it, hanging off one shoulder. Her hair was in her face and down her back. She hadn't taken off her studio makeup, and what was left of it blotched her eyes and cheeks. There was a wet and raw red area by the corner of her mouth, oozing bloody fluid.

He turned on a light, and she squinted.

'The report said something caustic in your toothpaste. Did it get into your mouth?' he asked.

'No.'

'They're checking out the tube. What happened, you felt it before you started to brush?'

'Mm-hm.'

With hands on her shoulders, he moved her under the light and leaned close to see the sore.

Her mind was a still camera, seeing and noting but not reacting. It registered the fingers on her bare skin, the warm breath on her cheek. It picked up the odors of shaving cream and sauerkraut.

'Must hurt like hell,' he said.

She didn't answer. But she yawned, and that did hurt, and she gave a little cry.

'Didn't they give you stuff to put on it?'

'Yes.'

'Where is it?'

'In the bathroom.'

He went and got the ointment and dabbed it on with a Q-tip.

'Let's sit down,' he said.

She followed him into the living room and sat in an armchair. Mike sat opposite her.

'When did you buy that toothpaste?' he asked.

'I just bought it at the drugstore downstairs. I already told the police.'

'So somebody got to it there. Or was in here. But only your brother has a key.'

She rested her tangled head back. She was so terribly worn-out.

Mike stood up and thumped her knee. 'Talk to me, Lynn. What's wrong with you?'

'I'm tired.'

'You're apathetic. You're worrying me.'

The camera clicked at the alarm in his voice.

He said, 'We have to figure this out. You have to wake up and do it. Somebody is trying damn hard to hurt you, and working harder at it now, and we have to know who. Are you *hearing me*?'

'Yes. Your list.'

'Let's make it again.' He took out his notebook and a pen. 'Kara. Mary. Orrin. His wife. Your brother –'

Lynn pulled herself out of the chair and went to the kitchen, supporting herself on chair backs.

Mike watched her, open-mouthed. 'Where the hell are you going?'

She didn't answer. He followed and found her at the refrigerator, drinking Coke from a two-liter bottle.

He said, 'I would have gotten you that.'

She finished her drink and reached to put the bottle back. It slipped from her hands. Mike jumped to catch it, but missed, and it landed on Lynn's bare foot and spewed Coke all over the floor and the cabinets and both of them.

The pain in her foot seemed to turn on a switch. Suddenly Lynn could feel it, and the sticky liquid on her legs. Her eyes teared up as she was engulfed in a terrible desolation.

Mike led her back to the living room. She was crying and shivering. He went to the bedroom and yanked the blanket off the bed and tucked it around her on the chair.

When the crying subsided, he said, 'I know you hate the list –'

Lynn wailed something he couldn't hear.

'What?' he said.

'You aren't on it!'

'What do you mean?'

'I mean, are *you* the one doing this to me?'

He stared at her.

'Isn't the list just another piece of the truth according to Mike?' she yelled, tears streaming. 'You were in here! Did you poison my toothpaste? Are you the real sick one? Did you let me believe it was Greg, when it was you?'

Mike was out of his chair.

'You think *I* would hurt you?'

'You've controlled all the information! All my security! No matter what locks and doors and passwords you arrange, things keep happening!'

'I dropped other work to help you! I worked thirty hours a day! I stood by you when nobody did!'

Fury made him shake. Above the neck of the sweatshirt, cords of tension stood out.

'Damn you! What planet are you on? I fought a maniac for you, Lynn! I almost *died* protecting you!'

He strode to the door and pulled it open. 'You can go straight to hell!'

March 27, 1993

It isn't enough for me to make her pay in pain. I want the chance to tell her exactly what she cost me.

I will keep her alive until I tell her.

I want her to know that it was all her fault that Greg didn't come back to me.

He would have. He left all the others, and he would have left Lynn too. But because of her, he is dead.

339

She made sure I'd never get him back.

I hate you, Star. I hate having you next to me. I hate seeing you in living color.

I didn't think it would be this hard to be around you. I thought I could work my plan without letting you get to me. But hiding my grief from you was harder than I ever could have imagined. I have to be nice to you, when all I want to do is watch you die.

My hate grows all the time. After you killed Greg, I couldn't even write about it. My hate filled me so, it couldn't make words.

But it is nearly impossible now to hide it.

I hold on with all my might to who I am supposed to be, because to show my real self too soon would cost me yet again.

I can do it, though. I do it so well, sometimes I forget both my selves are me.

Lynn yearned to have the numbness back again.

All these feelings were unendurable.

There was nothing she wanted to do but sleep, but as soon as her eyes closed, terrors pricked at her. Voices whispered. Her burn was worse, the wound a creeping, growing entity that wouldn't let her move her mouth without excruciating pain.

She hated to take any more Percodan, had said no when the last ER doctor offered medication. But it was that or faint from the pain.

By Saturday evening she could remember having swallowed four of them.

Some vestige of her intelligence insisted it must have been more, because inside she was getting numb again. But the diminishing of the horror was so seductive. Rather than risk losing it, she chose not to examine its cause.

And her mouth, her mouth. The mirror showed a big

blistered ridge of upper and lower lip on one side. To open it hurt so much that she ate nothing. When she was thirsty, or to swallow pills, she inserted a straw in the good side.

She dreamed of Mike.

Not bad dreams, but hazy soft ones, the only breaks in the black films that bombarded her.

In one she was lying on her sofa, back home in her harbor apartment, with a headache so intense she couldn't open her eyes. Mike kept massaging her head, and everywhere his fingers pressed, the pain disappeared.

She was awake for a while on Sunday afternoon. Her mouth was very swollen. She tried to clean off the crusting discharge gently with cotton and peroxide, but even that faint touch made her cry out. She looked for her ointment, but couldn't find it.

She tried to eat a little yoghurt. She gave up after finding she couldn't open her lips wide enough to admit the spoon.

She considered dumping it into a blender with some milk and liquefying it enough to drink; at least she'd have the nourishment.

But even thinking of dragging out the blender was too complicated.

All she really wanted was to go back to sleep.

Heading for the bedroom, she detoured to the bathroom to take another look for the ointment, but quickly gave up on that too.

Her last act before collapsing back into bed was to lean over the bathroom counter at the mirror. She had always been able to make contact with herself that way when necessary – either to calm irrational anxiety or to direct her attention or address a problem.

She lifted her sagging shoulders and pushed her hair out of her eyes. She tried to focus on them. She had a show to do tomorrow.

Her body knew what she couldn't face: there was no

chance she could go on the air.

Instead of communing with her mirror image, she found herself on the floor over the toilet, emptying her already empty stomach.

She thought she phoned Kara. But when she was finally awake again at seven Monday morning, she wasn't sure whether she had actually made the call or dreamed it.

She dialed Kara's number now, and got her machine.

She tried her own extension at the station. No answer.

She couldn't bring herself to call Dennis.

Every ten minutes she tried her extension. Finally Pam answered.

'I hurt my lip,' Lynn told her. 'It's swollen and ugly, and I can't talk well. I couldn't reach Kara; she must be on her way there. She'll have to do a rerun.'

Lynn could hear the lisp, and the pauses between words that seemed several seconds long. Druggy speech. She considered trying to explain to Pam about the intolerable hurting, and the painkillers.

But why should she bother? Did any of them believe a word she said anymore?

Exhausted from her busy morning, her mouth exploding, she took three Percodans and went back to bed.

'I can't leave,' Mary said. 'I'm stacked full today. I don't have time to pee.'

'This is an emergency.' Kara glanced at Pam, who nodded. 'Pam said she sounded completely wrecked. We have to go over there. No one else will.'

'Damn it. All right.'

In her dream, Lynn came out of the bathroom and got hit, but in the mouth instead of near the eye. She didn't see who hit her. It didn't knock her out right away. The blow came again and again, until she wished she could lose consciousness rather than be awake for this agony in her mouth.

Then Mike appeared, and took her hand, and pulled her away from whoever was hitting. He led her out of the apartment, and immediately through another door into Nancy Jean's.

There she heard lovely music. The friendly food smells and the smoke fog surrounded her and Mike as they moved onto the dance floor. It was only the tiniest space in the dream, and as they danced on it, Lynn noticed that they were the only people in the place. No one else, not even Nancy Jean, just Lynn and Mike moving to the sweet music.

Instead of the dance position, they held each other with both hands. Mike's arms were around her, so tight it was hard to take a breath, but when she took one, the hug loosened just enough.

Mike's cheek against hers was bristly. His skin was cool. His hair felt nice on the back of his neck where she realized her hand was. Her other arm was around his waist, holding him as close as he held her.

They moved in step to the angelic swells and dips of the music, as if their bodies were attached at each point of motion.

She became aware that all the people who weren't in the place were outside, trying to get in. She could hear them. She lifted her head and saw them through the glass, their faces pressed to the panes.

Mike said something, but Lynn couldn't hear over the sounds the people were making, banging on the door.

She was waking up.

She realized the sounds were real.

She opened her eyes and saw bloody smears on her pillow, wet and fresh.

Her impulse was to jump out of bed, but she could only follow it very slowly. All her movements were leaden.

People were at her door.

343

She touched her mouth. It didn't hurt quite as much, but her hand came away wet with blood.

She made her way to the bathroom. She had to keep one hand on the wall at all times.

Blood coated her chin and streaked her nightgown. She watched herself in the mirror, taking a towel and holding it to her mouth.

She reached the apartment door the same way. Once there, she leaned against the wall to rest a second.

'Lynn! Open the door!'

'Can you hear us?'

Kara and Mary. Her friends.

Weren't they?

She couldn't remember a goddamn thing.

Working the lock with limp fingers, Lynn got the door open.

Kara gasped. Mary gripped Lynn's arms. Lynn let go of the door and started to fall.

They helped her into the bedroom. Mary flipped the bloody pillow off the bed and moved the clean one over.

'Now,' Mary said, when Lynn was lying back, 'what's the story? What happened?'

'Someone ...' That was a word not to use, Lynn vaguely recalled. She started over. 'There was ... acid in my toothpaste. It burned my liff. Lip.'

Kara was crying. Lynn heard her sniffle, and looked over and started to cry too. Her tears seemed to be in the same other dimension as everything else she was trying to do. They trickled out in heavy slow motion.

Mary sat on the bed. 'Did you see a doctor?'

Lynn nodded. It hurt, and she winced. 'The police came. I went to the emergency room. My second home.'

'Which police? Mike Delano?'

'No ...'

'Did the doctor give you medication? Is that why you're so groggy?'

'Not ... this doctor ... I had some –'

Mary scanned the night table and pounced on Lynn's bottle of Percodan.

'You're pretty out of it. Have you been taking these since Friday?'

'Yes.'

'Before Friday too?'

'Once in ... a while ...'

Mary turned to Kara, but Kara had moved to the window. She was looking out, still sobbing quietly.

'I'm going to call your brother,' Mary said. 'We need to get you some help.'

'Mike too,' Lynn said through nearly still lips. 'Call Mike.'

Mary looked away. 'I don't think –'

'Yes!' Lynn hissed. Every word was a task. 'I need to ... tell him –'

'The person you need right now is your brother. He cares about you.'

'Mike ... cares ... about me!'

Mary got off the bed. She sighed, glanced Kara's way again. Finally she said, 'No, he doesn't. He's not on your side.'

'Yes, he –'

'Listen, Lynn. I never repeat what's said in my office, but right now I have no choice. You're my priority.' Mary clasped her hands together. 'Mike is not your friend. He thinks you're behind your own harassment, doing the things yourself.'

Kara had turned from the window and was listening.

'Mike came to my office yesterday,' Mary said. 'He insisted on a Sunday appointment. He spent over an hour picking my brain about you. Asking me all kinds of questions about why a woman would have the type of mania that causes her to do these acts.

'Of course, I only gave general answers. I made it clear that I would provide no personal information whatsoever.

'But Lynn, he obviously believes you had some stake in prolonging the stalking. The criminal is dead, but the acts go on.'

'What a bastard Mike is,' Kara said.

Mary nodded. 'You've been through enough,' she told Lynn. 'You don't need the extra betrayal of considering someone your advocate when he's your enemy.'

Booboo sat on her bed and held her hand and cried with her.

'I should have forced you to stay with us. I should have chained you.'

Mary came in. 'They have a bed at Laurel Glen. God, I hate these names. As if going to a place that sounds bucolic makes you better.'

'I don't want to go,' Lynn said.

'I don't blame you,' Mary said. 'But it isn't what you expect. The place is comfy, and the staff are respectful. You won't be the first celebrity whose admission there was kept very efficiently secret.'

Booboo asked, 'Will you be her doctor, officially?'

'If you want me to be.'

He turned to Lynn. 'Does that help at all?'

'I still don't want to go.'

Booboo stood. 'Maybe,' he said, 'I should do what I wish I had done sooner. Maybe I ought to truss my sister up and kidnap her to my house. My wife and I can take care of her there.'

'I don't advise it,' Mary said. 'She's going to feel lousy as the narcotic leaves her system. There's a lot in there. That kind of care is business as usual at the hospital. And they're set up to treat this wound that looks dangerously infected.'

Mary told Lynn, 'You need to rest in a therapeutic setting, with appropriate nourishment and medication. And you'll be safe at Laurel Glen. No one can get in there to hurt you.'

* * *

They left Lynn alone in the bedroom while Booboo went for the car and Mary and Kara straightened up and packed a suitcase.

She lay back on the pillows and closed her wet eyes.

She hadn't had any pills in hours, and her mouth was horrible, burning like fire.

'*You'll be safe at Laurel Glen. No one can get in there to hurt you.*'

No one could get into her two apartments either.

Who was there to trust? Who would protect her, if she couldn't protect herself?

Or would she no longer have to worry about that, because her tormentor would succeed and she would be dead?

There was still some narcotic barrier between Lynn and her thoughts. Their power to agonize was limited. But that would change. Nothing would cushion her at the hospital.

Thank God her brother was here. Her wonderful, caring brother whom she trusted.

Was there anyone else at all?

'*Mike is not your friend ...*'

But he was. Lynn truly believed he was. He had told her so in every way, and she had treated him abominably, kicked his trust away.

She thought of Mike in her apartment, helping her headache. Giving his time, applying his skills to her danger. Faxing and phoning and questioning. Following Greg, confronting him.

Mike had almost been killed, for her sake.

Mary had to be wrong.

But why – Lynn rubbed her eyes and tried to concentrate – why had he pumped Mary about her? Why had he said he suspected her of pretending someone was still after her?

Could she *herself* be the one who was wrong?

She groaned and tried to roll over, but it hurt too much.

So often lately she really wasn't sure what was what.

Wasn't sure even what was, or should be, in her own mind.

So she shouldn't consider herself sure of Mike either, should she? Maybe he *did* think she was a disturbed, attention-seeking lunatic.

Carefully, she edged over and reached for the phone. She dialed clumsily.

Mike's machine answered.

She couldn't think how to condense a message, so she broke the connection and called the police station.

'Detective Delano's not in, ma'am.'

Lynn worked her lips around to try to loosen them. She hated the way her voice was coming out. 'When ... when will he be there?'

'Can't say. Who's calling?'

Before Lynn could pronounce her name, she realized it was not smart to identify herself when she sounded like this.

For that matter, she probably shouldn't talk to Mike when she sounded like this.

But she wanted to.

'Hello? Do you want to leave a message, ma'am?'

She needed to hear why, if Mike trusted her, like he said, he was asking Mary those questions.

She needed to tell him how sorry she was for the awful accusations ...

But the dial tone buzzed in her ear.

March 28, 1993

What a tragedy that my darling had so little time left.

Lynn took it.

Well, now she is out of time too.

I am taking hers.

It's almost over.

* * *

All the rooms at Laurel Glen were private. Lynn's was on the second floor, overlooking a garden of flowers and herbs.

Booboo insisted on staying there with her. He slept in short stretches on a folding cot and watched over her and took care of her, relinquishing the job to a nurse only when it involved an IV needle.

By Wednesday morning he was sick himself, coughing and feverish, and they made him go home.

'Stay in this room. Don't let anyone in,' he told Lynn hoarsely as Angela waited outside to take him back to Salem.

Lynn was sitting at the window when Mary came.

'Where's your brother?'

'Home, sick.'

She read Lynn's chart and took her pulse. She examined the scabbed mouth.

'I hear you're not eating. No appetite?'

'No,' Lynn said.

'What can we do about that?'

Lynn turned back to the window, away from the cheery energy.

Mary said, 'How about a steam bath? I'll take you to your club and drive you back here afterward. You can have one of those treatments you like. I'll make an appointment right now. What's the number?'

'Booboo said not to leave here.'

'It's okay. You're with your doctor.'

Mary would be relentless if she said no, Lynn knew. She pulled on her sweats and put her hair in a rubber band.

Mary watched her with a frown as they went down the stairs at the Broome Club. Lynn moved like a sleepwalker, holding the banister, not watching where she was going.

Elizabeth Vail came out of the treadmill area. She

349

started to greet Lynn, then went silent, the shock clear in her face.

'What happened?'

'I … was hurt.'

Mary watched Lynn's unfocused movements, the lack of coordination. 'I think I'll stay around here and wait for you.'

'You don't need to,' Lynn said.

'You shouldn't be alone.'

'She won't be,' Elizabeth said. 'I won't leave her.'

'Well … all right, then. I'll be back in – what do you think, an hour?'

'We should be finished by then,' Elizabeth said.

She led Lynn into the massage room. The lighting was the usual restful glow. Heat from the next-door steam room warmed the air. Elizabeth adjusted the sound to find the waterfall tape she knew Lynn enjoyed.

She helped Lynn onto the table, peering at her red and swollen mouth.

Lynn waited for the questions she wasn't up to answering.

Mary kept referring to her depression, but was this really depression, this mental whitescape? She felt hopeless. Everything she had worked so hard for was all but gone.

And she had no hope this would change. No clue as to who was hurting her.

Elizabeth pulled the straps from their openings in the table and fastened them, one across Lynn's chest and arms, the other over her legs.

It was uncomfortable not to be able to move at all, not even to scratch.

'Did Mary tell you I needed to be strapped in?' Lynn asked.

Elizabeth stared down at her, and Lynn thought she hadn't heard. She started to repeat the question, but stopped, her mouth half open in confusion as Elizabeth moved aside and began to undress.

Lynn's heart thumped, some physical sensor responding to the danger before her mind caught up.

Elizabeth had removed her shorts and was peeling off her spandex tights. Slowly she pulled her right foot out of the fabric. She held it up for Lynn to see.

On her ankle, in blue and red, was the tattoo Greg had made Lynn get: the lips and the initial G.

Sweat formed under Lynn's straps. Her frozen brain was trying to work, struggling with the questions slamming into it.

Elizabeth leaned close to Lynn. Her face was so different suddenly, her eyes not blinking, mouth pursed inward.

'You killed him,' Elizabeth whispered. 'You took him and kept him, and he died, and it was because of you.'

'Greg,' Lynn croaked.

'It was me he loved. I was his Tina. That was his love name for me. He saved my life; he rescued me from a man who always hit me.

'Greg broke up with me. But he would have come back. The other women were meaningless. But *you* ...' Elizabeth's face pulled further into itself as the hate took over. 'You were on *TV*, everybody *loved* you.' She spat the words in a taunting singsong. 'You set it up so he couldn't resist you.'

'I tried to get *rid* of him,' Lynn protested, heaving against the straps. 'He wouldn't stop. He wouldn't leave me alone. He sent pornography, he –'

'I know. I know everything he did.' Elizabeth started to pull her clothes back up, but changed her mind and straightened. Her half-naked body was pale in the dusky light, the leg muscles pearly ridges. She put her hands on her pelvis and thrust close to Lynn.

'This body was the one he really made love to! Not *yours*!' She hit Lynn's belly hard, and Lynn cried out.

351

'Don't bother yelling.' Now Elizabeth rearranged her tights. 'Your pain hasn't even started yet.'

Lynn couldn't absorb it.

Her trusted trainer flipflopping impossibly into her enemy – her tormentor, her would-be killer ...

Not Kara, Dennis, Mary ... Mike ...

Elizabeth. Elizabeth, who always made her feel better. Elizabeth, who was alone with her now for an hour.

'I'm going to wheel you in for your steam. Enough steam to show you what real pain is before you're dead. You can holler if you want, but you'll only force me to use my other toys – like the cleanser I put in your toothpaste. I'll burn off the whole rest of your mouth before anyone can hear you.'

Horror washed through Lynn.

Her brain shot to life at last, racing around, grasping for a way out.

Elizabeth started to turn the big table toward the steam room door.

'Wait,' Lynn said. She was weak and helpless beneath the straps, but she could still talk. She was good at talk. 'I don't understand. You have to explain. You had a relationship with Greg, then he met me –'

'Not right then. There were others. But he left the others. That's why I kept looking for him; so I'd be there when he realized he wanted *me* back.

'I kept going to all the places we'd been together. And sometimes I found him, and I could see the truth in his eyes: the others were nothing. Then' – she made a frightening guttural sound – '*you* ... that night at Geoffrey's –'

'You were *with him* that night in LA?'

'Yes.' A desolate whisper: 'You looked right through me. Greg was looking through me. Greg and I were sitting together, with that bunch of people at the table next to yours ... and all he could see was you.

'He was surprised to see me at Geoffrey's that night. But he asked me to sit with him. And when he told me to go home, he said to wait for him, he'd be there. But he never came.'

Elizabeth gave a choked sob, then drew in breath in a shuddering spasm.

'Then I realized he had lied to me. He wasn't glad to see me. But he had to pretend he was, or I might have acted up and drawn attention to him. And then – then – he would have missed his chance to get next to you.'

She sobbed again, and seemed about to give in to a flood of crying. But as Lynn watched, Elizabeth pulled herself back to the hot rage that vibrated under her every word.

'I only met Greg for the first time that night,' Lynn said, scrabbling to keep Elizabeth motivated to talk. 'We didn't have a date until he came to Boston. How did you know he and I were together here?'

Elizabeth leaned over the table and spat the words in Lynn's face: 'I saw your tattoo. The perpetual kiss. On TV in Los Angeles. Then I knew where my Greg had gone. And I came here, and got this job.'

Elizabeth smiled. For a startling second her old sunny look was back, but it was quickly replaced by a mask of mean triumph.

'I *manipulated* my way onto your show, with that tape. I had it produced for practically nothing in LA, without me in it, in case Greg watched your show that day. Then I manipulated you into joining the club.'

Elizabeth started to wheel the table again. She was breathing hard. Sweat showed on her face and neck.

Lynn groped for another question. 'Did Greg know you were in Boston?'

'He almost caught me once. At your friend the doctor's place. But he never knew.' She swallowed. 'He died before I could tell him.'

353

Would this talking get her anywhere? Was Lynn just postponing the inevitable?

There was nothing else she could do.

Lynn said, 'I never even thought of you.'

Elizabeth hit Lynn's cheek with a rigid chop of her hand. The pain was a rocket burst. 'You should have figured this out, a smart TV star like you! You know any jerk can get a job at a health club – people have bitched about it on your show. You even know where the master key to the lockers here is – you've seen me use it when someone gets locked out. See, I'm smart too – smart enough to copy all your keys and Bernadine's. Smart enough to listen in on phone calls. Smart enough to know what to do with pictures that *you're* dumb enough to leave in your locker!'

Elizabeth kicked the table, and Lynn felt the force reverberate through her.

'Smart enough,' Elizabeth said, 'to fix it so a sick, weak, confused person can make a mistake with the control in the steam room.'

The waterfall sound was louder.

Elizabeth opened the door. Immediately Lynn felt the advancing blast of hot, wet air. Panic exploded, and she pushed against the straps, grunting with the strain.

'Give it up!' Elizabeth hissed, backing into the doorway, pulling the table after her. 'That was all crap about no heavy weights. I knew a wuss like you would buy it. I used to work in *real* gyms. I'm extremely strong. If you got out of that, and you won't, I could kill you with my –'

Straining upward with her head and neck, struggling to see what was coming, Lynn suddenly saw Elizabeth knocked sideways, off her feet, by a rush of water.

Was something broken? Were they both going to drown in a flood in the steam room? Lynn screamed, and felt steam settling on her, all over her, and screamed again …

… and realized she wasn't the only one making noise.

People were yelling in the steam room. Water was spraying full force all over the place. Lynn coughed as a shower hit her. She strained up higher, as high as she could.

The table was knocked out of the doorway as a grappling pair of people fell on it.

Elizabeth – and Mike Delano. With a yell from deep in his throat, Mike pinned Elizabeth's wrists and slapped handcuffs on her.

'I had to fight my way through police cars to get in here,' Mary said. 'What *happened*?'

'The person who was trying to kill me. She tried again, with the steam room. They arrested her. It was Elizabeth.'

Mary sank onto the bench Lynn was sitting on. 'The *trainer*?'

Lynn nodded. She had her knees drawn up and her arms wrapped around them to stop her shaking.

'My God,' Mary said. 'My God. She – Are you all right? Do you feel faint?' She took Lynn's hands and located her pulse. 'I don't understand why they left you alone here.'

'They didn't,' Mike said, coming around a corner. He was holding his back. 'I was only gone a minute, while we took Vail out.'

Lynn dropped her legs and sat up. 'You said you'd explain,' she told Mike. 'Tell me now. Tell me everything that –'

'I'll explain on the way to the emergency room.'

'I am not going to another emergency room.'

'Not for you. For me. I cracked those ribs again.'

Lynn said, 'You told me you believed me. Why did you ask Mary all those questions about me?'

Mike turned to her, winced, and shifted his position in the driver's seat. 'Not about you. About Vail. I was trying to put her shtick together. Mary thought I meant *you*?'

'Yes. She warned me you weren't on my side.'

355

'She's a jerk.'

'She doesn't like you either.'

Mike pumped the brake at a red light and winced again.

'I tried to call you after she said that,' Lynn said. 'They wouldn't tell me where you were. I thought you were avoiding me. I know I said awful things to you.'

He hesitated. 'For about a day I wanted to kill you myself. Then I started to realize that was your fear talking.'

He looked at her, then back at the road. 'I bet you didn't know I had someone covering you.'

'You mean guarding me? Where?'

'Around. I wanted you watched. I wanted to see if anyone tried again. When Mary put you in Laurel Glen, I figured you were safe for a while. Norm Lee was covering you today. He didn't know there was any problem with you going to the Broome Club, because I didn't tell him what I was working on. So he never got around to telling me you were there until it was … almost …'

Lynn expected him to say 'too late,' but he wasn't saying anything. She stared in amazement at what was undeniably Mike Delano trying not to break down.

She had to look away. Her blood pounded. She didn't know what to say or do.

Mike cleared his throat. 'When you couldn't reach me,' he said, 'I was in Los Angeles, checking out Elizabeth Vail.'

'But why?' Lynn said. 'How did you fasten on her?'

He shrugged, made another pained face.

'Let me drive,' Lynn said.

'No. I'll stiffen up if I sit still. Remember what I said to you that first day you came to the station? When you made that crack about Tufts?'

'"Don't ever assume that what's in front of your eyes is the truth,"' Lynn quoted promptly.

Mike nodded. 'I kept harping on the goddamn list. You insisted it couldn't be your friends or family. Finally I said to myself, stop assuming she's wrong.'

'Watch that taxi.'

'I see it. So I started going over what I'd seen of your life, trying to shake out pieces that didn't freeze. Any pieces – not just ones that fit my assumption. You know what kept falling out? That dumb conversation at the gym. When I went there to bring you the child abuse statutes for your pilot. Vail kept yapping about small weights, but I knew she was an experienced lifter. She put the weights on the bar outside in, like the muscle guys do. They like to see their numbers. It pumps 'em. She talked like one of them, too. She used terms you hear in the macho gyms. And she was no little spa exerciser. Did you look at those pecs? She's strong as a lion.'

He tapped the horn and passed a slow-moving Honda. 'At the time, I shrugged it off. But then I started to wonder why someone hides their experience. I thought, maybe you do that if you're covering other secrets besides.

'I checked her Broome Club file, and found out she had recently relocated from LA. Then I started peeling off layers. I was right – she worked at two gyms there. She's not a well person – she's been institutionalized three times. But what really rang the bell was her timing. Greg meets you in LA, starts up with you, doesn't share the fact that he lives here. Vail relocates here, worms her way onto your show and into your life. Greg croaks, someone carries the banner.'

Mike looked at her. 'Nobody else *wasn't* in your life before then. Nobody except me.'

Once again Lynn felt a hot flush of shame. 'I'm so sorry –'

'Never mind.'

After a minute Lynn said, 'Elizabeth was always so nice to me. Supportive and lovely.'

'She was waiting.'

'Waiting for Greg. She told me he was going to come back to her. Did they have a real relationship?'

Mike shook his head. 'No more real than any of his. But

by the time she got finished revising it, he was the love of her life. That's what I think.'

'So the questions you asked Mary –'

'I needed to know about victim pathology, jealousy, and obsession and mania. I was testing a hypothesis. We see sex assault victims all the time who have inappropriate feelings about their attackers. It's temporary, just the mind struggling to absorb the experience in some familiar frame. So I thought, what if the victim is a wackball herself? What if the feelings aren't temporary? That's what I believe happened with Vail. And you became the hated rival. She wanted to torture you and destroy you.'

They were quiet while Mike circled the emergency area parking lot, looking for a space.

'She was really going to kill me,' Lynn said, rubbing the bruised area on her chest where the straps had bitten in.

'Might've come closer too, if that hose hadn't been hanging there in the steam room. I needed to surprise her, in case she had a weapon out. I was just about to open the door and get her with it when she saved me the trouble.'

'You heard what she was saying to me?'

'Not much. I just got there.'

He looked away, out the window, and Lynn thought he'd spotted a space. But when he turned back, his eyes were red and wet. He took her hand and squeezed it.

'You can move back to the harbor now,' Mike said. 'That must feel good.'

'It does. I'm still kind of woozy ...'

'You look different. Sparked up.'

'I'm a mess. My hair, these sweats, no makeup. This burn on my mouth. I look terrible.'

'Not to me.'

'Thank you.'

He shrugged, made a face, held his newly retaped side. They were tangled in rush-hour traffic.

'I have to move back to my temporary apartment before I can move home,' Lynn said. 'I'm still officially a patient at Laurel Glen. Mary has to discharge me.'

'Shit.'

Her hospital room had been prettily made up in her absence, as if she were just out on a field trip. The bed was tight and crisp. Hyacinths from Angela perfumed the air.

The nurse who had escorted Lynn and Mike to the room smiled and left.

Lynn got out her suitcase and started folding her clothes.

Mike closed the door. He put his arms around Lynn and wrapped her close.

She was so dizzy.

But a different kind of dizzy. Someone had hefted a bushel basket of rocks off her shoulders. Impulses were coming to her, like children to a parent, testing. This? Can I do this now?

Mike's hands dropped to just beneath her waist and pulled her in against him.

She moved away. 'The door doesn't lock.'

Mike took handcuffs from his belt. He looped one side around the door handle and the other on a wall-mounted clothing hook.

'Now it does,' he said.

He touched the healing wound on her mouth. 'Does this hurt?'

'Not much.'

He took her hands and lifted them over his shoulders. His hands moved all over her back as he kissed her neck, her chin, her mouth.

Without letting go of her, he drew back and searched her face.

Lynn knew just what he was thinking. She had the same anxiety herself. 'You think I'm going to stop,' she said.

'Are you?'

She touched his face. Her finger traced his heavy, coarse brows, then his lips.

He made a sound and pulled her in tight again, kissing her mouth, using his tongue. Then, just as abruptly, he ended the kiss, pulled her hard to his shoulder.

'Answer me,' he demanded angrily in her ear.

'I don't want to stop,' she said softly.

She found his mouth again, and this time it was her tongue that was the aggressor. He allowed it, welcomed it, showed his pleasure in the eager way he looped his hands in her hair to hold her there.

The window was open. The garden scents wafted in, mixing with the hyacinth fragrance. It was getting dark, and the last bird chirps could be heard in the trees and eaves. It made Lynn think of her apartment, of the excitement of Mike's kisses that first time.

The taste of his mouth, the firm-soft warmth of his tongue ... the slight tremor she felt in his body ...

A chill began in her stomach. She extricated herself and stood there, confused, her breathing still quickened.

'What is it?'

'I'm not sure,' she said. 'A weird feeling.'

'If we're going to stop, it has to be now.'

His chest rose and fell beneath his shirt. A curl of black hair showed at the neck.

'Now. You have to decide now.' His dark eyes pinned hers. 'If you want to wait, we'll wait. I won't like it, but I'll do it.'

Lynn's dizziness was back. She rubbed her forehead.

'I won't lie, Lynn; I would kill to make love to you right now. But you have to want it.' He folded his arms. 'Maybe you don't. Maybe you still need to protect yourself.'

It came to Lynn then that that was exactly what had

been lifted: the need to protect herself. It had fallen away, was still falling as each shred loosened ... would probably continue to fall for a long time.

She had never needed to protect herself from Mike. She would never need to. Beneath his stony exterior was a giant capacity for caring and generosity.

'There's no putting the brakes on now,' he said. 'I've waited and waited. We're going down this road together, the whole way, or we're not going at all. Do you get that?'

'I get it.'

Still he didn't move or touch her. 'Say it. Say what you want.'

'I want to make love with you.'

His eyes closed. He drew her in and fitted their bodies together.

Lynn found the bandaged area on his back and caressed it gently. He reached back and pressed her hand, to show she didn't need to take care.

'I don't want to hurt you,' she whispered.

'That's what I'm supposed to say.' One corner of his mouth turned up. 'It's just like you to be afraid of hurting *me*.'

'Well,' she said, 'why not? You've been doing all the protecting.'

'Not quite.' He put his hands on her face. 'You're so brave. I love you.'

Tears spilled. She had no hand free to wipe them. They ran over his fingers. 'I love *you*.'

He turned her around so her back was to the wall and pressed against her. They kissed, their bodies meeting full-length.

Finally Mike stepped back and took the bottom of her sweatshirt and pulled it over her head. Lynn didn't wait for him to unhook her bra, but reached back and did it herself.

'I really didn't look at you that time in the bathing suit,' Mike said. 'I'm going to look now.'

He watched her slide off the bra. His hands went to her breasts and she drew in a shaky breath as the hardened fingers moved over them.

But after a minute he stopped. 'We both still have too many clothes on,' he said, his voice not working well.

Lynn got out of her pants and went to work on his.

When they were finally together on the sweet-smelling sheets, Lynn was the one who wouldn't wait. She pulled Mike over her.

He reached down and pushed her legs open, and was inside in a second. He groaned in what could have been pain.

'Are you all right?' Lynn gasped. She touched his bandage.

He didn't answer, but moved in an irresistible rhythm that compelled her to follow.

She gave up caring. Her hands moved down his back and her fingers dug into his thighs. Mike's mouth was on hers. She didn't realize she was making noise against it, but he silenced her with more pressure as he moved faster, pounding her body with his.

At the last moment he lifted his head, his breath escaping in a hiss as he drove deeply into her, and she was beyond understanding, as Mike clapped his hand over her mouth, that he had heard her yell before it escaped.

April 2, 1993

I look at my tattoo every day.

It used to give me strength. It doesn't anymore; nothing does.

The perpetual kiss has lost its power.

There's no power in anything for me now. I have accomplished nothing.

I even have to watch her on TV here.

Lynn is alive, Greg is not.

And me? I seem to be neither.